# FOR AELITA

## FEU DRAGON

ISBN-13: 978-0692446164
ISBN-10: 0692446168

For Aelita
Copyright © 2014 Feu Dragon
All rights reserved. Published by Feu Dragon
Covert Art by Nathie Block

Printed in the U.S.A.
CreateSpace, June 2015

The type text was set in Book Antiqua

# ACKNOWLEDGEMENTS

I am always grateful to the following people for their selfless help and love:

To my father, Dad, thank you for always being there for me no matter what, I am who I am today because of you.

To my mother, Mom, you are and will always be the greatest and most beautiful mother in the whole universe and thank you for being my mother.

To my sister, Mimi, thank you for always putting up with my impish side and being the best older sibling.

To GPT&GMJ, I can never thank you enough for all the supports and love you've given me since I met you. You will always be my angels.

To my best friend, Laurel, thank you for existing. You've taught me the real meaning of true friendship.

To my kitten, U, thank you very much for being there through all those times.

To the Armands women, thank you for all the help and supports you've given me.

To my dear fanfiction readers, thank you so much for reading my stories.

# 1

## COLTON ICE'S POINT OF VIEW

"Good night, Colton." Veronica murmurs, kissing me once more before getting out of my car. I then make my way back to my home. It's Friday evening, the weather is nice. The sun is setting, dying the sky red and orange. The birds are flying away to the opposite direction as if they're afraid of something. I glance at the sky for a moment and I feel as if it is warning me, as if it is trying to tell me something. I shake my head and scoff at myself feeling foolish.

My name is Colton Ice. I am a twenty two years old engineer who owns the most successful company in Terra. Terra is a corrupted, resourceful island in which the rich make the rules. I am a wealthy person and have more money than I need. Most people praise me, fear me, and respect me. Women throw themselves at me every day. I possess everything I could ever ask for and I take great pride in all my belongings except one thing: my wife.

She's the only thing I wish I never had. I never wanted her from the beginning, but if I didn't have her, her father wouldn't sponsor me and I wouldn't have become successful.

Don't get me wrong, Aelita is a very beautiful girl. She is a twenty-one years old girl with a flawless, glowing dark skin, long curly golden hair and gentle honey brown eyes. She has the face of an angel. I must admit, she is prettier than all the girls I have been sleeping with. Well, her face and her hair and her dainty hands that is. I have seen nothing more than that. I have never seen her naked, and I have never touched her or shown her any type of affection or done anything a husband is supposed to do except provide her food and shelter. Why is that? It's because Aelita isn't the woman for me. She is mute, too fragile, too gentle, too weak.

I have known Aelita ever since we were kids. It used to be me, her and our best friend Forest always hanging out together. Since childhood, Aelita has always been too kind and too forgiving. She always seeks peace and avoids quarrel. She allows herself to be easily influenced by others. She has no self-confidence. She feels inferior to everyone. At school, she used to get bullied because was mute and too kind and Forest would always defend her. That was until Forest died in our second year of high school in a car accident. And then, it was her and I. The bullying never stopped on her side and she never stood up for herself. I defended her few times because that was what Forest would do but I grew tired of her always crying and letting others take advantage of her. It continued for so long, and I was fed up. I had enough of her not defending herself. Then one day, during our third year, I yelled at her and told her to grow up and stop crying. If she did not like the way she was being treated, then she must defend herself because Forest wasn't there anymore and I had better things to do than protect her. Ever since that day, I have never seen her cry about anything. She kept on getting bullied and since I stopped sticking out for her, she started to stick out for herself in her own way. Aelita would smile at those bullies and bring them little presents or cookies the next day. She would forgive them and they would hurt her again and she would forgive them and the same thing would happen over and over. She was too kind, too gentle, and too fragile. She was weak, and I have learned to dislike her more and more.

Now she's my wife. A mute kind wife who stays home and plants flowers. She has turned my mansion into a zoo and a garden. She loves to plant and decorate and she also has a passion for animals. She is raising four dogs, seven cats, three horses, lambs, goats, chickens, hamsters, pigs, you name it. She raises and takes care of them.

At first I wasn't too happy with my home being turned into an animal shelter, but then our butler told me it made her very happy. She was alone, had no friends, I was never home so connecting with nature made her life better and since I knew for a fact that I couldn't make her happy myself but cared for her, I let her have it her way.

I dislike Aelita as my wife. She is weak and too kind, but I care for her. I made a promise to her family to satisfy all her needs and well, I'm doing most of it. I can give her whatever she wants, but I can't love her. That's the only thing I can't do.


I park my car in the garage and make my way in the mansion. Today is Friday, the servants and butler always have Fridays off, so tonight will only be me and Aelita in the house.

Fridays are just like any other days when I come home from work. Aelita will always be the first to welcome me in the house with that kind, gentle smile on her face and a ridiculous amount of flowers in her hands. She will always give them to me and hug me. I will never hug back, or kiss her or ask her how her day has been. I will just wait until she lets go of me and go to my room, then eat, then go to my office and never come back out. It seems like today will be like any other Friday.

Except it isn't.

Aelita isn't there to greet me with flowers. I look around the foyer and I don't see her.

"Aelita..?" I call her name, knowing she can't utter a sound because she is mute but I still hope for her to show up in front of me. I never thought it will trigger an unpleasant feeling from me not seeing her.

"Aelita?" I repeat, now rushing toward the garden area, hoping to find her planting something.

She isn't there.

I walk into her bedroom since both our rooms are separated. I am the one who has decided this way because I do not want to wake up in the morning and see her face.

She isn't in her room either.

But then I feel stupid and ridiculous for worrying about her. What do I care? She's probably somewhere in the house either taking a nap or playing with her pets. It's not her duty to greet me every time I come back from work. I am not the most loving husband to her. Why am I worried, and a bit irritated then?

I go to my bedroom and change, brushing away the weird emotions that have come over me. I will find her later.

I walk upstairs to my bedroom and open the door without looking around. I start to unbutton my black dress shirt and turn around. That is when I see her sitting on the white carpet facing me with those beautiful honey brown eyes.

I have never seen her look so frightened.

I frown staring down at her confused, what is she doing in my room? Then, it takes me few seconds later to notice she isn't alone. There is a man sitting behind her.

5

He has medium dirty blonde hair and disturbing brown eyes. His skin tone is just as pale as mine and he is wearing a simple blue jean on a long sleeve polo shirt. The blond man is playing with her golden curly hair.

Anger is the first feel triggered in me. Seeing someone else touch her, touch my wife is something I never want to see and something I will never allow. It doesn't matter that I don't love her. No one touches her.

Before I even move toward them, I feel a gun pointed to my head. Someone else is behind me. "Don't move," the person behind says with an icy tone and I freeze.

I understand what is going on, now. We're being held hostages.

I stare back at Aelita, who is stiffened, scared, and slightly trembling. I tighten my fists and clench my jaws.

"What do you want?" I growl at the two men in my room. None of them answer me. Instead, the dirty blonde haired man behind Aelita smiles at me and lazily stands up. He yawns, stretches as if he has just been awoken from a nap, then he pats Aelita's hair once more making me angrier.

"Do *not* touch her," I snarl at him glaring. The man turns to me. His brown eyes are cold and full of resentment. He smiles again and then slaps Aelita, making her delicate body fall on the floor.

"You fucker!" I lose all reasoning and my body moves on its own ready to beat the living shit out of that man, but then I feel a sharp pain on my neck, making me lose my balance and fall on the floor. The man behind me has just hit me with the gun.

I look up and stare at Aelita to see if she is okay. She isn't. Her eyes are frozen, and her lips are trembling. "Are you all right?" I ask her, forgetting that she can't speak.

"Colton Ice," the man who hit her earlier finally speaks. His voice is calm and playful, "it is nice to meet you. I am Hunter. The man behind you is Jago. How are you doing today?"

My eyes never leave Aelita, who is still lying on the floor not moving. Her eyes are wide open and her whole body is trembling uncontrollably. I have a strong urge to hold her in my arms and make her feel safe and protected. I don't like the sight of her scared.

I don't know why those men are in my house, why they are pointing a gun at me, hurting my wife and I don't care at the moment. All I want to do is have Aelita leave the room and be somewhere safe.

"Leave my wife alone, let her go. I don't know what you want, but I'll give you anything."

Hunter smiles at me once again sadistically, "I never pictured you as the generous type, Mr. Ice," his face darkens. "Tie him up."

The hell they are.

Jago, the dark skinned man behind me is about to do what he is told to but, I don't let him. I thrust my head forward and back, powerfully hitting his face. I am sure I broke his nose.

He grunts and takes few steps back. I stand up, and turn toward him, ready to punch him. Those guys are underestimating me. They come to my home and take my wife hostage and hope for me to just stay there and watch? Like hell.

I punch Jago hard, causing him to fall on the floor and let go of the hand gun. As I lean down and try to pick it up, I hear something click. I turn and see Aelita being lifted up by Hunter, his left arm wrapped around her small body, keeping her still while holding a gun to her head.

"You pick that and I'll shoot her,"Hunter threatens.

I glare at him and he removes the safety off the gun. That is when I put my hand in the air in defeat. I can't fight them, not when Aelita's life is being jeopardized.

"Don't hurt her," I tell Hunter as I drop the gun and put both my hands in the air.

"Jago, tie him up," Hunter orders Jago who stomps toward me and gives me a hard punch in the stomach. I cough out and fall to my knees and let him tie me up. He forces me to sit down on the carpet across my wife, and I am staring at her in the arms of another man.

Hunter retrieves the gun from her and pushes her down on the floor. Poor Aelita's body is shaking even more violently. I think she is trying hard not to cry. My heart sinks, she's innocent. She has done nothing wrong.

"What do you guys want from me? Is it money? I'll write you a check," I negotiate with Hunter as he walks around Aelita, staring down at her with a look I don't like. After hearing me, he draws his attention from her and walks toward me. I feel a bit relieved.

Hunter looks down at me and says bitterly, "I don't want your money, Mr. Ice. I want revenge."

I frown, not knowing what I've done to this man. I have never met him in my life. Yes, I am an intimidating, cold leader to all of my employees, but I take good care of them. I don't remember ever doing wrong to anyone—at least not intentionally.

"What have I done?" I ask him, but then realize it doesn't matter, "It doesn't matter. Whatever I did...I am sorry." On any other occasion, I will not apologize so easily. I am not the type to say I am sorry, but again, an innocent person's life is at stake and I cannot let anything happen to Aelita.

But, it seems that an apology will not do it.

"You will be," Hunter growls. "You don't know what you've done?" he is walking back toward Aelita again.

My heart sinks once more as that dangerous man approaches her. She stiffens, and looks up the man, then gives him a kind and nervous smile.

No Aelita, not everyone deserves your angelic smile.

The man smiles back at her and plays with her hair once more, "you're an exquisite lady."

Aelita smiles again.

"Don't touch her!" I yell at Hunter, and Jago punches me.

"Shut up!" Jago yells.

Hunter keeps petting her head and continues to smile at her, "you have not said a word since I captured you. Are you scared of me?"

Aelita nods at him, still smiling with her trembling lips.

"You should be," he continues to caress her hair. "What is your name?"

She doesn't answer and then he slaps her one more time, sending her body flying across the room. I feel so angry, so helpless, so frustrated. He's hurting her, and she doesn't deserve it.

He walks toward her again and roughly grabs her by the hair, "what is your name?" he repeats with a stern voice glaring down at her, ready to hit her again.

"She is mute!" I shout at him. "She can't speak! She is mute! Leave her alone!"

Hunter stills and raises an eyebrow, "mute?" he looks down at the trembling Aelita.

"Are you mute?" he asks her. Aelita weakly nods her head and his eyes and grip on her soften.

"Oh. I am sorry," he apologizes to her then turns to face me. "Anyways, Mr. Ice. Does the name Veronica Cross rings a bell to you?"

Veronica. Yes, the girl I have been sleeping with. What about her?

"She's my wife," Hunter announces.

Oh.

"You've been showing her a good time, lately. You've been fucking her, mocking and disrespecting me," his face is dark and angry.

"I didn't know she was married," I explain.

"Didn't know, or didn't care?" It is a rhetorical question. "And, I am not the only one whose wife you've been screwing around with. You've fucked Jago's wife, three of my friends' wives, and many others. You've been destroying lots of marriages and making a fool out of lots of faithful husbands, Mr. Ice," Hunter continues, his voice saddens. "Veronica doesn't even look at me anymore, she doesn't even respect me...all she does is leave the house and come back in your car...do you know how much I love her? How much I fought for her? And you just destroy our relationship like this in the blink of an eye without a care in the world," his face darkens. "I want revenge, we all want revenge."

"She came to me," I argue, glaring at the man. "She chose to fuck me. It isn't my fault if you can't keep your wife happy."

He glares at me with fury and resentment. Then, he smirks and gets closer to Aelita. His lips are on her ear and he is licking and tugging it, "eye for an eye, Mr. Ice."

Aelita's eyes widen in horror as if she understands what is about to happen to her, and so do I.

No, no, no. This is not happening.

"No," I plead. "No, please. Don't touch her." I begin to struggle, and try to break free from the plastic handcuff cables, but they are binding me so tightly.

"Please, she did nothing to you..." I keep on begging.

"I didn't do anything to you either, Mr. Ice. Yet, you hurt me," Hunter responds sarcastically.

"Aelita's innocent. Please. I am so sorry, I apologize. Please, Please. Leave her be. It's me you want; I'm the one who wronged you. She didn't. Take your anger out on me, please."

He ignores me, and kisses Aelita on the cheek. "Why would your husband go fuck other men's wives when he has such a beautiful woman like you, huh? Do you not make him happy?" his voice is gentle with her. He helps her up and unbuttons her white dress. He is caressing her body and watching me while doing it.

"I'm going to fuck your wife, Mr. Ice–and you're going to watch."

No!

"You can't! Please!" I beg harder, my voice pleading. I have never felt so hurt, so broken inside, so guilty in my life, and what is killing me even more is the look in Aelita's eyes. She stares at me once more, her body completely still and calm with a faint reassuring smile on her face, as if she is telling me that is okay. That she forgives me...then she breaks her eyes away from me and becomes an emotionless person.

No! I'll be damned straight to hell and back if I let this innocent girl take the blame for me.

"No! Stop it, please! She's a virgin!" I plead still trying to break free, but all my actions are in vain.

Hunter stops for a moment and his eyes widen in disbelief.

"No fucking way," he chuckles and turns to Jago. "Can you believe this? He fucks every girl in this island and his wife is still a fucking virgin...!" he laughs and looks down on Aelita, "this is just getting better and better!"

Aelita doesn't react. Her eyes are looking somewhere, far into space, as if she is not part of this world anymore, as if she is escaping this cruel reality.

Aelita...

"Aelita! I will get you out of this, okay?" I call her, still trying to break free. "Don't be scared. I won't let him lay a hand on you anymore!"

Hunter looks at me with a mocking smile and then says "alright, Mr. Ice. Since you want to save your wife so desperately, I'll make you a deal."

"Anything you want, I'll give you anything!" I respond immediately.

"Alright, how about this," he takes out his phone. "For half an hour I'm going to beat your wife while you get down on your knees, bow your head and admit that you're a coward and you're sorry ten thousand times. If you do that, I won't pop your sweet wife's cherry."

I stare at him speechless not sure if he's joking or not, but then he grabs Aelita by the neck and starts to slap her and throw her around.

"No!" I cry, "stop it! Please stop it!"

"You know what you have to do," Hunter replies.

So I get down on my knees, bow my head and start apologize fast. "I'm a coward and I'm sorry! I'ma cowardandI'msorry!ImacowardandImsorryImacowardan dImsorryImacowardandImsorryImacowardandImsorryI macowardandImsorryImacowardandImsorryImacoward andImsorryImacowardandImsorry" I continue to say it again and again nonstop, for as long as I can as I continue to hear Aelita's body being thrown around. When Hunter's phone alarm sounds, I stop talking and look up. Aelita is wounded and so weak, unable to fight for herself.

No...

"It has been half an hour already?" Hunter grins, sounding surprised. He wipes his bloody hand on his shirt and breathes heavily, and then he turns to Jago. "Did he say it ten thousand times?"

Jago shrugs carelessly.

"I did!" I respond, although I am not sure. All I know is that I have been begging for the past half an hour so Aelita doesn't get hurt.

"Well, Jago wasn't counting, and neither was I so..." Hunter gives me another cruel smirk and walks back toward the wounded Aelita, "I guess none of your bullshit counts."

"No...Please, don't hurt her anymore," I beg as I realize that he is going to rape her anyways. "Please, Mr. Cross, please I'll give you anything you want."

"What I want, Mr. Ice, is to hurt your wife in front of you," he responds as he forces her up and makes her face me. She's breathless and looks so tired and lifeless. Her nose and mouth are bleeding and I can tell that he might've fractured her bones.

"Please, Hunter. *Please*," I plead once again.

He stares at me with another mocking smirk and in a blink of a second, he rips off her dress as she holds her breath. Then, he takes out a knife from his pocket. I hold my breath and he slowly circles the blade on her bare body. She doesn't budge.

"It's okay," he whispers in her ears. I keep on yelling, pleading, threatening him to stop this, but he ignores me, and then brusquely cuts through her bra and underwear and I gasp.

So does he.

Aelita's body is divine, golden, amazing and flawless. I have never seen something so amazing, so appealing. Her breasts are full and round, her waist is slim and small, her legs are long and lean and beautiful. She is a beauty. No woman I've slept with will ever compare to that girl's body. And, I have never touched her...and she is about to be tainted.

If fury is what you think I am feeling at the moment, then you are understating it.

"Look at her body!" Hunter gestures to Aelita, admiring her, drinking her in with his perverted sick eyes. "You have a damn hot wife, and you still don't fuck her?"

"She's innocent," I snarl.

Hunter smirks and then runs his hands all over her body, her breasts and her thighs.

"Don't you fucking touch her! DON'T YOU FUCKING TOUCH HER!" I roar, breaking, trashing, and trying everything I can to free myself, but in vain. Jago is staring down at me smirking.

"Get a taste of your own medicine, Ice," Hunter spits at me, then pushes Aelita down on her knees, then down again so her body is smashing on the cold floor. She is calm and still like a statue.

Her back is facing him as he kneels behind her, undoing his zipper.

"Please! Don't do this!" My voice is now trembling, hurt, scared, "I'll give you anything you need! Take my company, take my money, take everything but please don't hurt her!" I beg once again.

He grabs a fistful of her hair and yanks her head up so she can face me as he adjusts her hips in his hands. Aelita is not even flinching. She doesn't look scared. She doesn't look like she is giving in. She is being strong.

"I want you to watch as I take her virginity," Hunter snarls. "I will be rough and I will hurt her and make her scream. After I'm through with her, she won't be mute anymore."

He then places a kiss on Aelita's hair and tells her. "This is nothing personal, Mrs. Ice. I hope you understand that."

Then he powerfully thrusts inside of her.

I freeze and my mouth falls open as I watch in horror what he is doing to my wife.

Her eyes widen too, showing shock as she digs her fingers inside the carpet. She purses her lips, not making a sound, not crying, and not giving in.

He starts to ram inside of her, gripping her tightly, holding her body firmly, and bruising her.

She doesn't cry. She doesn't move.

I am trashing around, yelling, screaming and begging him to let her go! Please, let her go! She doesn't deserve it! Aelita's innocent, Aelita is kind. She is fucking innocent! She doesn't deserve this! I try to break free, pulling on the handcuffs, but I can't. The more I pull, the more it's digging inside my flesh, bruising my wrists, drawing blood. I curse him out. I curse Jago out! I beg, I threaten, I scream in her place. I ask him to stop in her place. I even promise to keep away from any girl. I promise to God to be good to Aelita from now on. I promise to God that if they let her go, I'll come every night to her, I'll go to church every Sunday and worship Him like a dog. I'll donate all my money to charity, I'll help the world, I'll help Aelita, I'll be God's disciple if he just spares Aelita. But my prayers are not reaching God's ears. Hunter keeps on assaulting her, thrusting inside, grunting to his own pleasure as Aelita stays still, closing her lips tight, her eyes struggling to keep strong. Why is she being so strong? Why is she not breaking? Why is she not crying? Come to think of it, I have never seen her cry since our third year in high school. Since I told her to stop being a wimp. It is because of me. She is being strong because of me. The weak Aelita I have always rejected, known and hated is being strong right in front of me while I am the one being weak. She doesn't deserve this.

So, I cry in her place. Angry, furious tears fill my eyes as I scream in her place, as I beg in her place. I have not cried when Forest died. I have not cried when my parents died, I have not cried when my older brother killed himself. I have never shed one tear, and here I am now whimpering like a child for Aelita.

17

"I'm so sorry...Aelita..." I sob out, crying and crying and crying while he keeps on tainting her.

"Ah damn, your wife is tight!" Hunter grunts as he orgasms, pouring himself inside of her. I glare at him with fury and hate. My heart pounds restlessly against my chest as I feel my own blood boil through my veins and arteries. I begin to tremble, but this time not out of fear. My mind becomes filled with a dark and diabolical desire for... bloodshed. I want to kill him with my bare hands. No, not kill him...killing will be too easy...I want to make him beg and cry and suffer and regret what he's doing to Aelita...I want to annihilate him, pulverize him and his entire family...I want to make him pay for this. I will not let him get away with this. I will avenge Aelita.

He lets her fall on the floor after he finishes with her and he zips up his pant, "that was one good fuck I received from you, Mrs. Ice. Thank you." He smirks down at her and then at me.

"You don't know what you're missing," he says.

"Fuck you!" I snarl at him, with a murderous glare. I want to hurt him. I want to destroy him.

Then I glance down at Aelita. Her naked body is still beautiful, even after being bruised and tainted. She is trembling, and her eyes are closed as if she is resting from all this.

"Aelita, it's okay. It's over now..." I try to reassure her, comfort her in any way I can.

"What makes you think I'm finished with her?" Hunter asks raising an eyebrow at me. My heart sinks and I look at him appalled. He smirks, appreciating the look on my face.

"Come in," he shouts out loud and the door of my bedroom opens. Three guys come in, looking hungry but not for food. They're much bigger than Jago and much more muscular. I stare at them in disbelief as they gaze down at Aelita.

*No.*

*God, no.*

*No.*

*NO!*

I start trashing again, yelling and cursing. "NO! Fuck, no! You can't do this to her! That's inhumane! You've already made your point! You've already punished me! Why are you doing this!?" I yell at Hunter.

"Again, Mr. Ice I am not the only guy's wife you fucked. They had wives too," he turns to Jago. "You can do it too if you'd like."

Jago shakes his head.

"Heh, whatever. Have your fun with her, you guys. I'll be back when you're done. Enjoy the show, Mr. Ice." Then Hunter leaves the room and the three guys start laughing, and walking toward Aelita.

"No! Get away from her! Get away from her! You'll break her! She can't handle you guys! She can't! She's too fragile! Please! Please! She can't handle this! Don't you touch her! Don't you lay a finger on her! I'll kill you! I'll kill you!" They all ignore me and stalk after

Aelita, who is trying her best to get up. She is scared, and she is not hiding it anymore, and there is nothing I can do. I can't protect her from those guys, I can't do anything...I am a horrible husband to her.

All she has ever been to me is sweet, kind and comforting. She has been there for me when my whole family died. She has been there for me when I have been sick, she has taken care of me... has protected me, and has always put me first no matter how cruel and ungrateful I have been to her.

She is always the first one to wish me happy birthday on my birthdays. Well, she doesn't speak, so she gives me so many flowers, so many roses, to the point where I began to hate flowers because I found it so annoying.

She has always been gentle, and kind and supporting even when she knows I always sleep around with other women, even though I am never home, even though I am never there on her birthdays. I have never shown her any sort of affection. All I do is ask my assistant to buy her something. I never take the time to buy anything for her myself...I have never paid attention to her. I have always avoided her like a plague. I only saw her as a burden, a weak human being that I felt the obligation to take care of because her parents asked me to.

But now, I wish I can take all this back. I wish to be kinder to her. I want to receive more flowers from her. I want to smile back at her, I want to come home to her every night and make sweet and gentle love to her. I want to buy her presents myself. I want to be there for her.

"AHH!" I hear her scream, bringing me back to reality.

I gasp. This is the first time I have ever heard a sound come out of her. Her voice is horse, shot, and broken.

Her eyes are filled with tears, wide open, her face showing how much pain she is enduring, her mouth is open, gasping as the men ram inside of her like animals. She is not being strong anymore, she is hurt, she is abused, she is tainted, and she is broken.

And it's all because of me. I can't watch this. I can't...this is too much...I turn my head away from her, and close my eyes and try to ignore the faint screams I am hearing from her. I can't watch this.

I keep on hearing her scream for a while, as the guys are grunting and laughing, calling her names and enjoying themselves. How can they do this to someone so innocent...how can anyone enjoy hurting Aelita? I want them dead. I want them all to perish.

When they finish with her, they let her drop on the floor like an empty bottle of water. Jago unties me and as my bloody wrists are freed, I rush to her instantly, and embrace my arms around her tainted body. She looks up at me, her eyes are shot red, filled with so much tears and pain. Her lips are trembling and I can't help to think she still is beautiful after all.

I hug her tightly as she cries quietly in my arms. I want to take the pain away from her. I want to protect her. I want to kiss her and make her feel better. Having her in my arms and seeing her hurt like this makes me realize that I love her. I don't know what that means. I don't know if I'm in love with her, or if it's just simple love...all I know is that I want to care for her.

"It will be okay. I'll fix you...I'll be there for you..." I whisper in her ear, calming her. I don't know for how long we've been like this but when I hear the door open and Hunter enters, I realize things are not over yet. Hunter walks toward the rest and the other men whisper to themselves as Hunter glances at us few times, mostly at Aelita. Then he shakes his head, nods, and walks toward us. Aelita stiffens in my arms and I hold her tightly while glaring at Hunter.

"Get away from her," I snarl at him. He ignores me and looks at Aelita, his face softens.

"You've had it rough, huh? I'm sorry it had to come like this," he takes an earplug out of his pocket and wants to reach toward her, but I stop him. My hand grabs his, attempting to break it.

"Fuck off," I growl again. He glares at me.

"Listen, what I'm about to tell you, she can't hear. It'll be better for her, so let me do this."

I slowly let go of his arm and feel my heart sinking once more.

*What now?*

Hunter gives Aelita a tentative smile, "you're going to listen to a very calming music, alright?" then he puts the earplugs in her ears and raises the volume loud. I hold her tight in my arms, bringing her face to my chest.

Hunter stands up and walks behind Aelita, facing me. He is looking down on us. His eyes are filled with regret.

"Listen, Mr. Ice...I never thought your wife was a virgin, or *this* nice," he starts, clearing his throat. "I regret...hurting her."

"Fuck you," I growl. This motherfucker has some fucking nerves apologizing after damaging her.

"I wanted to hurt you so bad because Veronica is leaving me. I was in the moment, I wasn't thinking straight...you're right, Mrs. Ice doesn't deserve this. She's innocent."

"It's too late to take it back now, asshole," I snap, still glaring, still holding Aelita tightly. "I promise you, will waste you," I glare at the rest, "Every single one of you. Mark my words."

"No...It's not too late," he shakes his head, not looking concerned or scared for his life. I raise an eyebrow, and when he draws out a gun, I understand what he's thinking.

"No..." I shake my head, my voice changing from angry to pleading again. No. Anything but this.

"She's broken...damaged and this will have a psychological effect on her for the rest of her life," Hunter explains. "What we've done to her...is...unrepairable. I don't want her to suffer...I think it's better for her this way."

"No," I refuse firmly. "She will get through this, she will get better. She is...strong." I whisper the last word quietly. Is she? Will she really get better? Will I be able to face her or look at her in the eye after all this? Will she hate me?

Yes, she will hate me.

"You have no say in this, Mr. Ice. We'll stop hunting you down after this, you'll live to think about the damages you've done. Think of it as a sacrifice, as your punishment for wronging others...and I sure as hell know you don't deserve her...She's too good for this world and for you..." he pauses and looks at me again, "you have thirty seconds to say your goodbyes to her."

"Can we please..." I am trying to bargain.

"29," Hunter points the gun at the back of her head. She can see nothing because her face is buried in my chest and she cannot hear what we're talking about. My eyes sadden, and I gently push her away. I remove the earplug from her ears and take a gentle hold of her chin in my hand then kiss her.

It's the first time I have ever kissed her. She tastes sweet, gentle and her mouth is warm and comforting. I feel like I am kissing an angel.

An angel, yes...that is she is. A broken angel suffering in this world because of me, the demon. I wish I could spend more time with her and get to know her more.

"Aelita, you're a very kind girl," I start, tears filling my eyes as I wipe hers away.

"I'm sorry I've been a terrible person to you..." I sob. She smiles painfully and brings her hands to my face, caressing my cheeks. Her hands are so small, so fragile, and so delicate. I kiss them.

15 seconds.

"I want to garden with you...I want to play with all of your animals together...I want to buy you presents myself...take you out on dates...there's so much I want to do..."

Aelita frowns not understanding why I'm talking this way, but when she hears the click behind her, the sound of the gun safety being off, she stiffens and understands and her eyes are wide open in fear. Her body trembles even more.

She shakes her head at me, her eyes wide open in shock and horror and tries to turn around to look at Hunter. I grab her face with both my hands on either side of her cheeks, holding her in place. She is trembling and shaking her head viciously, letting me know she doesn't want this...she doesn't want to die. Her breathing quickens and more tears are sliding down her face.

"Hey, hey...it's okay. It's going to be okay...it's alright..." I reassure her as we both cry together. "Just relax, Aelita." She's agitated and shaking her head at me, begging me not to let this happen. "Relax....look at me. Look at me, Aelita. Don't worry about them; it's going to be okay... Don't think about anyone else...look at me and remember, remember all the fun times you and I and Forest had, remember..." My voice is breaking now, thinking about Forest...Forest is gone and Aelita is leaving me too...I will be all alone. I will have no one...

5 seconds.

She stares at me, and stops fighting, I can see the regret, and fear that her teary eyes are showing me. Her entire body is trembling, and so is mine. I kiss her quickly one last time.

3 seconds.

"Aelita, thank you for everything," I whisper to her before hearing the gun shot. Her mouth opens wide for a quick second and her eyes even wider. Both her hands that are holding my shirt slowly fall on either side of her.

I freeze in place as I stare at her honey brown eyes slowly losing its vivid, lively color with my hands still holding her face. I can't speak or do anything...all I can do is watch as her blood splatter on my face and drip down on hers. Her body slowly crumbles on top of me seconds after and I hold her in my arms unable to move unable to register what just happened me...to her...to us. No, I can't believe it. This is not happening, this is not real. Just earlier this morning, I saw Aelita wait for me at the garage to wave me goodbye with a proud, happy smile on her face and now...here I am holding her dead in my arms. I can't believe this. No, this is surreal. This is not happening. This has got to be a nightmare. This is not real...no...no...no.

"Shit, the cops!" I hear Hunter curse and they all suddenly run out of the room. I am left alone with Aelita in my arms with her eyes closed...her body is getting colder. I say nothing as I hold her and look at her. I trace my hands on her face, her soft lips...then her neck and I feel her gentle, slow pulse fading away. This is real...she's gone. She's not with me anymore. I lost her.

# 2

I am sitting on the chair in the waiting room lifelessly staring down the floor. I feel dead inside, I feel as if my whole being and energy has been sucked out of my body. I am locked in a haze, still trying to make sense of what had just happened two hours ago. Aelita...my wife, my childhood friend...did all this horrible things really happened to her? I don't know. I don't know anything anymore. My mind is faded and shut down and I don't even remember how I came here.

"Colton, thank goodness you're alright." I hear Mrs. Fire's worried voice. I turn around and see the beautiful tall and lean black woman with short grey hair and distraught honey brown eyes running toward me with a pained expression on her face. Behind her, is walking Mr. Fire with the usual poker face he never wears off. He is a lean tall man with a pale white skin, short golden hair and robotic brown eyes. I can't tell if he is shaken, worried, scared, sad or angry. I can't tell anything from this dangerous man's expression. I can never tell.

"Mrs. Fire," I whisper, a bit surprised that Aelita's parents are both here in less than two hours. They live about three hours away from our residence.

"How is she?" Mrs. Fire asks me. "We've heard there has been a robbery in your house, how is my daughter?"

I am speechless. I don't know what to say to her. That is not what happened.

"Esmeralda, it's alright." Mr. Fire finally speaks nodding at me as if he understands something. "You stay here and wait for our daughter to wake up. Ice, you come with me."

He doesn't know either. He doesn't know what happened. It wasn't a robbery and there is less than one percent of chance that his daughter will wake up.

"Sir, I'd like to stay and wait for the doctor," I say to him but he doesn't listen to me. He walks out of the waiting room, expecting me to follow him.

I swallow and give a nod to Mrs. Fire and follow Mr. Fire out to the waiting room. He presses the elevator button and takes out a cigar.

I am nervous, very nervous.

Mr. Fire is the only person I have always been afraid and intimidated of. He is...intense, intimidating and most of all dangerous.

Dangerous, because he is the Lord of Terra. Terra is an island that has another island inside of it. It's called The Fire Island and Mr. Fire owes that land, making him the most powerful and feared individual in the kingdom of Terra. The Fire island is the powerhouse and the nucleus of this entire kingdom because of the natural resources it possesses. The Fire Island is the only land in Terra that can grow healthy plants, vegetables, medical herbs and it also possesses vast amount of petroleum and minerals. Moreover, Mr. Fire is the commander of a brigade of thousands of dangerous, deadly, psychotic soldiers who only answer to him and no one else and protect Terra from invaders. Terra has been able to maintain peace, order and prosperity because of Mr. Fire. Everyone is at his mercy, even the King of Terra worships him. However, Mr. Fire is not all good. He is a cruel, heartless person. He thinks he is a God. He loves to be feared and looked up to. Those who don't, those who step on his toe are annihilated along with their whole family. Mr. Fire is the scariest man in Terra.

People know he has a daughter, but don't know it is Aelita because no one has ever seen her with him. Even though Aelita favors her father over her mother, the two of them do not interact much. It has to do with the fact that they are both so different. He's very scary, but loves his daughter. I don't know what is going to happen to me if he ever finds out what happened to his precious innocent Aelita.

When he handed over his electric company to me to take care of, he also handed Aelita in my care and he told me to take good care of her. He knew I didn't love her and he didn't care. He just wanted me to take care of her, spoil her, and be her man because Aelita loved me. I needed the company because it would make me the most powerful CEO in Terra and Aelita was the price to pay to get that title. I gave him my word that I'd take care of her and not let her get hurt at all. Wait until he finds out what really happened. I am so screwed.

The elevator door opens, and he makes his way in as I follow. He doesn't say anything for a while. He is so quiet, so calm and my heart is suddenly beating at an alarming rate. I can feel myself sweating and all my senses are coming back to me. My hands are slightly shaking. I don't know what he is thinking, and it is very nerve wracking.

"Relax kid," he tells me as the elevator door opens again and we make our way out. His voice is calm and neutral as always. I follow him outside the hospital into his notorious automatic flimousine. He is the only one that owns a car that can fly like a helicopter and I am the one who engineered it.

I seat across him and the flying engine departs. He is not looking at me, he is not talking. He is not saying anything and I don't dare to speak either.

A while later, I see him get a bottle of scotch and pour it in a glass. He hands it to me.

I politely refuse. "I don't drink, sir."

"Take it," he finally speaks, his voice is calm. "You've had a very painful day."

It is not a request.

My shaky hands reach over and take the glass from him. "Thank you."

"I had to lie to Esmeralda about what happened to our daughter," he starts to speak as I take a small sip of the very bitter burning alcohol.

"Esmeralda's health is very fragile; the small amount of stress in her life will send her back to the hospital. That's why I couldn't tell her that our daughter was raped and shot in the head hours ago."

I start to choke and cough on the drink. My throat and lung are burning due to the fact that I am not used to drinking and the fact that...

*He knows.*

"How did you find out?" I ask him moments later.

"She's my daughter. It is my job to know what happens to her," he replies as if my question is a stupid one.

I gulp, not knowing what else to say. He still doesn't show me any kind of emotion.

"The police caught all of them before they even tried to run," he scoffs. He doesn't seem happy about that which confuses me.

"I had to call in a favor to the Head Chief so the Terra Police Department could let them all go," he continues.

What? Why did he let those animals out? I don't understand. They raped Aelita.

I am confused, and my head is spinning.

"I also had to pay a lot of golds to make sure they don't escape from this island. Gangsters, mafia organizations, the police, the government are all making sure they don't escape from Terra."

I frown, still confused. What is he doing?

"I will explain everything to you son, for now just drink and relax," Mr. Fire says and looks out the window and ignores me for the rest of the trip. I look down on my drink, my head is clouded with so much emotions and thinking. I am twirling my thumbs and, my leg starts to shake again.

What is going on? What is Mr. Fire up to? Right now, I don't care. Right, now I don't care about those animals who hurt Aelita. I will deal with them later. All I want is to go back to the hospital and listen to what the doctor has to say about Aelita. That is all I care about.

The car descends in front of a thirty story tall tower and we get out. It is the Fire Headquarter.

The tower is covered with guards, hundreds and hundreds of them all in navy blue jumpsuits with a red flame symbol encircled with an ouroboros snake on their left chests. They have black utility belts around their waists as well. It's the standard uniform of Lord Fire's soldiers. They're known as The Sparks.

They all kneel on one knee and harmonically bring their fisted right hand to their left chest and with their left hands, they salute Mr. Fire as he steps out of the car.

"Follow me, son. I want you to witness something," he says walking toward the gates of his humongous tower.

We are in a very dark big room. The carpet is red, the walls are dark. It looks like a dungeon. There are two men hanging backward in the air, with their heads facing down the floor and their legs facing up. They're completely chained, unable to move and are muffling and whimpering. What disturbs me the most is the fact that they are both...naked.

I am standing by the door as it closes behind me. I blink over and over again. What the hell am I witnessing? Is it the alcohol? I barely had three sips.

"Ice," Mr. Fire says, walking past the hanging naked men and toward the desk across. "Do you know who these clowns are?"

I glance at them and glance back at Mr. Fire. "No sir," I nervously say. "I have never seen them in my life."

He faintly chuckles and shakes his head. "They're your sorry excuses of security guards who let the rapists in the mansion."

Oh.

"Ice, you don't even know the faces of the people you hire to protect my daughter when you're not home with her." I hear a small growl from Mr. Fire. He still has a poker face, but I know he is angry. "Anyways, they were not even doing their jobs. You pay them what, thousands of gold an hour to just sit and watch the camera all day long? Did you need to pay them extra for actually paying attention to who is coming in and out of the house my daughter lives in? They did not even know my daughter was being raped. They had no clue when you came in the house either. They were just jerking off to some porn."

The men are grunting, struggling to talk, but in vain.

"It wasn't until they heard her scream that they realized something was up. Yes, my daughter screamed," he whispers.

I remember Aelita screaming when the three guys started to assault her. I shudder at the memory of it and my head hurts as I recall how pained and tortured her voice sounded.

"Those animals made my daughter scream," Mr. Fire repeats. I can see his jaws clenching and his fists tightening as he stares out in space with blazing eyes. He then shakes his head and opens a box that is on the wooden desk. "You see, gentlemen, your mission was to protect Mr. Ice's wife who is also my daughter," Mr. Fire starts. He is talking to the naked men hanging in the air who are grunting and desperately trying to move. "You know, I have a problem with people who don't take their job seriously. Especially when it concerns my family...Your job was to protect Aelita Fire Ice, or die trying," his voice is raw. "And gentlemen, your performance on that special mission was mediocre," his eyes darken once more. "I don't forgive those who don't take their work seriously. Gentlemen, I'm going to waste you."

I swallow and glance at the two shuddering men who are now crying, grunting louder, and trying hard to move. Mr. Fire ignores them and from the box, he takes out a very large metal object that looks like a cigar cutter.

"Gentlemen, this is called a cigar cutter," Mr. Fire says admiring the tool, "it's the largest one I've ever seen, and it has a story. It belonged to friend of mine who died of a very embarrassing death. His name was Mr. Krause, and he had this obsession with chopping things off. He used to chop plants and flowers and especially cigars. He wouldn't smoke them, he would just chop the head off and he was so out of control that one day he ended up chopping his finger off," Mr. Fire looks at the hanging men slightly nodding at them because he is really into his story, "you would think that he'd learn his lesson and take it easy with his special cigar cutter right? That's not what Mr. Krause did. The very next day he hosted a party and flooded his brain and body with drugs. He was high and out of his mind and running naked in his house and then got hold of his cigar cutter and chopped of his own testicles simultaneously while laughing."

I gulp.

"He bled to death and died that night," Mr. Fire continues to contemplate the cigar cutter. "What an idiot he was. Anyways, I learned two lessons in that story. First lesson is: don't do drugs. Second lesson is," he stares at the men with the smirk of a maniac, "Mr. Krause's cigar cutter is big enough to chop off testicles."

My mouth falls open and I start to sweat.

The poor men start to struggle, sob, grunt and muffle something that sounds like pleading.

"It's going to be quick, but painful," Mr. Fire starts to walk toward them slowly and silently taking his time as the naked men are dangling, shaking and trying to free themselves.

I am frozen in place watching the scene in horror.

He is now in front of them, staring at their balls as they keep on grunting and moving around. They are scared shitless.

Heck, I am even scared for them.
"Shh, shh, shhh..." Mr. Fire says gentling patting down on one of the man's leg. "Don't be cowards, real men are not afraid of pain."

And he starts seconds after. The men are grunting harder, piercing my ears with their painful cries. My chest tightens painfully as I look away from the atrocious scene before me.

I can't watch this. I've seen too much today. I feel nauseous.

"Now, now, it's over." Mr. Fire says minutes later.

I turn around and glance back at the men who are still dangling in the air. They are barely conscious and I see a red liquid trailing down from their legs. They are whimpering.

"Go on, Zero." Mr. Fire says as he starts washing his bloody hands with a bottle of water. In a glimpse of a second, I see a very pale man with long hair darker than mine wearing a Fire uniform come out of the shadow with a gun and places two bullet in each of the men's head.

"Shit," I whisper and cannot hold down my stomach anymore. I turn around once again, fall down to my knees and start to vomit.

Fuck, Mr. Fire is worse than I thought. If this is what he does to those two men who had nothing to do with what happened to Aelita...I cannot imagine what he'll do the real animals...to me.

I am scared.

"You're alright there, son?" Mr. Fire is taking steps toward me.

I rise up slowly and wipe my mouth, "never better."

"That's a very insulting answer, Ice." Mr. Fire glares at me, growling. "Zero," he says ever so quietly and before I even know it, the pale guard who executed the two men is in front of me, staring at me with ghostly, emotionless grey eyes then he punches my jaws so hard that I dislocate it, lose a tooth and fall down.

He doesn't give me any second to get myself together. From the corner of my eyes, I see him raise his foot and with an inexplicable power, he kicks my face and once again, I lose another tooth. I am under shock, half conscious still trying to register what the hell just happened. When I manage to rise my body up from the floor, I look at the grey eyed man with an astonished look, and in return, he blankly stares at me, and with his foot, he throws me another merciless blow on my chest. I cough out blood as I am struggling to breathe and control the immense pain my body is feeling at the moment. He doesn't stop there. I feel his hand take a vicious fistful of my hair and pull it, making me rise up. I grunt in pain and feel his knee colliding against the other side of my jaw, relocating it. I grunt again still in shock. This guy is...awfully and overwhelmingly strong making me believe that he is not a human. He is not even reacting nor breathing hard while he continues to beat me up, stomp on my face, pick me up to just punch me right back on the floor again and kick me like I am a piece of dirt. It hurts, it hurts so much and I don't have the energy to fight back or defend myself at all. My entire body hurts so much, and I taste nothing but blood in my mouth. My nose too is bleeding as well as I find it hard to breathe normally. I start to gasp, eyes wide, unable to tell him to stop. I am kneeling on the floor helplessly; head bowed down as I try to pick up my breathing, but he viciously stomps on my head once again, stepping on me like a fly.

"Enough, Zero." I faintly hear Mr. Fire say but Zero doesn't stop, he doesn't listen to his commander. He lifts my head up by grabbing me by the throat and punches me ruthlessly, then again, he continues to kick me and kick me and kick me, and stomp on me again, and again and again and I start to believe that this is personal. That he is not just beating me up not only because he was ordered to, but because he personally resents me. I begin to feel frustrated and furious at him. I glare up at him with blazing eyes, wanting to beat him to death. He stares down at me with the same emotionless, psychotic grey eyes of his and he stomps on me again, making my face crash on the floor hard.

"Zero, stop." Mr. Fire orders once again with a warning tone and this time, Zero listens to him. He abandons my half dead body and walks toward Mr. Fire who pats him on the back. I am lying on my stomach, breathing and gasping hard and feeling my numb face drenched in my own blood. I feel as if I am slowly drifting away, but Mr. Fire's icy tone brings me back.

"Now listen Colton, I am going to explain you what is going to happen from now on. There are ten people who planned the rape of my girl. They're all in Terra. Five of them that the police caught are going to their niches right now, thinking they got away with the stunt they've pulled. They have no worries in the world. They have no idea what is going on yet. They don't know who they've messed with and I will crucify each and every one of them," he dangerously groans. I can feel the hatred, the desire for bloodshed in his voice, but it's nowhere near as strong as mine.

I close my eyes and think about Aelita and relieve the horrible moments. I relieve the moment when Hunter put his dirty hands all over her body, when he grabbed her breasts, when he thrust inside of her...when she screamed...when she cried, when they mocked me, tied me up and I wasn't able to do anything.

I am angry. I remember promising myself to avenge Aelita and suddenly, all the rage, all the hatred I had before come back all at once. I want to be the one to make them all suffer. "No," I growl, slowly and painfully rising my body up. It hurts so much, and I am still seeing double, but I rise up anyways. To tell the truth, I needed that beating. I'm completely awake now and aware of what is really happening. I'm not letting Aelita's father take revenge for her while my heart is still beating. I am standing on my feet, glaring at Mr. Fire, with Zero standing behind him. I feel my own eyes darken as manage to walk toward them. "I am going to destroy them."

Mr. Fire raises an eyebrow at me.

"Aelita is your family, I...get it." My breathing is still hoarse, "but she's my wife too. She holds my name. She is my responsibility...and I was there when all this happened...I watched." I look away, my voice is slightly trembling, "and it's my entire fault. I'm the one who created this whole mess..." Then I look at him again dead in the eyes, "I'm going to clean it. I will take care of them."

Mr. Fire looks at me for a moment, and I think he understands that I am serious.

"Alright then," he says nonchalantly. "I'll let you kill them all."

I hear myself chuckle darkly, "kill them? Who says I want to kill them?"

He looks at me bewildered.

"Killing them means that they're not going to feel anything, Mr. Fire." I explain fixing the collar of my black dress shirt. "When they're dead, they won't suffer anymore, like those guys you've just ordered to kill," I point at the two dead men still hanging in the air. "They're gone. They don't feel anything anymore. They don't feel pain. They're just dead. Killing those animals who hurt my wife is sparing them. It'll be too easy, Mr. Fire," I turn back and stare at him seeing the faint astonished expression on his face, "I won't kill them. I will hunt each of them, and I will torture them physically, mentally, emotionally...I will make them think hell is heaven," my voice is darker. "I will make them beg me to kill them after I'm through with them."

I see Mr. Fire's eyes widen a bit in shock and horror as if he is not expecting me to say something like this, "and people say I have a messed up mind," I hear him whisper to himself, he then looks up and gives me a quick nod. "That's fine by me, son. You do what you have to do. You have my support. However, you will be taking no more responsibility over my daughter," he gestures to Zero whose ghostly grey eyes never break from me. "He will be her personal guard. I will triple the security around your house as well. Until you take care of those men, Aelita will be under my protection...if she survives."

I swallow and nod slowly.

"I'd like to go back to the hospital now if you don't mind," I say.

"Before you go, I'd like to tell you a story," he says.

I look at him and nod, "of course, sir."

"You know, even though I order the execution of hundreds of people...I have only taken one life with my own hands," he begins with his usual poker face. "He was Esmeralda's first husband. I fell in love with her the minute I set my eyes on her at a gathering, and I know she fell in love with me too, but she was a good woman. She was faithful to her husband and never once betrayed him even though she had strong feelings for me. She was a good wife to him, and the bastard was a delusional drunk who used to beat her almost every night. I didn't know it at first until one night she came running to me for help and her face was swollen. I left the house that night and walked straight to his home. I knocked down the door and I saw the bastard screwing another woman. You know what I did? I beat him to death and strangled him with my own hands. Then, I ordered the execution of his mother, his father, his friends, his brothers, his cousins, his newborn nephew, his neighbors and everyone close to him...just for laying a finger on the love of my life, I killed everyone he ever knew."

Why is he telling me this?

"You know son, when our Aelita was born, she was unique and very different from the rest of the surrounding children, and she couldn't speak. She was a very sad girl as a child. She never wanted to go outside or see the world or meet new people or make new friends because she thought she was different and no one would like her. Then, she met Forest whose parents came to visit me for business. Forest took a like in her and used to try to talk to her and get her attention, but she would always run away and hide, and you know Forest...once he wants to be friends with someone, he would do anything to get the person's attention. He never gave up on her. He always came to visit her, follow her, play with her, try to talk to her and eventually, Aelita started to feel comfortable with him and accepted him," his eyes are traveling back in the past. "I really hope this kid rests in peace."

"Anyways," he continues. "Forest was Aelita's first and only friend and when he found out she was turning seven years old on the same day as him, he decided to have a big birthday party in our home as an opportunity to get her to meet more people."

That's how I met her.

"That's how she met you, Colton and from the moment she laid eyes on you, my daughter completely changed. She wasn't reluctant or afraid to go outside anymore. She even wanted to start going to elementary school so she could spend more time with you two. That is how you three became the ultimate trio, right? It was always you, Forest and Aelita."

I remember...I found Aelita a very strange girl at first because she couldn't talk and the only reason why I hung out with her was because my best friend, Forest was always talking about her and always wanted to be around her. I had no choice.

"You two boys were always by her side, you watched out for her. You defended her when she was being bullied," it was mostly Forest, "then in high school, the tragedy happened, Forest died in that horrible car accident, and the trio was broken. You know, I thought she would be sad and take pity on herself because her best friend died, but instead, my little girl was worried about you."

I stiffen at what he says.

"She wanted to know how you were doing, how you were holding up, always thought about you first. Then in the third year of high school, I don't know what happened between you two, but you suddenly stopped visiting my daughter and she was alone once again. However, she never ever stopped thinking about you and in the same year, when both your parents died, she came to me and wrote me a letter. She asked me for a favor. That was the first time my girl ever asked me anything. She asked me to take you in, to be there for you and to protect you."

I look away with guilt.

"That was when I realized she loves you, and you being okay was what made her happy. So I did it. I nurtured you, I paid for your education, I helped you make your own company, and with your godly brain, you became a successful electrical and mechanical engineer. Then, you became power hungry, you liked being CEO, owning the business world...so you ask me to hand over my company to you, so you could merge it with yours. I did not want to in the first place because I was angry with you. Aelita, wanted to spend her eighteenth birthday with you and visit a foreign country.

You knew she wanted to spend some time with you, and yet, you chose to abandon her and spend time with some other girl. You broke her heart."

My heart is sinking.

"But she asked me to give you the company anyways because all she wanted was to see you happy...and I wanted to make her happy. So, I made this deal with you. I would give you the company if you married her. I knew you didn't love her, but she loved you...and I knew you were smart enough to know that if you didn't care for her, there will be consequences. Aelita was happy being married to you, she was happy with just being by your side. You didn't love her. You didn't cherish her, but my baby girl was still happy being with you. I didn't mind because she was happy," his voice suddenly darkens once more as he turns and glares at me. "But then, you go around and piss off other lowlifes and *my* daughter ends up getting raped and shot in the head in return. My baby girl...gets hurt, gets her innocence taken away...gets broken...because of you. All she ever offered you was love, and this is how you repay her," his eyes are the coldest. "Colton, whether my daughter survives or not does not matter to me anymore. It's still the same. You made her suffer. You're the reason all this happened. Do you think I care about killing those animals? Do you think they're the real person I want to destroy?" His voice is bitter. "You're the one who hurt her. You're the one who hurt my daughter and Colton, when it comes to blood, I do not forgive. Once you're done with those animals, I will take your life with my own hands."

# 3

## HUNTER CROSS'S POINT OF VIEW

"Damn it, turn this shit off already!" I yell at the guys who are drinking and yelling and celebrating and watching the tape over and over again. They are laughing at Mrs. Ice screaming, and mocking at that Ice kid pleading. They had recorded the rape and are now watching for their own pleasure. Why am I the only one feeling guilty and uneasy?

"Come on, Hunter! Cheer up, look at this! Look at how her tits are bouncing?" Hidon says, smirking at me and back at the TV.

"Damn, she was tight, man," White Stone agrees. "You're lucky you're the one who popped her cherry, huh Hunter?"

I shake my head, losing my nerve. I cannot believe those idiots. I stand up brusquely from the couch and give a hard punch on the wall, making the room fall silent. They are all staring at me.

"Hey, what's the matter man?"

"WHAT'S THE MATTER? WHAT'S THE FUCKING MATTER? ARE YOU GUYS DUMB? DO YOU NOT SEE SOMETHING IS WRONG?" I fume at them. I can't be the only one who has a problem with us being freed.

"What are you talking about?" Hidon asks me.

"They let us go. They caught us, they know we've raped and killed Ice's wife and they lock us up in jail and half an hour later they let all of us go? Do you not see something wrong with this?"

"It's because Stigma is on our side," Hidon grins and raises his beer bottle to call out for a toast to his 'spirit guardian. "To Stigma!"

And the rest follow as well. "To Stigma!"

"Jesus Christ, you're all dumber than I thought," Zeus opens the front door and enters the house. "No wonder why your wives cheat on you."

Everyone turns to him and snorts. Not many people like Zeus. He's very tall, giant man with a bald head and a blind eye. Zeus is a gangster. He is mean and grumpy but we both go way back.

"Zeus," I say walking toward him, man hugging him. "What are you doing here?"

Zeus nods at me and at everyone else, then grabs a bottle of beer, "I heard the news. You got your revenge on Mr. Ice," Zeus finally speaks after taking few sips of the beer.

"Yeah, we got it on video!" Hidon turns the television back on, and the tape starts playing again.

"Pretty girl," Zeus nods, but somehow, his voice is sarcastic. "You all did her good."

"We made that son of the bitch cry," Jago finally speaks. The only thing he cares about is seeing Colton Ice suffer. I think he is the most satisfied of all. Everyone else in the room agrees and toasts again, and Zeus smiles bitterly at them. I know something is wrong.

Then, he puts down the beer and starts to clap very slowly and awkwardly. His voice is bitter and very sarcastic as he speaks,"congratufuckinlations."

We all look at him, and Hidon is starting to lose his nerve, "hey, man what's your problem? Why are you talking like that? We got our revenge!"

"You sure did," Zeus agrees, "you went in Colton Ice's home, tied him up," he is looking at the tape, "made him cry, made him beg, fucked his wife in front of him and shot her in the head...you sure got your revenge."

"Yeah man!" Hidon can't stop grinning.

"There's only one thing wrong in this picture: the wife," Zeus continues.

I knew something was wrong.

"What about her?" I finally speak.

"You've not only raped and killed Colton Ice's wife. You've raped and killed Lord Fire's daughter."

The room falls silent and Hidon's mouth falls open as he drops the bottle of beer that is in his hand. It falls on the floor and breaks into pieces. Jago's eyes are wide, his body is frozen, and he does a double take. White Stone loses balance, and he lets himself fall back on the couch. Lazar, who I thought was drunk or high on something is now wide alert, frozen like everyone else. I am seeing my death. I am seeing their deaths. I am seeing our dooms.

"Oh, you all quiet down now, huh?" Zeus gives us a smile that does not reach his eyes. He stands up and then walks toward the TV.

"I'd like to explain you your situations, dumb-fucks," he says. He then takes the remote and starts flipping through the channels. We are too frozen, too shocked to ask him what the heck he is doing. He stops flipping when he gets on Wild Life channel. There is a documentary on lions.

"Watch this carefully guys," he tells us as we all watch at the documentary. It is about lions hunting their prey. Where is Zeus getting at?

"See this lion?" Zeus points at the lion who has caught a fawn. The fawn is still alive, still moving around, but the lion has one sharp grip dipping into the fawn's body, and pulling it back effortlessly.

"It's playing with its food before killing it. It's enjoying it." Zeus continues, "and the fawn is desperately trying to run for its life, it's trying to survive, but it's at the mercy of the lion and it's pretty much doomed."

He then turns to us, "you guys are the antelope."

"Shit," Hidon finally speaks running his hand through his hair, "The Lord's daughter? I thought his daughter was married to some high class man!"

"Yeah, and that high class man is Colton Ice, you dumb-fuck," Zeus retorts.

"No wonder why she was a virgin…" White stone whispers.

"So what's going to happen to us?" I ask.

"Well, the lord paid a lot of money for the TPD to release you."

I knew something was wrong with this picture.

"Why is that?"

"You'll be safer in prison than out in Terra," Zeus explains.

"Then we gotta get the fuck out of here! Come on, Lazar. Let's go!" Hidon says, trying to leave but then Zeus starts to chuckle and then laughs.

Hidon stops moving and turns to him. "What the fuck is funny?"

Zeus continues to laugh, "you never cease to amaze me with your little shit mind, Hidon. If you think you can run from this…" he shakes his head.

"What do you mean, what's happening Zeus? Talk to me," I say walking toward him.

Zeus looks at me dead in the eye. I think I see a bit of pity and sadness. "You really fucked up, Hunter. You really fucked up," he turns to everyone. "Look guys, there's no way out. The Lord paid the mafia, the gangsters, the illegal organizations, the government and the cops, special units, whatever you can think of, he paid them to make sure you guys don't flea from this island. You're going to be watched, stalked daily until the lord decides to kill you all."

"Shit man..." White curses.

"You guys are fucked," Zeus says again.

"Why are you telling us all this? You're part of a gang squad..." Jago asks, looking at Zeus distrustfully.

"Yeah, are you here to rat us out?!" Hidon starts yelling too.

Zeus scoffs, and I raise one hand to quiet everyone else down, "why are you here, Zeus?"

Zeus takes a deep breath and shakes his head, then looks at me again, "because I owe you, Hunter. You saved my life once, and I am returning the favor...well not exactly..."

I remember how I met Zeus. It was about four years ago, I think he was running from the police, they were shooting at him and he ended up hiding in my house. I didn't know him. I could've rat him out to the cops, but I didn't because I knew he was going to die if they caught him. I let him hide in my house for about two months until everything quieted down. Since then, he and I became sort of friends.

"You're a good kid, Hunter," Zeus tells me. "But you're stupid. You think with your heart and not with your head and that girl Veronica, she doesn't love you. She never did, she doesn't now and she never will."

I feel like he is stabbing me with a knife as he says that.

"What you did was pointless, kid. Veronica still doesn't give a shit and the Ice kid is still getting richer at the end of the day. The only thing you've done is put yourself in even deeper shit."

"So they're going to kill us," I conclude. Zeus nods.

"Veronica, and everyone else's wives and kids...are they in danger as well?" I ask carefully and Zeus nods again.

*Jesus fucking Christ.*

"My kids...they're going to kill my kids too?" Lazar starts to speak, his voice is broken.

"God damn it! No!" Hidon punches the wall.

I am shuddering uncontrollably. I never saw this coming. I never even thought of consequences. I was impulsive...I was in the moment...I raped Aelita...I wasn't thinking...I was too angry, all I was enjoying was seeing this Ice's pained face...I was enjoying seeing desperation in his eyes...I never meant all of this to go down this way...I never meant to kill her...I just thought...it would be better off...I fucked up, and now everyone I know will pay for it. No, I cannot let that happen.

"We can't let them hurt Veronica and Lazar's kids, or everyone else's family...or my brother..." I feel a deep knot inside my stomach as I think of my little brother Noah.

"Yeah man, they're innocent!" Hidon agrees.

"Well, the Lord's daughter was innocent too." Zeus shrugs.

"What do we do, Zeus? W-we cannot just stay here and wait for them to k-kill all of us," I say. "I don't care what happens to me, I just don't want Veronica or Noah or other innocent people to pay for what I've done. Zeus, you gotta help me," I beg him.

He shakes his head, "there's nothing I can do."

"Please," I plead.

"Look Hunter, this is beyond my power. I am putting my own life in danger by coming to talk to you. There's eighty percent of chance that I have been followed here, meaning that there's a hundred percent of chance of me getting killed the minute I step out of this house."

We all frown.

"It's okay, I got cancer anyway," he says after seeing my pained, guilty face. "I was going to die sooner or later."

"Why are you doing this, Zeus? Why are you risking your life for me?"

Zeus shrugs, "you risked your freedom for my life."

"I don't want to just sit there and wait for them to come and hurt others who have nothing to do with this...Isn't there anything else I can do?"

Zeus sighs and looks at the tape. "From where I see it, you pretty much have two choices in this."

"What are they?"

"First choice is to kill yourselves," he starts.

We all stiffen and swallow.

"If you die, then they won't have any reason to hurt your family or loved ones, because you won't be there to see it, or feel the pain."

"Suicide is against my religion," Hidon refuses.

"But raping and killing isn't?" Zeus snorts at him.

"What's the other option?" Jago asks.

Zeus smirks, "you fight back, you blackmail them."

White laughs bitterly, "you're shitting me right?"

"I never shit around, kid." Zeus says, his eyes are dead serious.

"With what?" Hidon asks.

"The tape," Jago answers. Zeus nods at him.

"You can use the tape as blackmail. You see boys, the lord's daughter's honor, reputation and respect to them is more important than your pathetic lives. If you threaten them to show the rape of their late daughter's rape to the world, they'll back down a bit," Zeus explains. "Of course, it's a very stupid idea and will only add fuel to the fire and rush your deaths but it might just work to save your loved ones' lives."

"That might work," Hidon agrees with excitement, but I can't.

"No," I refuse. They all look at me.

"Why not?" White asks me.

"..." I don't know how to say this.

"Hey, spill it!" Lazar yells at me.

"We hurt the girl bad enough...let's just let her rest in peace," I answer.

They all quiet down, and stare me furrowing their eyebrows in confusion.

"Hey Hunter," Hidon is the one to finally speak, looking at me like I'm a kid. "She's dead. She's not going to know."

"It's not right. I don't want this for her...we took her innocence, her life...let's leave her reputation and honor alone. Please," I shake my head.

"Well it's either that or kill yourselves," Zeus says. "And killing yourselves seems more suitable but anyways, those are the only two options I can think of. If you have something better...knock yourself out, kid."

"Yeah, man...and think about this, it's for the safety of Veronica, of your brother, of my ex-wife...we have to do this..." White presses.

"We have no other choice," Hidon agrees.

I take a deep breath. I don't know what to think...I mean, too much has happened today. I've raped and killed and got arrested and got freed and I find out my victim is the daughter of the most dangerous man in this world and I'm the fawn, they're the lions, now I'm in deep shit and so is everyone I love that has nothing to do with this, and now I have to either take my own life to spare everyone else or go piss off the lion even more...this is too much.

I start to gasp, I cannot breathe, and I think I am having an asthma attack. I fall down on my knees and start to gasp even more, my head is spinning, and my lungs hurt. I need air.

"It's okay, kid. It's okay, come on...breathe in and out...come on, breathe in..." I hear Zeus softly say, kneeling beside me, soothing me.

"Here's the inhaler," I think it's Jago who's giving me my inhaler. I take it and start to use it, inhaling through the tube. My lungs and throat are relaxing now, and I feel a bit better.

"There, there," I feel Zeus and Jago helping me up and laying me on the couch.

"You're alright?" Zeus pats me.

No. "Yes."

His phone buzzes, he looks at it sighs, "I've got to go," and then tells everyone, "okay, you guys need to take maybe a day to think about all this. Lot has happened. I'm gonna go, good luck Hunter, you need it."

"Wait," I cough out. "I'm worried about you. Are you sure you're going to be okay?"

"Don't worry about me," Zeus smirks. "I'll come back and check up on you tomorrow. Be safe," he pats me and before he leaves, I call him out once more.

"Zeus, thank you."

He smirks and leaves.


"Holy shit man," Hidon lets himself fall on the couch. "We are all fucked."

"What are we gonna do?" White asks.

"I think we already made the decision. We're retaliating," Lazar says. "No way in hell I'm killing myself or letting my family suffer. What we did back there to that Ice kid was right! We made our point, we made the rich boy cry and the wife was delicious! I still don't regret fucking that Negress's brains out back there–"

"LAZAR, SHUT THE FUCK UP!" I roar at him, making everyone startle.

"No, you shut the fuck up," Lazar stands up.

"You got a problem with me asshole?" I stand up too.

"Yeah, I fucking do. You're a fucking hypocrite, you fuck that black bitch, put a bullet in her brain and now you're worrying about her honor? I could give two shits about her honor!"

That is it. I lunge myself at him, he punches me, I punch him, we're on the floor, rolling and rolling and hitting, and somehow, I am the one on the top, beating the crap out of him.

"Alright! Alright! I'm sorry!" He pants as he reaches his limit after I punch him again.

I am panting too, so I stand up and grab the inhaler to help myself breathe. Everyone in the room is quiet, looking at me with a bit of fear.

"I don't want to hear anything about Mrs. Ice from anyone's mouth ever again. Have I made myself fucking clear?"

They nod. "Take a chill pill, Hunter," Hidon whispers and a minute later, he speaks again. "Well what do we do now?"

I take a deep breath. "First we go warn the others who helped us planned this, and everyone go check if your wives and kids and family are okay...come back tomorrow morning at eight am. I'll tell you all what I decided on then. Now get the fuck out my house, I need to rest."

They all start doing so.

I fall back on the couch once again massaging my head because of my sudden headache.

"Later man," Hidon says, looking back at me. He isn't watching where he's going, so he bumps into Jago's back who is standing at the exit of my house.

"Hey man, watch where you're-" Hidon is about to scowl Jago who is frozen in place, and now Hidon is frozen.

"Holy shit," White curses.

I stand up, "what is it?" They don't answer. They're all looking down on the floor at the front step of my house. I walk toward them and look down to where everyone's attention is. My heart sinks at my discovery. I feel sick.

"Who would do...something like this?" White asks, horrified.

"Dude, do you really need to ask?" Hidon's voice is sarcastic. Not only do I hate myself even more as I look at Zeus's decapitated head, I am now angry. They killed him because he came to us. He had nothing to do with what we've done and yet they killed him. It is starting to sink in. Everyone I know and love and care for will be killed soon just like Zeus, if not, even worse. If I don't do something about this...there will be a lot of bloodshed.

"White," I growl. "Make copies of the tape."

# 4

## COLTON ICE'S POINT OF VIEW

"Colton...Colton..." I hear someone's gentle voice wake me up. I open my eyes and look around disoriented. I am lying on the waiting room floor and there is a nurse who is standing, looking down on me. Everything that happened yesterday comes back to me all at once. It's so painful.

I stayed at the hospital the entire time after having that intensive talk with Mr. Fire. I spent the whole time in the waiting room while Mrs. Fire followed the doctor in the operating room.

"Nadia," I stand up brusquely, a bit too quickly, making myself dizzy in return.

"Are you okay?" Nadia supports me. I ignore her question. My focus is only on Aelita.

"Is she...?"

Nadia takes a deep breath. I swear to you that my heart, my brain, my whole body system stops for a moment, anxiously and agonizingly waiting for her to tell me the news.

"She is alive," Nadia says.

Oh.

I don't know if that's good news or bad news. And, I am even more worried when I see Nadia's pained expression.

"But...?" I ask her

"It's nothing..." she shrugs. "It's just that she looked so pained...when she realized she was alive…it was as if she didn't want to be..."

I inhale.

"Come with me, the doctor has more to say to you," she starts walking toward the elevator door. I am still standing, frozen in place. I can't make my legs move.

"Colton, you're coming?" Nadia asks me after she realizes that I am not by her side.

I don't answer. I am still frozen in place, so she walks toward me with a sympathetic smile on her face, and she hugs me.

Nadia is a very good friend of mine. We've had history together since high school. She was Forest's girlfriend. I was Forest's best friend. You know the typical story: one day he finds his girlfriend screwing his best friend, and he gets upsets and runs away from the site. The next day, I find out he died in a car accident.

After this happened, Nadia and I sort of stopped talking out of guilt but after we graduated high school, I still wanted her. I was going to propose to her after Mr. Fire gave me his company but not everything went my way.

Plus, Nadia was never really interested in me like I was into her. It was just a high school crush. She quickly got over me, focused on school, got married to William Smith, and is now living happily ever after.

After sleeping around with at least a hundred girls during the first month of my marriage with Aelita and maybe another hundred later on, I found a way to get over Nadia. Now we're just friends. Mature friends.

"You need to be strong for her right now," she whispers in my ears and looks at me with those greens eyes of hers.

Honey brown eyes are better.

"Colton, do you hear me? You need to be strong for Aelita."

I nod, "yes...of course, sorry. Let's go."

She smiles at me and gestures me toward the elevator. We make our way into the elevator and then to the floor where Aelita's room is. As soon as we step out, I see Mrs. Fire talking to the doctor. She looks distraught and pained. When I walk toward them, she turns to look at me and her pained expression turns into pure resentment.

"You son of a bitch!" She hurries toward me and grabs me by the throat, pushing me back against the wall. My whole body still aches from Zero's beating. I never knew Mrs. Fire was this strong and this ferocious. I guess she found out what really happened to her daughter.

"Mrs. Fire, please stop it!" Nadia and the blonde doctor are pulling her away from me, but she has such a strong hold on my throat that I know if they pull her away, she will end up breaking my neck. She doesn't just stop at my throat, she is scratching and slapping my face with her vicious nails that I see as claws now. I don't struggle her, I know she has every right to.

"Good Lord, Esmeralda. Get your beautiful hands off Ice." I hear Mr. Fire say in the background. The way he pronounced my last name makes me feel like a vermin. It's the same as him saying: 'get your beautiful hands off that virus.' Mrs. Fire does so. She is angry, and tears are falling down on her face. Mr. Fire comes toward her and kisses her hair and hugs her, "it's alright, dear. I'm sorry I didn't tell you. I just wanted your health to be stable...how did you find out?" he gives a cold look to the blonde doctor.

"I am not just some weak woman that you have to protect, Henry. I am a mother," she glares at me, her words are as deadly as venom. "A mother who loves her child" she turns to Mr. Fire, "I want his head on a plate, Henry! I want it now."

I swallow hard but no emotions seem to be running through me. I don't feel pain, fear, anger, sadness, happiness, relief...I am numb. I don't feel anything expect the soreness of my chest, and neck and the burns on my face from her slaps and scratches.

Mr. Fire hugs his wife back and assures her. "You will get it soon, honey. I promise, it's just that Ice has lots of things to take care of first."

I find it a bit funny that they're talking about wanting me dead while I'm right in front of them.

"Ahem," the doctor clears her throat, getting everyone's attention. She then turns to me with a very sympathetic smile.

"Would you like to come to my office? I'd like to speak with you privately, Mr. Ice."

"We're coming with you," Mrs. Fire says, it is not a request.

Dr. Penn looks at me, asking for permission. I nod.

"I'll wait for you here, Colton," Nadia squeezes my hand. I nod at her and follow Dr. Penn and the couple who want me dead to a more private room.

"Mr. Ice, it is a miracle that your wife is alive. We've never seen anything like this. The bullet went straight through her brain with no damage. It's almost as if the bullet is transparent…either that or her brain is, I don't know what to tell you," she starts, sounding amazed. "Residues of the bullet ended up being stuck in the broca's area of her brain and somehow it happens to be a good thing. Mr. Ice, do you know what the function of the broca's area?"

"Speech," I answer.

"Correct, Mr. Ice. Well, we've removed the residues, and we've noticed that the malformation on her broca's area has been fixed."

"What do you mean?" Mrs. Fire asks.

"She's not mute anymore. She can speak."

Everyone sighs in relief and Mrs. Fire starts to cry.

"It's a miracle; it is as if her bullet healed her instead of hurting her. She is intact. There's an angel watching over her."

"Oh thank Goodness," Mr. Fire says. He is very relieved.

"But," Dr. Penn clears her throat. "There is a problem." Of course there is.

"What is it...?" Mrs. Fire asks, her face is now pained.

"The rape damages..." Penn answers carefully. I start to stiffen.

"Even though her body can heal faster than the average human, the rape damages are still atrocious." Even Dr. Penn's face is pained. "Her vaginal walls are torn and viciously ripped. It's even more painful for her because she was a virgin."

...

"She's going to be in a lot of pain for the next few months. It's going to be hard for her to move, to walk, to do anything..."

I can't listen to this. I just want to leave the room.

"Are you listening to what she's saying, son?" Mr. Fire calls me as I look down on the floor. His voice is so bitter.

"Yes sir," I reply.

"I strongly suggest, Mr. Ice, for your wife's benefit that you don't engage any sexual activities, at least for the first three months. Meanwhile, we're going to be giving her lots of antibiotics and pain medications to ease the physical pain," she then sighs. "But that's not what I'm worried about. The physical pain can heal with time, but the mental, the emotional pain...what this young girl has been through… it's going to take quite a while to heal her. That is why I am talking to you, Mr. Ice."

I can't speak.

"What do you recommend?" Mrs. Fire says in my place.

"I recommend her being put in a safe institution. She is psychologically broken, and I am concerned for her safety. Since you're the husband, Mr. Ice, we need your signature to put her in a–"

"In a mental hospital? You think my daughter is crazy?!" Mrs. Fire's tone is vicious and angry. She is getting up from her chair, shouting at Dr. Penn.

"Esmeralda ..." Mr. Fire starts.

"No. We are done here! I will take care of my daughter's mental state. I will help her heal emotionally. I am her mother and I know what she needs!"

"I am afraid that it's not your decision, Mrs. Fire. It's the husband's," Dr. Penn politely says.

"I could give two shits about what this sorry bastard thinks. My daughter is under my care now!" Mrs. Fire roars.

"Esmeralda," Mr. Fire stands up as well, trying to calm her down, but she doesn't listen to him.

"No. Listen, all of you! My daughter is under my care now. No one is taking her away from me! I will get her through this. She is strong!"

No, she is not.

"I'm taking her out of this hospital as soon as she is cleared. She will be staying at our house, and will be under the family doctor's care."

Wait what? Mrs. Fire is taking Aelita away from me?

"No," I finally speak. "She'll be staying at our home."

Mrs. Fire raises an eyebrow at me. I know she is thinking about aiming for my throat once again. "I'll stay in a hotel," I explain. "Aelita is raising tons of animals and a garden and she is very attached to it, so I think...it'll be in her best interest to stay at our home. I will stay in a hotel. Mrs. Fire, you're in charge of her, I will not get in your way," I don't want to argue and again, I feel nothing.

"Of course I am," she snarls at me. Then, she turns to her husband, "she can't have any males in the house for a while, so fire all those male servants, Zero can't be around her either. Not even you, dear," then to the doctor, "Dr. Penn, I need you to transfer all your paperwork and reports of my daughter to our family doctor."

Dr. Penn nods.

"And you stay the hell away from my daughter," Mrs. Fire is snarling at me again. Seems like I won't get to see Aelita. I am telling myself that it's alright, it's for the best. I don't think I can face her anyways. However, another part of me seems to be craving to see her.

I want to see her. I want to hold her and touch her hair and look at her honey brown eyes and hear her talk. I want to hear Aelita talk. I want to know what her voice sounds like. I really do. "Yes Mrs. Fire," I nod.

She is about to say something else as if she wants to curse me out or call me names but she shuts her mouth and walks out.

"I'll be right with you, dear," Mr. Fire calls after her and then looks at me, signaling me that he wants to talk. "Penn, I told you to keep my wife in the dark," he growls at Dr. Penn who is a bit stiffened. She is about to say something, but he doesn't give her a chance to. "I'll deal with you later. Let's go, son."

I stand up and nod at Dr. Penn and follow Mr. Fire. He walks me out of the hospital.

"I'm worried about Aelita's safety," I start to talk. "Most of the security guards you've hired are males, and I think if..."

"Son, don't worry about it. My wife knows what she's doing. She'll do a better job at protecting Aelita than you could ever try to," he's insulting me with his famous poker face.

"You look like shit, Zero gave you a good beating yesterday, didn't he? He's my favorite, always performs an outstanding job," he turns to look at me. "Go book a hotel room and shower and rest, enjoy yourself...do whatever used to do before the incident and don't forget to eat," his tone is starting to be mocking. "Come to church with me tomorrow son," he tells me. "My daughter is miraculously alive. We need to thank God. Then, we'll talk."

"Yes sir," I tell him and get in the car that is waiting for me.

"I'll get the penthouse for you, Mr. Ice," the hostess tells me as I try to book a room.

"No, it's not necessary. Just one room is fine," I tell her.

"Lord Fire insists on giving you the best hospitality we can give you, sir," she says with a fake smile.

I feel suddenly irritated, "fine, bill it to me." I don't have my credit card with me.

"That won't be necessary. Lord Fire is paying for it."

I clench my jaws, "alright."

"This way, sir." Two other women start to direct me toward the elevator. I follow them inside, and once the door closes, the two girls start to get close to me.

"Mr. Fire wants us to show you a good time..." One girl murmurs in my ear and starts tugging it.

*What the fuck?*

"He told us you've had a really hard day...and we were hoping to make you feel better," the other girl purrs.

I recall his words before coming at the hotel. "*Do whatever you used to do before the incident.*"

"That won't be necessary. I don't need your service," I tell the girls.

"We already got paid for this; if we don't...we're in trouble."

"Not my problem," I glare at them and step out as soon as the elevator door opens. They are about to step out as well, but I press the button sending them back downstairs. I enter the penthouse and look around. There's a fancy baseball bat hung up on the wall as a decorative item. I grab it and start breaking things.

I break the glasses, I break the vases, I break everything I see.

I am furious. Henry Fire is insulting me, devaluing me. He thinks I don't care about Aelita. He thinks all I want to do now is go sleep with more girls and forget about what happened while my wife is in the hospital. He thinks I'm just some trashy guy and I only think about my fucking dick. He's putting me on the same level as those rapists and that really fucking pisses me off. I care for Aelita! I care for her! Yes, I won't deny that I never wanted her to be my wife. I've been an asshole and an inattentive husband to her but I care about her. What those animals did to her, what those monsters made me watch...they have no idea what effect it is taking on me...to hurt an innocent girl...to make her scream while I watch...that is the worst thing that has ever fucking happened to me. Not even my parent's death or my brother's death can compare to what happened to Aelita.

I fucking care for the girl and her parents are bashing me...treating me like...some scumbag.

The baseball breaks and I am still angry, so I am using my fists to punch at the wall, break more things, draw blood on my knuckles. I think I even got few glass pieces jammed in my flesh from all the punching but I don't stop. I feel as if all the emotions I was lacking when I was in the hospital are coming at once. I am hurt, I am angry, I feel insulted, I feel like I am an enemy, I am scared for Aelita and how bad she will be suffering from now on. I can't even look at her. I can't do anything to help her. I can't support her. I can't do anything. I feel helpless...I feel useless...I start to sob through my punches.

I think of what Lord says earlier. Wanting me to come to church with him and praise God? What the fuck did God do in all this? I prayed for him to save Aelita, the most innocent person I know. I prayed for God to help her, to have mercy on her, to spare her while Hunter was tainting her and what does he do? He fucking brings out three more monsters to destroy her completely then he makes them put a bullet in her head. What for? Why? Why God? Why do this to her?! Why fucking do this to her?! What the fuck did she do!? What has Aelita ever fucking done to him? Huh? Why should I go to church and thank him for letting Aelita get raped huh?! The least He could do was let her die and rest in peace. But no, he decides to bring her back to life! She's going to be scarred...her innocence? Gone! Her smile? Gone! Her love for animals and plants and nature? Gone...She is going to look at this world in a different way... What did she ever do to God...to anyone...? Why? Why....?

"Why...God..." I keep on sobbing out, letting myself fall on the carpet. My hand is bloody, I am crying until I fall asleep.

When I wake up...the sun's rays are piercing through the window down on me. It takes me about ten seconds to gain complete consciousness and awareness. Ten seconds of peace of mind.

"Ugh..." I grunt and raise myself up. My hands are in so much pain, I feel like asking someone to chop them off. I feel weak and dizzy and try to take my phone and glance at the time but then I remember I have nothing with me. Not a phone, not a wallet, no clothes to change...I have nothing at all. I must go back to my home and get my things.

But, Aelita the lion cub and Mrs. Fire, the ferocious overprotective lioness might be there and I don't think they will enjoy seeing me. But I really need to gather my things. Maybe I'll try to sneak in my own fifty million gold home and not get shot.

I turn on the television to see what time it is. I furrow my eyebrow in disbelief. It's not the time that startles me.

It's the date.

Monday. I slept from Saturday to Monday? That's a first. And I also realize I didn't make it to church on Sunday with the Lord. Deep down, I don't regret it and I don't care at all. Why do I need to go to church and worship someone who doesn't hear my prayers? Why do I need to put up with the Mr. Fire's indirect, clever insults? I don't have time for this shit. I have people waiting for me to make their lives a living hell.

I enter the shower and clean myself. I clean the dried up blood from my hands and try to pull out the jammed glass pieces from my knuckles. It hurt so much. So I let it stay in. I'll go to the hospital later.

"What the hell are you doing here, Ice?" Mrs. Fire is at the gate of my home. My hands are up in the air, in defeat. I have completely understated this woman as a ferocious woman. She's a *crazy* ferocious woman. She's pointing a rifle at me. I think she is controlling herself not to shoot.

"I just want to pick up my phone, my wallet and some clothes, Mrs. Fire," I say quietly and calmly.

"Why weren't you at the church yesterday?" She asks me, "we thought you killed yourself."

*You all wish that, don't you?*

"I overslept," I reply. She frowns and glares at me, then withdraws the rifle.

"You have half an hour and make sure you eat breakfast before leaving. You look pale and malnourished."

*And you care?*

"Thank you," I say as we enter my house. I have this ridiculous hope that Aelita is going to be at the front door with a bright smile on her face and flowers to give me like she always used to do. I bet my life that will never happen again. I miss that. Well you don't know what you have until it's gone, right?

"How is she doing?" I ask carefully as Mrs. Fire stalks me to the stairs. I glance at the door all the way at the end of the hall. That is where Aelita's room is. Far, far away from mine.

"What do you think?" Mrs. Fire retorts. We're now at the front door of my room and I find myself asking. "Has she spoken? Did she say anything?"

I see a faint smile on Mrs. Fire's lips, "her first word was 'mom'..." Mrs. Fire seems very emotional as if she is about to cry all of a sudden. "Hurry up and get your things, Ice." She snaps at me and walks away.

I am now alone in the hall, staring at the door of my room. Last time I was in there...I don't want to think about it. I don't want to, so I shield my mind and my memory from everything as I enter the room. I'm going to make this fast.

I rush in, grab a suitcase, open the drawer and start to take some clothes. I am trying hard, very hard not to remember the things that happened in the room...I think I'll have to burn this room down if I ever get to come back and live in here. I am about to leave the room when I see one of Aelita's dog.

He is a golden German shepherd. I think he's one of Aelita's favorites because I used to see him the most with her. The dog is standing at the door and it's growling at me. I faintly smile. It hates me too. Why wouldn't he hate me? I let his master get hurt.

"Hey boy," I tap my knees, signaling the dog to come. He does so, and I kneel to level with him and look at his collar for his name.

Forest.

I shake my head and almost crack a smile. Aelita named her dog after our late best friend. I should've seen that coming.

"You look like him," I start the pet the dog. "Alert, hyperactive," the dog suddenly bites me. My bloody, painful hands. "Annoying!" I grunt trying to break free from his grip but he's not letting go. It hurts so bad. I try to struggle, grunt, warn the dog, but he doesn't let go. It's suddenly starting to drag me out the room with my hand in his fangs. "Ah, damn it! Stop this, Forest!" I growl at him and grab onto a tall plant that is in the corner with my other hand to not let myself get dragged anymore by the psychotic dog but the plant is a cactus and I get hurt even more.

Wow, everything wants me dead here.

I give up trying to fight the dog. I let it drag me to wherever he wants me to be. Probably in a room with the rest of the animals so they can all gang up on me and kill me…

Only it isn't where Forest drags me to. We're at Aelita's front door, and he lets go of me. He is barking at the door.

"Geez, you could've just said you wanted me to open the door for you," I glare down at the shepherd. I look at the door and think for a minute. Aelita's behind that door...probably on the bed, bruised up, either sleeping or crying...

"No, I can't open it." I shake my head but then the dog growls at me again and keeps on barking at the door. I have a sudden feeling in my heart that the dog is desperately trying to enter the room.

So, I turn the door knob and slightly open the door. I don't dare look inside. I just open the door wide enough to let the dog in. But, curiosity takes the best of me. I peek at the edge of her bed to catch a glance of her foot. That will be enough for me. The thing is, I don't see anything. I open the door a bit wider, and still no sign of any part of her body, so I open the door completely and she isn't in her bed. The dog is barking again, louder now, and it's barking at the bathroom door that is closed. I heard the water running...She must be taking a bath...But, something tells me it's not it.

I am about to call her but then I see something that takes me to hell and back. Water is dripping and running under the bathroom door drenching the bedroom carpet with a red color.

It's blood mixed with water.

I suddenly recall what Nadia said earlier about Aelita: *It's just that she looked so pained...when she realized she was alive, it's as if she didn't want to be...*

I also recall what Dr. Penn said: *She is psychologically broken, and I am concerned for her safety.*

Now I understand why the dog is barking at the door.

"NO!" I cry out and rush toward the bathroom door. I force open the doorknob, but nothing happens to it. It's shut tight. "Aelita! Aelita! AELITA!" I shout her name and am now slamming my body against the door, trying to force it open. "Aelita!" I cry out in desperation.
I turn to Him again for help. No, no, please God. Please God, let her be okay. Let it not be what I think this is! Please.

I slam my body down again and again on the door but it is not working so I take few steps back and then run forward and collide my body as hard as I can against the door. I dislocate my shoulder while doing it, but it doesn't matter at the moment. The door breaks open, and due to the force I applied on it, I fall on the bathroom floor—a very wet bathroom floor that is running blood. It's like a small river.

I get up, my eyes are wide open and dilated, my heart is beating at an alarming rate as I rush toward the bathtub, where her body is laying naked. Her eyes are closed and she is drenched in the bloody tube. I see a knife fall down from her hand. I rush toward her with agony and pain, trying to get her out of this blood bath. Once again, He chooses to ignore my prayers. Once again, He lets her get hurt.

# 5

"God damn it, Aelita! God damn it!" She is naked in my arms on the wet bathroom floor and unconscious. She is bleeding out of her inner thigh. She cut her femoral artery with the knife and I am using my hand to put pressure on the wound. The dog is still barking and circling us.

"Forest! Go! Go get help! Go get Mrs. Fire! GO!" The dog obeys and runs out of the room as I bring my attention back to Aelita. She is getting paler and paler by the minute.

"Aelita...why..." my voice is faint and broken.

I realize the water is building up, so I decide to take her back in her room, which is going to be really hard because I can't take my hands off her bleeding thigh. If I do, the bleeding will continue. So, I decide to wait for Mrs. Fire.

God damn it, where is she?!

"Aelita..." I say her name, looking down on her beautiful, gentle face.

I'm reliving the events that happened after they shot her in the head. When the rapists left, and I was holding her. She was so cold, so peaceful....so relaxed and I felt kind of happy that she wasn't shaking or screaming or trembling anymore. She was calm. She was peaceful, and I wished she stayed that way.

But now, now that she's survived and is trying to take her life again...I can't. I don't wish her to stay that way. She needs to wake up. I need to see those honey brown eyes again. Please.

"Aelita, I swear I'll get those animals who hurt you...I swear... I'll make them pay for what they did to you but please wake up...This is not the way...wake up...please..."

"Oh dear..." Mrs. Fire is frozen on site for a moment. She is staring down at us as if she does not believe what is happening. "Oh, dear...OH DEAR!" She is now realizing what is happening before her.

"Well don't just stand there! Help me get her on the bed!" I yell at Mrs. Fire when I realize she is still frozen.

She rushes toward us and I see her hand shaking. We manage to lift Aelita's body up and we slowly and carefully lie her down on the bed. I lay beside her, my hand still in between her thigh, applying pressure on her open wound. It's viciously and deeply cut. I can almost feel the dark emotions she was feeling while cutting her own flesh with the knife.

"Oh...God...what...what...happened....?" Mrs. Fire asks, her voice is starting to break.

"She tried to kill herself...we still have a pulse, but she's bleeding out, I need you to call the ambulance!"

Mrs. Fire is shaking, her eyes are starting to twitch and roll back in. I think she's about to have a seizure.

"Mrs. Fire! Not now!" I yell at her. "You can't go down on me. I need you!" Her body is starting to become unbalanced."Listen! Your daughter is going to die if you don't help her! You have to be stron-" She falls on the ground and her body begins to shake. Shit. "GOD DAMN IT!" I roar out. I can't leave Aelita. If I release the pressure on her inner thigh, she's going to bleed out completely and might die before I even come back for her. I need help. I need someone to help me, to call for a doctor. "HELP! SOMEONE! ANYONE!" I scream out. Then, I see the golden German shepherd climb on top of the bed; he is making a squeaky sound as he starts to lick Aelita's face.

"Hey, Forest. Please tell me you're a smart dog... go get help please," I beg. The dog stares at me and tilts its head to the side, then barks. "Please..." I plead again. It doesn't budge. "Look, Forest. I'm sorry I screwed Nadia behind your back. I was a dumb and stupid and sorry bastard and I still am. I'm sorry, but right now it's not about me...it's about Aelita. Please go find someone, anyone!"

*Why the fuck am I talking to a dog?*

To my surprise, the dog barks and stands up and runs out. I narrow my eyes at him.

Damn that Forest. I turn my attention back to Aelita and start to pat her hair with my other hand. I kiss her head and whisper with a trembling voice, "it's going to be okay." Then, I glance back at her wound, but then realized her inner thighs have more than one wound. I see darkish and reddish bruises in between her thighs. I inhale as I realize they're from the brutal rape.

Memories of them grabbing her, thrusting inside of her, pulling her hair, spitting on her...calling her names...all come back to haunt me again, "I'm going to make them regret this, Aelita. I swear, I'm going to get them...I'm going to..."

"Jesus Christ!" A dark skinned woman with brown eyes wearing a white coat is at the door, with the golden shepherd. That dog sure is handy.

"What happened?" The doctor says, rushing toward Aelita and me on the bed. She is rather young. Perhaps my age. She's the family doctor?

"Her c– Her femoral artery is cut. She lost a lot of blood."

"Okay...okay..." The doctor takes a deep breath and starts to open her medical kit. "Oh shit..." she says as she glances at Mrs. Fire's shaking body.

"She had a seizure..." I explain.

"Yes, she has epilepsy," she keeps on glancing at Mrs. Fire's body.

"Come on, help Aelita!" I press the doctor.

"I have to stop the seizure..." she is walking toward Mrs. Fire.

"WE DON'T HAVE TIME TO WASTE, DOC!" I roar at her. "MY WIFE IS BLEEDING OUT! MRS. FIRE WILL BE FINE. SHE WOULD WANT HER DAUGHTER TO BE TAKEN CARE OF FIRST!" She looks at me, still wasting time. "I'll make sure you get your money if Mrs. Fire dies," I snap at her, my eyes are glaring and she is glaring back at me.

"It's not for the money," she snaps at me and rushes toward Aelita and I after grabbing some tools from her bag. "On three you let go of the wound, okay?" She tells me. I nod.

"One, two, three!"

I do so and the blood starts to gush out again, splashing the doctor on the face, her coat and everything around is red. "Gosh!" She grunts, but then uses a medical tool and inserts it in her wound.

"I'll stop the bleeding. You take care of her mother. There's an injection in my bag. It is called Fosphenytoin sodium injection. Take it and stab it in her neck. She'll be okay then," I am reluctant at leaving Aelita's body.

"GO!" she yells back at me. I glare at her and comply. I do as she tells me to and inject the needle in Mrs. Fire's neck. Thirty seconds after, Mrs. Fire is grunting. Her body relaxes and she opens her eyes, scans around and then looks at me, brusquely rising up and hitting my nose with her forehead.

"Oh, I'm so sorry. It wasn't on purpose," she lies and stands up from the ground. "Dr. Brown, thank goodness you're here! Aelita, how is she?"

"I need some quiet, she'll be fine," Dr. Brown seems to be a bit stressed. "She lost a lot of blood, we need blood transfusion."

"Take my blood," I stand up from the floor and walk toward them. "I'm O negative."

"So am I," Mrs. Fire glares at me.

"You're in no way near healthy enough to give blood, Mrs. Fire." I press.

"I'm not letting you save my daughter's life by infesting her body with your rotten blood!"

"She's my wife and I need to take care of her, don't make it personal right now. It's about Aelita, not you!"

"Oh now you realize you need to take care of her?" Her voice is rising. I try really hard not to yell back at her.

"Mrs. Fire," I take a deep breath and grit through my teeth, "she is my wife, she still holds my last name and I make the call."

"Until death tears you two apart!" she growls at me.

"PLEASE STOP!" Dr. Brown starts to yell at us, "I JUST NEED BLOOD! I DONT GIVE A SHIT WHOSE!"

"I'll give her my blood," Mrs. Fire snarls at me and walks back toward the bed. "Get out," she orders me again.

"No," I refuse.

"No, seriously Mr. Ice. Get out." The doctor yells at me too. I inhale and exhale angrily and walk out the room. I slam the door behind and breathe deeply once more, then punch the wall. "AH!" I cry out in pain as the jammed glass pieces that were stuck in my knuckles pierce deeper into my flesh. "Ugh...ugh...ugh..." I pant, trying to control the pain. I look at my hand and realize it's drenched with blood. Aelita's blood.

Her blood is on my hand. Her blood is on my hands. Her. Blood. Is. On. My. Hands. I start to shake, feel sick all of a sudden. I stand up and run to the nearest washroom and start to vomit...only that there is nothing in my stomach to bring out. I spit in the toilet and wash my bloody hands in the sink. It's not coming off. It's not...coming off...It's not coming o–

Toc toc. There's a sudden knock at a door.

"What?" I snap, opening the door, glaring at the servant. She's a beautiful young Asian girl with long black hair put into a pony tail. She stiffens; her eyes are wide and frozen. "Y-you have a car...waiting for you outside. It's from the Lord."

One after the other. They won't give me a break until I die, huh?

"I'll be right out," I slam the door at her face. Before I leave, I need to find out if Aelita's going to be okay. I open the bathroom door a catch a glimpse of the servant who's about to leave.

"Hey!" I call after her. She turns back and I walk toward her, "I need you to go in my wife's room and see if she's going to be alright."

She doesn't budge. "Now," I snarl at her, "or you're fired."

Her eyes are just as cold as mine, "I don't work for you. Mrs. Fire hired me." Then she walks away. I look at her in disbelief and swallow my pride. This is for Aelita.

"I'm sorry," I call after the servant and she stops. "I'm sorry I yelled at you and slammed the door on your face. I shouldn't have. I'm sorry."

She turns around, nods at me and walks toward Aelita's room. She goes in and comes back to me minutes after. Her eyes are broken and teary.

*Oh no.* I think of the worse.

I walk toward her, "Wh-what happened?"

The servant shakes her head, "she's...alive. They're giving her blood."

"And what else?" I ask again. She looks so distraught and appalled and I have the feeling there's more.

She shakes her head again, "it's just that...I've never seen anyone so broken...so..."

"Don't finish that sentence," I don't want a stranger to pitying Aelita, "thank you."

"My name is Hinata, and you're welcome," she smiles, bows and walks away.

"Have a seat." Mr. Fire says with a very serious cold voice. I am guided in Mr. Fire's dark and intimidating office. I am a bit surprised that he's not greeting me and telling me that I look like shit. I do as I'm told. We're both sitting down on the sofa and facing a big screen TV.

"Zero, put the tape on and leave," he orders Zero.

"Yes sir," Zero nods and does so. His voice is cool and calm. Everyone in the room leaves except for me and Mr. Fire.

"What is it?" I ask him.

"We're about to find out. One of my daughter's rapists' dog carried this tape in his mouth and left it outside my property."

I clench my jaws and tighten my fists.

"They have balls. I'll give them that," Lord Fire says as he presses play and the tape starts to roll. We see a person wearing a mask seating on the chair. As he starts to speak, I recognize the voice.

"Hello," Hunter says. "What you're about to see next, will be broadcasted on the internet in forty eight hours if you don't let our loved ones flee out of this island in peace, unharmed. Please know that we're deeply sorry about what happened to your daughter. If we could take it all back, believe me we would...but unfortunately we can't. We can't erase the past and save Mrs. Ice so we can only focus on the present and the future. Mrs. Ice is dead," I want to enter the television and grab this guy's throat and rip it apart.

"However, her honor is still intact and unknown to the world and I am sure that as a father and a powerful man, Lord Fire, you wouldn't want the world discovering what happened to your daughter in a very detailed way. If you don't leave our loved ones in peace, I will destroy the small dignity that is left of your dead daughter by broadcasting this. We need you to answer us in forty eight hours, let us know we have your word. We're willing to stay in Terra. Us: the ones who are responsible for your daughter's death. We're willing to get killed, but not our family. They had nothing to do with this. I hope you understand that."

Then, the clip ends and another starts and what we both watch shocks and infuriates me to the point where I cannot move, or blink. They have a tape of Aelita getting raped.

And she's screaming.

And the guys are laughing.

And I'm watching it.

And so is Mr. Fire. He too, is still in his chair. His poker face is gone. His brown eyes widen and blaze with anger. His eyebrows are furrowed and his face becomes wrinkled. His mouth is pursed so low that it makes the form of a low arc.

Those bastards. Those fucking bastards! I cannot believe this. I cannot comprehend their cruelty, their cowardliness, and their guts! I can't! Why the fuck would they do that? I want to kill them. I want to hurt them. I need, I really need to see them bleed. I need to see them cry and beg. I want to hurt them so bad. I have never, ever in my life wanted something this bad. I want to kill them all. I want to kill their families in front of them and hurt them in any way possible. I want to destroy them. And I will.

Oh, yes. That is something I am going to accomplish thoroughly and perfectly. I'll make a deal with the devil if I have to. He can take my soul after I'm through with them. I don't care what happens to me anymore. I don't care about the Fires wanting me dead. I just want those animals to bleed. I want to make them all perish.

Mr. Fire shuts off the TV and stands up. He is pacing through the room.

"God damn it!" he kicks a chair, causing it to fall. "Zero!" he roars.

Within seconds, Zero is in the room.

"Gather the A-Squad. We're wiping all of them out. Tonight!" Mr. Fire orders.

Like hell he is. "No," I refuse, standing up walking toward Lord Fire. He glares at me. "Sorry kid, they just crossed the line. They're pissing on my name and my daughter's."

"I said no. They're mine to kill," I snarl at Mr. Fire, grabbing the front of his shirt. Zero points a gun at me. I don't even flinch. My eyes are still glaring at Mr. Fire. He raises one hand to Zero, gesturing him to put the gun down.

"Get your filthy hands off me, Ice," Mr. Fire warns dangerously.

"Not until you give me your word that you won't interfere," I growl.

"Son, they have a tape of my daughter being raped, THEY FUCKING SENT IT TO ME AND ARE THREATENING ME AND MY DAUGHTER'S REPUTATION AND YOU WANT ME TO STAY STILL? WHO THE FUCK DO YOU THINK I AM?!" He is fuming at me so loudly that my ears start to hurt.

"Killing them right now is a very reckless move," I start. "We don't know if they have extra copies or who has the copies. The minute you go on a killing rampage is the minute someone puts this out to the public. We can't kill them yet!"

"So you want me to just sit there and give them what they want?" he snorts.

I shake my head. "I'll take care of the tapes, I give you my word. I will have all of them sent to you so you can burn it yourself. I won't let them use the tape. I promise you. I need you to let me handle them, sir. Please. I really need this," my tone is stern and firm. His face is changing from the angry Grinch to the same old poker face. "I want to be the one making them suffer. I want to watch them cry, and scream. I want to see despair in their eyes. I've...never wanted something this bad..." I am shaking, "I am your prey, Mr. Fire. I'm the one you want to kill. Not them. Let me take care of them."

He looks at me a bit impressed, "get your filthy hands off me before I cut your throat, kid," he snarls at me again. I do so, and he fixes his tie. "You can have them," he tells me moments after. "But Zero's going to be your assistant in this. I am not taking no for an answer."

I glance at the very pale Zero, the guard who beat me half dead last Friday. He stares back at me with the same creepy, emotionless grey eyes.

"Alright," I reluctantly accept.

"Zero, you're under his order now." Lord Fire tells Zero.

"Sir." Zero salutes Mr. Fire, then me. His eyes are suddenly cold, full of unashamed hatred.

"Mr. Ice," he says, with a cold respectful tone. I nod at him too angry at the rapists to give a shit about what Zero thinks.

"You have twenty four hours to get the copies, Ice. Now get out of my office. I need to blow off steam." Mr. Fire snaps at us and we do so, instantly.

"Where are we going, sir?" Zero asks me when we get in the car.

"Right now, to the hospital," I show him my very swollen knuckles, "then we'll take care of business."

He doesn't say anything else for a while, and then he speaks again. "May I ask what's in the tape?"

I glare at him, "It's none of your business."

He glares back at me, clenching his jaws. The trip to the hospital is silent afterwards.

"There, the ointment and the antibiotics should kill any infection. Come back in three days to take off the stitches Colton," Nadia tells me after treating my wound.

"Thanks Nadia," I gratefully thank her. She smiles back. "How is she doing?" I don't say respond. All I do is look down.

"How are you doing in all this, Colton?" She puts her hand on mine, squeezing them. I still don't answer her.

"Colton, you know you can talk to me about anything, right? You know we're still good friends, right?"

I nod at her. "Thank you, Nadia," I stand up. "I'll get going now." I walk out of my hospital room and I'm about to make my way toward the elevator when I catch the glance of someone who is on my blacklist.

I do a double take as I see Jago walking in a room. The first thing I feel is a deep knot in my stomach. I feel my blood starting to rush through my veins faster than the speed of light. My eyes glister in fury and resentment and I clench my fists.

I run toward him and grab him then give him a good hard punch, feeling his bones break. Then he's on the floor and I am kicking him and kicking him and I sit on top of him and I am punching him over and over, then I'm biting his ears off, making him scream out in pain and then I'm ripping his chest open with my bare hands and grab his heart and crush it.

Well, all this is happening in my head.

I am about to do exactly what I imagine doing to him, but then I realize something. Jago is the weakest link of all. He didn't rape Aelita back there. He was just obsessed with seeing the pained expression on my face.

That guy was just into seeing me hurt and cry. He didn't touch Aelita. He seems like someone that has a bit of conscience.

I slowly and discreetly stalk him to the room he enters. Before the room closes, I catch the glimpse of a brown haired woman who is lying on the hospital bed.

"Hi sweetheart," I read Jago's lips after he kisses her on the forehead and puts down the flowers on the table. Then the door closes completely and I can't see them anymore.

"Sir, shall we go?" Zero joins me. I am staring at the door and Zero glances at it and back at me with confusion. "Is there a problem with the door?"

"Zero, get a complete profile on Jago and his family," I order Zero as we are making our way out of the hospital.

Zero is impressive. It takes him less than fifteen minutes to tell me everything about Jago's life, and his connections. Everything he tells me about this sorry pathetic bastard is enough to help me get the tape from them.

"We're going to his house and wait for him there." I tell Zero. He frowns at me as if he'd like to understand what's going on, but I don't tell him anything. I just have a very small smirk on my face. I feel like the devil has answered my prayers and accepted the deal.

We're in the bastard's dirty, disgusting house. It doesn't look like it has been cleaned for years. It smells and is trashy and is sickening.

I have been sitting down on the sofa for about two hours waiting for him to get home. I look at my watch and if Zero's information is liable, Jago should be back here in 5...4...

I hear the keys in the door starting to unlock.

3...

The door knob turns.

2, he opens the door and sees me.

"Welcome h ome Jago," I tell him with a deadly smile that doesn't reach my eyes.

# 6

## JAGO PARKER'S POINT OF VIEW

"Jago, I need you to come meet me and the boys tonight at my place," Mr. Hunter Cross tells me on the phone.

"...What time? I'm kind of busy tonight," I tell him not really wanting to gather with them. They all think we're friends and united because we're on the same fucking boat with the Lord.

"8 pm. There's some shit we need to talk about."

"Does it concern me?" I question reluctantly. I am not much of a social person. I don't like any of them.

They're stupid, dumb and reckless. This entire thing happened because of them. I didn't vote on killing the Lord's daughter. I didn't even vote on raping the girl at first. It wasn't until we got to the house that Hunter told me what they were going to do. I disagreed at first, but after seeing that bastard suffering, crying and begging for mercy, I didn't mind seeing the girl hurt.

Now I'm being put on the same boat with them.

"Yes Jago," Hunter's tone is sarcastic. "It concerns you. Whatever is going on with us from now concerns you. We're in this together."

"I don't know if I can make it tonight."

The end of the line is quiet for a moment, and then he finally speaks. "Jago, I know you're angry and scared about all of this but I worry about you, man. You can't withdraw yourself from us. We're stronger together; we need each other right now. It's us against the whole entire world and we need you. I need you. You need us. We need each other."

I am silent. I am not sure what he means by I need them and they need me. I am a loner. I don't have friends, no one needs me and I don't need anyone. Well, maybe someone needs me...but it's not them.

"Jago?" Mr. Cross calls me, "you're there?"

"Yes, yes. I'm there. I'll be there at eight," I answer him. I can hear the smile in his voice, "that's really great, man. We have a surprise for you."

"I'll see you soon," I hang up and place a kiss on my beloved Fiona's forehead who's asleep on the hospital bed. "I'll get us the money someway, and I'll keep you safe. I promise," then I leave the hospital.

I choose to take the elevator. Five people enter and when I step in, they all step out instantly.

It is as if they know who I am and what I've done.

Of course they do. Everyone in the town is avoiding me like I'm a plague. I can't even go buy myself a bottle of jack at the liquor store without the store owner giving me dirty looks.

Even the old lady I go buy milk from refuses to open the door to me earlier this morning. Everyone I thought that was nice and cared turned their backs on me because they're afraid of the Lord. See what I mean? Everyone watches out for themselves. No one is united. Hunter Cross is delusional.

As I walk outside the hospital, I try to catch a cab to go home. The cab driver stops, and as he sees me, he drives away immediately. I should expect this. The same thing happened when I was coming to the hospital. Oh well, I don't need a car to get home.

I'll just walk.

It takes me about an hour and a half to get home. I feel a bit tired and hungry. I think I'll take a nap and then get ready to meet Hunter and the rest.

I open the door and close it behind me and the first thing I see is my mortal enemy sitting on my sofa with a smile on his face.

"Welcome home, Jago." he tells me.

At first, I am frozen in place and my heart begins to beat really fast. I start to sweat.

"Please, have a seat," Colton Ice tells me. His voice is as sour and deadly as acid. I can feel the hatred and the self-containment in his voice. It is as if he is keeping himself from ripping my heart out but I ain't afraid of him. I still hate him.

"I don't take orders from you," I snarl at him.

His glare intensifies with a death wish. If looks could kill, I'd be dead. He brusquely stands up, getting me to stiffen.

"Jago Parker," he starts walking toward me like a predator. I try hard to stand my ground and show him I'm not afraid but I find my legs moving backward by themselves.

"You've been raised in a church because your crack-whore mother did not want you," he starts.

I stop walking backward and I frown, why is he telling me this?

"She was supposed to abort you when a kind, good-hearted nun convinced her not to. They gave her money in exchange of your life, so you could be born. The crack-whore took the money from them, gave birth to you and gave you up," his eyes are mocking and insulting, "your own mother sold you for drug money, Jago. Two days later, she was found dead due to overdose."

I clench my fists, "shut up."

He smirks and shakes his head at me, then starts to circle me, looking down on me, degrading me. "You were never loved from the beginning, Jago. Even the orphans at the church hated you. They always bullied you, ganged up on you. You never made any friends. You were a piece of shit. You were once framed for dealing drugs when you were in high school by one of your fellow orphans and they believed him instead of believing you because your mother was a crack whore."

"Shut up..." I don't want this son of the bitch talking about my past.

"Everyone betrayed you since you were born, you've always been all by yourself. That's pathetic if you ask me," his eyes are glistering, "then, you become even more pathetic, you were a smart kid, had tons of scholarships waiting for you to put you to college. You wanted to get into one of the best Universities in the world and you had a competition, my older brother. Small world isn't it?" he smiles, "of course, unlike you, Caleb Ice was a prodigy child and our family was wealthier and got his back and had some connections. Caleb obtained the scholarship and you were forgotten...that's really sad if you ask me because Caleb didn't even want to go to college, he hated school and was grateful for nothing at all. Then, you drop out, give up on your studies and decide to get an old part time job and become the pathetic loser you were destined to be."

"Shut up!" My voice is trembling. This Ice kid has no idea how much I hate him and he is talking to me this way! I hate him! I fucking hate him! What right does he have talking about my life, judging me! What right?!

"And then, you meet Fiona Frances," he starts, his voice becomes cold.

"Don't you talk about her..." I threaten. He can say whatever the hell he wants about me, but he can't talk about Fiona. He can't.

"You fell in love with her somehow and you guys got married, only that the marriage wasn't a happy one. You were poor, you couldn't afford to take your wife out to dinner, you couldn't afford to pay the bills, to buy her nice things, to make her happy. You weren't happy, and she wasn't happy either. Poor Jago," his tone is sarcastic "And then, as if things weren't bad enough...she gets cancer. You couldn't even afford to take her to a decent hospital or get a decent doctor for your wife...so she had to take matters in her own hands. She became an escort to rich men in Terra," he smirks at me. "That's where I come in. She slept with me for money and with the money I gave her, not your money Jago, *my* money–an Ice's money, with that, she was able to get herself taken care of. She is now under the care of a decent doctor and is resting at the hospital, thanks to the money I gave her. You hate me, don't you? You hate the fact that your wife chose to fuck me for money, just like your mother sold you for money...Hm, I don't blame you, friend," he stops circling me and looks at me dead in the eye. "You want to know the funny part of this?"

My breathing is harsh. I am clenching my fists and losing control.

"She probably fucked me better than she ever fucked you and I don't even remember the whore's face," he smirks.

That is it. I can't control myself anymore. "YOU SON OF A BITCH!" I roar, throwing myself at him. We stumble on the floor and I am on top of him ready to beat him to death when I feel a gun pointed to my head. I freeze for a moment.

"This feels like a déjà vu," Colton says bitterly then shakes his head at the man who has a gun pointed at me. He then turns to me, "it's alright. Beat me up. Take out your anger on me. I deserve it; I've disrespected your sweet pussy."

I punch him hard. I can feel his cheekbone crack at the contact of my knuckles, but it isn't enough. I want to see him bleed! I want to see him cry and beg for mercy again like last time. I want to make this son of a bitch pay again! I want to kill him! I keep on throwing punches at his face, drawing blood, cutting his lip, swelling his cheek. I don't stop. I am beating him up over and over again. I hate those Ices. I've always hated them since I was in high school.

His brother won the scholarship and internship to the University that I was supposed to go to because his parents knew the Dean of the University. They accepted him without even thinking twice and told me to apply next year. It's because of them I dropped out of school. It's because of them I don't have a decent job! It's because of them I couldn't take care of my wife! It's because of them Fiona looks down on me and doesn't even acknowledge me as a man! It's because of them she left me...she told me she wished she was Colton's wife instead of being with some pathetic loser like me...she told me that to my face...all because of those Ices! I hate them! I hate him! I am so glad his parents died in a plane crash and I thank God every day that Caleb killed himself. I am so glad!

I don't know how much time passed since I have been punching him. My hand is bloody and painful and I am breathless. He never once tried to fight back, or flinch or grunt out of pain. He just let me take my anger out on him.

I stop beating him and get up and so does he. "You punch like an old lady," he tells me. I ignore him and try to pick up my breathing.

"What do you want from me?" I finally speak as I start breathing normally.

"I want to make a deal with you," his voice is serious, "you know about the tape, don't you?"

I nod.

"And you know the Lord wants all of your heads and your family's now more than ever right? That was a stupid move you made."

I can't deny it, "so what do you want?" I snap at him.

He gives me a sarcastic look. "The tape and all the copies, the duplicates, everything. I want you to give it to me by tomorrow morning. In exchange, I'll spare you and make sure your wife gets treated by the best doctor in the region and I'll put half a million gold in her account so she can live the most luxurious life you've always wanted to give her."

I chuckle. He thinks I'm stupid. "So you want me to be a rat?" I laugh bitterly.

"Not a rat, Jago. A good, protective husband to your wife."

I stiffen. I feel like he is blackmailing me.

"Here are your choices, you get me the tapes and duplicates and I spare you and I make sure your wife has a happy life. If you refuse the deal, I'll make you seem like a rat."

I glare, "how are you going to do that?"

He smiles at me. "I'll give your wife a special treatment. I'll get every doctor and everyone to start taking care of her, and once your friends find out that sweet Fiona is getting special treatment while the rest of their families are living in fear, they'll think you betrayed them in some way."

I stiffen.

"They'll eventually kill you and once you're dead, I'll make sure Fiona spends the rest of her life outside, homeless, alone with no one to protect her. She'll eventually die and it'll be because of you."

My hands begin to tremble. He has me cornered against the wall.

"Don't think too much about it, Jago…" he tells me as if I'm a child who's confused about making a silly decision, "I am giving you a chance to be a good worthy husband to your wife. What you're doing is not betraying those animals; you're fighting for your wife's safety. They don't care about you. They just pretend to because they're scared. They will happily give you and your wife up in heartbeat if I ever ask them to in exchange of their lives. They don't care. You're on your own, and always will be."

I start to think about it. I don't really care about what happens to me, it's just Fiona...I just want her to have a good life you know? And Colton Ice is right...I'm on my own and I've always been. People hurt me and betray me all the time...it's time for me to stick up for myself.

"I have your word you won't let anything happen to Fiona?" I ask him.

He nods and gives me an empty look. "I cross my heart and hope to die."

I am silent again.

"It's for her, Jago. For once, you'll be doing the right thing and take care of her."

"Why are you...doing this? Why are you sparing me?" I ask him.

His eyes become cold and hurt and lost, "you didn't touch her," he says.

I look down. "I'm sorry about your wi-"

"Don't talk about her," he warns me. His voice is suddenly colder than before. I retain myself.

"Do we have a deal?" he asks me dryly.

"Yes we do," I nod at him.

"I'll come back here tomorrow noon. If I don't get what I want, you know what will happen," he threatens. I nod at him once again. He gives me another cold hard and walks toward the door.

"Let's go, Zero." He says as his guard follows him.

I let myself fall on the couch as soon as they leave. I am in shock. I cannot believe what just happened...what I've just agreed to. How the hell am I even going to find the copies and duplicates? Hunter is the one who has it with him and I don't know where and how many copies...I don't know how to get them. I am in deep shit.

I have to find a way to get it, and I don't have much time. I have until tomorrow noon. If I don't give him all the copies of the tapes...Fiona will suffer the consequences. I have no choice but find a way. I have to do the impossible and I hope Fiona's angels help me.


"What are you celebrating?" I ask Hunter as soon as I enter his house. There is music playing and they're all drinking beer and celebrating. There are familiar and unfamiliar faces, children and women and family members from all. I feel rather angry at them for being so easy going, so relaxed. Even after what Zeus told us, they're still acting like they're invincible and they're getting their entire family in even greater danger by doing this.

"Jago, I'm so happy to see you!" Hunter says, hugging me.

"What are you celebrating?" I ask him again.

"We're not dead yet!" he answers. "We sent them the tape about twelve hours ago and we're all still alive.

That means they're thinking about making a deal with us!"

Only if he knew. Hunter is a stupid kid.

"This is good news, Jago! Smile! Here, have a drink!" he gives me a bottle of beer and then continues, "I wanted to tell you something at the end of the party but I can't wait anymore. Come on, come with me," he directs me and I follow him. He stands on top of a table and gets everyone's attention. "Everyone! My love ones! Listen up!"

They all do so.

"We've lived in fear for the past three days and nothing has happened to us. We've stood against the enemies today and yet we're still alive. You know why?"

"Because Stigma is on our side!" Hidon roars raising his beer and everyone does so.

"To Stigma!" they're all cheering, and then when they quiet down, Hunter continues.

"Yes, Hidon. It may have to be because of your protector, but it's also because of one thing: we're all united and all in this together. We're a family now. We're all on the same boat, we all share a common enemy and unison gives strength! This is revolutionary, guys. It's literally us against the world and we're going to put up one hell of the fight!"

"Yeah!" they agree with him. These guys are idiots.

"We're all a family now everyone. We're all going to watch our backs and protect our loved ones no matter what. We won't let anyone, or anything scare us! We're going to fight back, retaliate, and do whatever it takes to protect one another!"

They are cheering again and clapping. "Now I know we've done some fucked up shit and that's the reason why we're in this deep shit, but we can't take it back. What happened, happened and I get the enemy's anger...but we can all agree that we can't let them hurt our children, our family members, our loved ones. That's wrong, that's no way of settling things. What we did to them today is just a tip of the iceberg. We will keep on retaliating...we will fight to protect the ones we love or die trying! I give you my word; I won't let anything happen to our innocent children. I will fight, we will fight! We're all family! And Jago,"

He looks down at me as I am staring up at him, "I want you to belong to this family. I want you to trust us. I want all of us to be united. That is why, Jago, we've made you the Keeper of this Family."

I raise an eyebrow at him.

"Hidon," Hunter nods at Hidon and Hidon walks toward me with a big box in his hands.

"Here, take it," Hidon grins at me.

I take it and ask them, "what is it?"

"Jago, this is all the duplicates of the tape we have. All of them. And we're giving it to you."

I stare at them in awe. How did I even end up being in the same boat as those brainless pieces of shits? "Why...why are you giving all this to me?" I ask, still appalled.

"Because, we trust you Jago. You're the smartest guy we know and we want you to know that we trust you, man. We want you to feel like you're family to us," Hunter explains. Everyone nods and is looking at me with appreciation.

"Plus, I thought about it and you're the only guy in the tape who hasn't raped the Lord's daughter so I think you might be the last person they'll come after."

*Oh Hunter, you are wrong on so many levels.*

"If anything happens to us, if anyone tries to hurt one of our loved ones, we want you to just put this tape out there for the world to see," Hidon tells me.

"Can you do that for us, Jago?" Hunter asks me. Everyone falls silent and looks at me for an answer.

I have no choice. "Yes, absolutely," I say and they all roar and cheer and some people are hugging me, tapping my back, and ruffling my hair.

"Welcome to the Family, brother! We'll take care of you and your wife, we promise!"

I nod and chuckle at myself bitterly. I am feeling a bit of guilt.


The party gets wilder and crazier, they are trashing the place, laughing, getting drunk, kissing, some are having sex right in front of the kids, it's a mad house and it's disgusting and I feel sick. I am only relieved that I have what I needed–the copies of the tape and the original. As soon as everyone passes out, I'll be off to my house. I am not part of them. They're not my family. They never will be.

"Hey, you're leaving bro?" Hunter catches me opening the door. It is 12:30 AM, and I thought everyone was asleep.

I have the box in my hands.

"Uh...yes," I reply to Hunter.

"Why don't you stay here for the night? It's late."

I shake my head. "No, I'll be fine. I just need to go home now and put the box in a safe place," I tell him nervously. I cannot afford to stay here for the night.

"Alright, I'll give you a ride," Hunter tells me.

"That won't be..."

"I'm not taking no for an answer, bro. I know you don't have a car to get home. Walking for an hour in the middle of the night all by yourself won't be safe. Plus you have the tapes with you...if it falls in the enemy's hands...we're all doomed and tripled fucked. This is all we got to survive. I'm taking you home."

I don't argue with him.


The car ride is silent. Hunter is yawning and half asleep and I am holding the box tightly and protectively like my life depends on it. Well, it actually does. It's not only my life. It's Fiona's.

Hunter parks in front of my home and turns to me.

"Alright, man. I'll see you in two days. We have something important coming up."

"What is it?"

"Zeus's gang members are hooking us up with a shit tons of weapons."

*What?*

"What? I thought they're on the Lord's side."

"Well, after finding out that their most favorite member was beheaded, they're kind of feeling a bit hostile. It's a discreet deal. No one will know."

"What are...you going to do with the weapons?" I ask him. I hope he doesn't amaze me more by saying he wants to go on shooting rampage.

"Give it to everyone in our Family for protection. If by any chance they come after us and start to shoot, we won't have any weapons to counter attack or defend ourselves with. Plus, it'll make a lot of the rest at ease knowing they can defend themselves."

I sigh and nod. It makes sense, but..."why do you have a sudden change of heart in all this, Hunter? You were feeling bad about what you've done to the daughter...you didn't want to use the tape in the first place...why all of a sudden you want to fight back?"

He sighs and looks at me. "I still feel bad for what I've done to Aelita. But she's dead now and we're all in danger and even if blackmailing the lord using the tape is a dirty move, I realize I have to do what I have to do to keep my loved ones safe. I need to get over this guilt and do what I have to do to protect my brother and Veronica. I have no other choice. It will get me killed in the end, but I'm willing to die for them. I just want them to be safe, and I'll do anything for them. I'll do the worse."

Looks like Hunter and I share something in common.

"Alright. Thank you for the ride," I tell him.

"No problem. Let me know if you need a ride anywhere, alright? I'll see you in two days."

"Ok," I say and get out of his car. He drives away as I enter my house.

I put the box on the table and sit on the couch and stare at it.

Do I really want to be a rat? Do I really want to betray them? They seem to believe in what they're doing. Even if they're idiots...even if they're all going to die, they still believe in something. They want to protect their loved ones from getting hurt...if I give Colton the duplicates...they'll all be doomed but Fiona and I will be spared.

If I don't, then Fiona will suffer the most and I can't allow that. I can't allow my woman to suffer any more than she's already did...I love her. I love her so much.

Hunter and the others would have done the same. They won't think twice before doing it...one to his own. There's no such thing as family in this world. You just watch out for yourself. This is for Fiona.

It is 12:00 PM the next morning and there is a knock on the door. He's on time.

My hands start to shake and my stomach starts to turn as open the door. This decision I'm about to make will be either the best one, or the worst one.

"Do you have it?" he asks me as soon as he steps in my house. He is straight to the point.

I nod.

"Let's double check they're not fakes," he tells me.

"They aren't."

"Do you have a video player?" he ignores my statement and looks around the house. I shake my head.

"The TV isn't working."

"As I thought," Colton says quietly. "Zero," then his guard comes with a fancy computer and lays it on the table. "You may go now," he tells the guard, and the guard does so.

"What are you doing?" I ask him annoyed, "I said they're all real."

"I'll be the judge of that. Come on, have a seat. We'll watch all of them."

I look at him in disbelief, "there are about a forty of them."

He nods, "Yes, thank you Jago. I see that too. And they're about fifteen minutes each. We have the whole entire day."

I glare at him in disbelief. Arrogant Ices. I ably and seat across the laptop as he puts on the first disk in the computer. It starts to play and Hunter is talking, threatening and then the rape scene starts to play. I had no problem watching the tape with Hunter and the others, it didn't really made me feel bad or nauseous or sad or guilty...but now, now that I'm seating next to the girl's husband and watching it together with him, I feel awful.

"Don't take your eyes away from the screen," he retorts at me with a cold glare. I do as he says. Colton's body never stops shaking while watching the video. I know it is torture to him. I can feel the anger coming out of him and filling my living room. It is almost hard to breathe.

We finish watching the last tape around six pm. He brusquely stands up and runs toward the nearest garbage can and starts to vomit.

"Zero..." I hear him call and the guard enters the house immediately. Zero walks toward Colton and hands him a bottle of water and a hand towel. Colton takes it, drinks, cleans his mouth and breathes deeply for a moment.

"It's all real," he nods at Zero and Zero rushes toward the table and takes the box.

"I knew you could do it," Colton tells me. "Good job. You saved your wife."

I exhale deeply with relief. Then I see him take out a gun.

"On your knees." he orders me. My eyes widen in horror and in shock and I suddenly understand he's going to kill me.

"Hey! Hey! That wasn't p-part of the deal! Y-you said you'd spare me and my wife!" I yell at him backing up. I glance at the door thinking if I could make a run for it, but Zero is at the door.

"Believe me, I am sparing you," Colton answers. "I am going to put a bullet in your head and it will be quick and painless and you'll be dead, you won't suffer. I am sparing you from the cruel, intentions I have in mind for the rest."

My throat tightens and my heart starts to beat fast. "Y-you gave me your word you wouldn't hurt Fiona."

"I didn't hurt her," he replies quietly. "Right now, at the moment she is getting in a helicopter and is being transferred to another hospital in another country. There's half a million gold in her account at the moment and she will be taken good care of. She will survive and live her life happily ever after because you let that happen."

I don't trust him, "H-how do I know you're telling the truth?"

"If I wanted to hurt your wife, I would've done it in front of you. Just like you all did," he snarls coldly at me. "On your knees."

"I...I want to see her one last time," I beg with tears rolling down my face. I just want to make sure she's really alright.

"We recorded a video of her. She has a message for you," he tells me and I gasp.

"She doesn't know anything that happened, what you did. She was told that you won the lottery, and you were still working hard that's why you couldn't come say goodbye. Zero, play it," Colton tells the guard and Zero does so. He puts a disk in the computer and when it starts playing. I see my beautiful Fiona in a wheel chair, her lovely hair is glowing and she looks happy, she has a smile on her face. I barely get to see her smile. I gasp and start crying.

"Thank you, Jago. I can't wait to see you soon. You're a really good mam," she tells me looking at the camera and I start to sob. I feel so happy, so relieved and so accomplished.

"You were born a loser and you're dying a good husband in the eyes of your wife," Colton tells me and there's a click on the gun, "on your knees," he repeats and this time, I do so...slowly.

I am ready to die. I am at peace. I know Fiona is alright, and that's all that matters.

"I'll see you in hell, Jago." Colton tells me, walking closer and pointing the gun at me.

I hear the gun go off and everything goes blank.

# 7

## COLTON ICE'S POINT OF VIEW

"Give the copies to Mr. Fire and show him the body," I order Zero after Jago falls on the ground. I shoot him twice again in the head to make sure he really dies since my wife survived.

"Yes sir," Zero tells me and effortlessly picks up Jago's body and goes out with it. I thought I would feel disgusted with myself. I thought I would feel guilty since it's my first time taking a life but I don't. I don't feel anything. I am emotionless, but very dissatisfied with my performance.

I killed Jago and made his wife richer. That doesn't seem like revenge. I feel like I don't have enough hatred inside. I felt bad for Jago...for his past and I'm pretty sure most of those animals have a similar history behind them, if not maybe worse. I can't let my good conscience take the best of me. If I do, I won't get revenge. I'll just pity all of them and spare them as well. I need to get rid out this soft heart of mine. I need to be darker for Aelita.

I glance at the copies in the box and take one. I always get angrier and thirsty for blood whenever I watch the tape. I think if I watch it more and more, it will motivate me and turn my heart black. I quickly sneak one of the copies in the pocket of my jacket and Zero enters the room. He takes the box and I follow him out.


"When I'm done reporting to Lord Fire, may I have the day off, sir?" Zero asks me while we're in the car.

"Why is that?" I ask him out of curiosity. I don't know much about this guy, and he's awfully quiet. Quieter than I am.

"I...have someone...important to visit," he tells me carefully.

"Girlfriend of yours?" I ask him. However, I doubt he has one.

"I wish," he slowly whispers and then adds "a friend."

A friend huh? He has friends? That's a bit surprising. I guess he isn't much of a cold hearted killer after all.

"That's fine," I tell him. I need the rest of the day off as well. I've killed a man. I need to let it sink in slowly in my conscience. "Just make sure you meet me tomorrow at seven am."

"Thank you, Mr. Ice," he replies.

The first thing I do when I get in the hotel is take a shower. It's the second time today that I am showering and I am sure I will clean myself later on again. Since I left Aelita to the doctor and her mother, I have been obsessed with cleaning myself. I can still feel the warmth of her blood drenching my hands every time I stare at them. I feel so dirty and disgusting every time I am alone, and I can't stop washing my hands for about half an hour.

Aelita is alive and safe. I called my house last night to ask about her. Her mother of course did not want to talk to me, but thankfully, Hinata did. She told me that Aelita was now on a twenty four seven surveillance. Mrs. Fire decided that someone had to always be around her at all times. I was relieved that no one will leave her out of sight. I was however upset when Hinata told me that Mrs. Fire was going to hire a psychologist to come talk to Aelita. Talk about what? They're just going to make her suffer even more. She doesn't need a psychologist. What happened to her won't ever go away. The pain she is feeling now will not go away. Ever. Mrs. Fire is just wasting time and money.

As I step out of the shower an hour later, I check my phone and realize I have about three missed called from my company rival, Cain Smith.

Cain Smith is Nadia's cousin. We get along because we're somewhat alike. We're serious about our companies and work and we're always competing against one another. He's a good friend as well. Not really close of a friend, but he is one of the few I can trust because he is almost as smart as I am.

I decide to call him back.

"Colton, finally. I've been trying to reach you for so long. How are you?" he asks.

"...Is there a problem, Cain?" I ask him quietly.

"I'm just a bit worried about you, listen, we need to talk. It's about your company. Meet me in half an hour at the cafe across the flower shop?"

Well, I have nothing better to do today. Why not?

"Sure."

"Great, I'll see you soon," he tells me and I hang up.

"You look horrible," Cain says. We're sitting outside the cafe. It's 4 pm, and the sun is still shinning bright. The weather is nice, to Cain. I don't see much of an importance to it.

"What about my company?" I ask him, changing the conversation. I don't want to talk about my personal life.

"Always straight to the point," he smiles at me but then gets serious. "Are you okay?"

"Do I look okay?" I retort.

"No," he shakes his head. His blue eyes show worry and fear. "I heard what happened to Aelita. I'm sorry, Colton. She was a very nice person."

*Was*? I guess Nadia didn't tell him she's alive. I am not surprised. Mr. Fire probably paid quite a lot of money to the hospital and doctors so they can keep their mouth shut about Aelita's survival. It's probably for her safety. I can't say I'm against that.

"She was," I answer back coolly.

"When's the funeral?" he asks me, his eyes boring into mine as if he is really interested.

"It'll be private. Only family members are going to be there."

"Then that means lots of people are going to be there since the Lord considers everyone in this island as family," Cain smiles. I'm not sure if he's trying to be funny.

I glare at him, "what do you want, Cain?" I ask once again. The waitress comes and gives him his iced tea while she pours me water.

"Thank you," Cain smiles at her. The waitress bows to us and walks away.

"I want to talk about your company," he starts. "I'd like you to let me take over."

I raise an eyebrow.

"Just for a while, until you're ready to get back to work," he adds quickly. "You haven't been to work for quite a while and you've missed five important meetings and your employees don't know what to do. You've not been answering calls from your personal assistant and she had no choice but call me. I know you're going through a though time right now, and this is my way of helping you. I don't want my rival's company to fall while I can do something about it..." his eyes are boring into mine again. "You need time to heal, Colton. I can't imagine what psychological effect it's having on you. I just want you to take time and heal and get over it without worrying about anything," he continues. He is so convincing... or maybe I just don't care anymore.

"I killed a man today," I announce. His eyes widen in horror. "He was one of the guys who hurt her...I put a bullet in his head...and the strange part is...I don't feel anything," I continue. I am staring into space. "It's my first kill, but I feel like it's not a big deal."

We're silent for a while and then I realize he is frozen. Maybe I shouldn't have said this to him. We're friends, but not that close of friends.

"I'm sorry," I apologize.

"No, it's fine," he says. "You need someone to talk to. I'm glad you're telling me this," his voice is a bit shaky. "However, if I may...I don't think revenge is the right path to choose. Killing them will not bring Aelita back. It won't fix anything."

"So you want me to just stay there and do nothing?" I glare at him.

He nods, "let God take care of them."

I snort. "Where was God when Aelita needed Him? I don't think He gives a damn about her."

"Maybe it's not about her. Maybe God is testing you," Cain continues.

I frown, "so God will choose to destroy an innocent's life just to test me?"

"He has very strange ways of influencing us, Colton."

If God is really testing me, then I am happy to be failing. I rather rot in hell with the Devil when I die than spend time with him in heaven. He let Aelita get hurt. He sacrificed an innocent live just to 'test'. What are we, his toys?

"Since when did you become so religious?" I snort at Cain, but don't give him a chance to answer. "Never mindthat. I'll sign my company over to you, temporarily."

I see a flash in his eyes, "thank you for trusting me. I will take good care of it while you're recuperating...I just need you to sign this."

"I'll read it over and give it to you by tomorrow evening," I tell him.

He smiles and nods, "fair enough."

"Thank you, for trying to help," I say.

He nods and takes out his wallet to pay for his drink.

"I got it," I tell him.

He smiles once more and then stands up, "I have somewhere to be, I'll see you tomorrow evening."

I stand up too, to shake his hand. "Yes."

He then walks to his car and drives away from the coffee shop, while I sit back down to finish my water.

I hear some girly giggles across the coffee shop. It's a girl and a boy, they're in their early teen years and the boy is buying a single rose for the girl. She looks so happy, so pleased, so loved.

I think about Aelita all of the sudden. Aelita loves flowers, she adores them. She built a garden in our home and she used to spend most of her time there, planting flowers and taking great care of them. I smile as I remember how she used to always give me tons of flowers when I come back home from work. I never liked her flowers. I never liked getting flowers from her. Out of respect and not wanting to hurt her feelings, I used to take them and when I get into my room, I always threw them away in the garbage.

She once caught me throwing her flowers out before going to work and I felt a bit guilty. I thought she was going to cry or be angry at me but instead, she smiled at me and at the flowers and just picked them up from the garbage. I thought she would stop giving me flowers because of the dick move I made, but to my surprise and annoyance, she had more flowers for me when I came back home. I was annoyed back then, so I snatched it from her and was going to toss it in my room, but then when I came to my room, I saw even more flowers all over. There were tons of flowers on my bed, on the floor, in my closet, in the bathroom, on the window...my room looked like a flower shop. I thought it was her way of getting revenge. As if she was trying to say "try throwing all of them out now!"

I find myself smiling at those memories, and then I frown. Come to think of it, I have never given her flowers. She has always been the one. I never came home to give her flowers, even on Valentine's Day. I never gave her anything. I always made my assistant buy Aelita presents on her birthdays and the assistant had to be the one to remind me most of the times.

My heart starts to clench. I've been such an ass to her. I've been so unfair, so mean, so careless of her feelings. I need to make it up to her.

"Are you buying flowers for your girlfriend, sir?" The florist asks me. I look at the old lady and blink twice as I realize I am at the flower shop now. When did I even leave the coffee shop?

"Sir?" the florist calls me again.

"Uh..." I don't know what to say to her. "They're for my wife..." I find myself saying.

"Ah," she smiles. "You seem like you have no idea what to buy her."

I awkwardly nod.

"You've messed up, haven't you?" she brusquely says.

I look at her stupefied.

"You have this guilty look on your face. Is your wife mad at you?"

"Uh..." I clear my throat. "Yes, something like that."

"Okay," she looks around her shop for some flowers and then gets a bouquet of red roses and hands it to me. "Here take this. She will forgive you in an instant. Red roses always do some kind of magic to a woman's heart."

I faintly smile at her and take the bouquet. "Thank you. How much do I owe you?" I ask the old lady. She shakes her head.

"It's on me," she says. "I love seeing responsible men like you care about their wives' feelings. Not so many men do that anymore."

I smile at her once more, this time painfully. I am not a responsible husband.

"Have a good day, ma'am." I am about to leave the flower shop when something that catches my eyes. Behind the flower shop main entrance, I see a written sign. "FORECLOSURE." I frown at that and then turn back to the old lady who is fixing her flowers and not paying attention to me.

"You're losing your business?" I ask her.

She turns to me and glances at the sign and turns back to me. "Oh!" she dismisses. "It's nothing to worry about. I'm getting old for this anyways."

"But you love flowers; you love your business, don't you?" I insist.

She nods. "Of course I do, son. I've been doing this before you were born....I love selling flowers...I love flowers....but what am I going to do? I don't have the money...I spent all my money to put my grandson to college..."

I remember how much Aelita loves flowers.

I take out my wallet and a check, "how much do you owe?" I ask the old lady.

She's not looking at me. She's staring at the flowers sadly. "About...a hundred thousand gold," she says. I write the triple of that and hand her the check.

"Here," I tell her. She takes it and looks at me confused.

"Save your flower shop and enjoy yourself."

"Son...that is too much," she refuses trying to give me back the check. "Plus I don't even know you, I can't take this."

"Please take it," I plead her. "My wife also has a passion for flowers and I'm sure she would have done the same if she was here."

"I..." she is about to refuse again when I give her a look. She gives me a smile and hugs me. "Thank you, thank you so much," she is crying. She shouldn't thank me. She should thank Aelita. It's because of her I'm doing this.


I am getting out of the cab. Instead of taking my car and drive to my home, I take a cab because I'm afraid Mrs. Fire will be expecting me and probably throw a grenade at me. I think she wants me dead more than her husband. She never really liked me anyways.

The cab driver stops few blocks away from my house and I decide to walk discreetly and carefully. I can't believe I am sneaking around to get in my own home. Also, I haven't really thought of how to give Aelita the roses when I get there. I thought to maybe call Hinata and ask her to give them to Aelita, but deep down, I want to be the one to give her the flowers. I want to see a smile on her face. I want to see her reaction.

I am slowly and carefully walking toward the gate when I catch a glimpse of Mrs. Fire opening the door.

Shit.

I immediately hide in the bushes by the fountain so she cannot see me.

She isn't alone. There's a guy at the front door who is talking to her. It takes me seconds to recognize the person. It's Zero.

I raise an eyebrow. Why is he visiting Mrs. Fire? Does she want to know about Jago as well?

It's when I see the basket of flowers in one of his hand and a puppy in the other that I realize he isn't here to visit Mrs. Fire. He's here for my wife.

I feel something click in my brain and my heart starts to beat furiously fast. Zero is now on my "to be killed" list.

Why is he giving flowers to Aelita? What connection or relationship does he have with her? How come I've never heard about him? How come Aelita never told me about him? Who is that guy?

"Zero! It's so good to see you," I see Mrs. Fire hug him and kiss him on the cheek. She's very warm and friendly with him. She never kissed me on the cheek before. She only used to hug me when we were once in good terms.

"How are you doing, Mrs. Fire?" Zero asks her, his voice is surprisingly gentle and cheerful compared to the way he behaves when he's around me.

"I'm alright, aw..." Mrs. Fire is looking at the baskets of flowers. "This is so wonderful, Zero. This is so beautiful. You're such a sweet boy! Aw, and you got her a puppy as well?"

"After hearing that one of her dogs died...I thought this might cheer her up," Zero answers timidly.

"Zero, you're the best. It will bring warmth to her heart. I am so sure of this. Those flowers are beautiful...I have never seen such beautiful flowers."

Mrs. Fire is right, and it is taking a lot of pride swallowing to admit it. I have in my hand, about eight red roses formed into a bouquet, and he has a large brown basket full of all types of flowers: roses, daisies, lilies, carnations, gladioluses, asters, tulips, and sunflowers and they're colorful, they're mixed, they're beautiful just like Aelita decorates and mixes the flowers she gives me. She will definitely love it. And as if it isn't enough, he is giving her a puppy.

I drop the bouquet of roses and tighten my fists. I hate him. I hate Zero. He likes her. He wants what's mine. Aelita is *my* wife. I don't care if my feelings for her are not the same as her feelings for me, I don't care. She's still mine. She holds my name, and no man is allowed to make her smile or give her presents...no man but me.

Yes, I am jealous. Very jealous, actually. And I really want to kill Zero. Once I'm done with killing the rapists, I'll put a bullet in his head as well.

"How is Aelita doing?" he asks Mrs. Fire, his voice holds concern.

"She's...hanging there," Mrs. Fire replies vaguely.

"I'd like to see her if that's possible," he asks.

I frown angrily. I swear, if Mrs. Fire allows this guy to see my wife while I am not allowed to even ask about her, I will wreak havoc.

"I'm sorry sweetheart," she apologetically tells him. "It's just too early to see her. She's not ready yet. Once she is, you will be the first person I'll inform."

Wow, Mrs. Fire. Just, wow.

"I see..." he sounds disappointed. "Well, please tell her I stopped by and I miss her and I am thinking about her."

"I definitely will, honey." Mrs. Fire hugs him once again and kisses him on the cheek and on the forehead again!

"Have a lovely evening," he tells her and walks away as Mrs. Fire enters the house with the basket of flowers and the puppy. I narrow my eyes at Zero's back as he is enters his car and drives away.

I glare at the roses I was thinking about giving her and sigh. There's no way I, her husband could give her something this simple when some guy is giving her a better version.

I toss the flowers away on the grass and decide to walk back to my hotel.

I am contouring my home, looking down on the floor and pouting angrily. Zero and Aelita? I still can't grasp the idea of the two of them having some kind of relationship. How does she even know him? He's a cold psychotic killer who doesn't know how to demonstrate emotions. He is not human. And Aelita is the sweetest, pacifist person I have ever met. I still don't understand how those two know each other or even get along.

I stop at the back of my house, where Aelita's garden is. I stare through the bar fence at all the lovely flowers and plants. She used to spend most of her times there. I remember coming home from work early one afternoon, she didn't know I was home, so she didn't come and greet me. I went to her garden to check up on her hours later and she was so serious and so into watering her plants and caring for the flowers. She adored them so much. When she turned around and saw me, bliss and joy was written all over her face. It was as if seeing me was the best thing that had ever happened to her. She stood up and smiled genuinely at me and she was beautiful. I thought I was seeing an angel that evening. Aelita is the most beautiful woman I have ever met.

I stare at the garden feeling nostalgic. I am about to leave and go back to my hotel when I see her.

She is in the middle of the garden, wearing a giant grey hoodie on a blue jean. Her curly golden hair is being swayed slowly by the wind. She is sitting in the mud, staring at the flowers angrily and sadly. I can see tears rolling down her face.

I frown and get closer, both my hands securing around two bars as I am staring intently at her.

She is looking at the flowers with so much anger and repugnance that I am panicking. I have never seen her angry.

Why is she looking at the flowers that way? Why? Those are the most precious things to her. She loves flowers...I thought her garden would be her sanctuary and help her feel a little better...

"Aelita honey," Mrs. Fire comes in the garden. "You stepped out of the wheelchair?" she asks Aelita and then I see a wheelchair by the entrance. "You're going to get your jeans dirty honey," her mother continues, but Aelita is not even staring at her. She is still angrily staring at the flowers.

"Aelita...Zero stopped by earlier and gave you this..." Mrs. Fire says gently, approaching her with the basket of flowers. Aelita doesn't even glance at the flowers. She is still sitting on the mud with that pained, angry gaze. Mrs. Fire comes closer and crouches beside her so Aelita can see the basket of flowers.

"Aren't they the loveliest?" her mother tells her gently, but Aelita does something that surprises me and makes me think I am living a nightmare. She smacks the baskets of flowers away from her mother's hand and they fall on the grass. The flowers are dispersed everywhere.

*Good Girl*, a part of me thinks. I know it's immature of me, but I feel a bit content that she is rejecting another man's gift. She probably would do the same if those flowers came from me but still I am satisfied she isn't accepting Zero's flowers.

Another part of me, the bigger part of me is appalled, pained and so hurt. Aelita is angry. She isn't like this. This isn't her. She never acts violent...she is gentle, she is calm, she is sweet. But, I shouldn't be surprised. What happened to her...what she went through is dark enough to cause this...I shouldn't be surprised...but I am...and I am so hurt. I don't like this side of Aelita. I like the old Aelita better. I want to bring her back.

Her mother gasps too, not seeing this coming. "Aelita...?" she says to her but when her daughter doesn't answer, Mrs. Fire smiles at her painfully and starts to pick up the flowers. "It's alright honey...I'll just go put them away somewhere else, when you're ready to see them I'll show them to you...also, he got you a puppy... when you're ready to see the puppy, I'll show it to you, alright?"

Aelita doesn't answer. Her head is still bowed down, staring at her garden.

"I'll be right back sweetheart." Mrs. Fire says and is about to leave when Aelita grabs the end of her skirt, stopping her from leaving.

"What is it, sweetheart?" Mrs. Fire asks her. With amazement and a tiny bit of happiness, I see Aelita's lips move. She is speaking to Mrs. Fire. She is saying something to her mother but I can't hear it at all because she is faintly talking. I can't hear her voice at all. I forgot she can speak now. I tighten my grip around the bars and stare at her as she talks to her mom. I want to hear her voice. I want to hear her talk to me. I would give anything to hear her talk to me.

"I'll give you the scissors once I come back, alright? You know why I can't leave you alone with sharp things."

I suddenly remember seeing Aelita in the bathroom...unconscious and almost bleeding to death. I shudder and my heart clenches painfully.

"I'll be back honey," Mrs. Fire tells her and exits the garden.

Aelita is now alone, with me staring painfully at her. She is glaring harder at the flowers and out of nowhere, she starts to snatch them away with her own hands. I gasp horrified at what I'm witnessing. No...why is she destroying her own garden? Her sanctuary? Why is she doing this?

Angry tears are flowing down her face and she doesn't stop yanking away the flowers, the plants, the roses, everything! She is so angry, so hurt, and full of hatred...and it is hurting me even more because I know it's my entire fault. I caused this pain...I am the reason Aelita is not innocent anymore...I am the reason her pure heart is turning black...

I am so sorry.

She is still snatching and destroying her flowers and suddenly she gets on her hands and knees like a baby and starts to crawl. Why can't she walk...?

I remember what Dr. Penn told me, it will be painful for her to walk on her own for a while.

I shudder once again and my throat is aching me.

Aelita is moving a bit toward my direction. She is glaring angrily at the plants in front of me. She wants to destroy them too. She makes few more movements toward me, and then for some reason...she looks up and our eyes meet.

# 8

As my eyes meet Aelita's...I have a sudden flash back of when I first met her.

————

It was fourteen years ago, on Forest's seventh birthday. He told me he was celebrating it with his girlfriend.

"Girlfriend? You don't have a girlfriend," the eight years old me told him smirking. "What girl in her right mind would want to hang out with you?"

"No, no! I'm serious! You'll see her. She's beautiful, but she doesn't talk," Forest was desperately trying to convince me.

"That's because she doesn't exist," I stubbornly refused.

"You'll see her today, really!"

"Heh," I smirked at him and the car dropped Forest and I in front of a ridiculously enormous mansion.

"Come on sweetie, let me fix your little bowtie." Mrs. Guardian told Forest crouching down to fix the seven years old's bowtie.

"Thanks mommy!" Forest grinned. I was awed at the size of the Fire's mansion. It was like a castle and I fantasized that I was the knight of the castle and I was going to save the princess. It was because Forest and I watched an animated movie the night before.

"Oh look at all those munchkins!" Mrs. Fire said as we entered the house. I couldn't stop gawking around. It was huge and the stairs, the statues, the walls, the paintings, it all seemed like a fairy tale..

"And aren't you the cutest of all?" Mrs. Fire tells me, kneeling down to look at me. She pinched my cheeks playfully and started to baby talk with me. "You're so cute, yesh you are, oh yesh you are!"

I gave her an annoyed look and thought she was annoying. She wasn't the only mother who fell under the spell of my adorableness. Even Mrs. Guardian used to hold me hostage in her arms and never wanted to let me go whenever I came to play with Forest.

"Where's Aelita?" Forest asked Mrs. Fire.

"Oh...she was right here a minute ago," Mrs. Fire said standing up and starting to look around. "She must be hiding somewhere. She's not used to seeing so many kids of her age. It's her first time celebrating a birthday like this," she sighed and said "I'll go look for her."

"No, no no! Let's all look for her together, really!" Forest proposed, "It'll be just like in the movie, Aelita will be the princess and we're going to be the knights who save her. The first person who saves the princess is the ultimate knight!"

"Yeah!" the other boys and girls agreed, "we want to play too!"

"Heh," I agreed as well knowing that it was what I fantasized about. It was going to be fun, not because I was going to save Aelita...but because I was going to be the ultimate knight.

"Okay! Let's go!" Forest and the kids started to run around the mansion and I followed after.

"B-be careful!" I heard Mrs. Guardian shouting after us.

The rule of the game was simple. It was almost like playing tag. If one of the knights is touched by another knight, then he loses and the last person standing would win and hopefully find the princess.

It was fun, we were running around, hiding, dodging each other. I almost got tagged twice by Forest and Cody but I had a really quick reflex.

At the end, it was just me and Forest and I ended up getting tagged by Forest. "I'm saving the princess, really!" he stuck his tongue at me. I was a sore loser. I hated losing, and I was a kid back then. I was taking this game serious. I wanted to be the ultimate knight but Forest won. I decided I didn't want to play this game anymore or have the party. I just wanted to go home.

I was making my way down the stairs but I heard something fall in the room at the end of the hall. I was curious, so I decided to open the door.

The lights in the room were off and it was dim. I turned them on and realized I was in a bedroom. It was sophisticated and very classy and I assumed it was Aelita's parent's room. I thought it would be wise to leave the room immediately because I knew it was rude to intrude. As I was going to shut the lights back off, I caught the end of her long golden hair on the floor. She was hiding under the bed and I knew it was her. The friend that Forest wouldn't stop talking about. She was the princess in our game. I gave myself a wicked smirk as I started walking toward the bed. I knew Forest would be angry that I saved the princess first. I wasn't going to be a sore loser after all. I lied on the carpet next to her golden hair and looked under the bed.

She was shaking like a Chihuahua, but stopped shaking as soon as she saw me. Her honey brown innocent eyes widened in awe and contemplation as if she'd just seen an angel.

"I'm here to save you, princess." I told her, reaching my hand out under the bed to take hers.

And that was how we first met.

————

Now, I am staring at her again, and she is staring back at me with those same innocent honey brown eyes. They're filled with awe and contemplation as if she has just seen an angel.

Heh, I wish.

Aelita's eyes, that once held innocence are now holding nothing but horror, anger, embarrassment and repugnance as she stares at me. I have the sudden urge to turn away and hide my face from her. I feel like she's the beauty and I am the beast. I want to run away, or at least turn around so I don't have to look at those hating eyes of hers. It is breaking my heart that this girl's eyes are never, ever going to look at me the same way ever again. She is long gone. The Aelita I know died last Friday evening. Hunter  put a bullet in her head. This Aelita is someone else...this Aelita is a complete stranger.

We are both frozen in place, still gazing at each other. When it starts to get awkward and uncomfortable, I decide to be the first person to break the ice.

"Hello Aelita," I swallow. "It seems like you're renovating your garden." My sub-conscience glares at me and I mentally hit myself. *Stupid! Stupid! Stupid!* I haven't seen her since she the tragedy and this is the best thing I come up with to say to her? What kind of sarcastic joke is that? Why am I even thinking about joking around? I am a humorless person.

I gulp again, expecting her to say something so I can hear her voice. I am hoping to hear her talk to me. It doesn't matter what she says to me. She can curse me out, yell at me, ask me to get away from her. I will happily take it and it will all sound like music to my ears because I want to hear her speak—so fucking bad.

But she doesn't. Instead she quickly turns around and starts to crawl again, and she is trying so hard to hurry. I stare at her stupefied as I realize what she's doing.

She's running away from me. I feel as if she is taking a knife and jabbing it in my heart repetitively. To be honest, I wasn't expecting this kind of reaction from her. Every time I think about how our first meeting will go, I have so many scenarios. One of them is having her smile at me and run to hug me and tell me how much she misses me and needs me and to never ever leave her side ever again. Another scenario is having her grab a knife and stab me, curse me out and send me straight to hell.

I never ever thought about her running away from me. My eyes slowly trail away from her, feeling rejected and embarrassed. I decide to leave her alone.

I am about to turn around and walk away but when I give her one last glance, I see that she isn't crawling anymore. Her curly, perfect hair are caught and tangled in between the plants next to her and she is trying to untangle them.

"Aelita!" I find myself immediately climbing over the fence and rushing toward her to help her untangle her hair. "Let me help you," I tell her. She is stiff and frozen again as if she doesn't want me to be around her. I remember what Mrs. Fire said earlier. She isn't ready to be around any male...maybe that's why she's scared of me.

*I should go*, I tell myself, but I can't just leave her like that. I'm helping her detangle her hair. It would be rude to leave her like this.

The German shepherd dog suddenly comes out of nowhere and circles me and Aelita. He's wagging his tail at Aelita, signaling her that he wants to play but she completely ignores him as if he doesn't exist. It pains me once more.

Aelita is not looking at the world the same way she used to anymore. She is destroying her garden and ignoring her favorite dog.

I take a deep and painful breath and try my hardest not to look at her in the eye. When I'm done untangling her hair, she doesn't waste any second. She starts to crawl away from me again. I look at where she's crawling to—it's toward the wheelchair. I can't let her move like this when I, her husband, am right there. I snort to myself and walk after her.

"I'll carry you to your wheelchair," I say and pick her up from the floor, holding her bridal style. I feel her moving around from my grip and I convince myself that she is trying to readjust herself, not struggling away from me. She can talk—she can just ask me to let her go. Why isn't she saying anything? Why is so stiff and frozen? I feel offended. I try to ignore the awkward situation I am in with her and let my memory drift away to a more pleasant one. I am remembering the first time I ever carried her bridal style.

———

It was during the break of our second year in high school, a month before Forest died. Nadia transferred months ago from another school and when I first laid my eyes on her, I knew I wanted her in bed with me. Unfortunately for me, Forest was the first to charm her and steal her heart away. It took them less than two weeks to start dating. Forest was happy with her and Nadia too was happy, although she knew I was interested in her as well.

During our break, Forest invited me, Nadia and Aelita to go cliff jumping by the waterfall that was about half an hour away from our school. We were going to picnic and spend the whole day cliff-jumping, relaxing in water and sunbathing.

Nadia was wearing the hottest bikini I've ever seen. It was a black top that revealed a lot of her cleavage and a blue bottom. Her body was exposed and I couldn't help gawking at her curves, her hips, hers legs, her chest. She was very hot, and I wanted her even more. I was fantasizing about taking her away from Forest later on and hiding somewhere, maybe behind the cliff or in the bushes and making sweet-passionate love to her.

"You look stunning babe, really." Forest told her, kissing her.

"You're not bad yourself," Nadia smirked at him between the kisses.

"Aelita! You look so fancy and sophisticated, really!" Forest complimented Aelita. He had the habit of saying 'really' a lot. Aelita was wearing a diving swimming suit, and it was covering her completely from neck to ankle. There was nothing to see. Well, she had a bit of curve, but it wasn't much to look at since she was completely covered and reserved. Plus, she wasn't developing as fast as Nadia was. She was plain and boring to me.

Aelita gave a gentle thank you smile to Forest and Nadia. Then, she looked at me and looked away. I knew she had a small crush on me. Forest told me that earlier and wanted me to ask her on a date and I told him it was never going to happen. I wasn't interested in Aelita, I was interested in Nadia.

The day started really nicely. Forest, Nadia and I were diving, jumping into the waterfall, doing backflips in the air, splashing each other while Aelita, who was too shy to join us, preferred to sit on top of the cliff and watch us have fun. After having a bit of fun in the water, we decided to eat and rest a little.

While resting, we laid on the rocks and stared at the clouds.

"This really cloud looks like you, Aelita," Forest told Aelita pointing toward the sky. Forest would often say something, anything to remind Aelita that she wasn't forgotten since she was always so quiet and felt like an outcast from the three of us. He was sweet and protective of her, he treated her like a little sister.

"It does," Nadia agreed. "And this one next to Aelita looks like Colton," she continued.

"Ah! You're right!" Forest exclaimed then smirked at me. "It might really mean something..."

I knew what he was referring to. He was still trying to get me to go on a date with Aelita. I glared at him.

"Alright! Enough resting! Let's go take another dive, this time you're really coming, Aelita!" Forest told her, but she shook her head, refusing.

"Come on, Aelita," Nadia tried to encourage her and still, she kept on shaking her head.

"Alright, we won't be long and then we can go hike together or something, really." Forest smiles at Aelita.

So, we start jumping off the cliffs again, it was me and Forest and Nadia in the water, but later, Forest and Nadia kept on slowly and slowly swimming a bit away from me, giggling and chuckling and kissing each other. I didn't want to let them be alone, so I followed them.

Forest shot me a glare, "Um is it not really obvious that we're trying to have a private moment together?"

"What am I supposed to do, then? Swim by myself?" I retorted back.

"Make Aelita jump. Come on, I really feel bad leaving her up there all by herself while we're all having fun," Forest pleaded me.

"No way," I refused.

"Come on, Colton! I'll owe you one, really!" Forest begged.

I shook my head.

"Please Colton," Nadia was the one pleading me now and I couldn't refuse anymore.

"Fine..." I muttered and saw both of them snicker and swim away toward the bushes. Forest was living my fantasy.

I sighed and grumbled then walked back toward the top of the cliff. Aelita was sitting down under a tree trying to hide from the sun — it was getting hot.

"Hot?" I asked her. She turned around and smiled at me and nodded.

"Maybe you should go swim. The water is refreshing," I told her. She shook her head at me but then looked around. She didn't see Forest and Nadia and gave me a questioning look.

Forest and I learned to communicate with Aelita through her facial expression. She was easy to read.

"They're having sex somewhere," I answered her. I saw her smile a bit embarrassed and shake her head. I stared at her for a while and then blurred out. "Wanna have sex too?"

The reaction I got from her was more than amusing. It was priceless. Her jaw dropped and her eyes were wide open as if she couldn't believe what I just said.

"I'm just kidding," I reassured her moments later. She sighed a bit in relief and shook her head at me.

"But seriously, get in the water," I commanded her. She shook her head at me once more. I glared at her annoyed. She knew how to swim. Her father paid for our swimming lessons for the last three summers. It was Forest, her and I and she was good at it. If she didn't want to swim, what was the point of her taking swimming lessons?

"I'm not going to say it again, Aelita," I warned her. "Get in the water."

I never treated her like Forest did. Forest was the one who was pleading, gentle and always amending to her demands and caprices, begging her to do something and I always thought she was just acting spoiled and she liked people being concerned about her. I was the one who bossed her around and commanded her. I was never nice or gentle or begged her to do anything. I made her do things.

She shook her head at me again with a pleading look as if she was saying "Please don't make me."

I glared at her again, this time angry that she wasn't listening to me. So, I stormed toward her and picked her up. She was so light. She stiffened and blushed when I picked her up bridal style. I walked toward the edge of a cliff and gave her a cruel, mischievous smirked as I stretched my arms further. She realized I wasn't going to jump with her.

"Have fun," I told her and let her drop in the air. I looked down and watched her squint her eyes as she dropped in the water, making a small splash. I waited few seconds and then she resurfaced out of the water gasping. I smiled, rolled my eyes and turned around walking away. When I turned around, I saw Forest and Nadia. Forest was zipping his swim short and Nadia was adjusting her bikini top. I glared at both of them.

"Oh, you're really here!" Forest said as he saw me.

"Yes. Thank you Forest, I already knew that," I replied with sarcasm.

"Where's Aelita?" Forest asked, looking around.

"Swimming with the fishes," I answered.

"Why aren't you with her?" he snapped at me.

"I had enough of being in water," I snapped back and then he rushed toward the edge of the cliff to check on Aelita.

"Where's she?" Forest asked me once again.

I raised an eyebrow. "What do you mean? She's in the water," I rushed toward the end of the cliff and I realized Aelita was nowhere to be seen.

"Shit!" Forest immediately dived, and I followed.

I was so worried and so scared. I thought she was a good swimmer. I knew she was a good swimmer! How could she have drowned?

When in the water, Forest swam deeper and looked around and I was right behind him doing the same. Aelita was nowhere to be found. When our lungs gave out, we both swam back up for air. We were gasping and we suddenly heard Nadia's voice calling after us.

"Guys, she's alright! She's just here!" she said, waving at us. We looked forward saw Aelita and Nadia under the cliff, sitting on rocks. I felt so relieved. For a moment, I thought Mr. Fire was going to have my head. Forest sighed and swam toward the two girls. I followed shortly after.

Aelita was fine. She just stepped out of the water when I turned away because she saw baby frogs jumping around so she wanted to play with them. She gave us an apologetic smile. We spent the rest of the day in the water. This time, it was the four of us and the day ended without any more incidents. I was such a douche to her back then...

———

I am back in the present time and I am holding her in my arms while she is stiff, frighten and angry. I gently put her on her wheelchair. She immediately starts to use her hands to roll the wheels.

I still want to spend just a little more time with her. I decide to push her, but Hinata, the servant comes in. She is surprised and shocked to see me.

"Mr. Ice...What are you doing here?" she asks me. "Does Mrs. Fire know you're here?"

I shake my head at her. "I just wanted to see how my wife is doing."

"Oh," Hinata looks away in guilt. "Well you shouldn't be here. I'll push Mrs. Ice," she wants me to move aside from the wheelchair so she can push Aelita instead.

Before Hinata even gets the chance to walk close toward the wheelchair, Aelita violently pushes her farther away and glares up at her. Then, she uses her hands to move herself and before I know it, she disappears in the house.

She's angry and scared because of me.

"You shouldn't be here, Mr. Ice." Hinata tells me once again.

"Indeed you shouldn't," Mrs. Fire comes out of nowhere with a deadly look in her eye. "Hinata, go make sure my daughter is alright," she tells the maid, her eyes not leaving mine.

"Of course," Hinata says, bows to her and to me and then leaves the garden.

"What are you doing here?" Mrs. Fire asks me. Her voice is rather calm, and I am surprised that she is not aiming for my throat.

"I'm leaving," I put my hand up in defeat, not wanting to start a fight with her. I am about to leave using the way I came in when she calls after me. "Wait."

I stop and turn around.

"What was her reaction when she saw you?" Mrs. Fire asks. She's curious and interested.

"Not good," I banally reply. I know if I give Mrs. Fire the complete detail, she will make sure I never come back in the house ever again.

"What happened to your face?" she asks me. I forgot that I let Jago take his anger out on me yesterday. My lip is cut and I think my cheek is a little red, it's nothing serious.

"I got into a fight," I reply. I don't want to give her any more details than that.

"I heard you killed one of those..." she clears her throat, "men today."

I nod.

She nods back approvingly, "good. Onto the next one."

"If that's all, I'd like to go."

"I meant to ask you," she starts again. Oh God, what now? "How did you find Aelita in the bathroom, the other day?"

"Forest showed me," I reply glancing at the dog. He hasn't left the garden or followed Aelita. He is sitting my by side, his mouth wide open, his tongue stuck out and he is breathing through his mouth.

"Forest?" Mrs. Fire raises and eyebrow at me as if I'm crazy.

"Her dog — the German shepherd," I explain.

The expression on her face doesn't change. "The dog died last Friday protecting Aelita. They shot him when they invaded the house."

I look at her confused and glance down at the dog who is sitting by me.

"Then whose dog is this?" I point at the dog.
Mrs. Fire glances at the direction I am pointing to and she glances back at me, she is stupefied.

"What dog?"

# 9

"What do you mean what dog?" my eyes are wide and confused just as Mrs. Fire's. I look at the dog and he is there! He is seating by my side and I can feel his warmth on my leg.

Mrs. Fire looks down and looks at me again. "I don't see a dog, honey," her voice is suddenly gentle, soft and sympathetic. I don't believe this. Maybe she's playing a prank on me...trying to make me think that I'm crazy.

"It's not funny, Mrs. Fire!" I yell at her and crouch down to touch the dog. I can touch the dog, he's real! I know he's real! I can pet him, feel his fur. The dog is real!

"How can't you see it?" I gasp, my eyes wide open. It doesn't make any sense. The dog bit me days ago when I came to take my belongings. He led me to Aelita's room! He saved Aelita's life...he's real!

"He's real!" I repeat, looking at the dog. He is real. The dog stands up and runs back inside the house.

"Okay honey. I see it," Mrs. Fire says right after, looking down the direction the dog was seating seconds ago. "I see the dog, he's a good dog," she lies.

I clench my jaws and glare at her, "he went back in the house seconds ago."

She looks back at me with so much pity. I hate seeing people pitying me. Mrs. Fire walks close to me and puts both her hands on either sides of my face looking at me with concern.

"When's the last time you ate, honey?"

I don't know.

"Don't worry about it," I try to remove her hands from me, but she doesn't let me.

"You're paler than usual and you're starting to look like a ghost. When's the last time you ate, Colton?" Mrs. Fire repeats, now very serious.

I look down and whisper, "last Friday morning,"

She inhales, her eyes not leaving mine and shakes her head. "This is also hard on you, isn't it?" Her voice is filled with sympathy. She then faintly smiles and hugs me, "it's okay, you're going to stay here this evening and

I'm going to feed you, and you'll talk to a very good friend of mine. He's a psychologist."

I frown and look at her suspiciously. Why is she acting this way now?

"Why do you care?" I ask her.

"I don't," she shakes her head and then hugs me again, purring dangerously in my ears. "I just want you well and healthy until my husband kills you. I don't want misery or depression killing you first."

Then she lets go of me. "Follow me inside. We have to feed you."

"I thought you didn't want Aelita to see me," I say slowly following her.

"She won't," Mrs. Fire reassures me. "She's locking herself in her bedroom with Hinata."

We're in the kitchen and Mrs. Fire is serving me chicken noodle soup with toasted bread. I don't want to eat it. One reason is because I don't have the appetite. The other reason is because the woman who wants me dead is giving me food to eat. I'm not that stupid. I look at the meal suspiciously and stare at her.

"Eat up," she orders, pulling a chair across me and sitting down. When I don't obey, she smiles bitterly. "It's not poisoned. I promise you. I can't kill you until you're done with your duties, remember?"

She has a point. So I shrug, take the spoon and take a sip of the soup. It is delicious, I cannot deny that. I take a second sip, and another, and another. Mrs. Fire is a great cook. All of her meals I have ever eaten since I was a kid have always been my favorite meals. She is amazing at baking and cooking which is the complete opposite with Aelita.

Aelita really sucks at cooking, that's why the first thing I did as we started living together was hire a cook.

I remember one day, I came back home from work and expecting dinner to be ready, but the cook wasn't there and Aelita was the one cooking.

---

"What are you doing?" I asked her. "Where's the cook?" Back then, Aelita used to communicate with me by writing. She grabbed a small white board and a marker and wrote: Jane's daughter is sick, and I gave her the week off. I'll cook for you, Colton.

Aelita was so eager to cook but I wasn't. I knew how bad her cooking was. Forest was my witness. In high school, when Forest was still alive, she baked us brownies for the first time and Forest was so eager to eat it. As soon as he took a bite of the brownie, Forest turned blue and ran to the nearest bathroom. I knew then that it would be a bad idea to eat her brownies. I told Aelita I didn't like sweets and saved myself from eating her creation.

That night, when Aelita wanted to cook for me, I wanted to say no but I thought maybe she was better at cooking since it had been a long time that incident happened. Plus, she seemed very eager to cook, so I let her. She ended up burning everything, and she was about to cry. She was so embarrassed. I sighed and told her not to worry, I could cook. I was going to make us something simple when miraculously, Mrs. Fire stopped by to say hi. She ended up cooking for both of us and the meal was delicious and even better than our cook's and I was very grateful.

————

The one thing I have always loved about Mrs. Fire was and still is her cooking. She's amazing.

Mrs. Fire looks at me with satisfaction, seeing how eagerly I am eating the noodle soup. "Delicious, huh?" she asks me.

I nod, taking the last sip.

"Aelita's chicken was well raised. That's why the meat is so tasty."

I look at her eyes wide and I realize she isn't kidding.

"You killed her chickens? Those were her pets," I glare at her angrily. How could she? And she fed them to me! If Aelita ever finds out I ate her chicken, she'll hate me even more. That sneaky cruel woman!

"Listen sweetheart," Mrs. Fire is rolling her eyes. "I was born and raised in a farm and in my time, chickens weren't used as pets. They're food."

My accusing glare doesn't break from her.

"Don't look at me like that," she glares back at me. "Aelita didn't want to have anything to do with those animals anymore, anyways."

I frown. "What do you mean?"

Mrs. Fire's face saddens. "She wanted me to get rid of all of them."

Just like her garden...That's awful. My heart is clenching painfully.

"I gave away the dogs, cats, hamsters, turtles, parrots and monkeys to a non-kill animal shelter. They'll be staying there until Aelita is herself again. The horses and some of the goats and pigs are at the Fire Farm. I only kept the chickens."

I look down the bowl sadly.

"Until she's herself again?" I ask Mrs. Fire. "Do you actually believe she'll come back from this?"

Mrs. Fire glares at me. "Yes I believe that my daughter will come back from all this. You may see her as a weak and fragile little girl, but I know my daughter. Under all this softness and gentleness, I know there's a strong spirit hiding inside of her that will come out sooner or later and will surprise all of you," her voice is starting to get hoarse as if she is about to cry. "Heck, she survived a gunshot to the head, survived from bleeding out and is able to move around. Both Dr. Penn and Dr. Brown are amazed of how healthy and strong my daughter's body is! My daughter is *not* weak. I swear to you all, you have absolutely no idea what this girl is capable of," Mrs. Fire exclaims.

I listen to her carefully.

"She's just finding a way to deal with this on her own. The psychologist said that she's reacting as if she's lost someone, as if she lost herself...as if she was dead. First stage was denial..." Mrs. Fire starts to explain.

"That's why she tried to kill herself. She was denying the fact that she was alive, that something bad happened to her, she didn't want to believe any of this, she was trying to escape reality... but she's past that now. She now knows what happened to her, and that she survived. She's now on the second stage...anger."

I swallow.

"Aelita has been violent, snappy and rebellious toward me, the psychologist and the servants. That's why she was destroying her garden and that's why she wants nothing to do with her animals...she's angry at everything, at everyone, at me, at the servants, at everything. I will let her deal with it on her own way. I'm not going to stop her from taking her anger out on me as long as it helps her," she inhales. "Then, the next stage will be bargaining...it will be her most vulnerable moment through the stage, that's when she'll need me the most and I will be there for her day and night. Then, she'll go through depression and eventually acceptance. When Aelita reaches that last stage, I know she will transform into a stronger woman. When she finally accepts what happened to her, I know she'll be at peace and will come back from all this."

Mrs. Fire is so convinced that Aelita's going to be alright...but the truth is, I know her daughter more than she does. I know Aelita will never come back from this. When I looked at her eyes, the amount of pain and horror that was in her was too much. She isn't going to come back as a strong woman. I'm not being pessimistic. I'm being realistic.

"I hate you, sweetheart," Mrs. Fire says later, startling me. "I never really liked you ever since Forest died. You were never nice to my daughter, but she loved you. She loved you so much and wanted nothing but your happiness..."

I don't want to hear this.

"All she wanted was you to be happy and now look at where it took her..." Mrs. Fire has furious tears rolling down her face. "All because you couldn't keep that little dick of yours in your pants," she snarls. "You disgust me, Ice. You disgust me so much. I can't believe we trusted you to take care of her..."

I can see and feel the amount of hatred that woman has for me and I don't blame her one bit.

"I want to be there when my husband kills you," she adds with a serious look in her eyes. "I want to watch you die."

I look away and say nothing. The weird thing is, I am not sad or scared that I'm going to die soon. I feel rather relieved knowing that my life will be shortened. I will not have to spend the rest of my life thinking about what I've done to Forest, to Aelita...to so many people. I feel relieved.

"I'm calling the psychologist and making an appointment for you tomorrow," Mrs. Fire suddenly tells me, and I remember the incident with the dog. I feel goose bumps on my skin.

"I don't need to speak to a psychologist. I'm not crazy," I tell her stubbornly. "The dog is real."

"Well I didn't see any dog ," she snaps back.

"The dog was the one who led me to Aelita's room. He was the one who barked at the bathroom door, I never intended to go to her room in the first place. I knew you'd kill me...the dog saved Aelita's life."

She does not believe me.

"When I found Aelita unconscious, I asked the dog to go get you and he ran out of the room and you came minutes after," I say through my clenched teeth.

She frowns and shakes her head. "No dog came to me Colton," she starts. "I was wondering what was taking you so long to pack your things up, so I went back to your room and didn't find you and something told me to go look in Aelita's room," she explains. "No dog came to me."

That's impossible.

"What about the doctor?" I continue. I know I am not crazy and the dog is real. "When you fainted, I asked help to the dog again. I begged him to go get someone, anyone...and miraculously, the doctor came minutes later. How do you explain that?"

Mrs. Fire is shaking her head again. "Dr. Brown was already in the house. She was going to do checks up with Aelita. She stepped outside for fifteen minutes before you even came in the house because she had an important phone call. She was supposed to be there. The dog didn't call her. There wasn't any dog."

I don't believe this. I know this is real. I know the dog is real. I am not imagining things. I know the dog saved Aelita. "I'm not crazy," I grit through my teeth angrily.

Mrs. Fire nods her head in a sarcastic way and is going to say something when the phone rings. She picks it up.

I know I am not crazy. The dog is real. How come Mrs. Fire can't see it...?

Yes, she told me he was shot on the day of Aelita's assault...but it's hard to believe that because I've seen the dog and I know it's not a ghost. The dog isn't transparent or floating in the air. It's normal, alive, and warm and I can feel it when I touch it.

No, I am not going insane. There has to be some sort of explanation to this. Maybe it is Mrs. Fire's way to mentally torture me. Maybe the dog isn't even dead. I'll have to ask Hinata about this later.

"There's a car waiting for you outside," Mrs. Fire says after hanging up the phone. "Henry wants to see you."

Jesus Christ, it's always one after the other.

"Alright," I sigh and stand up, walking toward the exit of the kitchen.

"I'm still getting you to talk to a psychologist," Mrs. Fire says after me.

"Thanks for the food," I tell her and before closing the door behind me, she calls me and with a cruel smirk on her face, she says "By the way Colton, I spit in your food."

I sigh and roll my eyes then close the door behind me. It's better than poisoning me.

I am in Mr. Fire's office. He is standing in the middle of the room and Zero is behind him. I glare at Zero remembering that hours ago he was giving flowers and a puppy to my wife. I'll kill him, I swear.

In front of Lord Fire, on the floor, is lying Jago's dead body and Lord Fire doesn't seem satisfied. Not one bit.

"Good evening," I greet him.

His famous poker face is staring right back at me and he is not greeting me back. He's upset. "This is your idea of revenge?" he points at the body, his voice is angry. "This is what you mean by making the rapist of my daughter suffer? You let him beat you up, make his wife rich and put a simple bullet in his head just like that? Is that what mean by revenge?"'

"I made a deal with him," I explain. "If I didn't, he wouldn't give us the tape."

"You negotiated with one of the guys who raped my daughter," Mr. Fire is sounding angrier and angrier by the minute.

"He was the only one who didn't rape her."

"I do not care!" his voice is rising, and he is glaring at me. His poker face is slowly disappearing. "He was part of them! He was there when it all happened! He was with them! I don't care if he didn't hurt my daughter directly! He still hurt her! He is just as guilty as all of them, and you dare to take care of his wife and save her life!"

"She is innocent," I'm glaring back at him.

"MY DAUGHTER WAS INNOCENT!" He suddenly fumes, making Zero and I and the rest of the guards jolt. He is loud. "My daughter was innocent and yet they raped her, insulted her, hurt her, tortured her body and shot her like a dog so don't fucking tell me you're sparing the prick's wife because she's innocent! Bullshit!" he slams his hand on the table. "She fucked you, the husband of my faithful daughter—a married man! She's not innocent! My daughter was the only innocent one in all of this!" he is breathing hard, his eyes blazing at me. He spits on Jago's dead body. "I killed his wife an hour ago," his voice is a little calmer. "I showed her the body of her dead husband and she cried and then I had Zero strangle her."

I can't believe this.

"They're all going to suffer and go down in a painful way," Lord Fire growls. "Anyone who's related to those monsters, whether it's a newborn, a kid, an uncle, a grandfather, and grandmother, I don't care. They all have to suffer. They're just as guilty as the monsters because they're related to them. I want them all to suffer and die," he is glaring at me.

I inhale and painfully exhale. I want to make those guys suffer more than anything, believe me, but I also have a conscience. I know what's wrong and what's right...killing the families and innocent children isn't right. If we go this way, then we're no different from those monsters.

"I'm going to show you what it means to torture someone. I'm going to show you what it means to make them regret they were ever born. Follow me," Mr. Fire orders me and walks out of his office. Zero and the two guards are behind him and I slowly follow him after.

I'm in his limo with Zero. The two other guards are in another car, following us. I am anxiously wondering where we are going and what Lord Fire has in mind.

I think about Jago's wife, Fiona. Lord Fire killed her in cold blood...she was innocent. It doesn't feel right. I'm just glad Jago wasn't alive to see it.

The car stops about an hour and a half later. It's dark outside and we're at a port surrounded with lots of containers. The port is deserted. The atmosphere around us is eerie and nerve-wracking. Before exiting the car, I glance through the window and see a man chained to a light pole.

I recognize the man and my jaws tighten.

"You know him, son?" Lord asks me and I nod, still glaring at the man. He is one of the four men who brutally raped Aelita. He is the one who kept spitting on her while ramming himself inside of her, calling her names. He was enjoying her scream in pain.

"His name is Lazar Lazare. He has three kids, two girls, one boy. I'm going to teach you how to make someone suffer. You just watch and say nothing. Watch and learn, son," he tells me and I nod. Afterwards, we exit the car.

It's windy and a bit cold outside. The wind and dust are blowing on my face, but I don't care...all I care about is killing Lazar right there and right now. I feel so enraged, but I remember that Lord Fire wants to teach me something.

When Lazar sees us, especially Lord Fire, his face falls. "Oh shit..." he curses.

There are five of us standing few feet away from Lazar. Lord Fire is in the front, with a smoking pipe in his mouth. He is as calm as silence itself, which amazes because I in the other hand am trembling with rage, unable to keep calm.. I am few inches behind him, and next to me is Zero. On the left side of Lord are the two guards who followed us. We're all standing in front of Lazar whose body is starting to shake not because to the cool weather. When Lazar sees Lord Fire, he sighs and leans against the pole, slowly letting himself slide down on the ground, he raises his head up and stares up the dark sky. The expression on his face is readable. He knows he's doomed.

"Good evening Mr. Lazare, do you recognize me?" the Lord asks calmly and politely.

Lazar nods slowly and is still staring up the sky. "You're Lord Fire."

The Lord smiles at him, still smoking his pipe. "Well everyone knows that, but I don't want you to know me as Lord Fire, so please allow me to reintroduce myself. I'm Henry Fire, the father of the girl you raped and killed last Friday night."

Lazar swallows. His body is shaking even more.

"Mr. Lazare, do you have an idea of what's going to happen to you?"

Lazar nods in defeat with a painful smile on his face. He finally makes eye contact with the lord. "You're going to take my life."

Lord Fire doesn't respond to Lazar's assumption. Instead, he chuckles darkly for few seconds, sending chills down my spine. I can't tell what he's thinking. My best guesses of what Lord Fire will do to Lazar are that he'll probably kill him, cut off his testicles like he did to the other two guards, or have Zero beat him to death, or physically torture him in the most gruesome way possible.

"Everyone has a favorite part of their body," Mr. Fire starts, "Zero, right here," he gestures to Zero who is standing still like a robot, his face completely emotionless. "His favorite parts of his body are his hands. He loves to touch, and he has gifted hands. With his hands, he can perform surgery and heal any kind of animal, and with the same hands, he can easily, and I mean *easily* snap a human's neck," Mr. Fire takes out his pipe and smiles. "I too, have a favorite part on my body: my eyes," he starts to walk around. "You see, Mr. Lazare, I'm a very curious and a very visual person, I like to see. I don't like reading books, or listening to the radio, I don't like descriptions; I like to see things with my own eyes. So anyways, one of my chemists was giving a verbal safety presentation on dangerous chemicals and I remember him emphasizing how extremely dangerous and deadly sulfuric acid is. Do you know what sulfuric acid is, Mr. Lazare?" Mr. Fire looks as him.

Lazare is still seating down on the ground, his eyes are dead and he is sweaty. "It's an extremely dangerous acid."

Mr. Fire brings his poker face back. "Indeed, Mr. Lazare. Sulfuric acid or as I prefer to call it H2SO4, is an extremely strong acid that has the ability to char organic materials such as wood, paper…" his voice darkens. "flesh…"

Lazar turns pale and stares at him horrified. "Shit, you're going to kill me with sulfuric acid?"

Mr. Fire clears his throat. "Well not really…" he turns to one of his guards. "Spyros, why don't you explain him…?"

He is a talking to the shortest and youngest looking redhead man who might either be in his late teens or early twenties like me.

"Yes sir," the guard clears his throat and starts to speak. "You see, sulfuric acid is a sucker for water. It loves it so technically, it doesn't melt your skin. It is only after the water in your body. When in contact with your skin, it removes the hydrogen and oxygen and dehydrates your cells. The reaction gives off a lot of heat which causes burns. That's why your skin melts in contact with it.

"Thank you, Spyros," Lord Fire says and Lazar suddenly panics.

"You are one fucked up son of a bitch!" Lazar shouts

Zero is making a move toward him, but Mr. Fire stops Zero. Lazar glares at both of them and spits on the

167

floor, then gets up. "Fuck you! I ain't scared of any of you! You think I'm gonna beg for mercy? Well guess what? I won't beg! You can do whatever you want to me, I don't give a shit. I won't beg! I don't regret anything! I don't give a shit! I don't give a fuck!" He is shouting angrily, and Mr. Fire's poker face doesn't disappear. Everyone is calm and composed listening to him. Lazar seems angrier than scared and doesn't really seem afraid of Mr. Fire. He is nervous, but he is prepared to die and is not regretting anything which is making me angrier.

After Lazar stops shouting and cursing us out, Lord Fire finally decides to speak.

"Mr. Lazare, as we can all see, and as you just confirmed, we can all agree that you really don't have any deep remorse for what you're done to my daughter."

"Damn right!" Lazar spits again on the floor.

"Therefore, we can all agree that killing you at the moment will be like a slap on the wrist," Mr. Fire's face is dark and his voice is raw. The atmosphere is suddenly scary and menacing. I can feel the terrifying energy around us, and the wind is becoming colder and so cruel that I can feel the inner core of my body freeze. It is as if nature responds to Mr. Fire's emotions.

"Anyways," he continues, his voice now calm. "As I was saying, I am a very visual man and I like to see things. I was very curious and interested in the damages $H_2SO_4$ can do to a human body. I do not want descriptions, I want to see it with my own eyes," Mr. Fire nods Spyros. Spyros salutes Mr. Fire before walking toward a somber bluish container. He presses a button and the container automatically opens like a box. We see another transparent container side of it. It's smaller and narrower and has a human inside. It's a little girl, she looks like she's in her early teen years and she's very scared.

*Oh...shit.*

"Oh shit," Lazar curses quietly, his face is completely pale and blue and green. His brown eyes widen in horror and his jaw drops. "Oh no," he breathes out in horror, staring back at Mr. Fire in disbelief and back to the girl. "Erika, honey?" Lazar calls after her.

I realize it's one of his daughters. The girl is standing up and looking around disoriented. She is crying.

"Erika!" Lazar is trying to move away from the pole, but in vain. "Aw shit, Erika! Oh no!" he turns to Mr. Fire. "No! No! No!" Lazar is shouting. He is becoming sweatier. "Shit! No! God damn it! No!"

Erika recognizes her father and starts to bang on the glassed container. "...dad...dad!"

"Baby, no!" Lazar shouts again, he is starting to sob. "Oh no! No, no, no!"

Mr. Fire is still calm and unoccupied, still smoking his pipe. "Your daughter is imprisoned in a special type of plastic container that cannot be charred by sulfuric acid," he explains. "So her remains will be contained after she's liquefied."

I feel myself turn pale as I stare at the little girl who is banging against the cement, screaming for her dad.

"No, this is not happening..." Lazar is shaking his head and starting to sob. "Erika...no..." he sounds as if he is not believing what is about to happen to her. "No, no....AHHHHHH! TO HELL WITH YOU!" he starts to yell and scream angrily at us, his eyes are red and furious and he is struggling to free himself. I have a sudden feeling of empathy. I know exactly what he's going through. I was like this last Friday—when they tied me up and made me watch as they brutally raped Aelita. I know what he's feeling, and I'd be lying if I tell you that I feel any sympathy.

"AHH! YOU MOTHERFUCKER! YOU HEARTLESS MONSTER!" he continues to scream at Mr. Fire who is still smoking his pipe like he doesn't give a damn. Then Lazar's daughter screams louder for him.

"Daddy! Daddy! I'm scared! I want to go home! Daddy, help me! Daddy! Daddy! I'm sorry I sneaked out! Please! Please! Please, daddy! Please!" she's shaking and crying and trying to break the container, but in vain.

Lazar stares at her painfully and starts to sob. "I'm so sorry, sweetheart...I'm so sorry!"

"Daddy! Daddy!" she is still screaming.

Mr. Fire nods again at the redhead guard who is climbing in a crane truck, and maneuvering the crane. He picks up a barrel and drives close to the container, ready to pour the acid inside. There are small opening holes on top of the container.

"No, please!" Lazar shakes his head at Mr. Fire, begging him. I am so fucking glad to be witnessing Lazar like this. He stares at Mr. Fire and drops to his knees, his head bowed down and his hands touching Mr. Fire's shoes. "Mr. Fire, Lord, please have mercy. I'm so sorry. I am so sorry. Please let my baby girl go. Please, please, I am so sorry," he is begging, just like I was begging!

Mr. Fire looks down at him and raises and eyebrow as if sorry is not going to cut it.

"Please," Lazar looks up at him, still on his knees. "Please, lord. Please, sir. Please not her, not my baby. Please, please...kill me instead, pour acid on me, torture me please, I'm the one who wronged you sir, I'm the one who hurt your daughter, mine did nothing. Look at her, sir. Look at my baby girl, she's innocent, she's just a child, she doesn't know anything...please. Please! Sir, I AM BEGGING YOU! SIR, please...." his face is crumbled and his head is bowed down again. When he doesn't hear anything, he looks up at Mr. Fire who is still smoking his pipe and staring down at him emotionlessly. Mr. Fire raises up his foot and steps on Lazar's head, forcing his face on the ground. "You're very good at begging,"

Lazare nods his head. "I am, I really. I am so, deeply sorry sir. I am very, very, very sorry."

Mr. Fire's still has a blank expression on his face. "It's good that you're sorry, Mr. Lazare. But," his face darkens. "I don't know how to forgive," he removes his foot from Lazar's head.

Lazar is breathing deeply and looking at him with begging eyes.

The girl is sobbing in the background.

Mr. Fire turns to the redhead guard and nods at him. Seconds later, the redhead man in the crane truck throws the barrel full of sulfuric acid on top of the container and the liquid starts to shower the girl inside slowly. The girl starts to scream in agony.

"No!" Lazar shouts, looking at the container and watching his girl's body slowly melting and smoking. She is screaming and crying and wincing and running around the container to dodge the drops of acid, but she can't because the holes are everywhere. Lazar is crying and shaking his head, painfully staring at the container, struggling to free himself from the pole.

"Erika, no," he cries. "NO!" he shouts looking at his girl. He falls down to his knees and continues to scream his lungs out.

I don't feel any pity or sympathy. I feel justice. I agree with what Lord Fire is doing.

Seeing the man who raped my wife cry and in pain and feel what I'm feeling right before my eyes is so satisfying. Lord Fire is right. I have to make all of them suffer. I have to. The girl is running and screaming and trashing around as Lazar is crying "nos"

Lord Fire looks straight in the container with a very faint, satisfied smirk.

"DADDYYYY!" the girl is crying. And about fifteen minutes later, we can't hear her scream anymore, but her body is still dissolving. She is dead.

"Erika...Erika-ha-hahaaaa.....ERIKAAAAAAAAA" Lazar is sobbing, still on his knees, powerless and completely distraught.

Lord Fire walks toward him and talks down to him. "Mr. Lazare, now you know what it's like to lose a child," he takes his pipe out of his mouth and glares down at Lazar. "Believe me when I tell you that what you just saw is just the tip of the iceberg," he tells him coldly. "You still have two kids and a wife ready to pay for what you've done."

Lazar looks up at Lord Fire and glares at him. "I am going to pulverize you," he growls.

Lord Fire smiles in a mocking way.

"I hope that black bitch whore daughter of yours rots in hell!" Lazar roars at Lord Fire, wiping the smile off his face.

I clench my jaws angrily, wanting to kill Lazar for talking about Aelita that way.

Zero suddenly points a gun at him, ready to pull the trigger.

"No Zero," Lord Fire refuses. Zero withdraws the guns and Lord Fire throws a hard punch in Lazar's face. The punch is so hard that I can ever hear his bones breaking from feet away. Lazar is immediately knocked out. Lord Fire then stands up and walks toward me. He is staring at me with satisfaction in his eyes and I know he sees how satisfied I am as well.

"This is what I call revenge, this is what it means to make them cry and pay for what they've done to my daughter, to your wife."

I nod , completely agreeing with him.

"I don't usually give out second chances, son, but I'm giving you a second chance because I know you don't have blood in your hands and you're still new at all this. But, I know you have a twisted mind even worse than mine. You pretend to be a masochist, but deep down, you know you're the worst kind of sadist," he continues to smirk at me with approval. "Let it out. Free your cruel intentions, son. Bury away that good conscience of yours and let the bad ones come out."

I nod.

"This is your new crew," the lord stares at the three guards including Zero. "They're three of my best men."

"This is Warr," he points at the grey haired man who looks mysterious. His hair and eyes are the rarest. He has pure platinum white hair, and his eyes are orange and yellow at the same time, as if they're inflamed. The rest of his face and body are completely covered. He has a black cloth mask that covers from his nose downwards, including his neck. He is wearing on top of his navy blue jumpsuit uniform, a dark grey hooded poncho with the red Fire symbol imprinted on the left upper corner. He is also wearing black gloves hiding his hands. He looks older than Zero and very, very intimidating. He makes me a bit nervous because I have a feeling that he is a hundred times worse than Zero. Warr looks at me, and his fiery eyes soften as he nods at me respectfully, acknowledging me.

"This is Spyros," lord points at the short redhead guard who nods at me as well. Spyros has green eyes and I see freckles on his face now that he is closer. As I mentioned earlier, he is the shortest of all and looks very young. I can't tell how crazy he is compared to Zero. His young face and almost innocent eyes are probably deceiving me. Lord Fire said that they're few of his best men; I know Spyros is probably just as crazy and as psychotic as Zero is. He just poured acid on a kid.

I nod at the two of them. "And you already know Zero," Mr. Fire continues. I don't bother acknowledging Zero. "They'll be working and helping you. They're all extremely skilled guards and will follow your orders. You are the leader of this squad, and you can trust them," he then looks at me seriously. "I'm going to leave the rest to you. You're going to deal with his two other kids and his wife and when you're done torturing them, you'll kill them in front of him and then you'll kill him last. I want it all to be recorded and sent to me by within a week. If I'm not satisfied with what you've done with them, I'll kill you next and then take everything else in my hands. Understood son?"

I nod again. "Understood."

He smiles at me then pats my back. "I feel exhausted. I shall leave you gentlemen to clean up the rest of this...mess," Mr. Fire looks down at the unconscious Lazar and the liquefied daughter who is still in the container, then shakes his head. "H2SO4 huh," he puts the pipe back in his mouth and walks toward his limo, the chauffeur immediately gets out of the car and opens the door to him. Within seconds, Lord Fire and his chauffeur drive away from the site leaving me with his three psycho killers.

I turn to stare back at them and what I see surprises me.

"Warr!" Spyros, the redhead kid suddenly tackles the platinum hair man. Spyros hugs Warr tightly with a very happy and enchanted grin on his face. "I missed you! And we're going to be working together for a while! I am so excited!"

I am surprised of how attached and extremely happy Spyros is around Warr, seems like they're really close. Warr's eyes are kind and gentle at Spyros, and he is playfully ruffling his hair. "You've grown, Spyros!" Warr then turns to Zero and ruffles his hair as well.

"Look at you, Zero. You never stop growing every time I see you, you're almost my height now, what are you eating?" Warr speaks. His voice is gentle and calming.

To my surprise, Zero's blank expression fades, and he has a faint warm and welcoming smile for Warr. I can tell that he's happy to have Warr with him as well.

"Tsk," Spyros mutters, giving a dirty look to Zero. "What's up, Lord's pet?"

Zero's expression returns to the usual blank one and he gives a quick annoyed glance at Spyros, smiles, and then turns to me. "What will be our next move, Mr. Ice?"

The three of them are now staring at me, waiting for me to answer. I look down at the unconscious rapist's body and recall what Mr. Fire told me before leaving, that I should free my mind and let all the creative twisted ideas out. I find myself smirking slightly as I start to think.

# 10

## LAZAR LAZARE'S POINT OF VIEW

I feel sore, and my face is hurting like fucking hell. I start opening my eyes, everything is blurry at first, but with my sense of smell, I recognize where I am. I am at my home, in my bed. I smile, realizing everything that happened to my sixteen year old daughter was nothing but a nightmare. Oh...Thank Goodness...

My eyes find their focus and I look around. I am on the floor, tied up and next to me is Sukia—my wife. There's blood coming out of her right chest and her eyes are closed. I realize it wasn't a dream. They got me.

"Aw Sukia...." please don't tell me my wonderful wife is dead. Please...not her too..."SUKIA!"

I am yelling at her.

"Don't worry Lazar," I hear a cold voice say. I look around as my eyes adjust more. I see three men in my bedroom. One of them is Colton Ice, the billionaire kid. The two others are the guards from yesterday. One has white hair and is wearing a dark grey poncho. The other has long black hair—he was the one who pointed a gun at me.

I force myself to get up, but I don't have the strength in me.

"What did you do my wife?! You sons of bitches!" I yell. "Fuck you! You're all dead! I'm gonna kill ya'll! Fuck You!" I am yelling, spitting and cursing at them.

None of them even flinch, or break a sweat.

"Your wife is alive," the Ice kid tells me and I glance back at Sukia. She is groaning.

"Sukia! Baby!" I rush toward her and she opens her eyes.

"Lazar..." she says faintly.

The dark haired guard unties my wrist and I hold her. "You're okay?"

She faintly nods and I look at her wound, she is bleeding out. I turn to glare at Ice.

"I didn't shoot her," he says, his face cold and hard and remorseless. "Zero did," he points at the guy with black hair. "Your wife tried to shoot me with her gun as soon as we came in your home but Zero has very quick reflexes. He shot her, missed a vital spot on purpose," his face is colder, "so she can bleed out in front of you."

My glare intensifies and I spit toward the Ice kid who is sitting on my bed without a care in the world.

"You like spitting a lot, don't you?" he asks with a cold glare.

"FUCK YOU!" I roar at him. He ignores me and turns to Sukia and looks at her with such disgust in his eyes like she's a vermin.

"I don't get it," he starts. "When did I have sex with you?"

The way he is saying it is almost as if it was a crime for any man to have sex with my wife. It's true, Sukia is not the most beautiful girl in the world. She is too skinny-mostly skins and bones are left of her due to the fact that she is a heavy drug addict and barely eats healthy. She has a very poor hygiene, barely showers, her teeth are rotten because she smokes, and her face is a bit disfigured but I still love her. It's not about what's in the outside, it's all about what's in the inside. Sukia is my woman and I love her just the way she is.

"I know I don't remember the hundreds of girls I've been intimate with," Ice's disgusted gaze doesn't leave Sukia. "But I'm pretty sure I never bedded you, Sukia."

Sukia gives him a very dirty, hateful look. "That's because you didn't, rich boy," she fires back.

Ice narrows his eyes at her in confusion, and then glares at me with anger. "Then why..." he growls, "why hurt Aelita?"

I smirk, knowing that he's going to hate this. I know if I tell him why I did all this, he's going to kill me and my wife right here and right now which is exactly what I want.

Sukia has lost too much blood, she will die soon. I can't save her, but I can save my other two children. I understand that Colton Ice wants to see me suffer. The Lord told me it'd be too easy if they killed me. They want to hurt my children, my family and my legacy right before my eyes. That is something I can never allow. I know if I'm dead, they won't have any reason to hurt my children and that's what I want. I want them to kill me. That is the only way to save them, so I have to tell him the truth. I smirk and spit on the carpet again.

"WHY HURT AELITA!?" Ice fumes, his eyes and body are trembling with fury. I know he is angry.

"Because that's what I do," I snarl back.

"What?" Ice's eyes are wide, confused. "Make yourself clear, Lazar!"

"Baby...what are you doing?" Sukia asks me confused as well.

I smile at her. "It's okay baby," I tell her. "I got this."

Then I look back at Colton Ice and his confused, angry guards as well. "You see boys," I start. "My wife and I have some sort of fucked up addiction. She likes eating human flesh, especially young female flesh and I like raping young beautiful girls."

Ice is clenching his jaws, his eyes are blazing and I know he is trying to contain himself.

"That's how Sukia and I fell in love. We embrace our flaws and our addiction and we help each other. Thanks to our imperfection, we've become the perfect couple and unlike your marriage with your wife, ours worked and never stopped blooming. I rape young beautiful girls, and bring them to Sukia so she can kill them and eat their flesh. That was our little thing. At first, it started with just college girls, and then slowly we started killing models, actresses, and young successful business women. Then, one day...my friend Hidon who knows I have this sort of addiction told me about their plan to rape your wife. You were a billionaire, and so was she...and when I first saw her picture, I was so aroused. She had the face of an angel,"

I see Ice tighten his fists. His body is trembling and I know he wants to kill me.

Good.

"When I first saw her, I knew her pussy would be sweet, tight and delicious," I lick my lips with a sick smirk on my face. "So I told Hidon I was up for it, and Sukia too wanted to know how a billionaire trophy wife tasted like. Hidon managed to lie to Hunter and tell him you fucked Sukia too so I could come with them and that's how it all happened. I raped her, enjoyed making that sweet little wife of yours scream," my eyes are mocking then I close them and grunt in pleasure. "Oh, I can still feel the tightness of her warm pussy clenching on my dick...hmm I can just come at the thought of this..."

It's all true. I don't feel sorry for what I've done to that girl. I enjoyed it. It's who I am and Sukia loves me for who I am. The only reason I am sorry now is because my kids' lives are in danger. I've already lost one and there's no way in hell I'm going to lose the two others.

When I open my eyes, I see how inflamed Colton Ice is. It's not just him, the dark haired boy who shot my wife too is angry.

I know I am so dead.

"Too bad the police had to come after Hunter shot her, I was planning to take her body home with me," I add and I know Colton Ice can't contain himself any longer.

He brusquely stands up and rushes toward me. I know he wants to kill me with his own hands. He is glaring at me so hard that I can just die from his stare.

He is few steps away from me and is about to take another step when the grey haired man calls after him.

"Mr. Ice," the grey haired man's voice is quiet and warning. "He is provoking you so you can kill him first."

I glare at the grey haired man.

Colton stops moving, glares at me once again, his breathing is heavy. His whole body is shaking.

"If you lay a hand on him, it will be impossible for you to stop. You'll beat him to death and that is what he wants. He wants the easy way out," the grey haired man presses.

Ice's breathing slows down a bit, and then he rushes out the door, slamming it behind him.

He is trying to cool himself off.

I am left alone with Zero and the grey haired prick who are both glaring at me and not saying anything. I am smirking.

"What the fuck are you doing?" Sukia hisses at me.

I wink at her. "I got this babe,"

"You got what? He gonna kill you," she snaps. "He's gonna kill me!"

"You're already dead," I tell her, and she shuts her mouth. It's true, she's bleeding out.

"And I'm doing this for Sony and Kenna," my voice saddens as I remember my sweet little Erika. "They killed Erika before my eyes. They made me watch her melt alive from sulfuric acid."

Sukia starts to cry. "Oh no..."

"That's their plan...they want to watch me suffer and hurt what's most precious to me in front of me so I can feel pain and remorse. They want to make me watch our kids get hurt like the Ice kid watched his wife get raped...but I'm not going to allow it. They'll have to kill me first..."

"Are Sony and Kenna safe?" she asks me.

I turn to her and nod. "Yes. They're in good hands, baby. I got this all figured out," I promise her. Then I turn back to the guards. The grey haired man is keeping himself calm while the younger one, the dark haired one is glaring at me with the same amount of hatred the Ice had earlier. Ha, I guess he had history with the dead girl.

"If you got something to say to me kid, say it," I spit again. He inhales, still glaring. His lips are trembling as if he is keeping himself from talking. He wants to say something. But he doesn't.

Ice barges back in the room half an hour later. His face is completely calm, composed and expressionless...as if nothing happened earlier.

He is completely under control.

I don't like it.

He has to be unstable.

I have to make him kill me.

"If I had to rape your wife again, I would," I continue. "Matter of fact, if you don't kill me I'll go find her grave, dig her body out and fuck her. I'm willing to try on some new shit."

He doesn't even blink or flinch, or glare. His eyes are still cold and full of hatred, but I don't see any anger.

"You want to kill me, kid?" I snap at him. "Do it now!"

He stares, and whispers. "That'll be too easy."

I glare at him and I'm starting to panic.

"I'll hurt your two kids and make you watch," he smirks cruelly at me.

That's impossible. My two kids are safe. They're in a church, in the hands of the priest who baptized them. He promised me to hide them in the church and keep them safe. That nothing is going to happen to them. Erika, my oldest daughter was supposed to be with her younger siblings too, but she was so stubborn. She wanted to go say bye to her friends first...and she left...and now she's gone. I wasn't able to save Erika, but I know my two kids are safe.

"You can never touch them," I growl at Colton Ice.

He mockingly scoffs at me then quietly, he says. "Bring them in, Spyros."

With horror, I watch the door open and the third guard comes in. He is holding my two precious kids' hands as he guides them in.

"Oh no..." Sukia starts to sob.

"Looks like God is not on your side either, Lazar," Colton tells me with a mocking smile on his face.

"YOU SON OF A BITCH!" I stand up and I sprint toward Spyros trying to snatch my two kids away, but Spyros is faster and more agile than I am. It is as if he was anticipating me to do this. He pushes Kenna, my eight year old girl toward the grey haired man who grabs her and Spyros pulls a gun out on my six year old boy.

I freeze.

"NO! DON'T TOUCH MY BABIES!" Sukia is faintly yelling. "You told me they were safe, Lazar!"

"The whole town is against all of you," Ice explains. "The pastor informed us about your kids the minute you gave them to him."

That back-stabbing priest! I thought I could trust him! Fuck! "GOD DAMN IT!" I curse again. I don't want to see my kids suffer. I don't them to die. Not Kenna, not Sony. I just want them safe. I stare at them, and they are frightened and quiet. They don't talk that much. They're sweet kids, and they're staring back at me with those innocent eyes, hoping for me to save them or do something...just like Erika was expecting me to save her when she was being drenched in acid...

Oh God, no.

"What do you want me to do?" I turn to Ice, tears are filling my eyes. I am so scared.

He is staring back at me with his cold, onyx eyes. "I want you to be sorry for what you've done."

I nod and immediately get on my knees. "I'm so, *so* sorry," I plead.

He is faintly chuckling. "I don't think you are yet."

"I am!" I beg again! "I am! Please! I am so sorry!" I am crying and he is not buying it.

"Look, I'll do anything, please...don't hurt my kids, I've already lost one...please..."

"We're so sorry..." Sukia is crying as well.

"You will be," Ice finally says and walks toward the grey haired guard and takes Kenna's hand.

"Get away from her!" I am about to run after him when Zero suddenly hits the back of my head with a baseball bat, hard. I feel dizzy and I black out for a while.

When I find consciousness, I am tied up and I am next to Sukia who is silently whimpering. I jump up once again and look around and I see my two kids. They're alright. They're bouncing on the bed and the grey haired man is telling them a story, making them smile and laugh a bit. They're relaxed.

"You're awake," Ice tells me. He is sitting down my bed too, next to Kenna and playing with her hair.

"Don't you touch her!" I growl at him.

He smiles at me, a smile that doesn't reach his eyes. "You know, I was saying the same thing to Hunter last Friday when he was stroking my wife's hair."

I stiffen. "Let my two kids go, Ice...look at them. They're innocent. They don't know anything...they're clueless about what I've done..."

"You want to talk about innocent?" he glares at me. "My wife was the most innocent human being I have ever met."

I look down and nod. "Okay, maybe she didn't deserve this–"

He cuts me off. "You're in control of what happens to your children, Lazar," he lets go of Kenna's hair and nods at the grey haired man. The grey haired man suddenly puts and earplug in each of my children's ears so they can't hear what Ice is about to tell me.

"You have two choices," Ice starts. "First one, I tie you up and make you watch as Warr," he points at the grey haired man, "uses his famous blade to cut your little kids into pieces."

I freeze.

"And it's going to be painful to them. They won't die as quickly as their older sister did. Warr will take his time, and slowly cut finger by finger, then toe by toe, hand by hand and so on. They'll be screaming and will be in so much pain and you'll be watching and won't be able to do anything...and then the cutting won't stop...Warr will keep them alive for as long as possible. He'll then take out their eyeballs, cut their nose, their ears, then hands, their legs and their heads last–"

I can't listen to this anymore. "What's the second choice?" I start to cry again.

Ice is smiling cruelly at me. Zero gives him a knife, and he takes it and throws it at my foot. I look at it and look at him confused. "What am I supposed to do with this?" I ask.

"You're going to eat your wife in front of your kids."

I frown in disbelief. Is he for real!?

"What the fuck..." Sukia says. I look at her in horror and I realize she's still alive...

I stare back at Ice in disbelief.

"What....?"

His crazy twisted eyes never leave mine. "You heard me. You're going to take that knife, cut a part of her flesh while she's still alive, and eat her flesh raw in front of your kids, while they're watching. You're going to keep eating her until she dies."

That kid is fucked up.

That's horrible...why would he make me do something so fucked up in front of my kids?

"That's psychological torture to you and to your kids," Ice explains. "They won't ever look at you the same way ever again once they see what a monster you truly are. They won't ever run to you or call you 'dad' or tell you they love you. They will be traumatized, and that's what I want."

I start to sob heavily.

"It's either that or the first choice. At least I won't lay a finger on them if you choose the second choice," he presses. He wants me to choose the second one. He wants to see me eat my own wife while she's alive in front of my own kids. That is beyond cruel. That doesn't even compare to what I did to his wife or what the Lord did to Erika...

Colton Ice is worse than the Lord.

"If you don't make a choice, then I'll make one for you," Ice presses me.

My thoughts start to race. What do I do? What the fuck do I do? I can't eat my wife...that's fucking crazy...and I can't watch my kids die either...maybe if I take the knife and slit my own throat...maybe he'll spare them.

"Eat me, baby...." Sukia pleads weakly...she's dying. "For our kids..."

I nod at her, and nod at Ice.

"Okay, I'll do it."

He smiles and nods at Zero who unties me. Warr removes the ear plugs and helps my two kids off the bed. "Come on, munchkins. Daddy wants you to watch something," Warr says to them kindly.

Kenna and Sony are standing few feet away from me.

Kenna looks down on her mom and frowns. "Why is mommy bleeding, daddy?"

Sukia is pale and weakening more by the seconds, but she manages to talk to them. "I'm okay, honey. It's not blood, it's cool-aid. I spilled it on myself..."

"Are you okay mommy?" Sony asks. They're walking toward her and Warr keeps them from going to their mother.

"Please let me just say goodbye to them..." Sukia begs, but Warr doesn't let go of my kids.

"Alright Lazar, get to work," Ice orders me. I lean down to pick up the knife and I hear Colton say. "Remember, if you try to slit your throat or hurt yourself, Zero will stop you and then I'll choose the first choice."

Shit. That Ice is fucking smart.

I nod at him and take the knife from the floor and with trembling hands, I slowly walk toward my wife. She is smiling at me, nodding.

"I love you..." I cry.

"I..." she is slowly losing her consciousness. I just want her to be dead before I do this...I don't want her to watch me or feel me eat her.

"Actually," Ice starts. "Feed her flesh to herself," his voice is acid and venomous. "Give her the extra rare taste her own medicine."

I glare at that son of a bitch.

"Go on," he glares back.

I turn to my wife and kiss her lips, brush her blonde hair off of her face. "I love you."

"I love...too..." she says faintly, "start...with...my leg..."

I nod and I lift up her dress and take hold of her dirty left leg and with the blade, I slowly cut her skin.

"Ahh..." she moans in pain.

"I'm so sorry baby..." I tell her.

"What are you doing to mommy?" Kenna yells at me, panicking.

I can't look at her. I can't look at my kids...

"Make sure you look at your two kids while you're chewing your wife's raw flesh," the fucker tells me. With my trembling hands I cut off her flesh completely from her skin.

"STOP HURTING MOMMY!" Kenna is shouts, trying to come to me and stop me but Warr is holding her. Sony is crying.

"Eat her flesh," Ice growls at me, "and look at your kids in the eye."

I am crying, and sobbing and slowly...I take Sukia's flesh and put it in my mouth as I stare at them.

"No!" Kenna is crying and shouting at me.

"Mommy...." Sony is burying his face in Warr's coat, but Warr forces him to turn back around and look at me as I am chewing their mother's flesh.

"Stop...daddy...stop..." Kenna is crying. I am sobbing in so much pain and humiliation...Kenna and Sony are now damaged...they hate me, they think I'm a monster...their innocence is gone...and Ice is watching the scene with so much pleasure on his face.

He is so cruel.

I take few more cuts from my wife. "Feed it to her, she has maybe five minutes before dying," Ice tells me. And I do so.

Sukia is eating herself and crying too. I am sobbing like a child and she tells me she loves me one last time and stops moving.

"Sukia! Sukia!" I cry. She's not responding.

"You killed mommy!" Kenna is yelling at me, crying.

"I'm so...sorry baby..." I sob.

"Keep eating her," Ice orders.

"Stop!" Kenna is crying.

I feel nauseous and try to vomit, but nothing comes out.

"We injected you a strong antiemetic. It will keep your stomach down," Ice tells me. I can hear the mocking smile in his voice, and he gets serious. "Keep eating."

And with agony I keep on cutting her leg, taking her flesh and eating her raw while I'm staring at my kids. There's so much damage in their eyes...they hate me. They're tortured, they think I'm the bad guy...we can never ever get things back the way they were before...

Those two used to run to me, hug me, kiss me, and love me...now they think I'm a monster...

This is the worst kind of torture...

I take another bite of my dead wife's flesh from her left leg. It's the last piece of meat. There's nothing left but the bones of the leg.

"I can't....take another bite..." I tell Ice. I really can't anymore. As fucked up as it sounds, I am full.

He smiles and nods. "Okay," then he stands up.

What now? Is he going to kill me?

"I'm going to kill you after you finish eating your wife completely. You have until this Sunday to finish this meal. You can cut her into pieces and freeze her. You'll eat her every day, for breakfast, lunch, snack and dinner in front of your kids. I don't care how you choose to do it, fry her, bake her, whatever floats your boat. As long as you eat her in front of them. I also want you to sleep in the same bed as your kids. Spyros will stay with you to ensure this. If you don't...Spyros will kill the boy and make you eat him in front of the girl and if you don't...we'll torture the girl until she dies then kill you. Either way, you'll be suffering. You just choose how to."

"You're a monster..." I say to him.

He turns and smirks at me. "Oh, Lazar ...you have no idea who you messed with."

I let myself lay on the carpet, exhausted and silently crying. He is right. I had no idea...

Shit...

"You're in charge of this, Spyros," I hear Ice tell the redhead guard who brought the kids in.

The redhead guard nods. "Yes sir."

"Alright let's go Zero, Warr," Ice says and with that they're gone. I am now left alone with the redhead guard, my dead wife and my two kids who see me in a whole different way now.

# 11

## COLTON ICE'S POINT OF VIEW

"Mr. Ice," Zero says after I finish vomiting everything I ate from yesterday's soup to today's light breakfast. Zero, Warr and I just left Lazar's house. I was trying very hard to hold my stomach down until I arrive at my hotel, but I cannot anymore. As soon as we step out, I let it all out. This is the most gruesome thing I've ever done. I had no idea I had such twisted ideas in my head.

"What?" I snap at Zero. I am still very angry at him for visiting my wife, and I have not had the chance to confront him about this yet.

"You did not kill them," he says with a stern voice. Warr is handing me a bottle of water and a towel.

"Lord Fire wants you to wipe out the entire family," Zero presses, almost scolding me.

This guy is a bit over his head. Just because Mrs. Fire likes him more than me doesn't mean he can talk to me this way. "And I will wipe them out on my own way," I snarl at him, my eyes glaring.

"How do you plan to do that? I've recorded the whole scene and only the wife is dead," Zero argues back, he is not backing down. Warr stares back at me as if he wants to know what my plan is as well.

"I'm psychologically torturing both Lazar and his kids. It's mainly Lazar. I'm manipulating him, in the end, he'll make a decision that he'll never see himself make in a lifetime."

Both guards look a bit confused.

"Look, the most important thing to Lazar right now is the safety of his children. He doesn't care about what happens to him or his wife, all he wants is his children to be safe. That's why he's willing to eat his wife in front of them. I am making him think he has a choice. I am making him think he can actually let his children live. However, we all know that the children's mental states are gone. They will never be the same ever again and they're better off dead after witnessing something like this. I see it now, you see it too but Lazar doesn't see it yet. Right now, he still thinks his children are going to be better off alive. But if we give him time alone with his children while he is still eating their mother in front of them for breakfast, lunch and dinner, and sleep in the same bed as them, if we give him time to look into his children's eyes, he will realize the same thing as us and I bet you a hundred gold that on the day he dies, he will beg me to kill his children too. And guess what? I'll give him the honor of letting him do it himself."

Zero and Warr are looking at me in awe and amazement. I am sure I have convinced Zero.

"That's an impressive scheme," Warr admits. I give him a halfhearted smirk then turn to glare at Zero.

"Do you have a problem with me, sir?" Zero grits through his teeth. I take a dangerous step toward him while he is standing his ground, not looking a bit intimidated.

"I have quite a few, Zero. First thing's first you need to understand that I know what I am doing with those animals and I know how to handle them so don't you ever question my authority or else I'll have Lord Fire remove you from this mission. He doesn't care who is on my crew as long as the job is done correctly and if he happens to know that I cannot focus or get revenge thoroughly because you're messing with my temper, you know he will have you killed."

Zero smirks at me. "Hmph, I'd like to see you try."

"Zero," Warr tells calmly. His voice is slightly warning him, but Zero ignores him and continues to glare.

"Lord Fire doesn't just see me as some guard. I'm his favorite and he knows me on a personal level.

Nothing you can say or do can remove me from this case," Zero snarls at my face with a triumphant smirk.

I scoff. "And I'm guessing it has to do with my wife."

He doesn't say anything, which confirms my suspicions and makes me angrier.

"My wife was the important friend you visited yesterday. I saw you," I tell him, and his eyes widen a bit shock.

"I saw you giving Mrs. Fire flowers and a puppy to deliver to my wife," I am breathing hard, my eyes are blazing. "You've got a lot of balls, Zero. I don't care for the importance you hold in Mr. and Mrs. Fire's heart. If I see you anywhere near my wife again, I'll kill you," I have never been this serious in my life and I think he is a bit intimidated. "I'm not joking around," I add.

"I know," he answers with a blank face, and then he bitterly growls at me. "You have nothing to lose, because you know you're already dead."

I inhale, knowing what he's referring to.

"Zero," Warr calls out his name once again, but Zero keeps tuning him out. He is staring at me with his grey ghostly eyes.

"However, what I do, who I see, who I deliver flowers to is absolutely none of your concern."

"When the person is my wife, it is my concern," I snarl back. Heaven knows how hard I am trying not to slit this fucker's throat right now. He has a smart mouth; I didn't know he was the type.

"Mr. Ice, with all due respect, the only reason why she's still your wife is because everyone is too busy trying to fix the mess you've created to think about divorce. We all know that marriage is already over."

I am enraged and taken aback. As hard as it is to admit this, he is right. This marriage was over since last Friday. We're all too caught up in this mess to actually worry about it.

I don't know what else to tell him, but I can't let this guy get the best of me. I can't let this guy make me think that I am nothing to Aelita. I know she still loves me. I hope she does...

No matter what their relationship is, I know Aelita will never, ever be with a guy like him even if we get a divorce.

Something unexpected suddenly happens. Warr is suddenly in between us, and gives a hard punch to Zero, on his stomach. The punch is so powerful that Zero takes few sloppy steps back and brings his hand to his stomach.  He stares back at Warr with a stupefied expression on his face.

"What...the hell..." Zero says as he bends down and falls to his knees. Warr gets closer to him and catches him before he collapses on the floor. I stare at Warr appreciatively.

"I apologize sir," Warr calmly says. "Zero can be difficult and uncooperative sometimes."

I snort not sympathizing or caring about Zero's bratty attitude. Warr is still supporting the grunting Zero as he continues to speak. "Zero is very close to the Fire

Family and is struggling emotionally with the tragedy. Please, try to understand and not antagonize him."

"He started it," I snap, wiping my mouth with the towel.

Zero's phone starts to ring suddenly and we watch him as he starts to support himself. He looks up at me a bit disoriented, then glares at me and Warr. He reaches in his pocket for his phone, clears his voice and starts to speak.

"Yes Mrs. Fire?" I hear him say on the phone. I freeze and stare at him in disbelief. Why is Mrs. Fire calling him?

"Is she okay!?" he asks her again with worry in his voice. My heart sinks as I think of the worse. I know he's talking about Aelita. What could have happened to her and why did Mrs. Fire call him first?

I reach into my pocket and check my phone to see if maybe I have a missed called from her, but there's no missed call on my phone.

*Why?*

"Me?" he says again looking surprised. "I'll be right there," he hangs up and I stare at him expecting and explanation.

"It's Aelita," he tells me.

"What's wrong with her?" I glare at him.

"I'm not sure. Mrs. Fire says she's out control and..." he gives me an arrogant look and whispers. "She wants to see *me*."

I hold my breath and bite my tongue.

*Why?*

"I have to go," he says and rushes in the car.

"I'm coming with you," I say and he knows it's not a request. We both rush to the car, Warr is taking the driver's seat.

My thoughts are racing. What could have happened to Aelita? Is she being violent and angry at everyone again? If so, why is she asking for Zero? Seriously, why is she asking for Zero and not me, her husband? What relationship do they have together and how come I don't know about this? Why hasn't Aelita ever told me about Zero? Who the heck is he? Most of all, why the fuck does she want to see him?

By the time we arrive at my house, it is raining. I rush out of the car and run into the house. I climb upstairs and run to her room. I need to see if she's okay. I don't care if she wants to see Zero instead. I want to see her.

There's no one in her room, so I run to check in the bathroom.

Still, no one.

"AELITA!" I yell her name and walk out. There's a servant who's staring at me.

"Where is she?" I glare at the servant.

"Sh-she is in her g-garden," she stutters and I rush downstairs to her garden.

Mrs. Fire and Hinata and Dr. Brown are waiting by the door, with worry and sadness in their eyes. Aelita is outside in the middle of her garden, completely drenched because of the rain. She's crying. She's loudly crying, but I can't hear her. The rain is camouflaging her cries. I am frozen in place by the door like her mother, watching her with pain in my eyes.

"Colton, why are you here?" Mrs. Fire asks me, not expecting me to be the one to come first. Well sorry to disappoint you, mother-in-law.

"What happened to Aelita? Why...why is she...out there in the rain?" I demand, trying to open the garden door and bring her back inside. She will catch a cold, but Hinata blocks me from doing so. I glare at her.

"She had a nightmare, she was screaming in her sleep and when I woke her up she got angrier and started throwing things at me, she did this to me," Hinata shows me very vicious scratch marks on her neck. I refuse to believe that Aelita did this.

"When her mother came in, Miss Aelita screamed at her and asked her to get out, she wanted no one in the room but Zero. Then, she came to her garden and started crying there. She wants no one but Zero to stay with her. She has been asking for him and throwing things...at us. We had to close the door."

My heart clenches, I think I know what her nightmare is about. "I'm going to get her," I say, gently pushing Hinata away.

"No," Mrs. Fire refuses. "She wants no one, but Zero."

I glare at her. "I am her husband and I will be the one to take care of her," I snarl and force open the door, but the minute I am in the garden with her...I don't know what to do. It is like her pain and distress have completely taken over me and frozen me in place. I am just standing there in the garden, staring at her as she is lying down on the muddy grass and crying. She's in so much pain, and I can feel it. It's as if her emotions affect mine, I feel suddenly lost and scared and hunted. I feel cold and out of reach, as if no one is seeing me, as if no one is hearing me, as if I am all alone.

That is how Aelita is feeling at the moment. I want to comfort her. I want to take her in my arms and tell her I am here for her. I want to say something and take away the pain from her, but...I can't. I don't know what to do. My body has completely forgotten how to function. I am stuck in place, standing there and staring at her like an idiot. I don't know what to tell her...so I just stand there, ten feet away from her as she is facing away from me and crying.

*Move.* I tell myself. *Go to her, she needs you.*

But I can't. I am still frozen there like a statue.

Aelita turns around seconds after, and her face seems a bit relieved. She looks rather grateful. She suddenly crawls toward me with tears rolling down her face.

I feel happy that she is running to me for comfort. I am so happy. I know I don't deserve this from her, but I am so happy.

As she is getting closer, I am about to help her up when she passes me and keeps on crawling toward someone else. I stand there dumbfounded and unable to pick up what had just happened. Aelita just saw me and simply ignored me.

"Aelita..." I hear Zero's voice soften behind. I turn around and watch my wife slowly rise up on her knees, and touch Zero's legs as if she's imploring him. "Aelita, you're going to catch a cold," he takes off his rain jacket and puts it on her gently. He crouches down to her level, holds her and hugs her as she whispers something to him. I still can't hear her voice. She never spoke one word to me ever since she survived and she's talking to him.

"It's okay...It's okay. I'm here now," he tells her as she keeps on sobbing in his arms. "I won't leave you, I'm here for you," he then stands up and gently picks her up bridal style as she wraps her arms around his neck.

Last time she was in my arms she was so frightened, angry and so uncomfortable.

I can't how describe low, how rejected and how humiliated I am feeling at the moment as my wife is looking for comfort in another man's arm.

And, Zero is so caring and so gentle to her. He is telling her sweet, calming words and carrying her back inside the house. Everyone else follows, except me. I am still frozen in place, unable to understand why Aelita, the girl who has always been in love with me is ignoring me and going to another man's arm.

I am so jealous, so hurt and so resentful toward Zero. I want to be the one holding her like this. I want to be the one to soothe her, to make her feel safe and I am not. He is and I hate him for it. It's not the first time I've felt this way about her. The first time was in high school after Forest's death and that was the main reason I stopped being too caring and close toward her. I was denying, running away from that kind of feeling and now I can't anymore. Seeing her in another man's arm just made me admit it to myself.

I have feelings for Aelita. I am in love with her. I need her in my life.

I've always have been, I just never wanted to admit it. I've always denied it.

The first time I suspected that I might have feelings for her was the day before I broke all ties with her. It was in eleventh grade.

———

Ren, a classmate was trying to hit on Aelita after school. I was supposed to drop her home like I always did. I always waited for her to meet me outside the parking lot and she was always on time, except that day she wasn't. I sighed, realizing that someone was probably picking on her. I was starting to have enough of her always getting bullied and me always rescuing her. It was annoying and getting old and I wasn't in good terms with my family at home either. Eleventh grade was the worse school year for me.

I looked around the bathroom, the girl's bathroom, the basement, the usual places I would find girls bullying her, pulling her hair or teasing her. She wasn't at any of those places and then I tried to go back to my car, maybe she was there waiting for me. As I was going out of the hallway, I glanced in an empty classroom and I hear a guy saying perverted things to a girl.

"Come on, let me see the color of your pantie. I want to see it, come on," the boy was asking. I took no interest in what was happening until I hear him say the next thing. "Come on, just because you're mute doesn't mean I don't want you."

That was when I knew the girl getting harassed was Aelita and something struck inside me. It was anger.

For the first time, I felt rage toward someone else for harassing Aelita. It was usually annoyance or impatience. I never really took it personal whenever someone was bullying her or making fun of her because she was mute but this time, after realizing that she was being sexually harassed, I was furious.

I barged into the room and Ren, the classmate, jolted. Aelita saw me and looked at me with relief. She was scared and crying.

"Go wait for me in the car," I ordered her giving her my car key, my eyes not leaving Ren. Aelita nods and does so and I am left alone with him.

"Leave Aelita alone, don't ever come near her again," I told him and was going to walk out when he decided to argue.

"Hey Colton, come on," he starts. "Why are you still hanging out with her anyways? Forest's dead, you don't have to pretend you care about her anymore."

I didn't respond to him because I thought he was right.

"I don't see what's so great about her anyways. She's mute, plain and boring. Is it because her parents are rich? Or is it because she's good in bed? Have you guys done it already? How is she in bed?"

That was when I lost it and stormed toward him. The thought of having someone else talk about Aelita's sex life in front of me enraged me. I punched Ren so hard that he stumbled back and fell on the floor.

"Don't you ever...talk about her in that way," I snarled at him and he completely backed off.

"Dude I'm sorry, I'm just kidding. I didn't know something like that was going on between you two," he said scared, and that was when I realized I lost my calm because of Aelita.

I immediately let go of Ren and said. "Nothing is going on between us! She's not my type! Don't get any crazy ideas!"

And with that, I took off. It was clear that I had feelings for Aelita and once again, I did not want to accept that. She was not my type. Like Ren said, she was mute, plain, boring and lacked a strong personality. She as always crying, relying on others to save her. She never once stood up for herself. She was weak, and I hated her for it. I didn't want to acknowledge the feelings I had for her. I decided to destroy away those feelings and cut all ties with her because there was no way I could fall for a girl like her.

So the next day, when she got bullied and I came to her rescue, I yelled at her. I was so ruthless. I told her I was done with her. I was done coming to her rescue. I told her she disgusted me, and all she ever did was cry and cry and she should toughen herself up. I told her

Forest wasn't there for her anymore and I had enough of this. I yelled at her, I even cursed her out and I was so angry at her. I then told her I had it. I was not going to come to her rescue anymore, and that she was on her own. I told her I was not going to give her rides to school or spend time with her. I told her I was done. And I quickly started chasing after Nadia again, forcing myself to think that I still had feelings for Nadia.

I was able to convince myself. I suddenly became obsessed with Nadia and wanted to be around her all the time, but she fell in love with William. I still wanted to be with her. I was going to propose to her after high school but Lord Fire made me propose to Aelita instead. It made me angry because all I was trying to do was keep some distance away from her and now I was forcefully being married to her.

I resented Aelita. I blamed her for all this. So, to hurt her, and to convince myself that I didn't care about her, I started sleeping around with so many women...I told myself it was because of Nadia. I forced myself to believe that I was trying to get over Nadia. I refused to believe that I had feelings for Aelita and even when I 'got over' Nadia, I still wouldn't stop sleeping around. It was all I knew, and all I wanted. All I was doing was to destroy and deny the feelings I had for her.

I convinced myself to think that I cared about her as a friend, or a human being. That the feelings I had for her were more of a friendly love because we grew up together. Even after she was raped, I was still trying to deny my feelings for her...

But now that I am seeing her in the arms of another man...now that I am seeing her run to someone other than me for comfort...I cannot kid myself anymore. I have feelings for Aelita and I am afraid that it is too late to admit it now. She already fell for someone else.

Aelita is calming down and not crying anymore and Mrs. Fire decides to shut the door to give them a bit of privacy.

I snort angrily.

"Sorry you had to witness this," Mrs. Fire tells me in a mocking smile. "I never asked you to come."

I glare at her and I realize I am seconds away from strangling her with my own hands if I don't get the hell out of here.

So, I take off.

Warr drops me to my hotel and asks me what our next move will be. I am not in the mood to talk about anything, so I snap at him. "I'll call you!"

I rush into my hotel room and pace around angrily.

Why would Aelita do this to me? What was her relationship with Zero? Now I'm angry at her too. Maybe she wasn't a complete saint. Maybe she had an affair with him before all this happen. Maybe she wasn't a virgin.

I snort.

Whatever. It's all too late anyways.

After an hour of anger and pacing and pushing anything I see, I feel exhausted and I am close to taking a nap to cool off when someone knocks on the door.

"Who is it?" I snap.

"Colton, it's Cain. Open up," Cain Smith says.

Oh. I forgot to sign over my company to him.

I open the door.

"Hello," he greets and realizes how messy the room is. "Oh dear."

"It's not a good time," I tell him and rush toward the desk to look into my folders.

"Do you want to talk?" he proposes.

"No, Cain. I don't," I snap at him and find the contract. I am supposed to read it over and make sure everything's correct, but I am so angry and don't care and I want him gone, so I sign the paper angrily and hand it to him.

"Here," I say. "The company's yours temporarily. Take care of it."

He smiles triumphantly at me almost in a mocking way, but I am too angry to think deeply about it.

"I'd like you to leave me now if you don't mind," I politely request.

"Are you sure? You seem like you need a drink," he insists. "Why don't we go drink?"

I don't want to. Why can't he just leave? "No. Cain, I want to be left alone. Please," I snap at him.

He nods and takes the contract. "I'll take good care of it. I hope to stay in touch with you."

"Thank you," I say and he wishes me well and leaves.

I am about to lie back down on the bed few minutes later when I hear another knock at the door.

Oh that annoying Cain!

I angrily rise up and rush toward the door and open it.

It's not Cain.

It's Zero. He is glaring at me in disbelief and I am glaring right back.

"Was that just Cain Smith I saw leaving your room?" he growls at me.

"Yeah, so?" I glare back and he continues to look at me in disbelief.

"God, Mr. Ice do you even read the e-mails and intel I send you?"

I look at him confused. "What are you talking about?" I open the door wider to let him in.

"You do know that there are ten people involved in Aelita's assault, five of them were the ones you saw that night who actually did the raping. The other five are indirectly involved, correct?"

I nod.

"Well sir, Cain Smith is one of the other five."

I blink twice, not believing what I'm hearing.

"We were not able to identify him the first time because he paid quite a lot of money to our intel men to keep quiet and give us a false alibi. When I did my research on the guy Cain was framing, I realized he didn't even know who Aelita was and we were being made a fool out of, so the torturing unit tortured our intel to get the truth out of them and after he told us who the real man was, we killed him. It was Cain Smith."

I've just been played..."I've just signed over my company to him," I whisper quietly.

Zero closes his eyes and shakes his head in disappointment and frustration. "Sir, I sent you information on the complete names and profile of the other five. They were Jon and Otto Cooper, Peter Stone, Veronica Cross and Cain Smith. Why didn't you read them?"

I sigh and sit on my bed shaking my head. "Because I wanted to get rid of the ones I knew first, the ones that I saw with my own eyes that night... I didn't really think it would matter to know the other five right away."

Why Cain? Why the only person I thought I could trust?

"You don't seem to believe Cain had something to do with the rape of Aelita," Zero notices.

I shake my head.

"That wouldn't be the first time he tried to hurt her." Zero continues quietly.

I raise my head up and look at him in disbelief. "What are you talking about? How do you know this?"

Zero sighs and takes a seat on the chair across me. "That is how I officially met Aelita," he begins. "It was about ten months ago, when you travelled for a meeting to the Fall Republic and left her home alone. I had just become an Elite soldier and had my medical license,"

I frown a bit confused. "Medical license?"

"I am a veterinarian," he explains. Ah, Mr. Fire mentioned that before.

"I took care of the dogs since there wasn't much to do back then. One day, Lord Fire noticed that was really good with animals and he told me about his daughter who loved animals. He told me that she would really be pleased to meet someone like me and that I should go pay her a visit since you were gone and she might be feeling a bit lonely. I accepted, of course. Later in the evening, I stopped by her mansion and heard a dog barking. Since I'm a vet and understood animals, I knew the dog was barking out of distress. Something was wrong. I sneaked behind the house and entered in the mansion from the back and I pulled out a gun. I was looking around the house. I saw by the garden, a girl who was being held down at gunpoint by two masked guys. I tried to shoot them, and they saw me and took off and I couldn't run after them because I wasn't sure if other men were in the house," he clears his throat. "Aelita was scared. I told her I was a soldier serving her father and that I should call him and let him know what had just happened. Aelita shook her head and started writing on her pad, pleading me not say a word. She explained me that they were trying to scare her and stir things up between Lord and you. She told me it was business, and that your rival, Cain Smith was trying to take over your company and you wouldn't let him. Many other CEOs were trusting you and signing deals with you. She told me that Cain Smith was very jealous and would do anything to hurt you by hurting her. His plan was to hurt her, so the Lord would be angry, blame you and get you to give up the company or worse kill you. That was what Aelita suspected, and she did not want that happening," Zero's eyes soften a bit as he starts to talk about my wife.

"She is a peacekeeper and does not want any bloodshed, so she decided to protect you by keeping everything to herself. She made me promise to keep my mouth shut and not tell a soul about this. In exchange, she would always call or beep me if she ever suspected of being in trouble. That's how she and I became good friends. We bonded because we both love animals and I used to pay her visit three times a week in the morning so I could teach her how to heal animals. That's how she and I became friends and it had never been anything more than that."

I listen to him completely and I don't know how to feel.

"Why...why...why did she want to protect me that bad? And how come she never told me about you?"

"Because she loves you," he snaps at me painfully. "She told me herself in her writings once that if something ever happened to you, then she might as well be dead. She told me you are the only person who makes her feel like she has a purpose in life, you're the reason she has to be strong. And she never told you about me because you never bother talk to her. She told me how every time, when you come back from work she always tries to talk to you and tell you how her day has been, but you never bother to spend even one minute with her. You just take the flowers she gives you and go to your room and never come back out. You don't even talk to your own wife..." he is looking at me with anger. "And she never blamed you. She always thought tomorrow would be a better day. She never lost hope. I fell in love with her. Last Friday morning, I confessed to her. I told her I had feelings for her and I could treat her better than you. She rejected me and told me she was going to talk to you that evening and tell you how she really feels about you. She told me she was going to finally lose her virginity to her husband that Friday."

My heart is breaking into pieces again and I don't want to hear any more of it.

"I was angry that I was rejected... she felt bad and I didn't want her pity....she tried to call me that evening, but I ignored her calls thinking that she was trying to apologize or sympathize with me..." his voice is getting lower and lower. "She was in trouble...and reached out to me...and I ignored her..."

I know he blames himself, but it's not his fault at all. I am the one to blame for all this. Zero is great. He has always been there for her, he saved her life when I was away...he spent time with her when I never did...he cared about her...and I understand why now she chose to run to him for comfort instead of coming to me. I only bring Aelita nothing but pain. I feel so inferior to Zero.

"Anyways, I came here to explain you that there's nothing going on between Aelita and I. Nothing ever happened. She loves you and always has...I was just the friend she needed," he swallows painfully. "She asked to see me because she had a nightmare and it was about that night when I first met her. That's why she wanted to see me. She needed a friend, she needed comfort."

I sigh and we're both silent for a while.

"What are we going to do with Smith?" he finally asks me.

I chuckle darkly. "Oh....I don't even know if I want to kill Hunter last or him last....what I have planned for him..." I am going to hurt him so bad. Cain has always wanted everything that I had. I knew that. I knew he was jealous of my power and my never ending success. I never thought he would stoop this low to hurt me...and I trusted him like an idiot and signed my company over to him.

"Shall we go get him?" Zero asks standing up. "We can kill him right now."

I shake my head. "No. Killing him will be too easy. Let him think he's comfortable. Let him think no one is after him. Let him enjoy himself and know what it's like to be the owner of a great company like mine. Let him enjoy himself while he can. What I have planned for him....I'll get him when he least expects it, and I won't hurt him first."

I'm pretty sure his sweet cousin Nadia knew about this...and she was acting all worried at the hospital.

"I'm sorry," Zero tells me and I finally look up to him. "I have not been the fairest person to you and it's because I blame you for what happened to Aelita...but the truth is, I am just as guilty."

I don't say anything.

"Are we in good terms, Mr. Ice?" he asks me again a while after.

"Are you still in love with my wife?" I ask him.

He pauses for a while, looks at me and nods. "I don't think I will ever stop being in love with Aelita."

"Then no," I answer walking to the door and opening it for him to get out. "We're not in good terms."

# 12

It has been a day since I found out Cain Smith, my business rival and the man I thought was my friend, is actually part of the ten people who planned the rape of my wife. I've been so angry, so thirsty for blood since then. I want to torture everyone he loves with my own hands. I want to hurt him with my own hands.

My first intention was go to Nadia and confront her, but I knew it would be a mistake because I would kill her the minute I set foot in her home.

I told myself it would be better to cool down and think clearly.

I still don't know what I'm going to do to Cain, but today, I am calm enough to visit Nadia.

Honestly, I can't understand why Nadia wouldn't tell me or warn me about what her cousin was plotting. What have I ever done to her? She's the only girl I've ever been nice to.

I've had a crush on her the minute I met her because she was so beautiful, and I even went far enough and hurt my best friend in the process. I've never done anything wrong to her. Not even when I was trying to destroy my feelings for Aelita...Nadia was the first girl I came to. I cherished her and made her feel like a queen. I was the most romantic with Nadia during our last two years of High School. I've always been fair and nice to her. I've always respected her...why would she hide this from me?

It doesn't matter now. She's as good as dead, and it is breaking my heart that I'll have to kill the woman Forest fell in love with. But still, what reason could she possibly have?

I am at her apartment, the fancy one she and her husband William own. I'll have to eventually kill William as well since he's Cain's cousin-in-law. What a small fucked up world...

I knock and wait. It takes her less than thirty seconds to open the door. She is surprised to see me, and she is smiling at me.

"Colton! What a pleasant surprise!" she grins at me.

*Fake lying back-stabbing whore.*

"I went to see you at the hospital, but they said you took the day off," I say with a blank expression on my face. My voice is calm. She decides to take the day off from work after I find out her cousin is implicated in my wife's rape?

"Uh...yes," she says nervously. "I wasn't feeling well..."

*Liar.*

When I don't say anything or react, she continues "please come in!" she opens the door wide and let me in.

I enter her apartment and look around. There are two luggages on the living room floor, and lots of clothes all over the place.

"Going somewhere?" I ask sarcastically. She's trying to run away while she still can. She thinks I don't know about Cain.

"Yes..." she blushes. "William and I are going out on vacation for a while," she looks at me with excitement and happiness in her eyes. "I was going to tell you this after we come back...but I might as well now. Maybe it'll cheer you up..." she approaches me thrilled and dares to hold my hands in hers. "I'm pregnant!"

I widen my eyes in surprise and shock for a moment, just for a moment.

I almost believed her.

*What a good way to cover up your ass, Nadia.*

"Isn't that good news, Colton? I'm going to have a baby! I still can't believe it...William is so happy!" she is squealing and smiling innocently and I realize how good of an actor she really is.

When I don't answer or even show any kind of emotion, she becomes a bit serious.

"Is everything okay, Colton?How's Aeli—"

"Don't," I warn her quietly. She frowns, giving me a questioning look. I take few dangerous steps toward her, glaring at her with so much anger and hatred.

"Don't you ever dare say her name again," I snarl at her. She frowns looking confused, and a bit offended. That acting of hers has got to stop.

"What are you saying, Colton ...?"

"DON'T YOU DARE PLAY DUMB WITH ME!" I fume at her, making her jolt. Her happy, innocent face is now transformed into fear.

*Much Better.*

"You little lying bitch..." I growl, walking closer making her step back.

"Colton...what's happening?" her entire body is starting to tremble,

"You knew about Cain...you knew about him hating me, wanting to destroy me...you knew he was part of those people who hurt Aelita...and you kept quiet...you kept it away from me..."

"I don't know what you're talking about..." She shakes her head and I throw her against the wall, making her squeal.

"Please don't hurt me, Colton!" She cries.

I look at her in the eyes and see fear. In return, all I feel is betrayal and anger...if there was one person I knew

I could trust after Forest, Nadia would be the one. I thought I knew her, I thought we were good friends...I thought she was my friend...I can't believe it...I can't...

"I can't believe you helped saved my wife's life! I can't believe you were pretending to care!"

"Colton..." she is sobbing. "I don't know anything...I swear."

She is still denying it and it pisses me off. She's not admitting the truth...I never thought she would be such a good liar. I don't know her anymore...I don't know if I ever had friends. I've been alone all along, from the beginning. Since Forest died, my world fell apart...bad things happened to me...I cut all ties with Aelita, my family was separated...my parents died in a plane crash, Caleb committed suicide and I was alone...all alone and I thought Nadia was the one who saved me from loneliness...I thought she cared....I thought she was my friend...

I think I am feeling exactly how Forest felt when he walked into us...I can now say that I know what betrayal feels like. I never knew thought Nadia would...

*Why*? "Why, Nadia?" I ask her, my voice is pleading. I feel very emotional. I am begging for her to give me a reason, a reason why she would betray me. Why?

"What have I ever done to you? Why hurt me? Why hurt Aelita? Is it because of Forest? Is it that you're blaming me for his death? For convincing you to cheat on him?"

She starts to cry shaking her head. "No Colton...I don't know what you're talking about...I've never blamed you...it was my fault too...I'm the one who chose to cheat on him as well...I don't know anything about Cain..."

"SHUT UP!" I roar at her face, my breath is hot and angry and she stiffens. Her eyes are showing the incredible amount of fear she is feeling at the moment.

"I'm going to kill you," I promise her and she shakes her head.

"No...please..." she starts to sob and I talk over her.

"Yes, I'm going to kill you and that fake baby of yours. I'm going to hurt you so fucking bad."

"No..." she is crying harder and I am not buying it. "I didn't do anything wrong! I never talk to Cain!"

Bullshit.

"I doesn't matter, whether you're innocent or not, you're still going to be killed because of the fact that you're related to that fucker and so will William and so will William's family and everyone you know."

She is shaking her head. "Please...I am begging you..."

"Shut the fuck up!" I yell at her again. "If I hear any more sound come out of your mouth again, I will cut your tongue, understood?"

She nods.

I am furious and trying hard to contain myself. I never raised a hand on a woman, and I never believed in that...but now I am trying to hard not to beat that lying bitch to death.

"Now you listen to me and you listen carefully," I start. "You will say nothing to anyone, especially to Cain. He is not allowed to know that I know anything about this...I'm going to use you, Nadia. I am going to use you to backstab him like you backstabbed me and once I'm through with you, if I feel merciful, I'll put a bullet in your skull. If I don't feel merciful..." I bring my face closer to hers and I can smell the fear coming out of her. "Nadia, if I don't feel merciful, I will make you scream, I will make you suffer...I will kill William in front of you. I will cut open his stomach and make you watch as his guts leak out of his body and then I'll do the same to you."

She is holding her breath.

"It's all up to you, nurse," I tell her. "You can either choose to backstab your cousin, or watch everyone you love die right in front of you."

She is not moving, but her eyes are horrified as if she is begging me not to do this to her. I brush away the guilt that is starting to build inside of me and I convince myself that she deserves it. She is not innocent. She is affiliated with Cain. She's a lying, back-stabbing bitch.

"I'll give you till tomorrow noon to think about all this thoroughly," I say after I step away from her. "I'll be back, and you better have an answer ready," I turn around and walk toward the exit, before closing the door behind her I tell her "You can start unpacking, you will never be able to make it out of Terra," then I close the door and get into my car right after.

I am not satisfied with the way I handled Nadia. I really wanted to see more than tears and fear coming out of her body. I wanted to see blood and screams and agony and pain. I want to hurt her so bad.

Every day is getting worse for me. I can never be happy in this world...no matter what I do, no matter how hard I try to see the good in things, not to be like my parents or my brother...no matter how hard I try to be strong, to pull myself together, to get stronger...there is always something out there to bring me down further.

With each new day, I find myself growing darker, more alone, and distant from everyone.

I thought I was strong, I thought I was a survivor...

But I'm not. I am weak.

Just as weak as Aelita. That's another reason why I've been distant to her...because when she used to cry, I saw myself in her eyes. She always expressed the emotions I always hid...and I didn't want to admit that I was just like her, but I am weak.

I've been through so much.

I want to die. I want to get over this revenge as quickly as possible and let Lord Fire kill me. I've had it with this world...I've had it with suffering...

Why me? Why is all of this happening to me? I still don't get it. They say we all have a purpose in life. I don't get mine at all. What's the point of being brought up in this world if all I do is suffer and watch so many people die in front of me and be the cause of everyone's suffering? I mean is that really my purpose? To make people suffer?

I start to laugh out loud to myself while driving the car.

That's one hell of a purpose if you ask me...and if by any chance making people suffer is really my job in this world, then...

I chuckle darkly again.

I am so golden.


I walk back into my hotel room and decide to shower and cool myself down. Lately, cold water on my skin has been helping and relaxing. I feel so high, so blessed as the coldness of the water drips on my body, washing away my anger, my hatred, my sorrow, my pain. Temporarily that is.

As I step out of the bathroom, I don't dry my body. I let my skin absorb the water and dry by itself. I put on a white shirt and a simple casual jean and I take out my computer.

I am going to review every information Zero sent on the ten criminals. I won't make any more mistake. I will learn about all of them, I will know them, their family, their daily routines, what they like and hate and I will use it against them and take pleasure watching them suffer and bleed.

There's a knock on my door and I sigh a bit annoyed. It is probably Zero or Warr. We're supposed to meet today and discuss our next target. I want everything to be organized and planned from now on. I don't want to just choose randomly. That's disorder and I need order in my life.

I stand up, walk toward the door and open it. This world never ceases to throw me surprises, does it?

"Colton!" she barges in my room without waiting for me to invite her in. I close the door afterwards and try my best to keep myself composed.

She's so comfortable. While everyone is panicking, running for their lives, watching their backs, she has time to do her hair, get a more expensive pair of glass, dress up provocatively, and buy herself a new expensive bag and she decides to walk straight in her enemy's home. I gotta hand it to Veronica, she likes living life dangerously.

That's one of the reason I fucked her. She is a woman who is fearless, shameless and does whatever she pleases. Mostly, she is very good at covering up her ass...This time, she's not going to get away and things are not going to end up in her favor.

"Colton, I'm so sorry," she starts to tell me. I look at her with a smile on my face—a smile that does not reach my eyes.

I want to hear this. I want to be amused.

"I know you think I have something to do with what happened to your wife...but I don't."

One liar after the other, huh?

"Well I do, more or less. I knew the rape was going to happen, and I didn't warn you that Friday night because I thought it was for the best."

I raise an eyebrow.

"You never seemed happy with her, and I love you. From the moment we started sleeping together, from the moment I knew you were powerful...I've fallen for you. I wanted to be by your side. I wanted to be Mrs. Ice...I've fallen for you, and it angered me that you had a wife who wasn't making you happy. I hated her, and I was jealous, but mostly I wanted to take you out of your miserable marriage. Cain Smith is the one who planned all of this. He had been watching all of us, noticing how Hunter was angry with me and hated you. He decided to give Hunter the idea to get revenge, to sleep with your wife too, to give you a taste of your medicine. I knew about it and I didn't say anything because I thought it would help you divorce your wife and get out of this miserable marriage...I've been so stupid," she flips her red hair to the side and continues to stare at me with her blue eyes. "I had no idea they were going to make you watch or kill her...I swear...I just thought they were going to have sex with her and taint her so you would hate her and not want to have anything to do with her. I never knew they would kill her," she is looking at me with a pained face and she takes a step closer to me. "I'm so sorry. I am so sorry. I never meant for all of this to happen...I never meant for things to turn out this way..." she is now looking horrified. "I never knew she was the Lord's daughter for Christ's sake! I never knew who your wife was, Colton...I know you want revenge and I am begging you, spare me. I did all of this for you and it was a mistake, I know...I am so sorry...please."

I keep on smiling at her, my eyes look at her with disgust. When she doesn't get the reaction she hopes to get from me, she continues. "I'm on your side, Colton I'm willing to tell you everything that's going on with Hunter, Jago, Lazar, White, Hidon, Jon and Otto. They're like gangsters now...they call themselves 'The Family.' They want to fight you, they want to defy you. They bought weapons from Zeus's gang squad and are going to protect themselves...they're going to hurt you...and I can tell you anything else you want about the rest. Peter Stone and Cain Smith ..." she gets even closer and dares to put her dirty hand on my face, caressing it. "I can be your double agent...Colton I'll do whatever you want. Use me to get revenge, please. Kill them all, I'll help you...I'm on your side...but please, spare me. I'm the most innocent person in this story..."

The last thing she says is amusing and angering. I keep on smiling at her, and she smiles back tentatively. We're staring at each other and I can't control myself any longer. I grab her by the neck and slammed her against the drawer. Then, I stalk after her, pull her up by taking a vicious grip on her hair and I slam her face on the wall hard, hearing her nose break. She falls down on the floor, frightened. Her hand is on her broken, bleeding nose. She is looking at me with pain and disbelief. I crouch down and grab her by the throat once more, snarling at her face. I hate her more than I hate Nadia.

"If you ever put your dirty hands on me again, I will cut them off and if you ever call yourself innocent in front of me ever again, I will disfigure your face first before killing you."

Her physical appearance is the most important thing to her and I'm glad I have her nose broken. She nods her head quickly. She's scared. I'm still glaring at her with pure resentment.

My cell phone suddenly rings, and I stand up, leaving her sitting on the floor with a broken bloody nose.

"Ice," I answer the phone.

"Sir," It is Warr. "Spyros just informed me that Lazar is done with his chow."

I smile pleased and impressed. He ate her faster than I thought.

"Alright, I'll meet you and Zero at his house in half an hour."

"Yes, sir."

"You better have a hundred gold ready, Warr. I hope you didn't forget our bet,"

I can hear the amusement in his voice. "No sir, I haven't."

I hang up and turn to Veronica and my eyes glisten with excitement. I have suddenly an idea. I am going to make this woman crawl out of her comfort zone and peace of mind.

"Jago's dead," I tell her. "Lazar is going to die today."

She doesn't seem to care. Wait till I show her the way he will die.

"You're coming with me," I say and she shakes her head in horror. "No, No! Please don't kill me Colton! Please!"

I force her up, grabbing her wrist tight on purpose. I hope it breaks.

"Don't worry, I won't kill you today," I am dragging her out of the hotel and to my car. She expects to be sitting in the car. She thinks she has this kind of privilege. I open the trunk.

"Get in," I order. She looks at me as if I'm crazy.

"You're kidding right?"

I glare at her and start to take menacing steps toward her.

"Okay! Okay I...I'll go in," she says while shaking. She awkwardly gets in the trunk and seems uncomfortable because the space is very small. I am about to close the trunk when she puts her hand out, trying to stop me. She wants to say something, but I don't give her a chance.

I violently shut the trunk on her hand hard and I hear nothing but her faint screams. I smirk at myself while I get in the driver's seat.

"She wants me to use her," I explain to Zero and Warr as I arrive at Lazar's house with Veronica. Zero glares at me and then at Veronica then when he sees her crying with a bloody face and broken fingers, his eyes soften in pleasure and he nods at me.

We enter Lazar's house. The house smells like death and raw meat. It's disgusting. We make our way in the kitchen, where Spyros, Lazar and his two kids are. Spyros seems fine, but the three others...I can see the distress in their eyes. It's like they all want to die already. Even the kids! The innocent eyes they once held about three days ago are long gone.

The kids are gone. There is nothing left of them. Their soul, their mind, their conscience are all gone. They're just empty shells. Lazar looks worse. Saying that his eyes hold pain, sorrow and angst is a big understatement.

I whisper in Veronica's ears. "I made him eat his wife in front of his kids," I let her think about that for a moment as I bring my attention back to Lazar.

"I see you've finished your last supper," I tell him with a sneer. He doesn't reply. He's just sitting at the dining table with his children sitting across him.

I smirk at him. "What's wrong? Too full to speak?"

He glances at me. There's no emotion left in him. He's completely drained.

"Just kill me already," he says quietly as if he doesn't care. I nod at him.

"But please...do me a favor," he adds.

"Listen to this carefully, Warr," I tell Warr with a smirk. Warr is staring at Lazar in disbelief.

"Kill my kids too, but don't do it painfully...Just take them out of their misery," Lazar whispers.

I feel a bit of joy in my heart as I hear this. I've just made Lazar make a choice he swore himself to never make: kill his own flesh and blood. I've made him betray himself, his wife and his children.

Warr digs into his pocket and gives me a hundred gold. I take it and throw it on the table in front of Lazar.

"This is how much your children's lives are worth combined," I tell him. "I made a bet with Warr and I bet him a hundred gold that you would beg me to kill your children..."

Lazar looks at me with disbelief and anger. "You sick bastard..." he says.

"It's funny, don't you think? In the beginning, you were doing everything in your power to keep them alive, to not let anything happen to them....and now you want to end their lives. That's quite a transformation you've gone through," I scoff bitterly.

"You're going to hell," Lazar whispers.

I smirk. "I know. So are you."

Warr hands me a gun and I give it to Lazar. "I'll give you the honor of killing your own children."

He gives me such a hateful look. I know he wishes to see me die thousands of death. He takes the gun and looks at his children who are just sitting there emotionless. As I mentioned earlier, their state of mind is...destroyed. They are lifeless.

He points the gun at them and looks at them painfully, tears running down his face then he suddenly points the gun at me angrily and pulls the trigger.

No bullet comes out. Lazar looks at me and at the gun in disbelief and keeps on pulling the trigger again and again but nothing comes out.

I glance at Warr. "I've anticipated him to shoot one of us once armed," he explains me. I nod at him, although I'm not sure if I'm grateful for what he just did.

I turn back to Lazar and glare at him. "We're going to give you another gun, and you won't know if it's loaded or not. If you try to shoot anyone else but your kids, we'll make sure they die of a very painful death in front of you before killing you."

Zero hands me his gun and I give it to Lazar. Lazar's hands are shaking as he takes hold of the second gun. Tears are rolling down his face. "I'm so sorry..." he whispers to his children and then points the gun at them and pulls the trigger. The first bullet goes through his daughter's head and the second goes through the boy's heart. They both fall on the floor and stop moving. Lazar starts to sob painfully. "Just kill me already..."

I smirk. "I will, but don't expect it to be as quick and as painless as your children's," I say as Zero hands me an axe.

"Remember how I told you I was going to cut your children into tiny pieces?" I take a strong hold of the axe and walk toward him. "Well that's what I'm going to do to you, Lazar."

Then I glance at Veronica who is pale and appalled. "Make sure she watches this, Zero," I order Zero as I push Lazar off the chair. He falls on the ground and is not fighting back or struggling.

He is so broken.

I use my feet to adjust his body so he is lying on his back. He is emotionless, staring up the ceiling.

I have already destroyed him. Killing him this way is just dessert to me.

I am good at fulfilling my purpose.

I am *so* good at it.

I violently chop off his left hand to his wrist level and I do the same with his right hand. I can hear Veronica in the background gasping and crying out God's name.

Lazar is still alive, crying silently trying not to grunt in pain. I know that the physical pain is nothing compared to the emotional.

"All this is happening to you because you raped Aelita Fire Ice. I want you to think about this until the moment you die," I growl at Lazar. I cut down his foot, to the ankle side, then the next foot.

Then, his arms to the elbow side, then his leg to the knee side, then his upper arms to his shoulder side, then I separate his upper body from his lower body. He is already dead. But I can't stop. I keep on cutting and chopping and violently butchering him with the axe. I behead him and keep on cutting and cutting with his blood splattering all over me.

I am letting all my emotions out on him. Everything I've been feeling today, I let it all out on Lazar's dead chopped up body.

Once I finish with him, he looks like tiny pieces of meat. You can't even tell he was human.

I am breathless and my shirt is stained with so much blood. So are my hands and my face.

I drop the axe on the floor and spit on Lazar's chopped up flesh then glance at the rest.

Veronica is definitely out of her comfort zone. Zero, Warr and Spyros have a blank, neutral expression on their faces. They're like robots when working with me. They never let their feelings or personality merge out.

"I have something similar planned for you, Veronica," I tell her. She looks at me and starts to break down. I ignore her and turn to Zero. "Do you have it recorded?"

He nods. "Yes, sir."

"Good. Send one copy to the Lord and give one copy to Veronica," I turn to Veronica. "If you want to be 'useful' like you said earlier, you can walk to your man's house and give this copy to him and have him watch it with all his big happy family. Tell them I'm coming for them."

Zero hands Veronica a copy of the tape. She is about to take it from his hand but Zero lets it drop on the floor purposely so she can pick it up herself.

I faintly smirk at Zero. Well, he is the only guard who's having trouble coping with his emotions.

"Go now, Veronica." I tell her coldly. "If you don't disappear from my sight within fifteen seconds, you'll end up just like Lazar...today."

And with that, she stiffens and runs out the door.

I am still trying to pick up my breathing and for some reason, I glance out the window and I see a kid, maybe ten year old on a bicycle staring right back at me.

# 13

## HUNTER CROSS'S POINT OF VIEW

"Hunter," I hear Hidon call my name. I am in my room, stocking weapons in my jeans. Hidon, White, the twins Jon and Otto and I are getting ready to look for Jago and Lazar. It is Friday morning and the last time I saw Jago was Monday night after our small gathering. Since then, I have not heard a word from him, I tried to visit his wife at the hospital but the nurse wouldn't let me see her or tell me anything. Everyone thinks the Lord got him and his wife and took the tapes since we never received an answer from the Lord to let our family go.

But, I am the only one who does not want to believe this. I don't want to think Jago's dead. He's the type to spend time by himself. He's an outcast, a loner. Maybe he just wants to be alone. Maybe he's hiding from everyone for a while. I tried to convince the rest that he will be back by the end of the week, but now that Lazar never showed up to meet us and Zeus's gang members, now that we've tried to call him countless times and he never answered, we've been very worried and I have become anxious as well.

I don't personally like Lazar. He has a bad attitude. He doesn't regret what he did and I bet he'll do it again if he is asked to. But what I know, and what I respect about him is his love for his wife and his children. He will do anything to protect them and he loves his wife even though we all think she is a fucked up ugly lady. I know he cares for his family and that's one reason why I am worried about him.

We've all decided to go to Lazar's house and see what's going on. I just hope nothing happened to him or his family.

"Hidon, I'm coming. Be patient." I shout at the door a bit annoyed. Hidon is so impatient, hot headed and violent. I think he wants to retaliate the most. He's been staying at my house a lot lately and I have learned to know him more. He likes violence, and he is really looking forward to a bloody fight. He has no one to live for. No family, no kids, just an ex-wife who has no choice but stay by his side for protection. Does he still love his wife? I don't know. They've been fighting a lot lately.

Everyone's been fighting a lot and all of that is happening in my home.

White Stone and his girlfriend, Jon and Otto (the twins) with their partners and children, and Hidon and his ex-wife and family, all of them are now living in my home. We all thought it'd be safer if we were all together and protected one another. I thought it was a good idea, but not everyone agreed to it.

Lazar told us he had somewhere safer to hide his children, and he and his wife will be staying at their own house. He didn't want to show he was afraid, and he was too proud to ask for us to protect his family.

Peter Stone, White Stone's brother, does not want to mingle with us either. He thinks he is much smarter and much more intellectual than the rest of us because he has some sort of educational degree. He and White Stone don't get along at all.

Cain Smith, the mastermind behind all this, the rich one who has 'connections', has gone MIA. I haven't heard of him since it all went down. I have tried to contact him for help or advice, but he never answers. I guess he knew all of this was going to happen and he probably fled from the Island a while ago.

Rich bastard.

Veronica too doesn't want to mingle or affiliate herself with me. She is now living with her sister and does not want to see or talk to me. She hates me for killing Aelita and making Colton watch. She told me that she only let me rape Aelita because I was hating too much on Colton and I might feel better after getting his wife...I'm not sure if that's true but it doesn't matter, she did not sign up for the killing of Aelita Fire. She's innocent in this messed up story. I don't want her to be hurt and I still love her so very much. I will do anything to protect her. I just wish she can love me back...I miss her a lot.

"Veronica's here to see you!" Hidon says. I blink twice and rush to open the door and make sure my brain is not playing tricks with me.

"Wait what?" I see Hidon waiting at the door.

"Veronica's here to see you," he repeats. He looks a bit worried. "She's waiting outside, she wouldn't come in. She looks pretty scared man..."

*Oh no...*

I rush downstairs to the main entrance of my house and I see her standing outside all teary...Her nose is dislocated and bleeding and her right hand is swollen. She looks pretty bad.

"Baby..." I walk toward her. "What happened? What happened?" I try to touch her and she smacks my hand away and backs off.

"Don't you touch me!" she yells.

I ignore the fact that she is angry with me. "What happened to you? Who did this to you?" I ask her again.

She ignores my question and hands me a disk. "Colton wants you and your friends to watch this..."

I take it from her and then I clench my jaws angrily. "Did he do this to you?" I growl.

"Just watch the fucking video..." she snaps at me and is about to leave but I stop her.

"What happened, Veronica? You need to tell me what happened!"

She turns to me and with teary eyes, she starts to yell and push me with her left hand. "You wanna know what happened? *You* happened! It's all your fault Hunter! You have no idea how dangerous Colton has become..." her blue eyes are traumatized, "what...what he made me watch..."

She is trembling and I am growing angrier. He hurt her.

"What the hell happened?  What did he do to you?"

She glares at me. "I'll tell you what happened. I went to his place to beg him to have mercy on me! I told him I would do anything for him because I love him and you know what he did? He smashed my face on the wall, broke my nose, then he made me get in the trunk of his car, closed the trunk on my hand on purpose, drove me to Lazar's house and made me watch as...he..." she starts to sob as if she can't say what she saw. She's very scared...

"Aw baby..." I want to hug her and comfort her. I hate myself for not making her stay with me, for not protecting her...I hate myself so much for this. I want to make it up to her. I want to be there for her, I wish I could've been there.

I bring her close to my arm and for once, for a while, she lets me hug her. That's when I know she's really hurt. Veronica isn't the type to cry easily or let me comfort her.

"It's okay baby," I tell her. "I'll keep you safe."

She suddenly pushes me away as if she just realized she was in my arms, then she glares at me. "I don't want to have anything to do with you. Just watch the fucking video...you really need to know how dangerous Colton is."

She is about to walk away when I chase after her. "I can't leave you like this, Veronica. I want you to stay with me from now on."

She ignores me and I secure my hand around her wrist, stopping her from walking away. She turns around and slaps me with her swollen hand then screams in pain.

"Get away from me! I don't want to be around you ever, ever again! I hate you!" she is shouting, glaring at me, blaming me. "It's all your fault, Hunter! You are such a dumbass! I am not safe with you, I never will be! Just being around you will make my death come quicker and even more painful! I can't stand you! You're an asshole! I hope you rot in hell! I hope you and your sick stupid brother go down in a painful way!"

I try to tell myself she doesn't mean what she's saying. She's just angry and scared. Colton made her that way. He is the one to blame.

"Veronica, you need to be with me now," I try to reason her.

"No! I am never, ever being around you! I don't want to be part of you and your stupid friends! I am not fucking with you!" she's yelling

"Veronica," I say softly, trying to calm her.

"Shut up! Don't ever say my name ever again! I hate you Hunter! I hate you so much! I don't give a fuck you and your family! I don't give a fuck! I don't give a flying fucking fuck! Stay the hell away from me! Stay the fuck away from me!"

She is really angry, and I realize my presence is making her feel worse.

After yelling and cursing me out, she finally stops lowers her tone and warns me. "I am safer far away from you. Stay the hell away from me."

Then she walks away and I see her get in her sister's car.

I am outside, looking at the car driving away painfully...It feels like my heart is breaking into pieces...it doesn't matter how many times she spits those cruel words at me, it doesn't matter how much she hates me...I still love her.

I love Veronica so much...and I just wish she wasn't implicated in this. I just want to keep her safe.

"She hates you," Hidon says coming outside.

I glare at him. "Thanks, captain obvious."

He looks down and sees the disk in my hand. "What's that?"

"A message from Ice.Veronica said we should all watch this..." I say, walking back in the house. Hidon follows me and calls the others. We're all in the TV room. I am standing in the middle while they are sitting on the sofa, couch, chair, the floor and are anxiously waiting for the video to play.

And it starts...

And we all watch with horror...what happened to Lazar. We watch him eating his wife in front of his children...we watch Colton look at him with satisfaction...we watch Lazar beg for his children's safety....we watch him cry. And, we watch him asking for Colton to kill his children...Lazar asked Colton to kill his children...something I never thought he would do. I can see how broken Lazar was...and I watch as he painfully put a bullet in his own kids...and we all watch in horror...as Colton brutally slaughters Lazar with an axe...cutting him into pieces.

When the video ends...I feel sick and nauseous. We are all appalled, unable to react or to speak. I've never seen something this cruel in my life. Colton Ice is a sadistic psychopath...

No, he's worse than a psychopath...he's not a human being...he's despicable, he is the devil. What he has done to Lazar and his family is atrocious...And that's just to Lazar's family...

What will he do to me, the guy who killed his wife? To Veronica, the woman I love...to my family? To my brother...?

*To Noah...?*

No.

Please, God...I can't have Noah fall in the hands of this psychopath. No.

"We're all gonna die like this...?" White is the first to speak and everyone, the girls, the family members...they all are yelling and crying, realizing that they will all end up this way. Everyone is yelling, it's noisy in the room. Hidon is pacing, cursing and he is getting paler and paler almost to White's skin color.

There's so much terror in the house.

That's what Colton wants from us. He wants to terrorize us and let our imagination run wild and think of what's going to happen to us...he is deadly...

I thought Lord Fire was dangerous...but...Colton Ice just proved me wrong.

"We can't let that happen to our family...I can't..." Jon says. "I can't watch my children get mentally tortured like this...it may not be the same thing that might happen to us but...it'll be just as cruel, or maybe worse...I can't put my family's life in danger," he takes out a gun and points it at Otto, his twin brother.

"Jon, what are you doing?" Jon's partner asks him with worry. Jon ignores her and is speaking to Otto who is just as scared as everyone is.

"He is hurting our family to watch us suffer...if we're dead, they can't hurt our family," Jon explains.

"I love you, brother," Otto nods, accepting what Jon is about to do.

"I love you too..." Jon says and pulls the trigger on his brother and then shoots himself in the head.

I hear their girlfriends scream in horror, everyone is terrified.

"Did he just fucking kill himself and his brother?" White asks, his voice breaking. Before I know it, this situation we're in just went from worse to chaotic. I feel like I'm in hell, and Colton hasn't even touched me or my family yet...There's screaming and crying and children bawling and two dead bodies in my house and it's all a mess and I can't be there...

I have got to get out of here. I need to see my brother. I need to tell him I love him.

I need to see my poor suffering brother who has nothing to do with all of this.

I walk out of my house and leave everyone else screaming and trying to deal with the tragedy.

I am in my car driving toward our grandparent's home where Noah, my seventeen year old brother is resting. Noah is the most precious thing in my life. My love for him hurts me because it's a mixture of self-hate, self-blame, pity and regret. Noah has been through so much since he was born.

————

He was born premature because his insides were upside down and barely had a healthy beating heart. Our mother was in an abusive relationship with our father, and she was depressed when she was pregnant of Noah. She neglected herself and abused her body with substances and alcohol, and it led to Noah being born prematurely. Our mother died after giving birth to him, and I was the one who raised and took care of him. I was ten years old. Our father never cared about us...he was an angry drunk who was always in a bad mood. Our grandparents were the one who saved us. They took custody of Noah and me and brought us far away from our father. He was very upset about it, so he wanted to get revenge.

When Noah was barely three years old, he witnessed grandmother get beat and brutally murdered by our father. I was in school when that happened and our grandfather was working. After killing our grandmother, our father kidnapped Noah and was trying to run away and get out of the island with him. The police eventually caught him and tried to stop him, but he put a gun to the three year old Noah and threatened the police to kill his own three year old son if they didn't let him escape. The police was going to let him go because the life of a three year old boy was in danger, but our father was paranoid and deranged. He thought the police was still after him. So, he shot Noah in the chest and tried to kill himself, but the police stopped him and arrested him. Our father ended up being killed in prison because he probably pissed off someone. I never felt bad for him.

Noah had a bullet that damaged a part of his very weak heart, but miraculously he survived thanks to a very talented heart surgeon. His heart became weaker and extremely fragile. He needed a heart transplant, but it cost a lot of money, so our grandfather and I decided to just give Noah medicine until we obtained enough money.

When growing up, Noah took care of me and our grandfather. We were a broken family, and he was the strongest of all. Even though he had a weak heart and couldn't go to school or make friends, or live a normal life, even though he didn't have a mother or a father, he never once felt sorry for himself. He never complained about his condition...he never once whined or cried or blamed anyone for his misfortune.

I was the weak one. I was the one who was angry at the world, who was rebellious and emotional and hated everyone. During my teen years, I was troubled and lost. I didn't care about school and our grandfather used to yell at me and lecture me a lot. I used to fight with him all the time, but Noah never once blamed me or never once got angry with me. He was always by my side, always telling me how much he loved me and that everything will eventually be okay.

When he turned twelve, I was twenty-two, and that was when I met Veronica. I fell in love with her. She was as beautiful as demanding. She was interested in me because I was a wild one, I was badass and always got into fights and she liked it and I loved her even more because she was the only good distraction from my family. I thought that everyone would leave me eventually. My mother and father were dead, my grandmother was dead, my grandfather was getting weaker and older and Noah's heart condition was worsening...I thought that if I distanced myself from them, I wouldn't miss them when they die. A year later, our grandfather managed to work hard and get enough money to pay for a heart transplant for Noah. That was a lot of money saved for him and at the same time, Veronica and I were having a bit of crisis in our relationship. She was growing tired of me not spoiling her. She wanted to go on a vacation cruise and I couldn't afford it, so she said she was going to leave me and I panicked. I didn't want her to leave me. I didn't want to be alone. She was the only one who made my life better, so to keep her with me, I stole the money our grandfather had saved for Noah and spent it on Veronica.

It made her happy, and she married me right away during our cruise vacation because she was so happy I finally gave her life a bit of luxury. When I came back from vacation, my grandfather was furious with me and he couldn't believe I did something like this to my own little brother. I didn't really feel bad for Noah because I thought he was going to die soon anyways...I was so sure everyone in my family was going to die, and I was expecting Noah to hate me or get mad at me for what I did to him, but he never once blamed me or hated me...He was happy for me that I made Veronica happy. He told me it didn't matter what happened to him, as long as I was happy, he was happy. It broke my heart...

He was getting weaker and weaker by the year and my marriage with Veronica was in jeopardy as well. She grew tired of me quickly and didn't want to settle, she wanted to explore, experience more things, and that's how she started cheating on me...and by the time I've realized that...it was too late.

Noah was completely weak to the point where he could barely move on his own. When he turned sixteen, a year ago, he wanted me to take him to see the ocean since he had never been at the beach in his life...and at that same moment, Veronica called and demanded me to come pick her up from another city. She was ditched by her friends at a club. Noah begged me to stay and spend his birthday with him, but instead, I chose to go find Veronica.

I left him alone... and he had a breakdown. He fainted and lost consciousness that day and was in a coma for a while. He didn't die, he managed to wake up about three months ago, but he's going to die soon, and spend the rest of his painful life in bed... he is now broken...he's tired of suffering, he is sad and cries a lot. He whines, and doesn't sleep much, he feels bad for himself...he finally pities himself, and the heartbreaking part of all this is that he still loves me very much, still forgives me and still wants the best for me.

———

That poor boy has suffered his whole entire life; you do understand why I cannot let him in the hands of Colton Ice, right? You do understand that I cannot let Noah suffer any more than this. He is completely oblivious of what happened, of what I've done. He is innocent, and he has absolutely nothing to do with this at all. He just came back from a coma not even three months ago...he is dealing with his own problem and he doesn't need to be mingled in this... I can't let him suffer any more than he is right now. I just can't...

I want to see Noah and tell him how much I love him. I do love him a lot. I just couldn't show it. I was selfish and did not want to get too close to him because I knew I would suffer if he died...

I can't let that happen now. I can't let him die. I can't let him suffer. I have to make things right.

I park my car in the garage of our grandparent's home. My grandfather dislikes me a lot now and can't stand being in the same room with me. I have not seen him since Noah came back from his coma three months ago. I hope he is not in the house—grandpa will never let me see Noah.

I knock at the front door and I get no response. So, I look under the rock on the floor and take the duplicates of the key and enter.

"Hello?" I call but no one answers. I guess our grandfather is not home. I walk toward Noah's room and knock.

"Come in..." he tells me with a very faint weak voice. I open the door and see him lying on the bed. His blond hair is turning ashy and his brown eyes are so dim...so lifeless. He is so weak and so pale, and so sad...He looks so lonely.

He *is* lonely.

Grandfather has to work hard to support both of them so he is never home and I am never around to visit him and he has no friend. He is lonely...He has no one...

"Hi brother," I see a faint weak smile on his face. His puffy eyes that are blood shot from so much crying and suffering, soften at the sight of me. Seeing me brings him happiness...

"I've...missed you," he tells me.

I smile at him painfully and sit by his side. I put my hand in his weak and cold hand. "How have you been?"

"I'm better now that I...see...you..."he says. Talking makes him breathless because of his weak heart. Any small physical movement makes him sick.

"Don't talk too much..." I tell him. He smiles at me once again. I smile back and then I don't know how, but I just feel a rush of release. I feel as if it's time for me to let go. So I break down and cry. I start to cry really hard and harder and louder by the seconds...and when I feel his weak hand slightly squeezing in mine for comfort and I cry even harder.

He does not deserve this...he does not deserve to suffer. "I've messed up, Noah...I've messed up really bad..." I tell him in between the cries. "I hurt someone innocent...and now everyone I know and love will suffer for this...for my mistake...there's nothing I can say or do to change the things I've done....I wish I could take it all back, I swear...I'd do anything within my power, God knows I'll give everything I've got to stop anyone from getting hurt, but I am powerless...there's no way out of this mess I've created, of this dark place...there is no hope, no future for me and if I am alive, there will be no hope for you either....I can't see the light at the end of the tunnel...I can't face another day knowing you will be hurt..."

I look at him in the eyes, imploring him. "Noah...I let you down. You've always looked up to me, you've always trusted me, believed in me...and I let you down. Of all the things I hid from you, I can't hide this shame, this guilt I am feeling right now...I can't..." I stop crying and compose myself. "I can't let you get hurt...I just can't let you pay for my mistakes again. If I disappear, you won't suffer anymore. No one I love will suffer...I need to make this right for you. I have enough money saved to get you a new heart I will leave it to you. Once I'm gone I want you to take that money and–"

"No," he says. He is shaking his head and crying as well. "I don't... want to... survive...I don't want...to live either."

"Don't say that Noah..." I plead him. Don't break my heart any more than it already is...

He shakes his head, "I give up, big brother..." he starts. "Look at me...I am as good...as dead...I am...lonely and sick...and I have....no friends....I've never had a friend...no one...will miss me...when I'm dead...no one....needs me..." he stops to pick up his breathing. "Veronica and grandpa...they need you...they will need you...I don't...know what's going on...but you can't....just die...I want to die...I will be...better off dead...this...is not...the life I...want to...live ...so please...don't..."

He is breathing hard, but continues. "When I die...I want...you...to burn my body...and spread my ashes in the...ocean...that's...all...I...want from you...I don't...want you...to leave me..."

He stops talking because he can't anymore. He is completely breathless. I continue to cry. I can't keep his promise. Colton will never allow me to...all he wants is to see me suffer and he will do it by hurting Noah. I can't...

I have to do this.

I kiss him on the forehead and stand up. "I love you, brother. Tell Grandpa I'm sorry...Goodbye," then I make my way out of the room and before closing it, I hear Noah call out after me. He sounds angry.

"Goodbye...? You're leaving me...again...like you did on my birthday...? You're saying goodbye again...?"

I don't say anything. I don't know what to say to him, so he continues and this time, he is not breathless. He is using all the strength he has left to tell me this.

"I just hope you know that...if you say goodbye today...I hope it's true..." then he starts to sob. "You're not the only one suffering big brother...I am...and if you're saying goodbye...then don't...ever come back...I don't hope to see you ever again before I die....cause the hardest part of all this is leaving you..."

I can't listen to him anymore...I close the door behind me and run out while weeping.

Talking to my brother was the most painful thing I've experienced.

I thought I would feel better after talking to him and saying goodbye, but that's not the case. I feel so much worse and I want to die now, right now...Jon and Otto did the right thing by killing themselves. Their families won't be tortured if they're not alive to see it.

That's what I'm gonna do, and I'm sure that my death will bring a bit of happiness in Veronica's life. She hates my guts.

It will also bring relief and healing in my grandfather's life because the money I have saved for myself will be for him and for Noah and he won't have to work too hard anymore, and hopefully...he'll forgive me. I know with Noah, it'll take a while before he is happy again because I know how much he loves me, but I know that he won't die and won't suffer or be tortured, so he'll eventually heal with time.

It is decided. I am going to take my own life.

I want to say goodbye to Veronica too, but I know she doesn't want to see me...so I end up walking to the first place we met. It was at the cherry blossom tree park. I want to visit there once again and say goodbye to the small good memories I've had.

I am walking around the park and admiring the beauty of the trees and remembering when Veronica used to be so nice to me. After almost four hours of wandering around, I decide to leave and go take my life. I am about to go when I see someone I never expected to see.

The girl I killed a week ago. She's in a wheelchair and someone is pushing her. I blink and rub my eyes and pinch myself several times, thinking that I'm hallucinating due to the lack of sleep, but she's real.

My jaw drops and I feel a sudden kind of relief and happiness.

She's alive!

Aelita's alive!

I want to go run to her and hug her and hold her and tell her how happy I am to know that she's alive! But I have to contain myself. She's not alone, there's an older looking girl who is pushing her. She must be her servant. I have to separate the maid from Aelita.

Heaven hears my prayers. I hear the maid say something to Aelita and Aelita nods and the maid walks away toward the restroom. Aelita is now by herself sitting in the wheelchair and watching the leaves fall from the trees.

I am so happy that she's alive. Not just for me, but for her! I've regretted killing her. I thought I was doing the right thing because I thought she would be better off dead...but I had no right to make that call. I had no right to decide whether someone lives or dies...I was wrong.

And she's alive! Thank goodness!

I look around to make sure the servant is not coming back and I slowly rush toward Aelita.

She feels someone come toward her and she turns and her beautiful honey brown eyes meet mine.

Her eyes have changed. They're not innocent anymore. They hold pain, anger and sorrow.

I am the reason.

She freezes and stiffens as she sees me. I understand why she's scared.

"Don't be scared," I whisper to her softly. She looks around to try to find the maid, but there's no one coming.

"Aelita...I'm not going to hurt you," I reassure her as I start pushing the wheelchair so I can take her somewhere quiet and private so we can talk. I end up going deeper in the park and when I don't see anyone around, I stop pushing her. I turn to face her and she is shaking and frozen. I ignore that. I am still psyched that she's alive, so I stretch my hand to touch her golden curly hair and I realize she's real!

"You're real!" I tell her, gasping. Happy tears are rolling down my face. "You're alive, Aelita! I'm so glad! I'm so glad....!"

She looks at me a bit confused and puzzled, probably wondering why her rapist and killer is happy to see her alive. I am so happy and so overwhelmed that I start to have an asthma attack.

I gasp again and again and cough and I kneel before her. My throat is hurting me and my lungs are inflamed. I reach into my pocket to take out the inhaler, but it falls from my hand and rolls far away. I am too weak to chase after it so, I stay on the ground, gasping and choking on my own breath.

I'm going to die.

I see her push herself toward the direction where the inhaler is, and she picks it up. She's probably going to hold it and watch me die.

Hahaha, that is so ironic. I won't blame her at all for this...I think it's righteous to die in front of her.

I feel so much better suddenly. I feel freed.

To my surprise, I see her leave her wheelchair and kneel on the ground next to me as I am gasping for air. With her shaking hands, she gives me the inhaler and I take it from her and start to breathe in as she is gently and tentatively patting my back.

"There, there. It's ok. Breathe in slowly," she tells me gently with a very soft voice.

My eyes widen in shock.

She can speak!

As my breathing becomes normal, I stare at her in disbelief. "You can speak!"

She nods at me with a tentative smile.

I grin. "That's great, Aelita! That's really great! I'm..." I can't express my happiness. "Gee I'm so happy you're alive, Aelita...I'm so happy you're alive and talking... I'm really happy for you."

I can tell she isn't really happy about that.

I am so sorry for everything I've done to her...she's an angel...she's the greatest person I've ever met...she's just like my brother...I've hurt her so much in the worse way possible and she is acting as if I've never hurt her. I mean, she's scared...I can feel her shaking, but she's not yelling at me or screaming for help, and even better, she'd just saved my life! She has every right to let me die...but she doesn't...She is an angel. A real angel, a saint! And that saint is the answer to all of this mess.

I am suddenly on my knees. "Aelita," I start. "I'm not going to insult you by telling you that I'm sorry for what I've done to you. It is inexcusable, and I deserve the worst kind of punishment. I can't imagine what you're going through emotionally right now. I thought I was suffering, but I know you're the one suffering the most...and still you choose to act kind toward me, the man who's hurt you and broke you...I don't deserve your kindness, Aelita. It's not me you need to save. It's my family."

She frowns, a bit confused. She doesn't know what's going on.

"Aelita, your father, Lord Fire...he wants to hurt me."

She doesn't seem surprised.

"Him and your husband."

She eyes widen when I mention Colton Ice. She does not believe me.

"I don't blame them. I deserve to suffer for what I've done to you. We all do. We deserve to die...and I am prepared to be punished...but the way your husband is doing it is wrong. He's hurting innocent people to hurt us. He's hurting us by hurting our families, our children..." my face is pained as I think of Lazar. "I've just watched a video of one of the other guys who hurt you...Colton made him do horrible things, I can't tell you the details, it's too horrible, but what you need to know is that the guy's kids died. They were killed just to hurt him."

She frowns, horrified.

"That's what he's going to do. He's going to hurt our families and make us watch them suffer and die... but they're innocent. They haven't done anything wrong to you or to Colton. I have a brother, his name is Noah..."

I tell her the complete story of my little brother's life and I can see pain and sympathy in her eyes.

"He has gone through a lot already and I don't think it's fair for him to suffer and get tortured physically and emotionally just to hurt me...he is innocent and has no clue of what I've done...he doesn't deserve this, neither do the children of the others or the families...they're all innocent and they don't even know what we've done...they don't...so please, Aelita. I'm begging you. I don't care what happens to me or to those who hurt you, you can kill us, torture us do whatever the hell you want, but please, don't let the innocent ones pay for our crimes...please talk to your father, please Aelita. Please, please...please!"

I am imploring her, I am on my knees, crying and begging. She looks at me with a pained, gentle look on her face and places her soft delicate hand on my cheek. "Okay," she says.

# 14

## COLTON ICE'S POINT OF VIEW

"Mr. Ice, Aelita wants to go outside, today," Hinata tells me on the phone. As I hear that, I jump out of my bed and listen carefully. Hinata is my secret spy. She tells me everything that's going on with Aelita since her mother won't tell me anything. I honestly don't know why Hinata is choosing to help me, but I'm very grateful. Knowing how Aelita is doing helps my day and my state of mind better. She has been better since Zero visited her. Her violent act stopped, and she has been kinder to everyone around her. She is slowly regaining her smile and even started planting flowers. I don't know what Zero did to her, but it worked. I've realized he is very important to her. As much as it hurts knowing that he is the man making my wife feel better, I am grateful for Aelita finding a way to cope with her emotions. As long as it has a positive outcome on her, I will tolerate it.

"She's going outside? You mean in the city?" I ask.

I can hear the smile in Hinata's voice. "Yes. She told us she wanted to go spend some time at the cherry blossom park."

I smile happily. That's great, that's really great.

"She wants to go alone," Hinata adds and I stiffen.

"I'm...I'm not sure if that's a good idea," I say quietly.

"She said she needed to get away from everyone, that we're all suffocating her since someone is always with her all the time. She wants to breathe, she wants some fresh air. She wants to feel free."

I still don't think it's a good idea for her to venture herself alone in Terra...the criminals aren't all dead yet.

"Her mother refused to let her go alone, she wanted to come with her, but Aelita refused. She said she was tired of seeing her mother's face every day as well...Mrs. Fire had no choice but accept letting her go alone,"

What? Is Mrs. Fire out of her crazy mind?

"She said yes to Mrs. Ice to not upset her, but Mrs. Fire asked me to take the day off and go visit the park as well...if I happen to see her, then it will be a 'coincidence'. I'll keep an eye on her."

Oh...well that's better than leaving her alone.

"I guess that's fine."

"I'll call you and keep you posted if anything goes wrong," Hinata promises me.

"Thank you," I say and hang up.

It's Friday morning. It's been exactly a week since the tragedy. Those seven days have been hell to Aelita. She was raped and shot on Friday, she survived, tried to kill herself on Monday and survived again, was emotionally torn and tortured...and here she is now on Friday, wanting to go out and watch the cherry trees fall.

I smile at myself. Aelita is one hell of a girl. I want to tell her I'm proud of her. I want to speak to her...I want to see her, but I don't think the feeling is reciprocal.

My phone rings again and it's Zero. He and Warr and Spyros are waiting for me outside my hotel in the car. Lord Fire wants to give me his opinion on what I've done to Lazar and his family.

I could give two shits about what he thinks. But, I still have to go talk to him anyways since he's the father of my wife.

I shower and get myself ready, then walk out to get in the car.


Warr is driving, Spyros is seating in the front passenger seat and I am sitting with Zero in the back. I have learned to know a bit more about those three in only few days. Even though the three of them are psychotic killers, they have humanistic characters. Warr is very calm and very patient all the time. I have never seen him lose his temper. He is welcoming and his teammates, including me enjoy his presence. He has a strong sense of leadership. Moreover, he is a very precise killer. They all have their different style of killing, and Warr is precise, silent and very deadly. Furthermore, Warr likes to read a lot, only that he reads the same book many times. As soon as he reads the last page, he starts from the beginning again which is unusual. Above all, I think he is the one I trust the most between the three.

Spyros on the other hand is the complete opposite of Warr. He is loud, talkative, short-tempered, hyper, cheerful, sarcastic and loves to go crazy. He is very affectionate toward Warr. He thinks of him like a brother but he is a bully to Zero. He takes great pleasure at trying to anger Zero. It seems like they have known each other for a while. Even though Spyros is the most lively and foolish of all, he is however the smartest, and fastest. Don't get me wrong, Zero and Warr have an incredible speed, but Spyros is at least two times faster than them. Another unique thing about him is that, unlike the other two, Spyros only knows how to kill with weapons. He is null at physical combat. Instead, he carries a bag pack that has knives, guns, shirukens, tantos, grenades, swords and anything he can get his hands on.  And lastly, comes Zero.

Zero is quiet, cold and distant most of the time, but he is not a complete robot. He kind with Warr once in a while. He sometimes argues with Spyros and tries to tolerate me. Zero is very skilled, he thinks fast, he has the strength of a bear and can fight with his eyes closed. He is a natural born killer and I still believe he is the deadliest of all. I don't know much about Zero except that he loves animals and my wife. My relationship with Zero is...complicated now. We don't snarl or glare at each other anymore, but we still can't stand each other. I don't think he's a bad person, and I am very grateful for what he has done for Aelita. However, I still can't stand him because he wants to get in my wife's pants.

He likes her, he has strong feelings for her and even wanted her to divorce me last Friday so they could run away together and live happily ever after. Furthermore, he's trying to win her heart by bringing her flowers and cute puppies and staying over to console her. I know what he's trying to do. He's trying to take advantage of Aelita's dark state and make her like him and eventually leave me and end up with him. That's never going to happen. I'm sorry, but I don't see anyone with Aelita other than me. I just can't picture it. Aelita has always had feelings for me since I first met her. It will be hard for her to just forget about me and run with Zero—some guy she just met not even a year ago. No. There's no way Zero will have Aelita. Aelita loves me, so ha.

I sound very childish right now, don't I? I feel childish.


My phone rings and it is Mrs. Fire. I deny it and roll my eyes. I know why she is calling. She has been harassing me to come speak to Dr. Vancouver about my hallucinations.

The hell I am.

I am not crazy.

The dog is real.

"Hey Zero," I say. "You know Forest , right?"

He faintly smiles. "The human or the dog?"

I smile back. "The dog."

He nods. "Yes, he died protecting Aelita last Friday. He was shot down by those criminals..." he sounds very angry.

I frown. It doesn't make sense that Forest, the dog died...he bit me and I felt pain, and he saved Aelita's life. How can he be dead and still do all this?

And why the fuck am I the only one seeing the dog?

The phone rings again and it's Mrs. Fire. I put it on vibrate mode and ignore her call. I am not crazy.

"Why do you ask about him?" Zero asks me.

I shrug. "Just wondering if you knew him on a personal level since you like animals and you used to spend a lot of time with my wife when I was not around,"

He glares at me. "Yes, I knew Forest on a personal level. He was a good dog who loved and guarded Aelita. He died righteously. He died protecting Aelita, something that *someone* wasn't able to do."

*Asshole.* I glare back at him and decide not to continue this conversation.

"I am mind blown and satisfied with what you've done to Lazar," Lord Fire tells me. We're outside, in a junkyard and Lord Fire is smiling at me. I feel like I've won the lottery. Henry Fire is honestly smiling at me. "I knew your sick twisted mind would unravel, you just needed a little push."

I nod. "So does that mean I get full control of what happens to the rest?"

He nods back. "Yes son. And it also means that you get to live for three more months."

I stiffen a bit.

"I'm giving you three months to wipe all of them out along with their families. That's more than enough time, since you were able to kill two of them in just a week, isn't it?"

"I'll use the time wisely sir," I say.

His poker face is back. "How's the crew? Warr, Spyros and Zero, do you like them?"

The three guards look at me nervously.

I want to tell Mr. Fire that I don't like Zero, but it would seem very childish again. "They're very good at this job," I reply. I'm being honest, even though I dislike Zero and think Warr is too easy going and Spyros is way too energetic, they're amazing at what they're doing. They're perfect killers...I think they're fantastic.

"That's good son," Mr. Fire says and then looks at me seriously. "My wife spoke to me the other day,"

Oh God.

"She said she's concern about your mental health," he says carefully.

I sigh. "I am perfectly fine,"

As soon as I say that, I see the dog, running toward me with a tennis ball in his mouth. I look at the dog in disbelief.

What the hell is it doing here!?

"No you're not. No one is fine. I'd be worried if you were fine after all this...it's normal to be having a psychotic break down blah blah blah..."

I tune Mr. Fire out and stare at the dog that has the ball in his mouth. The dog is real. I just know it. It doesn't feel like I'm losing my mind and I don't believe in ghosts...I know the dog is real.

He drops the ball from his mouth and the ball bounces. I can see and hear the ball bouncing and it's rolling over toward me.

The dog wants to play huh?

I crouch down to take the ball and the minute I do it, I feel a rock fly above my head with a strong velocity.

"HEY!" I hear Spyros yell and I turn around and Spyros is chasing after a kid.

It's the kid on the bicycle from yesterday, the kid who saw me butchering Lazar. Did that kid just tried to kill me by throwing the rock at me? If I hadn't crouched down to pick up the ball Forest threw at me...I would've been hit and seriously injured.

Did Forest just save my life?

"Let go! Let go!" the kid is yelling and trashing around, trying to fight Spyros. Spyros seems to be having a hard time containing the child, so Warr comes to his aid. He effortlessly secures the boy's hands and drags him out to us.

"Do you have eyes behind your head?" Mr. Fire asks me stupefied. "How did you dodge that?"

"You wouldn't understand," I respond and look down at the boy who is glaring at me.

"Why did you do that for, kid?" Warr asks him gently.

"You hurt Sony and Kenna!" the kid shouts at me angrily, tears rolling down his face.

My heart sinks with guilt and remorse.

"Who's Sony and Kenna?" Mr. Fire asks.

"Lazar's kid sir," Zero responds.

"I see."

"They were my friends! I used to play with them! You hurt them!" the boy is crying.

I realize what I've just done. I've actually killed two innocent children yesterday. I've taken two innocent lives, and it's hitting me now. I haven't even thought twice about it, I haven't even regretted it until now that I am seeing the little boy cry. Sony and Kenna were his friends...and he watched them die...

I can't imagine how devastated and traumatized the poor boy is feeling. "I'm so sor-" I am about to say when Mr. Fire cuts me off.

"Kill him," he commands Warr.

Warr nods and points a gun at the child.

"No!" my eyes widen in horror and my heart starts to beat fast. Warr stops and Lord Fire glares at me.

"What is it, son?"

"He has nothing to do with this! Why do you need to kill him?" I object.

Lord looks at me with a cold face. "He is friends with the enemy's children and he tried to kill you."

I can't believe Lord Fire is reasoning this way.

"He's just a kid!" I argue in disbelief, "he doesn't know what he's doing. He is innocent. He hasn't done anything!"

"He tried to kill you son,"

"He tried to throw a rock at me, I'm sure it wouldn't have killed me."

"Maybe, maybe not. He still put your life in jeopardy and he is disagreeing with what you've done to Lazar."

"He doesn't know anything! He doesn't understand a thing about this. He's just a kid who's upset because his friends are dead! I would be too!" I shout.

"Watch your tone, son." Mr. Fire glares at me and nods at Warr. I turn to Warr.

"No, don't do it! Warr, don't!"

The kid is trembling and crying. He is afraid. "Please," I beg Warr. I know Warr is the wisest of all. I know he knows that what he's about to do is wrong. I have faith in him. I trust his judgements. I know he will not kill an innocent child.

He pulls the trigger and blows the kid's brain out.

I am stupefied and frozen in place as I see the poor kid's body collapse on the floor as blood leaks out of his head.

My eyes are wide open, trembling and my breathing starts to quicken. I can't believe it...they just killed this innocent child...He had nothing to do with this entire mess and they just killed him without thinking twice...

What kind of heartless monster is Lord Fire?

"Find out who his family is, bring his body to them and kill the rest of them," Lord Fire orders Zero.

"Yes sir," Zero nods and starts to drag the kid's body in the trunk with Spyros's help.

*Wait what?* "Why kill his family!?" I yell after Lord Fire who is walking his car. "Why do this? They're innocent people!"

"My daughter was innocent," Lord replies quietly.

Is he seriously using this as an excuse to kill people?

"That kid and his family had nothing to do with what happened to Aelita, he doesn't even know!" I argue.

"He went against what you've done and tried to kill you," Lord Fire glares at me. "I know he's innocent son, I know that damn well, but I need to send a message to everyone who tries to side with those animals. If you didn't know, a gang squad has been giving weapons to those animals so they could protect themselves. They're siding with them. I had to slaughter all of them including their families and children to send a message to all the gangs out there not to make this same mistake. This kid is doing the same thing. He is defending those animals. Whether he knows what happened and why you did it or not is not my problem. I am doing this so I can send a message to the community to not side or affiliate themselves with my enemies. That's the point of this."

But the child was innocent...

"Son, this is how I deal with things and people who stand in my way. Get used to it. Now if you'll excuse me, I have an important meeting to go to," he says and gets into his flimo.

I am left standing there frozen...I can't believe Lord Fire reasons that way. It's wrong, it's so wrong on so many level...he just killed that kid without even thinking twice...

"You don't have to come with us if you don't want to," Warr tells me minutes later. He is talking as if nothing happened, as if it was nothing killing this innocent child. I trusted him to be a person with a conscience...and he turns out to be otherwise. They're all the same. They're not humans. "We can get a cab to get you from here,"

"How can you be so calm about this?" I ask him with disbelief and disgust.

He shrugs and simply says. "I'm a killer. That's what I do."

"Kill innocent people?" I glare at him. "Does that sound right to you?"

"Killing is wrong either way," he replies. "It doesn't matter whether the victim is innocent or not. Taking any human being's life is a despicable thing to do."

I am even more confused. "Then why do you do it?" I look at him.

He doesn't answer the question. "Sir, would you like me to call you a cab?"

I glare at him. They're really going to kill his entire innocent family just to send a message? Over my dead body. I will not let this happen. "I'm coming with you."

We're in the car and Zero is looking for the address of the child. I am trying to talk to them, to reason them, to tell them not to do this, to think it over...that they already killed the kid. It is enough, but they are all ignoring me, saying that it's what Lord Fire wants.

I shake my head. No, I won't let them kill any more innocent people.

We're in front of a house, It two blocks away from Lazar's. We all get out and Zero opens the trunk and with Spyros's help, he drags the body out.

"It's not too late to change your mind, guys...we can just scare the family and tell them this is what happens when they mess with the Lord. We don't have to kill them."

"Mr. Ice," Zero tells me now annoyed. "This is what Lord Fire wants."

"And I don't want this!" I glare at Zero. How could he be such a sweet loving, caring man toward my wife and a cold hearted killer at the same time? How...can a human being be like this? I don't understand!

"We don't work for you, " Zero retorts.

We're in front of the house and Spyros is knocking at the door. I am sweating and very nervous.

"We can drop the child here and just leave guys..." I say again, desperately trying to convince them to stop. They all ignore me.

I have to stop them.

No one answers, so Spyros barges in. We're in the living room and there's a woman breastfeeding a baby.

Oh no.

"What the-" The mother says and then she sees her dead son being thrown on the floor and she starts to scream.

"Hugo!" she shrieks and starts to cry. "What have you done!?" she starts screaming at us. "Who are you people!? What has my son done to you!?"

"We're under Lord Fire's orders, ma'm. Your son has been retaliating and rebelling against us and we're ordered to annihilate him and his entire family," Zero says.

She freezes and looks down her dead boy confused. "Rebel? Retaliate? What has he ever done...? He's just eleven years old! He's a child! Oh no...!" she is sobbing, and the baby starts to scream too. I feel broken and hurt inside.

"Is there anyone else in the house ma'am?" Zero asks.

"No..." the mother is sobbing and crying her son's name.

Spyros goes and makes a tour of the house and comes back and shakes his head.

"Where is your husband, ma'm?"

She doesn't answer. Zero points the gun at her baby and I stiffen.

"Don't Zero..." I beg him.

"He's at work!" the mother cries. "Please don't hurt my baby..."

"Where does he work at?" Zero asks indifferently. His voice is so cold.

"At the pastry shop across the street..." she is sobbing.

When they get what they want from her, they are ready to shoot her, but I can't let that happen.

Warr is standing next to me and I see a gun in the back on his pant so I quickly grab it and point the gun at Zero.

"Don't Zero," I tell him. He is still pointing the gun at the mother and her crying child.

"Please...don't kill us...we didn't...do anything..." the woman is sobbing, scared.

"Zero please," I beg. It's not right what they're doing. I know they know this. I know Zero knows this...if Aelita trusts Zero, then that means he might be more than just a cold hearted killer. He has to have a good heart, he can't just–

Before I even know it, Warr grabs the gun from me and grabs me, keeping me from getting closer to Zero.

"NO!" I scream at Zero. "Don't do it!"

But he doesn't listen to me. He pulls the trigger and kills both the mother and her baby...

I fall on the floor and look at their bodies in disbelief...This is not happening...this is not happening...this is a nightmare.

*Why?*

How can Zero, Warr and Spyros slaughter an innocent family without even feeling bad? What makes them any different than the animals...What makes Lord Fire any different from them? What makes *me* any different from killing Sony and Kenna?

What...?

"Sorry Mr. Ice. It had to be done," Warr is trying to console me, attempting to touch my shoulder but I violently shrug it away, get up and walk out of the house.

I need a friend. I need someone who is sane and who has a good heart. I need Nadia.

That's right. I'm supposed to meet her in half an hour. I don't care anymore. I know she's innocent. I'm not going to kill her. I'm not going to hurt her to get back at Cain. She's innocent and has a baby coming up. There's no way in hell that I'm going to kill her. I can't. Not after witnessing this atrocious scene.

I don't think I can hurt any more innocent lives...

I am knocking at her door.

"It's open," I hear Nadia's voice faintly say. I enter her house. She's standing in a corner far from me with a gun in her hand.

"Close the door please," she tells me.

"Nadia, what are you doing?" I ask her carefully after closing the door.

"Don't take another step toward me," she points the gun at me. I raise my hands up in the air.

"Nadia-"

"Please shut up!" she says, tears trailing down her face. She is shaking.

"I'm not going to turn on Cain. He's family," she says.

I nod. "Okay," anything to get her to put that gun away.

"And, I'm not going to let you torture me or kill me and my child," she says.

I shake my head. "I won't, I promise."

"Liar, you were so angry and hateful toward me yesterday," she yells, clicking the gun.

"Because I was hurt that Cain had something to do with Aelita's assault and since you were related to him, I thought you were his accomplice and I am so sorry Nadia, I wasn't thinking...this whole week has been a nightmare to me."

"I can imagine," she says, still pointing the gun at me. "But I'm still going to get tortured."

"I won't hurt you," I promise her.

"If you don't hurt me, Aelita's father will!" She yells and shakes her head. "You're all hurt and angry and want revenge, I get that...but I'm not going to be your punch bag. I'm not going to be just a piece of your sick games. I refuse to die in your hands."

"Nadia, what do you mean?"

She points the gun to her head. "I mean I'm not going to let you make me suffer," then she pulls the trigger and kills herself.

I am shaking. "NADIA!" I scream and rush toward her unconscious body! "NADIA! Oh God...why...why you!?" I start to sob. "Why Nadia..." I am crying holding her body and cursing.

Why is all this happening? Why am I witnessing all of this? I don't get it...why am I always the one who make people suffer? Why do I bring pain in everyone's heart...Why?

God why?! Why is everyone I care about dying...?

Nadia...oh no. Why Nadia? Why? It's all because of me...

I don't get this...I don't get this...I don't want to be part of this world anymore. I don't want to have anything to do with all of this... I can't. I'm not a survivor. I've witnessed too much today.

I place a goodbye kiss on her forehead and I grab the gun from the floor and shove it in my mouth.

This is what I want. If I die, I won't hurt anyone else...Lord will get revenge and take care of the rapists and without me in this world, Aelita will be happier and will move on from this tragedy. My presence brings everyone pain.

I want this.

It's for the best.

I close my eyes and pull the trigger.

Nothing happens.

I pull again and again and nothing still happens...so I look inside the gun and notice there's no bullet left. She had only one bullet just for herself...

I begin to sob and stay by her side for an hour. She is innocent and still had to die...

I don't understand. Where is God or Karma or justice or the damn Forest dog? Why couldn't he save her? He saved Aelita and I...why not save Nadia...why not?

I feel my phone buzz in my pocket. I pick it up and the caller ID is Hinata. I answer and she sounds very alarmed.

"Mr. Ice!" she starts, her voice is panicking.

I stiffen and get up, letting go of Nadia's dead body. Please, I hope nothing bad happened to Aelita either...I can't make it through this day if something happens to her...

"What is it, Hinata?"

"It's Mrs. Ice. She's missing!"

My heart stops.

"Where are you right now?"

"I'm still at the park looking around for her."

"Don't move. I'll be right there," I say and hang up. I turn around and look at Nadia's dead body. "I'm sorry..." I tell her before leaving the apartment.

My attention is completely on Aelita. I take a cab and rush to the cherry blossom park. I call Zero and the rest and tell them about Aelita missing. They are going to meet me there.

"Oh thank goodness you're here!" Hinata says when she sees me.

"What happened to my wife?" I glare at her.

She stiffens and begins to shake. "I-I don't k-know...I just went to the bathroom for a minute and when I came back, she was nowhere to be found..."

"Shit," I hear Zero say. He is there as well with Warr and Spyros.

"Alright, let's all look for her around the place," Zero starts. "She must be close by since she's in the wheelchair. Maybe she's wandering alone. I'll look in the woods. Warr, you look around the four entrances and stores nearby with Spyros. Hinata, go check the restrooms," he then turns to me

"I'm coming with you in the woods," I tell him. He doesn't argue.

We all start to search for Aelita. I am worried and scared and sad for her, for everyone...for all the innocent people who died today...for Nadia. I still cannot believe she's dead. I still cannot believe the innocent family was slaughtered just like that...Today was horrible, it is almost as worse as what happened a week ago with Aelita.

As I think about what happened to Aelita, I shiver. She was the most innocent in this entire mess and they were so brutal to her...She suffered the most. Whatever I witnessed last Friday with her was in fact worse than what I've witnessed today. I can't still compare this kind of pain I feel for my wife to anything...I need to find Aelita and hug her and tell her I love her. I need her to be okay. I need her to talk to me. I need her to be my light in this dark world...I need Aelita.

And I find her.

I find my wife. She's deep in the woods sitting on the floor with someone else. She's with the man who raped and shot her last Friday.

She's smiling at him. She never smiled at me since the incident.

She's talking to him. She never uttered a word to me.

She's caressing his face.

I clench my jaws and I feel something starting to build up inside of me. All the emotions I have been holding back, all the anger, sadness, sorrow and frustration coil together into something dark and dangerous. I've been going through hell, and people are dying for her sake and here she is flirting with the enemy.

Hanging out with Zero is one thing...But bonding with Hunter...

For the first time since the incident, I feel something negative toward her. I am enraged, and she is the reason. I feel something strike inside me.

I go berserk.

# 15

I growl so low that I think I am sounding like a wolf. My eyes are glaring so hard at those two.

"Mr. Ice, where are you going?" Zero calls after me but when he looks at the direction I'm going in, I hear him faintly gasp and curse.

"Guys, she's over here!" Zero shouts in the background.

I pace toward them and the worse part is they haven't noticed me. What the fuck is wrong with Aelita Fire? What is this girl's problem?

"Get away from her!" I snarl as I finally reach Hunter and Aelita. I am in between them and I violently push Hunter away with so much strength that his body collides against a tree. I glare at him with a murderous intent and at the same time, I am breathing nervously.

Sudden memories of last Friday night crawl into my mind. I remember being tied up, I remember being forced to watch Aelita get brutally raped by him in front of me...I remember crying, begging, screaming and trashing around. My breathing suddenly quickens in fear again. I remember him telling me he had to kill her and made me watch as he shot her in cold blood...

I...I...

"Mrs. Ice! Thank God you're alright!" I hear Hinata shout and I am back in reality. Zero, Spyros and Warr are circling Hunter.

I pull myself together and turn back to Aelita.

I glare at her with fury.

She's not looking at me.

"Hinata," my voice is quiet. I am seething as I glare down at Aelita. "Take my saint wife back home," I am talking to Hinata but hissing at Aelita. "I will deal with her later."

"Y-yes sir..." Hinata stutters and helps Aelita on the wheelchair. Aelita is still not staring at me, but I can tell that she is displeased with the way I am talking. My gaze doesn't break from her as Hinata is pushing her out of the woods. I tighten my jaws and inhale. My back is turned from the monster.

"Sir," Zero's tone is so angry. I can tell he is controlling his wrath as well. "What do we do with him?"

"I-I'm s-sorry..." Hunter starts. His voice is bringing back those memories again. I don't want to go back to those memories...I don't want to recall any of this. I don't want to feel the way I've felt before. I am not afraid or traumatized or desperate anymore.

I am angry, enraged and bloodthirsty. I am not afraid of Hunter. I am not afraid of that bastard.

"Shut up," I turn around and glare at him. I take few steps toward him and he is trembling. That's right. He is the one who is supposed to be scared. The tables have turned now.

I grab him by the throat and lift him up and I squeeze him so tightly that I can hear and feel the pulse on his neck slowing down. He's suffering, he's gasping. I smirk as I am enjoying his reaction.

That fucker has some balls, talking to my wife and letting her touch him...as if nothing ever happened. He's acting as if he never did anything wrong, as if they used to be friends...that sick mother-fucking bastard. I hold on to him a little tighter and when I feel his eyes roll back, I know he's on the verge of losing consciousness and probably die.

No, I won't let him take the easy way out.

I let him go, and he falls on the floor and starts to cough.

"Round him and his whole family up and call me when they're all together," I growl at Zero and start walking away. I need to knock some serious sense in my very delicate, angelic wife.

"Where are you going, sir?" Zero asks, fearing that his guess might be right.

"To solve a domestic problem," I grunt then stop. "Bring Veronica as well," then I walk away.


"Where is she?!" I growl as I am storming inside our house.

"Sir...please, calm down..." Hinata tells me. "She's very sorry of what she's done. Please don't be mad at her."

"Where is she, Hinata?" I turn to her, grab her and shake her violently. My eyes are blazing with fury. I know Hinata will die of a heart attack due to my very intimidating, deadly gaze.

"In th-the TV room..." Hinata stutters. I let go of her and storm in the TV room which is on the first floor. I glance up and see Mrs. Fire coming downstairs. She looks confused.

"What is going on here?" she asks, but I ignore her and rush in the TV room.

Aelita is sitting in her wheelchair and looking out the window, her face is calm and composed.

Oh, she thinks this is a game?

I storm toward her. "What is the matter with you!?" I roar at her. She is not even moving or flinching or turning around.

"Did you hit your head? Do you have a fever? What is the matter with you, Aelita? Why were you talking to him!?"

She is still not acknowledging me, which makes me lose the tiny glimpse of patience I have left for her. I brusquely turn her wheelchair and make her face me. She is still looking away, avoiding eye-contact.

Tsk.

I lean forward, and trap her in her seat, both my hands on either side of her wheelchair. "What. Is. The. Matter. With. You?"

Still no answer.

I am becoming less patient and more furious. "So you will talk to him and still won't talk to me huh?!" I shout.

Still no reactions. She is looking away, but her face is not calm anymore. It's slightly frowning and wincing at the sharpness of my icy tone.

"ANSWER ME!" I roar. Her whole body winces then and I retrieve myself from her to calm down a bit. I run my hand through my hair with frustration.

I can't tell what she's thinking. I don't know what's going through her weird mind and she still won't talk to me.

"Why are you doing this!?" I yell at her again. "Why are you being nice to him, Aelita? Are you out of your fucking mind? Did you forget what he did to you? Did you really forget? Are you having memory loss or something? Aelita?! Hey, I'm talking to you!"

She grips the end of her dress tightly, but still not talking. I can read her facial expression. She's not sorry for what she just did.

*Why?*

"I want to slap you right now, Aelita. Really bad. And I want to shake you so hard that your brain readjusts itself so you can snap out of it!"

I am trying to understand that crazy wife of mine. Yes, she always forgives and forgets. That is in her nature. Since elementary school, every time she gets bullied or hurt, she immediately forgives the person. I get that she's has a gentle heart, but this is not the time. Those people don't deserve her forgiveness.

"This isn't high school anymore, Aelita." I continue to severely scold her. "Hunter is not just some bully you can forgive easily! HE RAPED AND TRIED TO KILL YOU!" My voice is rising. She winces again and then shakes her head as if she doesn't want to continue listening to my lecture. She starts rolling her wheelchair and moves past me, toward the exit.

I take a firm hold of the end of the wheelchair and this time, violently turn the wheelchair back toward me so I can yell at her louder. My words need to reach this girl's brain.

"SO WHAT THE FUCK HAVE YOU BEEN ANGRY FOR THESE PAST DAYS? HUH? IF YOU'RE GOING TO EASILY FORGIVE HIM AND TALK TO HIM AND FLIRT WITH HIM WHY THE FUCK HAVE YOU BEEN ACTING ANGRY AND DESTROYING EVERYTHING? IS IT FOR ATTENTION?"

She glares up at me. She's finally looking at me with her eyes—those deep honey brown eyes that I am not recognizing anymore. I feel like I'm talking to a stranger.

"Do you have any idea what everyone has been going through FOR YOU?!"

"What the hell is going here?" I hear Mrs. Fire hiss in the background. I turn toward her and she is glaring at me with a murderous intent. "Why are you yelling at my child?" she demands.

I don't have time for Mrs. Fire's overprotective behavior. She's too nice to Aelita and lets her do as she pleases. She is not helping her.

"Get out," I yell at Mrs. Fire. "This is between my wife and me."

She looks at me undignified. "How dare you!?" She is about to slap me when I grab her arm.

"Ah!" she gasps not expecting that. I don't have time for her. I am way too angry and upset to deal with Mrs. Fire.

"Get out and stay out of this!" I grab her and push her out of the room, slamming the door on her. I lock the door and hear her banging at it. "Colton you better open the door! You better open it! I swear if you hurt my girl I'm going to kill you! Colton!" I ignore her and I'm glaring at Aelita again.

She is staring at me, then looking away and staring back at me and looking away again. I can tell she's nervous. "Do...do you have any idea what I've been through this week just for you?! Do you have any idea how many people have died?! HOW MANY INNOCENT LIVES HAVE BEEN BRUTALLY TAKEN JUST FOR YOU?!" I storm toward her. "I'VE JUST WATCHED A KID DIE TODAY, HIM AND HIS ENTIRE FAMILY BECAUSE OF THIS MESS! THEY HAD NOTHING TO DO WITH THIS!" I step away and walk backwards as I say. "Nadia killed herself because of this!"

I hear Aelita faintly gasp.

As I think about Nadia and how she killed herself in front of me, I get angrier. "GOD DAMN IT!" I scream and begin to trash the TV room. I am throwing everything I can get a hold of, punching the wall, cursing, and finding a way to satisfy my anger toward Aelita and sadness for Nadia. But I can't. There is no way to express this dark, bitter feeling anymore. There is no way for me to control my emotions, my sanity. I mean… how can I protect and contain my only glimpse sanity when she is choosing to be insane?

Nadia just fucking killed herself because we are trying to get revenge. We're trying to avenge Aelita... "And you are just being the sweet old good hearted girl you've always been and decide to go forgive away and spread some love, huh?" I mutter at her, my voice is dangerously quiet. She is still not talking to me.

Tsk!

I race toward her and I am all over her face, giving her no room to turn her head around.

"Have you by any chance forgotten what happened? Have you forgotten what he did to you? Do I need to remind you how he stripped you naked in front of me and pushed you down the floor and fucked you brainless?!" she is wincing and her eyes are tearing up.

"Do I need to remind you how loud you were screaming when those guys rammed themselves inside of you? Spit on you and called you names? Remember Aelita! Remember that night! REMEMBER!"

She is shaking her head and trying to move away from me, but I am not letting her go anywhere. If I need to scare her shitless so she can understand how dangerous Hunter is, I fucking will. "Come on," I grab her wrist and pull her up from her wheelchair. "Get up! Walk!" I order her. I let go of her hand and she winces and I see how painful it is for her to walk, she stumbles and falls on the floor.

I brush away my worry and my instinct to help her and instead I shout. "It hurts to walk, right? Your body is still in pain, isn't? Does it not ring a bell, huh Aelita?"

She doesn't answer.

"If that doesn't ring a bell, why don't you come here, I'll show you yourself!"

I lean down and grab her hand and pull her up and force her to stand in front of the large mirror that is in the corner of the TV room. I furiously undo her pink waist wrap and let her kimono unravel. Her body is exposed, with her black bra and deep pink underwear. I am behind her, holding her in place as we're both staring at our reflection in the tall mirror.

"Look at yourself!" I command. She is trembling under my hold as I yank down her bra, exposing her full breasts. They are still amazing, but covered with bruises.

"Look at your breasts, Aelita! They did this to you! Look at your body! Remember what they did to you!" I hiss in her ear angrily. She still doesn't say anything, although I can see how pleading her eyes are. She wants me to stop.

Well not until I am sure she understands that Hunter is an enemy and not until I remind her what she's been through and what he did to her. Not until I get all that in that thick skull of hers!

I suddenly have an idea.

The tape.

That's right, the tape. The copy of the tape I stole from the box Jago gave me. I took one copy before Zero took the whole box away. I always keep it with me, all the time. I tell myself I'd watch it to punish myself, to motivate myself to hurt those guys in the worse ways possible. I've never watched it because I am too scared and do not want to relive those moments. At the same time, I do not want to get rid of it. So I carry it with me all the time in the pockets of my jacket. Every time when I am put my hands in my pockets, I can feel the tape and it reminds me of what happened to her.

Now I'm going to play it. And I will make her watch.

"Maybe this will knock some sense in you," I say and let her go. She crumbles on the floor while I walk toward the TV, insert the disk in the DVD player and turn on the TV.

Her rape scene starts to play and I stare at her. She looks at it in horror.

"Your rapists recorded this. Hunter tried to blackmail us with it. He threatened to show this to the whole entire world so everyone could see you," I snarl at her. She shakes her head furiously and starts to cry.

"Watch it," I command her. "I need you to remember and re-live that moment."

She shakes her head and covers her ears with her hands. Then, she closes her eyes.

"No, you don't!" I rush toward her, grabbing her face in my hands.

"Watch!" I tell her.

"No..." she says faintly.

Oh! She speaks! "Now you're talking to me?" I say sarcastically, but I am still forcing her to face the TV. I know this is cruel of me, but I really have to do anything to make her understand how bad and evil those guys are. I need her to see that.

"Watch, Aelita!" I growl at her.

"No," She refuses more forcefully, her eyes tightly shut.

"WATCH WHAT HE DID TO YOU! WATCH IT! YOU NEED TO REMEMBER WHAT A MONSTER HE IS! YOU NEED TO REMEMBER HOW HORRIBLE AND HOW BROKEN YOU WERE AND STILL ARE-" I am fuming at her.

She finally opens her eyes and glares back at me with so much anger, hatred and accusation and with a very loud, bitter tone, she yells back. "HE IS NOT THE ONE I BLAME FOR ALL THIS!"

I freeze at the sound of that and let go of her as she angrily backs away from me. She furiously crawls toward the TV and turns it off. I smile painfully at myself. *Ah, I'm the one she blames.* So this is how she feels about me huh? This is why she's been ignoring me, not talking to me, not acknowledging me. She hates me. I suspected that for a long time, but never really wanted to believe it. She hates me for all this. Aelita blames me. *Okay...*

I nod my head painfully. "You blame me," I tell her as she is wrapping her kimono back and glaring at me. She is not trembling anymore. It is as if she is completely relieved after telling me this. It's as if she has been waiting to tell me this for a long time. "That's fine," I continue. I am calm now, but that doesn't change anything. "You have every right to."

I walk toward her. She's sitting on the floor and glaring up at me. It hurts a lot. She never used to glare at me or hate me before all this. No matter how much of an ass, of a bully, of a bossy mean friend I was to her in high school. No matter how much I ignored her during our marriage, she never once gave me such a dirty angry, hateful look. But still, I can't let her hate me and think her rapists are the good guys in the story.

"However," I crouch down and look at her dead in the eyes. "I am not the only one to blame here, Aelita.

Hunter and the four other guys chose to hurt you. They could have hurt me instead. I didn't make them rape you. I didn't make Hunter put a bullet in your head. I am not the one who bruised your body and ruined you. They did. They chose to and they're not sorry about this. They're bad people,"

She glares at me and scoffs. "Really?"

It's so strange to hear her talk. Her voice is...unusual. It's mixed with softness and roughness, I feel like I am talking to a child and a teenager and an adult at the same time. "So you're the claiming to be the good guy in all this? Killing innocent children and family members of those guys make you the good guy?" her tone is sarcastic.

I scoff as I realize what Hunter has been telling her. He probably fed her naive brain and soft heart lies, describing how much of a monster I am so she can turn on me and ask me to stop.

*That manipulative selfish bastard.* "I do what I have to do to make them regret what they did to you," I snap at her.

She raises her eyebrow in disbelief. "So this is for me?"

I look at her and bluntly nod. "Yes, Aelita. I'm avenging you."

How can she not understand?

"Bullshit," she snarls at me and my jaw drops open and my eyes widen in horror.

Did she just curse?

Who is that woman and what the fuck has she done to my wife?

"Now you watch your mouth," I start to scowl her, but she doesn't let me finish. She is defying me. She is fighting back. It is as if the minute she opened her mouth she also opened the gates of hell and let the demons to possess her soul.

"I said that's bullshit!" she hisses again. I am getting angrier. I don't want to hear her talk like that, that's too painful. I rather have her mute again!

"Aelita!" I warn her.

"Bullshit! Bullshit! Bullshit!" she continues to spit out, glaring at me with those lost eyes of hers.

No...Who is that woman?

"You think you're doing this for me? By killing innocent children you're avenging me? By hurting other people you think you're doing the right thing? You're just as bad as all of them, worse, you're lower than all of them!" she degrades me.

"So you don't want them to pay for what they've done to you!?" my voice is getting louder.

"I..." she starts but then doesn't say anything else as if she is confused with herself as well.

"Aelita, whether you like it or not, those guys need to be hurt, tortured and killed for what they've done to you, my wife. This is justice!"

"Revenge is not justice. You just feel the need to hurt and get back at them. You're itching to hurt them. Revenge to you is just so you can feel better about yourself! You're just doing all this for yourself!"

She looks at me with eyes colder than a windy winter and hisses "You're not doing anything for me! You're doing all this for yourself! Because your pride has been hurt! You just want to hurt all of them because they hurt you, they made you cry and they made you feel low. This isn't about me!"

I look at her pained and offended. That is not true. Heavens know that is not true.

"You don't care about me, Colton! You never did, you don't now and you never will!" she continues while crying. "You just care about your own little pride!"

"That's not true..." I tell her softly.

"You never once cared about me!" she starts to cry while yelling at me. "All I ever did was love you! All I ever known, the reason I could wake up every day and put a smile on my face and seize the day was because I loved you! I wanted nothing; *nothing* at all but your happiness...and you...you just don't care! You never cared about me! You never will!"

"Be quiet..." I beg her.

"You've always seen me as a burden! You were probably relieved when he shot me, right? So you didn't have to deal with me anymore right?"

"Be quiet," I tell her again, my heart is clenching and aching at her cruel words.

"You probably thought about getting remarried to some girl who's ten times prettier than me and who can talk and socialize and be fierce right? I was never your type and you hate me for it...you hate me for surviving...you want me to die, you hate me don't you!?"

"NO I DON'T! I AM IN LOVE WITH YOU!" I roar at her and find myself pushing her down on the floor and claiming her lips with mine.

She is still and frozen beneath me as I am kissing her. This is the second time I've ever kissed her in my entire life and this time, her lips are still soft but they're missing something.

They're missing warmth and gentleness. Aelita's body is always warm whenever she's around me...but now all I feel is coldness. She doesn't love me anymore.
She is struggling under me, trying to refuse the kiss. It seems like she is struggling with herself more than she is struggling with me. It's as if she is trying to decide whether she wants to let me in her heart again.

My kiss is begging her for a second chance, for a bit of understanding. I am begging for the old Aelita to come back, to not hate me. My tongue is pressing on her lips, asking for entrance. I want to explore her mouth and her body, I want her.

I feel as if she is still struggling and still trying to decide. I can feel her hands on my chest, trying to push me away, but then I realize for a moment that she is still, and her hands are not pushing me back anymore. Her lips are slowly and tentatively moving against mine and I feel her submitting to this kiss.

I grunt and deepen the kiss, adjusting myself on her and running my hands through her golden curly hair. For a moment, the world stops around me. I forget everything that happened and everything that I witnessed today. I forget about Lord Fire and Mrs. Fire and Zero and Hunter and Nadia and Cain and my company and who I am...all I am focusing on are her and her soft, tasty sweet lips. Kissing Aelita Ice is the best thing on earth.

Suddenly, I feel her tense up beneath me as if she is realizing what she's doing with me. She pushes me away.

"No!" she gasps out and I stop.

I sit back on the floor and touch my lip. It feels warm.

"Don't..." she looks at me angrily, "don't make me fall back in l-" she is about to say something when she bites her tongue and looks away. There's so much regret in her eyes. "Get out, please," she tells me.

My heart is breaking. It's really over huh? I can never have Aelita love me again, can I? She is really over me...huh.

"Fine," I say quietly, getting up. "I'm sorry about the kiss."

No, I'm so not.

"I'll leave you alone from now on, however," I look at her seriously. "You're going to stay away from Hunter and all of them. If you want to go outside, you will take two guards with you. I will make sure of that. If you don't want any guards to follow you, then stay home. I am not going to let you anywhere near those guys again. It will be over my dead body."

She doesn't say anything. She is looking away with sadness in her eyes.

My eyes soften painfully as well. This is goodbye. I probably won't see her until I die. "Goodbye, Aelita." I tell her softly and walk out.

# 16

## HUNTER CROSS'S POINT OF VIEW

"Hey, this is a mistake! I am not affiliated with him or his family! Please let me go!" Veronica is shouting at the guards.

We're brought and locked up in a dark room in an abandoned building. It has been twenty four hours since we have been locked in here. It's me, Veronica, my little brother Noah and my grandfather. Veronica is panicking, going ballistic and is out of her mind. She has been yelling and begging and crying for the guards to let her go. She has been cursing me out, yelling at me, telling me that it's my entire fault.

My grandfather is just as confused as well. He doesn't know why the hell they pulled him out of work or what he did wrong. He doesn't know anything, and he's asking me questions, asking me what's going on. I am too numb from fear to answer anyone.

Noah is asleep. He has been unconscious since they brought him with us. The guards were nice enough not to wake him up after I told them about his condition. I am scared for them. I am scared for what's going to happen to us.

When Mr. Ice caught me talking to Aelita, I could see the amount of hate and desire for blood in his eyes. I did not mean to upset anyone or add salt to the wound. I didn't even know he was around. I was just talking to Aelita, begging for mercy for my family. She told me she would do whatever she could so no more innocent people would get hurt. She was too kind, too nice to me. I still don't get why or how she could behave this way to someone who made her life miserable.

I still feel as if it is a sin to beg her for forgiveness and I feel even more horrible that she forgives me, but this is for Noah and my grandfather and Veronica. I don't want them to suffer for what I've done.

"This is so unfair!" Veronica whines, sitting back down far away from me, Noah and grandfather.

"Veronica, please calm down..." I tell her softly.

"SHUT UP!" she yells at me. "DON'T EVER TALK TO ME!"

"Hey!" my grandfather says. "Have some respect for your husband."

"Shut up, old man," Veronica yells back at him.

Grandpa shakes his head and turns to me. "Hunter, what is going on? Why are we all locked up here?"

I sigh.

I don't know how to tell him that I've messed up. That we might all die today. I just want it to be quick.

"You wanna know why?" Veronica scoffs. "It's because of your stupid grandson! He's going to get all of us killed! He raped and killed the daughter of Lord Fire! Now the Lord and the husband want all of us dead and wiped out!"

Grandpa frowns and looks at me with disbelief.

"Is...that...true, big brother?" Noah asks me.

I turn and look down on the floor next to me where Noah's body is lying. He's awake and staring at me with a very sad expression on his face. My heart clenches with guilt and I look away.

"Is...that…what...you've…been...trying…to…tell me...yesterday?"

I can't say anything.

"Answer him, Hunter!" Grandpa demands. "Answer me!"

Tears start to roll down my face as I painfully nod and admit. "Yes...it's true. I'm...so sorry...." I start to sob. I am so ashamed and so mortified to admit something so horrible to them. Noah has always seen the best in me. He has always looked up to me even though I always mess up. This time I don't think he'll be able to forgive me. This time I don't think he'll be able to see past this and forget. I've done something so horrible.

"That's...really...bad....Hunter," Noah says. "Really...bad..."

"Noah, don't waste your breath on him!" Grandpa tells him while glaring at me. "I can't believe you would do something this horrible! You're just like your father! You're abusive and a murderer!"

I am sobbing, not daring to look up. I am so mortified.

"Every bad action you take always ends up hurting us!" Grandpa continues, he is really angry. I can feel his voice cracking as if he's about to cry. "Why are you such a reckless child? You've stolen money, and it led to your brother not being able to go through surgery and suffer! You've abandoned him on his birthday and that lead him to ending up in a coma for almost a year! And now you...you go hurt someone else's daughter and your brother and I still have to pay the consequences of your actions! Why?" he starts to sob. "Why..."

"It's okay, Hunter..." Noah starts. "I know...you...didn't mean....to...hurt...anyone...you...never do..."

I sob even harder. No, I don't want him to forgive me. I don't deserve it. I don't want his forgiveness...Grandpa is right. I bring pain and suffering to everyone near me. Everyone I know always ends up paying for the consequences of my actions.

"Hey..." Noah continues and I feel his hand touching mine. He weakly squeezes it. "It's...going to be... okay..." he says with tears filling his eyes.

"No, nothing is going to be okay!" Veronica shouts crying harder. She's trembling. "Noah, I get that you always see the bright side of everything but there's no fucking bright side in this mess. Colton is crazy! He's a psychopath! You haven't seen how he killed...he butchered...he..." she can't speak anymore. She is shaking violently and is very traumatized. All because of me.

Damn it.

"We're all going to die..." Grandpa sighs wiping away the tears from his face. "We're all going to die because of you, Hunter."

"Grandpa...stop...it," Noah scowls him. "Stop...fighting..." And then we're all quiet and we're crying silently. It's all because of me...

We've been seating and waiting in the room for hours and finally the door opens and a guard comes in. I stiffen and my heart starts to beat.

It's time...

"Mr. Ice wants to talk to you," the redheaded guard tells me coldly. "Let's go."

I swallow and nod and I am about get up but Noah's hand grabs onto mine.

"No...don't...go..." he says. He sounds scared

I smile at him. "I have to."

"I...want...to come with you...." he tries to get himself up but I don't let him.

"Hey," I say silently. "I'll be okay, just relax..."

"Let's go!" the guard snaps impatiently.

I squeeze Noah's hands in mine really tight once more and I say. "I love you,"

He starts to silently cry and he's shaking his head. "No...don't...go..."

I stand up and nod at Veronica and Grandpa. Maybe it might be the last time I see them.

"Move!" the guard tells me, pushing me out of the room.

I am sweating and my breathing is starting to pace. I wonder what Mr. Ice wants to tell me. He probably wants to see me cry and beg for him not to kill any more innocent lives...and then right after that, he'll probably make me kill one of my family members and make me eat them like he did to Lazar? Or make me kill them all myself...?

My brain is frying as I am thinking of all the worse things he can possibly make me do.

I'm pushed in another room. It looks like an office. He is seating on the executive chair and his eyes are lost in thought. They're sad and broken and filled with so much angst. This man is a very sad person. I feel bad for him. I wonder what happened between him and Aelita after they left yesterday.

"Take a seat," he tells me quietly. I do as I'm told and seat across him. The only thing shielding me from Colton Ice is the office desk. He finally turns to look at me. The eyes suddenly transform from sadness and sorrow to hatred and resentment. I feel as if I am being hypnotized by him. I feel like a fly, trapped into a spider's web and I cannot escape this trap. He hates me.

He wants to see me suffer the most, he wants to see me scream and cry and beg for mercy.

He hates me.

He wants to replace my laughter with cries, my peace of mind with terror.

He hates me.

Just from looking at his eyes, I can feel something dark and scary and unholy penetrating my body and my soul and terrorizing it. I see the devil when I look at him. He hates me so much that he's itching to decimate me and everything that is related to me. I can see his suffering, and his blood thirst. I can feel it deep in the core of my soul. I see the desire for genocide in his eyes. I am very much doomed.

"So I had a very interesting conversation with my wife yesterday," he startles me with the calmness in his voice. I am expecting him to growl or snarl or roar at me, but he sounds very composed, very quiet. "Why did you tell her about all this? Answer me honestly."

It makes him even more intimidating.

"I don't like the idea of innocent people paying the price for what we've done," I answer him truthfully. I am trying very hard not to stutter.

"Ah," he says again quietly. "You don't like the idea of innocent people paying the price for what you've done."

I nod. "No sir."

"Then why did you rape and tried to kill Aelita?" he is not being sarcastic. He is asking me truthfully as if he wants to understand me.

"..." I look down with regret. I don't know how to answer this.

"Answer me, Hunter. I want to hear your reasoning," he demands again quietly.

I swallow and look up "I...I wanted to see you suffer. I wanted to wipe the smile off your face...I wanted to terrorize you and make you pay for what you've done to my marriage with Veronica."

He is quiet for a moment then he chuckles and shakes his head. "So you understand why I am killing innocent people that are dear to you,"

I nod. "I'm very sorry for what I've done to Mrs. Ice," I say with honesty. I really am. If I could go back in time and take everything back, if I could just start over, I would. I really am sorry for what I've done to her. "I deserve to suffer in your arms, I deserve to have my smile wiped off my face, I deserve to be terrorized and I deserve all the hate you have for me. I deserve to burn in hell. I deserve everything horrible in this world and in the next. I am prepared to pay for my mistake. I am prepared to take responsibility. White Stone deserves it too, Hidon as well, and Lazar deserved to be butchered the way you butchered him in the video...but...his family and children did not," I say quietly. "They have not harmed you. The children didn't know anything about you or what we've done to your wife. Neither does Stone's girlfriend. Neither does Hidon's girlfriend, neither does my family, my brother, my grandfather. Please, Mr. Ice, I am begging you. Please don't harm anymore innocent people...please."

He listens to me calmly, clears his throat and then nods. "Alright,"

My eyes widen in disbelief. Is he serious?

"You're right. Innocent people don't deserve this, but I still want to see you watch someone you love suffer right before your eyes while you're helpless, begging and screaming for mercy. I need you to feel exactly how I felt before," he starts. His voice is somber. "So this is what I've decided. I'm going to let you choose one person out of the three to get beaten to death today while you watch."

I hold my breath.

"It can either be Veronica, or your grandfather or your brother," he continues. "Once the person dies, I'll let you all go and I won't hurt them ever again. I won't lay a finger on any more innocent lives. I give you my word. I just need you to sacrifice one of your loved ones for the sake of many."

What? I can't...I can't make that choice...I can't choose to hurt Veronica or grandpa or Noah...no! No I can't do that. I love them all.

I can't.

No...

"It's all up to you. If you don't sacrifice one of them, I'll kill them all in front of you and I'll continue to kill other family members as well and their deaths will be all on you," he shrugs indifferently. It is as if he doesn't care. Either way, I'll suffer. Either way he'll be satisfied. "Warr, Spyros, Zero," he says and suddenly the door opens and three guards come. They have each a baseball bat made of iron in their hands.

I stiffen as I realize they're going to beat one of my family member to death with this.

"Let's all go enjoy the show, shall we?" Mr. Ice stands up from his chair and smiles at me bitterly.

I stand up and reluctantly follow them out. I am leading the way and they're behind me as we're walking toward the room my family is locked in.

"I'd pick Veronica if I were you," I hear Ice tell me as one of the guards unlocks the door. "She's not innocent. She knew about the rape and I plan to make her life miserable if she gets out. What I have planned for her is much worse and much more gruesome than being beaten to death and it will be in front of you since you like her so much. It's in your best interest to choose her instead of your brother or your grandfather who, like you said, have nothing to do with this mess."

I swallow and breathe deeply.

The door opens and we all enter. I see Noah standing up, leaning against the wall for support. He is holding his oxygen tank in his hand weakly. His eyes are filled with fear and worry for me. Grandfather is by his side and patting his back with comfort. He stiffens in fear as well as he sees me and the others. Veronica, who is rocking back and forth in the corner stiffens as well, her eyes are wide and her body is shaking even more.

"You have one minute to decide who," Mr. Ice tells me and waits by the door with the guards.

My whole entire body is trembling as I walk toward my family. Veronica stands up from the corner and joins us.

"What's going on?" She asks me. I look at them and I am breathing with fear. How can I choose one of them to die?

"He wants one of us dead, in exchange...everyone else who's innocent will be spared," I say quietly.

Grandpa gasps "Good Grace" but then stares at me nodding. "You."

I wish.

I shake my head. "He has a different plan for me. It has to be...either you or Veronica...or Noah."

Grandpa then says. "Alright, pick Veronica."

"What?" Veronica glares at Grandpa.

Grandpa ignores her and looks at me. "She's not family, and I bet she has something to do with all of this. We don't. I'm not going to let Noah take the fall and I'm sure as hell won't die for any of you two."

I stare at Veronica who is looking at me with pleading eyes. "I'm sorry..." I tell her.

"No," she starts to cry.

Grandpa and Mr. Ice are right. Veronica has to be the one...not just because she's not innocent in this but because Mr. Ice told me he has something worse planned for her if she gets out alive.

I can't allow that.

"We pick Veronica!" Grandpa nods at the guards and one of them walks toward us.

"Please Hunter," she pleads, and it is breaking my heart. I don't want her to die...But I have no choice...

The guard comes and grabs Veronica, pulling her away from me as she is grabbing onto me. "Please Hunter! Please! Please!" she cries. "HUNTER! HUNTER!"

I turn my head away. I don't want to hear her scream for my name... It's too painful...

"Pick me..." I hear my little brother pant.

I open my eyes and look at him in disbelief. He is between Veronica and the guard. Veronica holds him tightly and is trembling.

"Noah, what are you doing!?" I yell at him.

"Noah, no!" Grandpa says at well.

"I'm...sorry..." Noah starts, he is glaring at Colton. "I don't give...a shit who you...are...or how...scary you are...you're...a coward...I can't let you...hurt a girl...you don't...get to...make...that call...so I...volunteer."

"NO!" I refuse, my eyes widening in shock.

No, Noah! No! Please! No!

"Sorry...brother...I just...can't let...the woman...you love...die..." he starts, he is silently crying. "I...am as...good…as...dead...anyways...plus...my...death...will save...many other...innocent lives...I'm happy...to be dying...for you...big brother...for something..."

"No!" I cry and I am trying to pull him but the two guards come in between and one of them is holding me and grandpa in place.

"Sir, who do I take?" the redhead guard asks Mr. Ice.

I turn to Mr. Ice and shake my head pleading him. I don't want Noah to take the fall. Please...Please...I pick Veronica ...I pick Veronica ...I rather have her die than see my brother hurt...please...

Mr. Ice looks at me with cold, unforgiving eyes. "The volunteer," he says quietly with a very cruel smirk. The guard pushes Veronica out of the way and starts to drag Noah away from us.

"NO!" I am screaming and trashing around and trying to take Noah away from them. The silver haired guard is holding me in place and so is Veronica.

"No! Please! Don't! Don't! Don't!" I yell. I don't want Noah to die! Please!

The redhead guard pushes Noah. Noah is in corner of the room and is breathing hard. His hand is holding the wall for support.

"Can't you see he's sick?! He can't! It's not fair!" Grandpa yells as they start to tie him up so he doesn't move. The silver haired guard ties Veronica up as well and the other guard is doing the same to me and I am struggling and trashing around.

"Not my problem," Mr. Ice says nonchalantly.

I am tied up, and they make me sit down on the floor across Noah. He is staring at me with a kind smile, nodding at me as if he's telling me that everything is going to be alright. Not to worry. I notice that he can't talk anymore. He is breathless and scared and cornered and trapped and he's crying too.

"He's innocent, Colton! He didn't do anything! He's just a kid! He's only seventeen years old! Please! Don't!" I beg and I am sobbing.

Colton smirks at me once more and says. "I'll tell you what, say you're a sorry good for nothing rapist twenty thousand times and I'll release your brother."

I stare at him in shock as I recall how I made him do something similar when he was begging for Aelita's safety. Colton gives me another smirk. "Eye for an eye, Hunter." he says.

The three guards grab the metal baseball bats and pull Noah in the middle of the room in front me. They are circling him, adjusting their baseball bats in their hands.

And the guard with long dark hair starts hitting him first. He hits him with the bat on his ribcage. I gasp in horror as I see Noah stumble, before falling, the other guard grabs him and pulls him back up.

Then another guard takes another hit.

Noah is crying and his face is crumbling in pain.

I get on my knees and start to plead. "I'm a sorry good for nothing rapist! I'm a sorry good for nothing rapist! I'm a sorry good for nothing rapist! I'm a sorry good for nothing rapist!"

I start to hear Noah scream loudly and cry. I look up and notice that they're hitting him harder and harder. They won't stop...

I am screaming and crying and begging and trashing around. He never did anything wrong! He doesn't deserve this! All he's ever done was love me and support me and look up to me...he never did anything wrong! Why is he the one suffering in my place? Why him? Why?

Please...no...

It's unfair...

Please stop hitting him. Please stop making him suffer...he has suffered enough!

*Please*!

They keep on beating him and his body is drawing blood. They're so cruel...three against a weak kid... that's not fair! That is not fair!

I can't live with myself anymore...I can't...I can't...Noah doesn't deserve this.

They keep on beating him in front of me. It takes less than five minute for Noah to fall down on the floor and not be able to get up again. Before he receives his deadly hit, he looks up at me. His face is swollen and bleeding and with the very last breath he has left...he manages to whispers "I love you, brother." Then they bash his skull and he loses consciousness.

"NOOO!" I scream. Grandpa is screaming and crying as well.

Even though Noah is dead, even though he isn't moving anymore, they are still beating his dead body with the baseball bats.

I glare at them and then turn to look at Colton Ice.

His eyes are already on me.

I glare at him and I feel something starting to build inside of me. All the remorse, regret and fear I had for him are all gone and they're now transformed into hate—pure hate.

I don't care anymore about what he wants. I want to avenge my brother's death. I want those three guards to pay. I want Colton Ice to suffer even more.

"Well, congratulations. No more innocent lives will be taken by me anymore," Colton says with cruel smile. He opens the door and before closing it, he tells the guards. "Set them free."

Then he leaves.

The guards untie me, my grandfather and Veronica. Grandpa rushes to Noah's broken and destroyed body and is starting to cry. My face is hard and angry. My eyes are becoming colder and colder and I feel my insides turning black. I look up and see the three guards who just beat my seventeen year old weak, defenseless and innocent brother to death and I tell them carefully.

"You can't kill me. Colton wants me dead and he'll kill me with his own hands. I will be the last one he'll want to kill, and there's nothing you can do about it," I keep in glaring in a menacing way. "Just know that before I fall into Colton's hands, I will make it my priority to find you guys hunt you, terrorize you and kill you."

# 17

## COLTON ICE'S POINT OF VIEW

I am in Lord Fire's headquarter. He has requested to see me immediately. It's probably because of Aelita. Mrs. Fire probably complained to him about how mean I was to their sweet innocent daughter.

Aelita...

I am still replaying everything she told me yesterday when I was yelling at her. She blames me for all of this. She thinks I hate her and don't care about her. She thinks I am doing all of this just for my pride. She thinks I want her dead. She thinks I don't see her as a woman worthy of my time. She hates me.

But when I was kissing her, for a brink of a second I could feel her kissing me back, I could feel her returning the same feeling I was giving her...and I thought for a moment that she still loved me.

She doesn't want to. There's nothing between us anymore. We can't be saved.

"So what happened yesterday? What did you do to my daughter?" Lord Fire asks me, his eyes are cold and angry.

I am not surprised. "Earlier yesterday, she went out for sightseeing with a servant and met Hunter, the man who raped and shot her, the man who threatened to show the videos to the whole world."

His eyes widen in shock.

"Hunter spoke to her and begged for forgiveness. He was trying to use her and ask you and I to stop getting revenge. Your daughter accepted and was smiling and talking with him as if they've been friends for a while," my expression is numb, and he is growing angrier and angrier. "I grew angry at Aelita and confronted her about it. I won't lie, I yelled at her and probably traumatized her again and made her cry but I'm not sorry for it. I can't let her–"

"Forgive those animals and let them get away with it," he finishes my sentence.

"Yes sir."

He shakes his head and sighs exasperated. "If it wasn't for the resemblance, I would never believe that Aelita was my daughter," he is frowning as if he's trying to understand something. "How can I, a cold hearted corrupted killer who's responsible for thousands of deaths and who doesn't feel sorry for it can have a child like Aelita? Someone who is the complete opposite of me... Someone so sweet, so gentle, and so innocent..." he shakes his head. "I can never understand this."

I don't say anything. I am emotionless. He looks at me and nods. "I understand why you yelled at her and tried to reason her son," he says. Then his eyes become cold again. "However, I cannot forgive you for making her cry, and grabbing wife and throwing her harshly out of the room."

Wow, Mrs. Fire did not miss a single detail of what happened.

Lord Fire is furious now. He is glaring at me with so much hatred and I can feel his body trembling. What is he going to do now? Kill me? Might as well. I got to see Hunter cry and beg...I think I'm ready to die today. He got to feel what I felt when he was hurting Aelita.

I'm a bit satisfied. What made me happier was the look he gave me after his brother died. There was so much hatred and anger and desire to hurt me. I think he's going to put up a fight.

"I don't care how nerve-wracking or how irritating Esmeralda can be. Nobody touches her," Lord Fire growls. "I am going to punish you for that." He is walking toward a table far in the back and opens the drawer. He picks up a hammer.

I feel a bit nervous.

"I'm going to break the hand you used to grab my wife, Colton. That's your punishment for touching her.

Consider it as a slap on the wrist," he takes few more steps closer. "Then, I'm going to shorten the time I gave you to destroy those animals. I gave you three months, but now that you've made my daughter cry, you've destroyed my patience and I am itching to kill you so I will give you just a month to kill all of them. However,"

*Oh what now?*

"My wife told me about how you've been avoiding her calls to see a psychologist about your hallucinations. Son, I need you sane and mentally healthy. I can't allow you to have delusions and go crazy anymore. You're in charge of killing those animals and I can't have your state of mind compromise that, therefore, after I break your arm and after the doctor puts a cast on it, you're going to be put in therapy for a week. Dr. Vancouver will be treating you and help you clear your mind. I think you need that," he gives me a smile that doesn't reach his eyes. "You're welcome."

Then he adds, "It means that technically, you have three weeks left to finish your job since you'll be using a whole entire week to heal your mind."

You've got to be fucking kidding me right? "I don't need therapy," I object.

"It's not a request son," he says sharply as he is directing me to seat on the chair in front of his desk. He slowly and gradually clears up his desk so there is nothing on it but the hammer. "I can't have seeing things that are not there while you're still alive. Believe it or not, I care about you."

I raise both eyebrows and stop myself from rolling my eyes.

"You've got no parents or family, so I take you as my responsibility."

Oh this guy needs to shut up.

"Alright, which hand did you use to grab Esmeralda, son?" he asks, the tone of his voice completely changes.

The left one, but I don't want my good hand to turn bad so I lay my right hand on the table.

"Just get it over with," I tell him coldly.

He breathes in and out. "Very well then," then he calls a guard's name. "Christopher."

A guard suddenly stands behind me and holds my hands in place on the table. Mr. Fire takes a strong hold of my arm with one hand, and with the other he takes the hammer and raises it.

"Next time you grab Esmeralda the way you did, I will cut off your arm," he growls. I look away nonchalantly. Whatever, he can do as he pleases. This pain won't hurt as much as the pain I feel inside.

I was so fucking wrong.

"AHHHHHH!" I hear myself scream and my body struggle as the hammer collides on my hand. It hurts, it hurts so fucking much. It is as if an entire building collapsed on my hand. Every nerve ending is highly stimulated, and the pain feels like a wave. It's starting from my knuckles then rushing through the whole entire length of my arm, to my shoulder, to my neck and into my brain. It is so excruciating.

And it's not even broken yet.

Christopher holds me in place as I am struggling to move my hand away. I want that fucking psycho to stop. Now!

I get another blow on my hand, this time it's an even stronger one.

"GAHH!!" I grunt and try to pick up my breathing. *Control the pain, control the pain, control the pain.* I tell myself, but it's no use. It hurts so fucking much! My whole entire body is alarmed and my arm is not just the only thing feeling the pain. My whole body, my eyes, my brain and mind are only focused on the pain I am feeling right now. Nothing else matters. Nothing else can come across my mind. All I am feeling and thinking about is the physical pain.

He slams the hammer once again on my arm, this time I can feel and hear the bones crunching and cracking. He slams again and I feel one of my broken knuckle pierce out of my hand. My hand is completely crushed and my body is shaking.

He finally stops.

No. I don't want him to stop. The pain is too addicting. I want him to continue. I want my whole body and mind to only focus on this kind of pain.

It was just like when I was kissing Aelita, when nothing else mattered. When I forgot about who we were and what happened to her and what I've done. That feeling is the same I'm having at the moment. My whole mind is liberated from all the angst, sorrow, hate, horror and heartbreak. All it is focused on is the throbbing, excruciating pain. I don't want him to stop...

No, please.

"That's enough. I think you've learned your lesson, son. Christopher will take you to the doctor in the other room and he'll treat your wound. Then you'll be sent to Dr. Vancouver's institution where you will be locked down, observed and rehabilitated for a week. I'll come to visit you when I have time," he pats me on the back and Christopher helps me stand up. My right hand is shaking and throbbing. I want to throw up.

That's fantastic. That's really fantastic. I never knew physical pain could be this addicting.

"I don't want any pain killers," I tell the doctor as he finishes casting my hand.

"Er..." he hesitates. "If I may sir, I think it will be best for you to take at least two capsules of pain killers until to arrive at your destination. I can't imagine how much pain your body is in right now."

"Don't worry about me," I dismiss the doctor and am escorted outside in a car by Christopher.

It takes about forty minutes to get to the institute. My whole entire body is trembling, and the pain is getting worse and worse by second. That's okay. I want this pain to last as long as possible.

"Welcome to my Institute, Mr. Ice." Dr. Vancouver tells me. He is a very tall skinny man with long brown hair and green lunatic eyes. Well, I guess working with lunatics turns you into one.

"I am Dr. Vancouver and I will be taking care of you during your stay here."

"I don't need to be taken care of," I snap at him coldly as he is directing me into my room.

He chuckles creepily. "Lord Fire was right; you are a stubborn young man with a lot of ego. Nonetheless, the Lord paid me quite a lot of money to heal that very disturbed mind of yours. He also gave me permission to take any measure possible to get you to collaborate with me."

What now? They think they have a right over me? They think I'm a child? I won't let them control me.

"The doctor who has put a cast on your arm called and informed me that he strongly suggests you to take a pain killer," he starts.

I glare at him. "I am fine. I can handle the pain. I don't need any pain killers."

He smirks and crosses his arm on his chest. "Don't need or don't want?"

I don't respond.

"Are you enjoying the pain, Mr. Ice?"

My eyes widen a bit surprise. How can he tell?

"Judging by the expression on your face, I am right, aren't I...Mr. Ice?"

I am standing in the middle of the hall speechless and frozen as he starts to circle me and profile me as if he knows everything about me. "You want this physical pain because you're refusing to accept the emotional pain

323

that is troubling your mind. That's alright, fear not. It's a strange behavior some humans demonstrate when close to losing complete control. You just need to feel alive."

"What's that supposed to mean?" I growl and turn to him.

"It means you're going crazy," he faintly laughs. He thinks it's funny? Who the fuck does he think he is?

"Shut up!" I roar, glaring angrily.

I don't know what took over me all of the sudden. He's so easy-going, so peaceful while everyone around me is suffering. I don't want him to be smiling. I want him to be hurt just as much as I am. I try to throw a punch at him with my left hand, but I'm in so much pain that my body stumbles and he grabs me and corners me against the wall.

"Sorry Mr. Ice, I don't like violence," he whispers and then stabs me in the neck with a needle. I lose consciousness right after.

### Day 1:

I regain consciousness and everything around me is white. I am disoriented for a moment and try to move my arms around but I find myself trapped in a white straight jacket. I look around again and realize where I am. I am in a white padded cell. Just like a crazy person.

I grunt angrily and force myself up. I realize that my complete body is numb. I can't feel the pain in my right hand. I can't feel the pressure on my feet while I'm standing. I am completely, utterly senseless.

"I see you've woken up, Mr. Ice," I hear Dr. Vancouver speaks through the head speaker in the white cell. I look up and look around but I don't see him. Everything is white.

"I'm sorry, I had to give you a strong anesthetic that can not only stop you from feeling pain, but also eliminate any physical sensation. At the moment, you're feeling as if you don't exist, do you?" I don't respond so he continues. "It is now Sunday. You have seven days left to spend time here in this white room. I will be communicating with you through the head speaker until you are ready to talk about yourself,"

"I need you to work with me, Mr. Ice. I need you to accept your feelings, your reality and whatsoever. This is the only way you can help me help you."

I say nothing.

"Can we talk about what made you upset yesterday?"

No answer.

"Very well then, what about the dog you've been seeing a lot lately?"

Still no answer.

"Very well, sir...would you like to talk about your wife?"

I glare up and say nothing.

"Alright," I feel him sigh exasperated. "Have it your way, sir. The longer you choose to say nothing, the longer you will be locked in. You can always press the white button in the left corner when you're ready to talk and I will be there to listen to you. Remember, Mr. Ice, I am here to help you," he then signs off, and I am left alone in the white room.

It's so white and so bright.

I sit on the floor for an hour and begin to grow impatient.

Get me out of here!

It's too white, too lonely, and too creepy. I'm not crazy! Just get me out of here!

I force myself up and start to try hard to move and walk but it's nearly impossible. I can't feel anything physically. I feel as if my body does not exist. I am so numb.

Get me out of here!

I continue to try hard, very hard to move around but I can't. I'm still numb and still alone with myself, with my mind, and all the horrible things that have been happening.

I begin to shudder in the corner as those painful memories of Aelita screaming, me crying, finding Aelita unconscious in the bathroom, killing Jago, making Lazar eat his wife, killing his children, butchering, the innocent family slaughtered, Lazar's daughter melting away, screams, Nadia shooting herself, Aelita yelling at me, blaming me, they're all crawling back into my mind and taking my soul hostage.

Stop...please...make it stop...I don't want to remember this anymore...make it stop...

**Day 2:**

I wake up and I am in the white room again. I still feel numb, but I don't feel hungry or thirsty. Dr. Vancouver probably injected my body with nutrients when I was unconscious. The room is so white it hurts my eyes.

I am sitting there, staring around. I don't like it. I want to go out. But I won't talk to that lunatic of Vancouver ...my business does not concern him.

The room is so white.

I miss Aelita...

Aelita...and her soft lips and smooth dark skin and tender breasts and her amazing, celestial body.

I miss Aelita.

### Day 3:

"Colton..." She's moaning my name as I am inside of her, completing her and embracing her. Her whole body is shaking under me as she digs her nails in my back. She has just orgasmed.

"I love you, Aelita," I rasp, kissing her soft cheeks, her neck, her nose, and every part of her body.

"I need you," she whispers half moaning and half demanding. "I need you to come. I need you, Colton...I need you."

And so I find my release inside of her and feel as if the two of us have just become one.

I open my eyes and I am gasping and sweating. My eyes adjust themselves as I find myself in the white room. Oh...

It was just a dream. It felt so real though...

I come to the sad realization that I want to fuck Aelita so very fucking bad.

I want her...I have to have her...Just for a little bit before I die.

I need her.

Come to think it, Zero told me she was planning to give herself up to me that night when they raped her. She wanted me to take her virginity.

I would've rejected her. I never touched her because I did not want to get too close to her or enjoy her or give into my hidden feelings for her. I would've dismissed her and scold her about it even...

Haha...it's funny how karma works...I did not want to take her virginity and someone else did that night, forcefully...in front of me.

I'm so horny right now. Is the drug working or not? I thought I'm supposed to be feeling numb and embrace my inner emotions?

I feel myself getting hard while the rest of my body is still numb.

I haven't had sex since the incident. Wow. I haven't been with any girl since the incident and I never even once thought about it or craved it, or missed it. That's weird to me because I used to have sex every day with different women. I never felt horny or craved sex because I always had women to satisfy me whenever I wanted...

Now I am left alone in a white room, with a hard on and I want Aelita.

I need Aelita. I need to feel the warmth of her body on mine. I want to run my hands   through   her breasts and inner thighs.   I want to lavish her. I want Aelita....

This room is very white.

## Day 4
I wake up finding myself talking...

"Aelita..." I say.

Why are my lips moving on their own...what drug did Vancouver give me...? I want Aelita....

"How is he doing?" I see Mr. Fire walk into the white room with Vancouver behind him. They close the door and the room is completely white again. Except for them...

Mr. Fire is wearing a black suit and so is Vancouver.

I want them in white.

"He is not collaborating with me, so I had no choice to give him sodium pentothal and other drugs to help him relax and talk and express out loud what he's really thinking," I hear Dr. Vancouver say.

Lord is standing in front of me with a poker face as he says "How arc you doing son...?"

"I..." I start, "I want to fuck your daughter...I want Aelita..."

I can feel his eyes blaze at me and he glance angrily toward Dr. Vancouver.

"H-he's under the effect of the d-drugs...it's making him express what his subconscious thinks..." Dr. Vancouver says in a very defensive tone.

Lord turns back to glare at me. "So all he's thinking about is..." he stops himself from speaking.

"Aelita..." I whine again.

Lord Fire crouches down to my level as he pats my hair. "I'm going to castrate you before I kill you, son." he promises while hissing at me.

"I want to fuck...Aelita," I repeat.

He breathes angrily and stands up walking away from me. "He's a mess! Is this even working?!" he's shouting at Dr. Vancouver.

"Right now no, because he's not helping himself...I can't just heal him within a week sir, I'd like him to stay a bit more if you're alright with that–"

"No. He has duties to fulfill. His guards will come get him out in three days. I expect him to be better by then, if not, I'd like him back how he was before he came in here...not crazier. Understood?"

"Yes, sir." I continue to hear them talk and disappear from the white room.

I want Aelita...

This room is so white.


## Day 5

I wake up feeling very sad and emotional and thinking about my family. They all left me so soon...and I think it's because of me.

Caleb was a very smart and talented brother and our parents had very high hopes for him. Everyone saw him as the prodigy child...but he wasn't happy with himself. He didn't want to go to college, or win scholarships, or become an engineer like our father. He just wanted to travel the world. He had no interest in whatever my father wanted for him...and I used to be mad at him because I thought he was taking things for granted. But, he used to listen to me. When he asked me one day if he should go to the school that accepted him overseas...I told him that he should do whatever dad and mom wanted for him. So he followed my advice and went to study overseas.

He was miserable because that was not what he wanted. He wasn't enjoying himself and didn't fit in, so his grades began to drop dramatically.

Mother and Father were very angry with him and wanted to go visit him overseas and lecture him for being such an insolent, ungrateful child. They never made it there. The plane crashed, and they both died.

Caleb blamed himself...he wasn't happy. He couldn't live with himself, so he took his own life right after.

I was alone. I was the reason they all died.

If I hadn't told my brother to please our parents...none of this mess would've happened...

People die because of me. Forest died because of me...Aelita almost died because of me, now she's suffering and resenting me. Mom and dad and Caleb died because of me. Innocent people are dying because of me. Nadia killed herself because of me. Everyone dies because of me.

I am always alone. I've been alone. I'll always be alone.

I can't be saved.

This white room is like my soul...blank.

## Day 6:

White is such a good color. It's so plain, so neutral, so comforting. I like being in this room. It's very white.

I want to stay here forever. I like white.

I want to merge myself in the walls and become one with the room.

It's so white. White is so unique. It's like it's very own personality.

It's stuck up I think...because it doesn't look good when merge with any other colors. It thinks it's better than every other color.

Is it? No...it's just very popular...

White is...white?

I like white...I think?

No...black is better or grey or green or yellow...or brown...yeah

I hate white. Okay maybe I don't, it's a good color...

I like white. This room is very white.

Is Aelita white...?

## Day 7:

I want to stay in this white room forever...But Dr. Vancouver  just untied me, lets me shower and change clothes and tells me I'm free to go. I feel so weird not wearing a straight jacket.

I feel so free. I can move my arms freely...well the left one that it. The right one is still casted.

"You're not okay, Mr. Ice," he tells me as he guides me outside. Everything is so colorful.

It's not white. I want to go back to white. I want to see white.

"I'd like you to take my card and call me when you're ready to talk. I really want to help you," I can hear sincerity in his voice.

Well good to know someone cares.

I want to go back to the white room.


It's so bright outside. It's not white. I see a car parked in front of the institute and I recognize Zero waiting outside.

He's very pale...he's close to white. Okay.

"Good morning sir," he greets me. I see sympathy and pity on his face.

I don't care what he thinks about me anymore. I don't care what anyone thinks about me. I just want to be back in the white room.

Zero opens the door for me and I enter the car. It's not white. I am silent during my whole trip. I don't know where we're going. I want to go back in the white room.

"Are you alright, Mr. Ice?" Zero asks me a while after. I don't answer.

"Lord Fire has given us the privilege of using the main torture chamber back in the headquarters. It's very amazing. I think you'll like it. We're going there now," is he trying to cheer me up?

"A-Aelita is doing fine. She's doesn't use the wheelchair anymore. She has been healing dramatically fast. She can stand on her own for a long time and walk slowly even. She's better," he continues.

*Ah, Aelita.* I wonder if I'll ever see her again.

White.

"We had a whole entire week of vacation not knowing what to do with ourselves," I hear Warr continue. "We're just so used to being around with you that we felt deprived. It's good to have you back again, Mr. Ice,"

White.

"To be honest, I can't wait to start torturing again." Spyros says.

White.

"Hm, sounds like you're doing it just for the fun." Warr is teasing him quietly.

White.

"Somewhat, hey I can't deny, I'm sadist. Spending years in the Fall Republic battle camp made me discover that," Spyros continues.

They're talking. Is it to cheer me up? I don't know. I don't know anything anymore but white.

"What about you, Mr. Ice...have you missed anything?"

I don't answer.

Have I missed anything? I don't know...I think the drugs are still in my system. I feel hazy.

"This is my new sanctuary," Spyros says as we're inside the torture chamber in the Fire headquarters. The chamber is filled with all kinds of torturing equipment, some I've never even seen. I am not very interested. I don't see the big deal.

White.

"Warr," I suddenly hear someone purr, it's a feminine voice.

"Lava," Warr replies gently and carefully.

"L-lava, h-hello," Spyros says shyly and nervously, blushing a bit but the woman ignores him and walks toward me and Zero.

"Well what do we have here?" she continues to purr as she stops in front of me. I don't pay much attention to her since my mind is hazy. "And here I thought I couldn't find any more handsome boys to play with," Lava continues to speak. Her breath is hot and cold at the same time. I glance at her and notice she has shoulder length wavy hair, piercing cold grey eyes, and is wearing a very red lipstick. She stares at me with hunger and desire.

"He's not for you, Lava," Zero tells her. "You don't want him."

Lava ignores Zero and continues to stare at me, she's now very close to my face and I can almost taste her breath. Her grey eyes darken as she tilts her head to the side and starts to caress my jaws. "Hmm," she murmurs. "You're a fine young man."

I continue to stare at her, but I am numb and my mind is filled with the color white. Nothing matters to me at all.

"You should call me sometime, when you feel like giving me your heart," she whispers her number in my ears and pulls back smirking and winking. "I promise you, I will take good care of it."

"Lava, I said no," Zero insists, his tone is firm and threatening.

"And since when do you get to tell me who I can or can't play with, brother?" Lava glares at him.

*Brother...?*

Zero doesn't reply for a moment, he stares at her for a while and she stares back, raising her dark eyebrow at him.

"He's Colton Ice," Zero replies to her sharply. Her eyes widen in shock and she turns around to stare back at me. "Okay, I'm out," she say backs away quickly. Zero gives her a triumphant smirk.

"You can play with me anytime you want, Lava." Spyros tells her, but she continues to ignore him. We watch as Lava exits the room and Spyros shakes his head and turns to Warr "She's so amazing..."

"Focus, Spyros. Focus." Warr gently scolds him and they both turn their attention back to me.

"Sir," Zero tells me. I see that he has been observing me for a while. His tone is gentle and careful. "Is there anything I can do? Do you need anything?"

I am silent for a while, then I find myself speak.
"White."

"...White?" he repeats.

"You want White Stone to be our next target, sir?"
Spyros asks with anticipation.

"We have a tracker on him — on most of them. We
could bring him in right now if you'd like," Warr
suggests.

"White Stone," I say quietly and look at Zero. "Is
he really white?"

He smiles nervously and Warr starts to laugh. "I
get your jok,." he says.

What joke?

"Sir, would you like us to bring White Stone and
his family?" Zero asks me once again.

I nod then shake my head. "...not family," I say
remembering Aelita's anger and disgust toward me.

"Warr, Spyros, bring White Stone only in. Mr. Ice
and I will stay here and prepare things," Zero orders the
two.

"Right away, Mr. Wanna be boss," Spyros says
with a bit of sarcasm, but seems very thrilled to go. He
really misses torturing people the most, huh?

They're gone and I'm alone in the room with Zero
staring at me creepily. I don't mind though, I don't care
anymore about anything.

"Are you...alright?" he asks me again.

I don't answer.

He sighs "I know we're not really friends or anything and I sort of hate you..." he scratches the back of his head. "But it's still my job to protect Aelita."

What does that got to do with me?

White.

"By making sure you're alright, I'm protecting and helping Aelita heal better and faster...you know," he says sadly. "She didn't tell me that, but I can tell that she thinks and worries about you all the time."

...

I don't want the guy who wants to get in my wife's pants talking about me or her. I don't want anything.

I just want white.

I look around the room and gaze at something is painted white.

White! Finally.

I walk toward it and stare at it. It's a giant bull. It's not a real bull, it's a metallic statue of it. I wonder what this is for.

"It's called a brazen bull," Zero starts. He is answering my unspoken question. "It was a torture and execution tool designed in ancient Greece," he walks around it and touches it. "Its color was originally bronze but Spyros painted it white because he wanted to 'decorate' and bring 'color' in this room," he is shaking his head as if he cannot understand Spyros. "He and Warr are very fond of this room. Anyways, as I was saying, the bull is made entirely of bronze with a door in one side," he points at the rear of the gigantic bull. "As you can see, the bull is in the form and size of a real life bull."

"How does it torture?" I finally ask. I find myself very intrigued by it.

"It's a very painful and slow way to die, sir," Zero continues. "The person is placed inside the bull through the door and a fire is set underneath it until the metal turns literally yellow as it is heating. The person inside the bull will slowly roast to death all while screaming in agonizing pain..." I see a flash in his eyes. He also enjoys torturing and hurting people, just like Spyros and Warr. He is no different. "The bull is purposely designed to magnify these screams and make them sound like the bellowing of a bull. It's one of my favorite in this room."

See? I told you he likes to torture.

I can't deny that I like this method of torture as well...White Stone will definitely suffer and die slowly. I'm using this.

It takes an hour or so for Spyros and Warr to return.

"L-let me go! Who are you people? I didn't do anything!" White Stone is shrieking. He's as short as Spyros with brown hair and brown eyes. Ah, yes he has a very pale skin. He almost blends to the color of my white cell. I find myself smiling. I haven't noticed how pale he was when he was raping Aelita.

Oh. He raped Aelita. He made her scream and made her cry and tortured her innocent body. He hurt my Aelita.

I frown and glare at him with pure hatred. His eyes finally meet mine and he recognizes me. I see fear and doom in his eyes.

"Oh shit..." he curses as Warr and Spyros push him down on the floor. He looks up at me and is very afraid. "I-I'm s-so sorry, please h-have m-merc-cy..." he stutters bowing down before me. His whole entire body is shaking. He is very white. I don't want him to be white. I want him to be red, then I want to roast him.

"Strip him naked," I order one of the guards. Spyros does so while White is protesting.

Meanwhile, I turn to Zero who is ready to obey my command. "I need a very sharp knife that can peel," I tell him.

"What would you like me to do with it?" he asks.

"I'll take care of him," I say again quietly and emotionlessly.

Zero frowns. "But your arm sir," he insists.

"My left arm is working fine. I'll use it."

"But sir–"

"Zero," I cut him quietly. "Get me the knife."

He looks at me for a while and then sighs. "Yes, sir," he complies.

"Also, be sure to get me lots of doses of adrenaline." I add.

"Very well, sir."

White is stripped naked and his skin is so white. It's very close to the color of the padded room I was in.

Actually, it is as white as the padded room. That's good, right...? But it doesn't look good on him.

Red looks better.

I order Spyros to tie White up so that he is standing and both his hands are tied up above his head with a chain.

Zero comes back and gives me a sharp knife. I take it with my left hand and walk toward Stone who is shaking, and he's crying already and I haven't even touched him yet.

What a crybaby.

"I'm so sorry for hurting your wife, sir!" he sobs, "Please don't hurt me! I'm so very sorry! There's not the day I don't regret what I've done! Please! PLEASE! Have mercy on me!"

I ignore his pleads and walk close to him. I draw the knife toward him and he's shaking.

"P-please...I am afraid of pain! P-please! P-please sir!"

I don't say anything. His words don't reach me. I am just very obsessed with the color white, you know...? And he's so white and I just want to take his whiteness away.

With my left hand, I draw the knife, and it touches his skin.

"AH!" he starts to scream, but I haven't even pierced his skin yet. Isn't he over dramatic?

It's funny.

"Stop! Please! God! Oh God! Have mercy! Please! Stop! Stop!" He is trying to struggle, and he becomes sweaty. I ignore him, then run the knife through his face, his neck, his chest and back up toward his neck again.

I start from the collarbone area and go down from there. I begin to peel his flesh with the knife. It's going smoothly. My eyes glow with excitement as I see blood coming out of him. He is not completely white anymore. He is stained with blood. He is turning red.

White is screaming, but I can't hear him. I can't hear anything. I'm not doing this to torture him or hurt him even though it *is* torturing him and hurting him. I just want to take away the white color of his skin away, you know? Somehow it bothers me that he's so white just like in the white room. It's bringing me bad memories...

I continue to peel him, and I am so focused on it. I am doing it perfectly and I am shutting the whole entire world out. I can smell his blood and his flesh. It reminds me of Lazar eating his wife.

Oh that was pretty sick wasn't it...?

I keep on peeling him, then I realize his body is not trembling or convulsing in pain anymore. Why is that?

I look up to him and see that he is unconscious. The pain is too much  for him to bare? No, he needs to feel it.

I administrate him a dose of adrenaline and wait. His eyes are closed for a while but seconds later, they're wide open and he is gasping. Then he starts to scream and cry.

Good.

I continue to peel his skin. I'm done with the chest and stomach area, and I start with his back.

He's screaming and begging and saying something I cannot understand because I am blocking him out. My mind is just very focused on the peeling — turning him red. The knife is completely drenched with blood and so is my hand and my shirt and my cast, I can even feel his blood drip down on my face because I rubbed my eyes earlier. Blood is everywhere on me.

I think I don't like white anymore. I prefer red.

Red is good right? Red. Hm red...

Nope. I still think white is better.

But red is all I'm seeing now...I can only feel red.

I want to feel white too.

No, I want red.

Ok ok okay...how about... I mix red and white together hm? It creates another color.

Red and white give pink.

Hmmm pink.

Pink sounds familiar.

Someone I know loves the color pink.

Who is that person? I know her. I can't recall her though...why do I feel so far from her?

Pink...Pink...

Ae...li...ta...Aelita?

Yes, Aelita! Aelita loves pink. Aelita is very pink...I like pink. I like pink very much because I like Aelita.

"Sir,"

I like pink. I want to see pink.

"Sir,"

I want to see Aelita.

"Sir!" I hear Zero's voice call me. I look at him and I realize where I am. I am in the torture room and I am torturing White Stone.

"What...?" I ask Zero.

"He's knocked out again," Zero tells me carefully.

I look up see White unconscious.

Oh. Okay, then I'll just wake him up again.

I grab another dose of adrenaline.

"Sir, if I may..." Zero starts. "I think you should put him in the bull right now. He might just die any moment due to the loss of blood."

Oh...but I'm not done peeling him yet... There's still his lower body and his face left...but Zero's right. White is just a coward who can't handle a little bit of pain. He's overdramatic. He'll die before he even gets his real torture. "Alright. Untie him," I tell them.

The guards do so. White is completely red and his flesh is exposed. He's a combination of white and red and pink...

So many colors. My favorite colors.

"Wake him up before putting him in the bull," I order the guard. I need him to be awake to feel himself roast.

After all this is torture right? This is what he gets for hurting my wife. Damn bastard. He deserves this.

They administer him another dose of adrenaline. "No. Two doses," I insist. I want White to stay awake as long as possible.

Zero and Warr look at each other and nod.

White is waking up and then he is screaming again. He is screaming so loud. I can almost feel his pain. His flesh is exposed and hyper sensitive to the whole world. Hm, good. I like seeing people like him hurt and scream. I like seeing him tortured. Am I just like my fellow guards?

Ha...hahaha....

They dose him once again and drag his body toward the giant bull. Spyros opens the rear of the bull and Warr and Zero—who are carrying White push him inside the bull and lock the door. White is already screaming, but it sounds like the bull is bellowing. It doesn't sound like a human screaming. Zero sets fire under the stomach of the metal bull and it is starting to slowly heat up. We wait and wait and about twenty minutes later, I see the metal turn yellow and the screams become louder.

He can't faint anymore because there's adrenaline running kicking in. All White can do is feel the agonizing pain and drive himself crazy and scream until he is roasted.

"I could go for a BBQ right now," Spyros jokes around snickering quietly.

Warr rolls his eyes and is stopping himself from chuckling. "I don't think you'll like it. You don't like your meat cooked, remember?"

"Ah, that's right. I like my meat rare, but I could go for medium well," Spyros says. The bull is still bellowing and they're talking as if nothing is happening.

"Ah," Warr agrees. "Must be very tasty."

"Yeah, let's go eat some BBQ pork after this, the four of us, huh Warr?"

"...No. Like Zero, I'm a vegetarian."

"Oh, I forgot..."

I start to not listen to their conversation and tune them out when I hear a bark. I freeze and turn and I see Forest, the dog.

The fucking dog—the reason why they locked me in the fucking white room and drugged me. "I'm going to go ahead and say that Lord wasted millions of golds on this, huh?" I say out loud, looking at the dog.

"Who're you talking to?" Zero asks me panicking. I ignore him. The dog is barking and alarmed. He always comes whenever there's trouble around me.

What is it now?

He is still barking then he runs out of the room. The door is open. I'm pretty sure Spyros closed it earlier when they came with White. Please don't tell me the dog opened it...

How's that even possible?

The dog is barking louder at me and I feel urged to follow him.

"Sir?" Zero calls after me but I ignore him.

I walk out of the room and out of the building and the dog is running out toward the street. Where are we going?

He's going fast, and still barking at me as if he's urging me to hurry the fuck up. I don't know where we're going. I suddenly feel something buzz in the pocket of my pant. I take it out and it's my phone. I look at the caller ID and it is Hinata. Is it about Aelita?

I answer. "Yes...?"I hear nothing for a while but then she starts to speak. Her voice is shaking and sounds panicked.

"Mister Ice come, hurry… h-he h-has us hostage..."

"What?" I can't understand her. I'm still hazy and numb from the drugs.

Then I hear a loud angry voice in the background. "Hey! You bitch! Get off the fucking phone!"

My heart begins to beat fast. Who's that?

"Sir..." Hinata starts to speak really fast. "He's in your home! And he's taking Mrs. Ice and her mother and I hostage! Please! He is killing people! Please! Come hurry please!"

Then I hear Mrs. Fire cry in the background "Please don't shoot her!"

Then the angry voice talks again "Get off the phone, you bitch!" Then I hear a gun shot in the end of the line.

"Hello?! Hinata?! Hello!?" I ask but then the phone is disconnected. I feel suddenly awake, I feel suddenly aware of everything around. I feel like my body is completely wearing the drug off by itself at an alarming rate and my heart begins to beat fast. My body is shaking in worry, agony and anger. Someone is hurting my Aelita. Aelita needs me.

# 18

## HIDON MARS'S POINT OF VIEW

"Hunter," I'm knocking on his door and I receive no answer.

It's been a week since he locked himself in his room. I don't know what happened to him but he has been really down.

He hasn't spoken a word and we're all scared and confused of what the fuck might happen next. After seeing Lazar's video, I know in my heart that we're all doomed. It's just a matter of time before we all die...but I don't want us to die in fear, despair and loneliness. I want us to die together, proud. I want us to fight, and not give in. I want us to strive.

But I can't lift everyone's spirit up. I'm not the leader type. I'm always angry and people end up getting angry at me as well. Hunter is the one who's more calm, more understanding and more people-oriented. He has what it takes to lead us, to comfort us and to set order when there's chaos. I need him back.

"Hunter!" I knock the door once again, this time harder. He still doesn't answer so I barge in.

He is sitting by the window and looking out somewhere in space. His eyes are the saddest things I have ever seen. They're lost, confused, and tainted. I see despair in his eyes, I see sadness, sorrow, I see hate. How can the leader of our group lead if he's filled with despair and loss of hope? Are we really that doomed?

"Hey, Hunt." I start. He doesn't utter a word.

"Look, man...we need to know what's going on with you. You're worrying us. You haven't come out of your room since last Saturday..."

He says something.

"What?" I ask, it's very low and faint.

"I said...Noah used to love the ocean," he repeats. His voice is anguished.

Noah? His sick brother...? Why is he talking about him?

Oh! He's finally dead. I understand Hunter's sadness...well the kid has been through a whole fucking lot from what I've heard. It's better if he's dead. At least Lord won't get him.

"I'm sorry about your brother, man." I tell him quietly.

"He took the fall for me and Veronica..." he says.

"What do you mean?"

His voice is as quiet as ever. "They beat him to death...Ice's guards...they took him away from me and beat him to death right in front of me...he...he was...in...so...much pain..."

I know that Hunter wants to cry, but it seems there aren't enough tears left for his eyes to release. He is crying, tearless.

"What...? They killed Noah?" my heart is hurting for the poor kid. That's awful.

"All because I begged Aelita for mercy," Hunter continues.

Wait, what?

"Aelita's dead, man." I tell him. Is he losing his mind?

"She survived," he says. His eyes are not even blinking or breaking from the long distant gaze outside the window. Far, far away, we can see the ocean.

"What?" I repeat.

"She's alive," he repeats. "Lord's daughter is well and healthy and glowing."

As I hear this, I start to clench my fists and furrow my eyebrows angrily. She's alive? Then why the fuck are people dying because of her? Why the fuck is the Lord trying to kill us all? Why is Noah dead if she's still alive and well? It's not fair.

She can't be living while people are dying. I need my death to make sense. I need people's death to make sense. I was okay with dying because I thought the bitch was dead and we probably deserved to die as well...but now that she's alive...

No. Fuck, no! "I'm gonna kill her," I growl.

I am expecting Hunter to say something, to stop me or convince me to not be reckless. That I'll only be adding fuel to the fire.

"Suit yourself," he simply says.

My eyes widen in shock and anger. Look at Hunter, he's an empty shell. He's lifeless. He doesn't care about anything anymore. His brother's death really did a number on him.

They're gonna pay. They're gonna pay for so what they've done to us, to Jago, to his wife, to Lazar and his children, to Hunter 's brother...they're going fucking to pay.

"I'm going on a suicide mission," I tell Hunter before leaving the room. "I can't let the dead's death be in vain. If they're killing innocents because we harmed their precious innocent girl, then I might as well make it right. I'll kill her. At least I will have a reason to be killed."

He doesn't say anything. He really doesn't care anymore.

"Goodbye, bro. See you in the next life." I tell him and close the door. I rush into my room and with hurry, I pack some weapons in my bag. I take as much explosives and guns as I can.

"What are you doing?" Elena, my ex-wife asks me. I look up at her and my eyes soften. I probably won't ever see her ever again. We hate each other so much...I'm still going to miss her. I zip up my bag and wear it on my back, walk toward her and kiss her.

"Fight until the end," I tell her after breaking the kiss, then I leave.


I'm three blocks away from the Ice Mansion. I am on top of a building and I am using binoculars to look around the house. It's guarded with only females. What the fuck is this?

Well, I take it to my advantage, since girls are weak.

The back of the mansion is more guarded than the front. I have an idea. I will create a distraction. I'll throw some grenades at the back of mansion since most of the guards are there. When the back blows up, it will make the rest of the guard rush there immediately, leaving the main entrance open for my invasion.

Good plan.

I follow my plan and it actually works. I think I blew several guards up when the grenade landed in the back of the mansion. There are screams and rushes and chaos and I see most guards deserting the front of the mansion. I take advantage of that and sneak inside the house.

"Hey!" I hear a guard yell after me when I am inside the house. She has her gun pointed at me. That's cute. It takes me less than three seconds to snatch the gun away from her.

"Where's Aelita?" I growl at her. She freezes and doesn't answer. Another guard appears behind her and is about to take out her weapon, but I shoot her down making the previous guard scream.

"I will shoot you if you don't tell me where she is!" I roar at her. She is refusing to talk, so I shoot her down.

What a useless peace of shit.

I want to start looking upstairs in the bedrooms but as I start to take steps toward the stairs, I see at the end of the hall three girls. One of them is Aelita, the other is dressed in a maid uniform and the other is a dark skinned older woman. They're pushing Aelita in the wheelchair.

I smirk.

That lucky bitch is so fucking dead.

"Come on honey, come on I know you can walk by yourself now but we need you to move faster that's why I'm putting you in the wheelchair. We need to get you somewhere safe," the dark skinned woman says. They don't make it far. I am in front of them, pointing my gun. The three of them freeze and Aelita recognizes me. Her body begins to tremble and she grabs the dark skinned woman's hand.

I'm glad she is still traumatized and scared. That means she hasn't forgotten our special night.

"In that room," I direct them in the nearest room.

They obey and the dark skinned woman is pushing Aelita while the servant is opening the door.

We're in a kitchen. There are two other maids that are cooking and something. I don't give them a chance to scream as they see me with a gun. I shoot both of them.

The dark skinned woman covers Aelita's eyes with her hand. "Don't look sweetheart," she whispers softly.

"SHUT UP!" I roar.

They're in the middle of the kitchen and the dark skinned woman is holding Aelita's hand and calmly patting her back while giving me a ferocious glare. "My husband won't let you get away with this."

"Oh so you're Mrs. Fire," I glare, smirking. This is just too good. I get two for the price of one. Thank you Stigma.

"I'm gonna rape and kill you too," I tell her. She looks at me horrified then I turn to look down on the golden brown haired girl seating in the wheelchair. I take steps toward her and her mother gets in front of her glaring at me.

"Get away from my daughter!" Mrs. Fire hisses at me.

"Oh give me a fucking break, don't be so impatient. I'll deal with you soon."

"My husband will kill you and make your life miserable first," she roars at me.

I slap her and she stumbles back. "Yeah well guess what, bitch?" I look down at Mrs. Fire. "I don't give a fuck what he does to me anymore. After killing you both, I'll die happily!"

Then I glare at the frightened Aelita. "You're so cozy getting people to push you around, take care of you.

You, you get to have a good night sleep and wake up the next day with all the servants at your feet...you have no worry in the world," I get closer to her and lean toward her. Her honey brown eyes are trembling. I can smell her delicious fragrance and I feel horny. I'll fuck her again before putting a bullet in her brain. No, not a bullet. Three or four or ten. I'll put as much as I need to until she's stays dead.

"While innocent people are dying for your fucking sake!" I hiss at her. Aelita frowns at me.

"Stop telling her that!" Mrs. Fire screams at me. I turn to Mrs. Fire and roar at her.

"SHUT THE FUCK UP OR I'LL BLOW YOUR BRAINS OUT RIGHT FUCKING NOW!"

Mrs. Fire becomes calm and then I turn back to Aelita. "You little bitch. You little bitch. Lazar's children were killed...They made Lazar eat his own wife's flesh in front of the children. They fucking beat Hunter's innocent sick helpless brother to death, you bitch! Innocent people have been fucking dying while you're alive living happily ever after..." I grab her face roughly with my hand and she gasps. "Guess what baby, it doesn't matter whether you're alive of not. We're still going to fucking suffer and die anyways and guess what, I'm okay with dying but I'll take you down with me. You and your mother so Lord Fire understands what it feels like to lose his family."

Mrs. Fire gasps. Aelita is looking at me with such sad eyes. I'm not sure if she's sad for herself or for me. *Whatever.*

I am about to undo her top and grab those full breasts of hers once again, but then I notice something. The servant who came in with her is not near us anymore. I rise back up away from Aelita and look around and see the servant on the phone talking to someone. I grow angry.

"Hey! You bitch! Get the fuck off the phone!" I yell at her. She starts to talk really fast on the phone. I point my gun at her.

"Please don't shoot her!" Mrs. Fire tells me but I shoot the servant anyways.

"Ah!" the servant moans in pain as the bullet pierces through her lower abdomen. She collapses on the floor.

I am about to shoot her once again in the head when Mrs. Fire suddenly kicks me in the nuts and starts to run toward the exit. "Ugh!" I grunt in pain and try to shoot her before she escapes. I miss. She's already out the kitchen.

Damn it! I have to go after her.

I rise myself back up and run outside the room but then stop remembering that Aelita might escape too. So I run back in the kitchen and stare at her. Her entire body is shaking and tears are rolling down her face. "Please...p-please...don't hurt my mother..." she begs me with such a tiny adorable voice.

How fucking annoying.

I take out a duct tape from my backpack and tie her hands and feet so she can't move from the wheelchair. "I'll be back for ya, bitch!" I say and run out. I try to chase around the house and look for Mrs. Fire. I really want her to be there when I rape and kill Aelita so she can feel what Hunter and Lazar felt when their family was being tortured. I want them to feel the same thing.

But I decide to stop chasing after her few minutes later. I realize I'm wasting time. They're probably going to send backups and more guards and police will come in to shoot me down. I know I'll die today. I don't care. I just want to take Aelita with me.

I rush back and run inside the kitchen to Aelita and I see the servant crawling toward the wheelchair, trying to untie Aelita. I glare at servant.

"You little bitch," I tell her and draw the gun at her. She's frozen in place and I'm about to shoot her when I feel someone behind me and there's a click.

"Drop the gun, asshole," Mrs. Fire says. She has another gun pointed at the back of my head. "Drop it!" She yells again. I do so.

"Turn around." She orders me and I do so. She takes few steps back "Walk toward me,"

"What?" I growl at her. "You don't want to shoot me now?"

"Not in front of my daughter. Come on, let's go." she hisses. She is walking backward nervously and not paying attention. She missteps on something and that is my chance.

I grab the gun from her.

"Ah!" She yells out of anger. I take the gun away and throw it out the window. I want to kill them with my own gun.

"You should've killed me when you had the chance," I smirk at Mrs. Fire. I'll tie her up as well. I grab her and I turn around when I see the servant grabbing my gun from the floor and pointing it at me. She pulls the trigger and I feel the bullet pierce through my shoulder.

"Gah!" I yell in agony and glare at the servant who is shaking with the gun on her hand. Before she gets another chance to shoot me, I somehow grab the gun from her and then shoot her in the chest four times. This time, she won't get up.

"Bitch!" I spit at her, then I feel a sharp pain on my back. Mrs. Fire just hit me with something. I turn around and glare at her, feeling a bit disoriented from the blow. She backs away from me as I start to stalk after her. She then runs toward the sink in the kitchen and opens the drawer to grab something. I pace after her. I'll kill this fucking bitch.

I am inches close to her and about to grab her when she turns around and stabs me with a knife in my stomach, twice and one time in my chest. I gasp and stare at her in disbelief, then stare at the knife again. She looks at me with frightened eyes as well and wants to run away from me.

I am getting angrier. I will fucking kill her. I will fucking kill that bitch. I pull the knife out of my chest and grab her by the throat.

"Oh!" she screams as I violently push her on the kitchen counter.

"You fucking bitch! You fucking bitch! I'm going to kill you, you fucking bitch!" I roar at her and I stab the knife in her arm.

She screams loudly. Yes, that's right. Scream for me bitch. Scream. I stab her again in the other arm, and then in each of her thigh. She's screaming hard and painfully. Good. I want to see that fucking bitch suffer.

I grab her by the hair and slam her head back and forth in the counter. I want to crush her skull.

She somehow finds a way to grab a fork and stab me in one eye with it.

"AH! Fuck!" I grunt and back away from her due to the pain. She's shaking and falls on the floor. I am grunting in pain while she's stumbling away from me. She won't get far. I'll get her!

I am about to storm after her when I see a man at the entry of the kitchen who takes her hand and helps Mrs. Fire up. He glares at me with the eyes colder and crazier than Hunter's. It's Colton Ice.

# 19

## COLTON'S ICE POINT OF VIEW

I knew they were in the master kitchen when I saw Mrs. Fire's gun get thrown out of the window. I am outside the house, trying to save a guard's life. Her whole body is on fire. I hear screams from the kitchen door and gun shots.

Shit.

"Go sir, go!" Another guard tells me coming to the burning guard's rescue. "I'll take care of her!"

"Thank you," I say and waste no time. I rush in the room and I am about to walk in the kitchen when I feel suddenly dizzy and fall down on the floor. The drugs...

I start to see white again and start to feel hazy. No...Not now. I can't give in to white. But it's so white...so fucking white…so white like the padded room I was in few days ago…white…I like white

I hear the dog bark at me again, this time louder and he's biting on my cast. I come back to my senses suddenly and force myself up. I have to save Aelita!

I rush in the room and see Aelita tied up in her wheelchair with tears rolling down her face. She's still as beautiful as ever. When she sees me, her eyes widen in surprise and relief. I am relieved she's alright as well.

I look around and see two cooks on the floor dead and see Hinata's body as well...she's dead. Then I see Mrs. Fire slowly crawling desperately away from Hidon. She's covered in blood and has cuts all over her skin. She looks up and sees me, for the first time, she's pleased to see me. I help her up. She is trembling in my arms. I then turn to glare at Hidon. I'm going to kill this mother fucker with my own bare hands.

He sees me and his eyes widen is horror and shock. He pulls out the fork from his eyes while grunting then starts to throw things at me and on the floor, to slow me down from coming at him. When all else fails, he decides to lunge himself at me.

"ARGH!" He yells and is about to stab me with the knife in his hand. I dodge him and throw a punch at him with my left hand since my right hand is casted. He stumbles back and I throw another punch, he blocks it and bangs his head against mine. It hurts so fucking much.

"Ah!" I grunt in pain and feel dizzy. He takes advantage of me trying to recuperate and pushes me down the floor. He's on top of me and I'm wrestling with one hand.

"Die, you fucking fuck!" he yells at me, trying to crush my throat. I don't let him, I grab his hand with my left hand and with a bit more of strength, I manage to lift up his hand from my throat. I am grunting and so is he. He forces his hand on my face, and I find myself biting one of his fingers off.

"AAAHH!" He screams again in pain and stumbles away from me.

I register around the room. Mrs. Fire is sitting on the floor resting, she's bleeding. Aelita is furiously using her teeth to undo the duck-tapes around her arm. I am about to stand up and help her when Hidon kicks me back down on the floor and this time he has a knife.

"You bit off my finger, you fucker!" Hidon roars at me, raising the knife and trying to stab me.

I use my left hand and try to grab his wrist. I am wrestling him. It's his strength against mine, and I can tell you that he's really strong since he's a body builder. But, I'm Colton Ice. I am stronger.

"GRRAA!" With all my might, I am pushing his hand back while he is forcing the knife toward my face. The knife ends up piercing through the palm of my hand as I am grunting, still trying to move his hand away from me.

"Fuck it!" he says and lets go of the knife and gets off me. I look around again and I see Aelita is not sitting on the wheelchair. I am about to scan around the room to look for her, when I see Hidon coming back and drawing a gun. I freeze. He's going to shoot me.

I don't mind dying, but this time I don't want to. If I die, I won't be able to protect Aelita. He's going to hurt her once again. I won't be able to save her.

"Die, motherfucker!" Hidon tells me looking down on me and is about to pull the trigger when Aelita suddenly throws hot oil on his face. The frying pan hits him, hot oil is all over his face, making it swell.

I look at Aelita and grin very proud of her.

"AAHH!" Hidon screams, grabbing his burnt face. He then does something that enrages me.

He strikes Aelita. "You bitch!" he growls at her as she stumbles back on the floor and falls.

There's a flip-switch inside of me and I find myself rising up all of the sudden. I stalk after him, and he turns around and sees me. He wants to shoot me again, but I smack the gun off his hand easily and use my head to violently head bump him.

"Ugh!" He cries out, stumbling backwards. He stumbles until he bumps against the stove. He is about to fall down, but I don't give him the opportunity. Instead, I grab him by the back of his hair and drown his head in the giant boiling water pot. I am angrily holding him down as he struggles to force himself up. He manages to lift his head up and gasp for air, but I give him no time. I force his head back inside the water. He is struggling and struggling and splashing and struggling. He wants to survive.

Then, I feel his hand move around to turn off the stove, but it ends up touching the second burner and I turn it on with my right hand. The fire burns his hand and I feel him starting to scream in the boiling water. His hand is burning and bleeding, it is starting to look like a blood bath. I lift up his head to hear him scream and I watch him in agony.

"AAHHH!!" He is whimpering and shaking as he tries hard to remove his hand from the burner. It's glued to it.

He manages to do so, but I don't let him rest. I punch him with my elbow and he stumbles back again. His face is disfigured and swollen from Aelita's previous attack and the hot water.

His chest and shoulder and stomach are bleeding out. Seems like Mrs.Fire did a number on him before I came. I should not be surprised. His right arm is bleeding bad, due to what just happened in the stove but I am not satisfied. I want to see him bleed more.

I punch him once and again and kick him with my knee. He falls down on the floor. He has no energy left to fight. I grab the meat tenderizer that is on the kitchen counter and I begin to smash his kneecap angrily and furiously with it. He is screaming and screaming.

When I see blood being drawn out of his jean, I stop and the I grab him by his auburn hair and bangs his head angrily against the wall back and forth and back and force and again and again and again.

Then I let him go and grab the knife he was trying to stab me with earlier. I stab him in his groin and he screams again. Next, I use the knife and shove it up his mouth then slice his mouth open. He's completely drained and can't move anymore. He can't run. He's close to dying.

I grab the wooden floor mop and then start to beat him with it over and over and over again. His swollen face is breaking, I can hear the bones cracking. I let go of the mope and grab the meat tenderizer again. I carve his nose with the meat tenderizer over and over and I see his face is smashing in.

It's not enough. I want to beat him more. I want to hurt him more. I find myself putting my hand under his pant as I grab both his balls and with all my strength, I rip them out of him and shove them in his mouth. I start to punch his very broken face again.

"You!" Punch. "fucking." Punch. "son" punch "of" punch "a" punch "bitch!" I breathe and growl at him as I am beating him senseless over and over again. He is not moving or breathing anymore, but I'm not satisfied. I am still punching, kicking, and cursing him out. I am forgetting and blocking out the whole entire world around me. All I want to do is beat that man until his body disappears.

He raped Aelita and now wants to torment her again!? He dared to fucking raise a hand on her!? No. Fuck that motherfucking fucker! I get up and my whole entire body is stained with blood — White Stone's blood and now with Hidon's.

I grab the mop again then I raise it up vertically and begin to beat and stab his body with it over and over and over again! There are holes in his chests and I can even see his intestines leaking out. I am still not satisfied. I want him to completely disappear.

I start to use my foot and angrily and mercilessly stomp on his face. I am stomping and stomping and stomping and each stomp becomes even more violent than the previous and I just keep on stomping on his face until the skull breaks, the brain is mushy and exposed, his face is caved broken and open and blood is leaking out.

I stomp on his neck and plan to do it again and again and again.

"COLTON PLEASE STOP!" I hear her pained voice plead me and I become aware of my surroundings.

Shit. I did all this in front of Aelita.

I stop stomping on Hidon's very dead body and then have the sudden urge to piss.

"Turn around if you don't want to see this," I tell Aelita and I feel her shift away. I open my zipper and start to piss on Hidon. When I finish, I spit on his body. I hope he rots in hell.

As I zip up my pant, I turn around and I'm about to check if Aelita's okay when suddenly we hear footsteps running in and Lord Fire and Zero come along with lots of guards and policemen.

Ahhh...why do they always show up *after* the damage is done, huh?

"Are you alright, sweetheart?" Lord Fire asks Aelita, holding her and hugging her. She nods at him, and looks at Zero.

Zero looks at her with concern and then his hard, blank face softens. He has a gentle, warm smile on his face. That kind of sweet innocent look is from a killer. I can't...I don't know how he is able to do it. Aelita smiles back at him and hugs him.

I try hard not to stomp on Zero's head too.

She lets go of him and then tentatively walks toward me. Her lips are trembling and she is stretching her arm to touch my face. Her touch is so gentle. I want more.

"A-are you alright?" she asks me softly with tears running on her face. She has the face of an angel. I can't believe I have been trying to keep my distance from her. I don't even know why I have been avoiding her in the first place anymore.

"Colton? Are you alright?" Aelita repeats. I nod at her. I can't find my tongue to speak. Her beauty and gentleness makes my mind go blank.

"Esmeralda, are you okay?!" Lord Fire's voice is filled with worry and pain. It's rare to see him like that.

"Yes..." Mrs. Fire replies faintly, smiling at her husband. "I put up a fight, and so did...Colton," Lord Fire kisses her forehead and stares at her bleeding body. He is growing angrier. He stands up and grabs the gun from Zero. He is storming toward me.

I freeze, thinking that he wants to shoot me. He's blaming me for all this. But instead, he moves past me and points the gun toward Hidon's dead body and starts to shoot him.

"AAHH, YOU BASTARD!" Lord Fire is screaming at him and shooting Hidon's body countless time.

I instinctively pull Aelita closer to me and hide her face in my chest so she can't see anything. I hold her tightly on my body and I feel her warmth. I realize I have to protect her. I really need to get myself together and focus more. There's nothing more I want than this girl's safety. I'll protect her until I die.

Mrs. Fire is sent to the hospital and my wounds are being treated as well.

Lord Fire and Aelita and Zero are also at the hospital, staying by Mrs. Fire's side. She's is going to be okay.

I think about Nadia, since she's the one who's usually healing me whenever I get injured.

I also think about Hinata she died as well. I liked Hinata, she was very helpful and supportive to Aelita and to me...but all her efforts led to her death. Getting close to me led to her death. Another innocent life taken away even though I made a promise not to kill anymore innocents...blood won't stop shedding until this war is over, huh?

People will continue to die. About a dozen of guards and servants died today. And Mrs. Fire got hurt as well. Aelita could've died today.

Shit. Aelita could've died.

I don't know what I'll do with myself if she died...if I lost her...I love her so much.

I need to get myself together, I want to get better. I need to clear up this foggy, crazy, hazy mind of mine. I want to be able to think clearly again. I don't want to think about white anymore.

White always leads to red.

No. I need help.

I want to leave and meet someone, but before that, I want to say goodbye to her, but I feel shy and unworthy of that.

"Keep an eye on Aelita for me, alright?" I tell Zero.

He nods at me with confidence. I know he will take care of her. I am about to go into the elevator and leave when I see her call after me. I stop and freeze and turn around.

She is looking at me with such sad lost eyes. Why is she looking at me like that?

"What happened to you, Colton?" she asks me sadly.

I don't know what she is talking about, but something is telling me that it had to do with the cruel beating of Hidon.

I sigh and look at her. I want to fix myself, and get help. "Aelita," I start. "I am going white, far into white because red won't let me go...but I won't give into white and red because pink needs me."

I don't know any other way to explain this. It makes complete sense to me, but it doesn't to her. She doesn't understand. She doesn't need to. "Take care of yourself, Aelita," I tell her before leaving the hospital. She is staring at me as the elevator door closes. I want to be around her every day.

I am urgently banging on his door. It takes a minute or two for him to open and see me. He is very surprised to see me.

"Ice? What a surprise," he tells me with a smirk.

"Dr. Vancouver," I start. "I'm ready to talk."

# 20

## AELITA FIRE ICE'S POINT OF VIEW

It's hard...It's so hard not to detest. It's almost impossible not to resent people, and not to feel angry at the world when all they do is demolish you and take pleasure in watching you suffer…

Especially when you did nothing wrong to them…

When everything, when the world, when people you love and people you don't know hurt you in a way that you can never recover from, when all hope is taken away from you, hate is only thing you have left.

However, I have witnessed many times what hate can do to an individual. It destroys him, breaks his spirits, and transforms him into a horrible, despicable monster.

And when that man completely transforms and sells his soul to hate, everyone around becomes affected and eventually do the same because hate is a very contagious disease.

Everyone around me is getting that disease and it is only getting worse...and before we all know it, even strangers hate. That's why I need to remind myself every day who I was before all this chaos happened. That's why I need to try hard, I need to struggle and fight this deadly, repulsive disease very hard so I don't become like everyone else around me. I need to be strong, I need to be different. I don't want to give into this disease. I don't want to be dragged in. I want to be strong. I'm Aelita Fire Ice and this is my story.

———

I was raped about two weeks and three days ago. It was a Friday night, my special Friday night. I was finally going to be brave enough to confess to my dear husband. I have never told him I love him, I have never expressed my feelings for him even though he knew. Our marriage was empty and lonely and he was never around me. He spent quite a lot of times outside, with other women and I blamed myself partly, because I felt like he was forced into this marriage. It was a gift from my father. He wanted to make me happy so, he gave me the love of my life as a husband. Only that Colton was not really into this kind of marriage. He was angry with me. I knew he didn't love me and I knew I was stealing away his freedom...I felt guilty. I tried as hard as possible to make this marriage work, to show him that I was a worthy woman and that I loved him. That night, I decided to be brave. I decided to be strong and courageous. That night, I was going to tell him that the sun and moon rose in his eyes. I wanted to hold him close to feel his heart beat and I wanted to tell him how much I love him. I wanted to make love to him that night.

That same night, I broke my very good friend's heart. He was brave enough to confess to me, he was actually the one who inspired me to confess my feelings to Colton. I could see and feel how pure and honest Zero's feelings were for me. They were just like how I felt for Colton. I rejected Zero and told him that I was going to make things better with Colton and I believed in the power of love. I knew that if I love Colton strong enough, if I fought and proved him that I was worthy of his heart, and loved him and was willing to become the woman of his dreams, I believed that he would actually fall in love with me.

I upset Zero and he left. Although, I was not worried. I knew he'd come back from this. I knew he'd forgive me.

I showered and waxed my entire body that night. I was so excited, and looking forward to seeing Colton. For once, that night, I loved my body and I felt confident and beautiful. When I got out of the shower, I went to my lovely garden and was going to pick out some red, passionate roses to decorate Colton's room, but then I heard Forest bark angrily.

That worried me because he wasn't the type to bark. So I went to the main hall, and I found a man glaring down at the dog. I froze and gasped, I wanted to scream for help, but my voice was gone. I couldn't talk. I tried to run, but they caught me. Forest was barking and biting and growling at them, so they shot him down.

I was scared. I wanted to cry because my favorite dog just died, but Colton hated it when I cried. He told me once that I was weak and disgusted him, so I trained myself not to cry. I was scared, but calm. Everything was going to be okay, I told myself. I tried to use my alarm button, a necklace that Zero gave me. It was an alarm system that I could just press whenever I felt like I was in trouble. It would reach his phone and would be like I was calling him. I pressed and pressed and pressed and hoped for him to come at any moment, but he never came.

The man with dirty blonde hair made me show them Colton's room. I wondered why they needed to be in his room...was it Cain's doing again? Was he sending those men to hurt me so Colton could be in trouble with my father?

The two men and I waited and waited silently in Colton's room. Colton eventually came in and one of the man started talking to him. The man told him how much he hated Colton. He told him what Colton did to him and his marriage. It broke my heart. Poor man, he had the disease. He had so much hate inside and he wanted to share it with Colton. So, he used me.

I lost my virginity, my dignity and pride that night to another man in front of the man I loved. I tried to be strong. I tried not to cry. I just wanted to make Colton proud. I wanted to make him believe that I was strong. That I was not the girl he used to know years ago...

He was the one crying that night...he was the one filled with hatred and sorrow...and angst. The disease was getting to him quickly. I wanted to resist the disease. I wanted to be strong, I thought I could handle his amount of hate but blond man was not the only one with hate...more came. And there was so much hatred.

Colton was hating, crying, begging, the men were mocking me, laughing, degrading me, ruining me...there was too much hatred for me. I couldn't handle it, my body, my heart, my soul and mind could not handle this amount of hatred. So I broke, and I found myself screaming and crying...I could not be strong anymore.

They broke me, they took away the small glimpse of hope and love and innocence that was left of me. They took it all and I was a mess.

I didn't feel human, I didn't feel worthy anymore. All my hopes and dreams and perseverance were shattered by those men.

Colton could not do anything, he was hurt and helpless and was trying to comfort me. For the first time ever, he tried to comfort me...

But then they killed me. They took away my life. The only thing that belonged to me. The only thing left that was precious, they took it. Hate won that night. I died.

Yes, I died that night. The sweet, innocent joyful girl died, and someone else, woke up. It was hate. Hate took over me and when I woke up, I regretted it. I wanted to be dead. I didn't want to survive. I wanted to forget about what happened to me that night. I did not want to live.

Even the doctors and the nurses agreed. They were gossiping about me in the room. They were telling each other how sorry they felt for me. *Poor girl, she's ruined. Poor girl, she can never come back from this. Poor girl, she's now a damaged good. Poor girl, poor girl...*

Poor me.

They were right, I was damaged and even my mother looked at me and spoke to me that way. She felt sorry for me. Everyone felt sorry for me, my father never came to visit me...Colton...I never saw him. I didn't want to see him. What would he think of me? I was broken, I was a damaged good...I was not worthy of him anymore. I could never come back from this. I mean look at my body...it's bruised and ugly and my face looked lifeless and my eyes were lost somewhere in another dimension. I wasn't Aelita anymore. I was an empty shell.

More gossips and pities continued when I was brought home. Mom took over and told me she was going to take care of me. That I wouldn't have to worry about anything anymore...She thought she understood me, but she did not. She didn't know what I was going through. She didn't even know the brink of how broken I was. The servants smiled at me with pity and sympathy and I found myself needing to wipe that smile off their faces. I found myself wanting to make them as broken as I was...I wanted all of them to get raped too. I was sad, and lonely and Colton wasn't there...Zero wasn't there...Forest wasn't there... dad wasn't there...I was alone and left to deal with the pain...all alone. I asked myself *Why? Why do I need to do this? Why should I care about my life? Why should I value it?* It was worth nothing anymore. So I forced myself up from my bed and painfully drag myself in the bathroom. I undressed myself and got in the bathtub to wash away all those dirty feelings...I could still feel them touching me...I could still feel their rough hands on my body...I could still feel them inside of me, so I couldn't take it anymore. I knew I would never get rid of this painful feeling and I didn't want to be strong. Colton wouldn't care anymore. There was no point of surviving...so I took the knife that mom used to peel me an apple, and carved myself deep.

It hurt so much, so much and I began to cry again. Pain was all I was feeling, mentally emotionally and physically and I wanted it to just stop. I wanted to put an end at all of this. I stared down my thigh and saw blood, blending with the water and taking the color red. I was numb and couldn't feel a thing...then slowly and slowly I lost consciousness and thought I was going to join Forest. But I didn't.

It was as if the afterlife did not want me. It was as if I was too stained, too damaged, and too used for any other world to accept me. Death didn't want me. So I was forced back to planet earth.

Mom was worried. I was in pain. Mom was crying and the doctor convinced her to get me to see a psychologist. He was a male psychologist because the female one was on vacation and he was one of the best. No psychologist or doctor in the world could help me take this pain away. I was going to suffer for the rest of my life. Nothing would make me feel better. Colton wasn't there with me.

His name was Dr. Piper. He was very nice to my mother and very kind toward me in front of my mother. He wanted to talk to me alone, with no one else in the room, like a psychologist would do. So my mother left us alone. She told me I was in good hands and I should talk to the psychologist. She told me everything was going to be okay.

She left the room and the psychologist locked it. The psychologist who seemed to be nice and innocent turned out to be a very horrible human being who liked to take advantage of the weak, lost and vulnerable ones. He gave me such evil, disturbing eyes...

"Poor, poor little girl, so broken...so lost...so unwanted. Don't worry...you don't have to feel unwanted anymore. I want you."

I was straddled and tied up in my bed and he drugged me. I couldn't move, or make a sound. I was there in my bed...lifeless, like a statue and he raped me. Colton wasn't there to see me, to help me, to beg for him to stop. No one was there. I was like a small island in the middle of a vast ocean.

When he finished, he untied me and drugged me again and I fell asleep. I woke up the next morning crying, realizing what happened to me.

*Poor me.*

*Poor Aelita.*

Why me? Why is the world trying to break me? Why is everyone taking pleasure in watching me suffer? Why me? Why...?

I tried to tell mom that I did not want to see the psychologist anymore. She smiled at me and told me I had to because she was worried about me. I wanted to tell her about what happened, but Dr. Piper was one step ahead. He managed to play with her mind and convince her that I was safe in his arms. When mom left, he raped me again, and again, and again... and Colton wasn't there to save me...and I stopped being an empty shell.

Like I said earlier, it's very hard not to resent or feel oppressed toward people when the only thing they do is break your spirit and take pleasure in watching you suffer. Hate and anger were the only thing left that made sense to me.

I gave my heart, mind and soul to hatred. I let my body become the host of that disease. When the doctor finished with me and left, I tried to tell mom about him raping me. But Dr. Piper was always one step ahead. He convinced mom that I was becoming delirious and had delusions of every men wanting to hurt me. He convinced her that I was unstable and would say anything not to get help. Therefore, because I was raped, broken, suicidal and unstable, my mother chose to believe Dr. Piper over me.

Sweet Hate...I welcomed it inside my heart. The Aelita Fire Ice everyone once knew was gone, I let hate take over me and transform me into something I never thought I would become. I became violent and angry and hateful toward everyone. I was enraged. I hurt servants who tried to get close to me. I even hurt my own mother. I wanted to destroy everything.

So, I started by getting rid of all the animals, then I started destroying the flowers. I did not want to see the good in anything anymore. Everything around me disgusted me. I was angry. I hated this world. I just wanted to rage, to destroy, to hurt, to watch the world burn with everyone in it.

Mom tried to console me, she told me about Zero, that he came to visit me and had brought me flowers. Fuck him! Fuck the flowers! Fuck this world! Fuck me! Fuck everyone! Fuck Colton...

I finally I saw him, outside the garden staring at me with those anguished lost and sad onyx eyes of his. He was just standing there, staring at me. I wanted to see him since the rape. He was the only person I wanted to see, the only person I thought I could find comfort and appeasement...but now that it was too late, now that the disease took over me, I did not want any of him anymore. He came a bit too late.

A part of me felt ashamed of myself because he had to see me in such an angry, hostile stage, and another part of me became even angrier. It was his fault after all. He was the reason why all this happened. If he didn't learn to keep his dick in his pant and stay faithful to his wife, none of that would've happened. It was his fault all of this happened to me. Why did I want him to comfort me in the first place? I hated him and I was scared of him, so I tried to escape.

I was pathetic...I couldn't even make it far and my hair was caught in between plants and he came to my rescue. He was being nice, he was being gentle...did he pity me? I didn't want him to, I wanted to hate him. I couldn't stand being around him. I couldn't stand that very sorry son of a bitch.

He carried me in his arms and helped me into my wheelchair. He was trying to be nice, and I wanted none of his sympathy. I wanted to yell at him and curse him out to not touch me. But I knew the moment I opened my mouth and spoke to him was the moment I would tell him that I blamed him for all this and it would be the moment where I would have to confirm that I hated him. I didn't want to say it. Part of me didn't want to tell him that I hated him.

The next day, I woke up and realized the psychologist was coming again today. No, I didn't want to see him. Not after seeing Colton yesterday. I felt the need of comfort. I felt the need of love. I didn't want to let

Dr. Piper break me again. I wanted to fight because I saw Colton yesterday. The small part of me wanted to fight. So I demanded to see Zero.

He was the kindest. He brought me flowers and new pet to comfort me. He knew what to do or how to act around me. He was my friend. I demanded him. I knew if he came, the psychologist wouldn't hurt me. I begged and yelled and trashed and demanded mom to get me Zero. And mom agreed to my demands.

The real person I wanted to see though, was Colton. That stupid part of me wanted to see him. I wanted him to be the one to comfort me. When the door of the garden opened, I saw him. I saw Colton and he was staring at me with pain in his eyes. I didn't think he was real. I thought my mind was playing tricks with me. He wasn't real. I asked for Zero, not for Colton.

*Colton doesn't care about me. Colton hates me.*

Next, I saw Zero rushing in the background and his eyes were gentle and compassionate. That was what I needed. So, I crawled to Zero and touched him and begged him to pick me up and carry me and comfort me and he did exactly what I wanted. When we were alone and I lied to him and told him I had a nightmare about Cain and wanted him to stay with me until I fell asleep.

The real reason was that I needed Zero to be there so Dr. Piper wouldn't come and harm me. Zero tried to comfort me and he thought he would ease my heart a bit if he told me about how much Colton was angry and full of hatred and wanted to avenge me. Zero thought I would be happy and pleased that Colton was making my rapists pay.

Boy, was he wrong.

Fuck Colton. He didn't give a shit about me. He was only angry and only getting revenge because his pride had been hurt. He didn't care about me. He never did from the beginning. He was never there for me, no matter how much I craved for his attention and for his love, he was never there...so no. Colton was not avenging me. I refused to believe that.

The next day, Zero wasn't there anymore and I grew scared. Dr. Piper could be back and rape me again...

But thankfully he wasn't back. Mom told me that he died in a car accident while coming here.

I...I cried.

Mom thought I was crying because I was sad that 'sweet' and 'kind' Dr. Piper was dead because he was such a 'nice' man. But no, the tears were not tears of sadness. They were tears of joy. I was so glad. I was so happy that man was dead. I was rejoicing his death. See what hate was doing to me?

The next day, which was Friday...exactly a week since the incident, I wanted to go outside. I was in a better mood. I wasn't happy, but just satisfied because Dr. Piper was dead. I wanted to thank Mother Nature for killing him. So I decided to go outside. I wanted to be alone I felt crowded and cramped with all those servants and my mother. Mom gave in and let me go to the park.

Hinata 'happened' to be there. I knew she was there because mother asked her to. It couldn't be helped. They were never going to leave me alone.

I was enjoying the view of the cherry blossoms and Hinata excused herself in the bathroom. That was when my first rapist came out of nowhere. My heart almost stopped and I was afraid. Oh no. Not again. I didn't want to get hurt again. Please no.

He came close to me and pushed me deeper into the woods. I was frozen and forgot to speak. I thought he was going to rape me again. I really thought this world was against me. I thought I was only brought up in this world to be hated and bullied and tainted.

But he didn't rape me. Instead, he broke down and cried happily. He told me how glad he was to see me alive. I was confused. Why would he...?

Then, he had an asthma attack and was on the verge of dying. His inhaler dropped from his hand and away from him. I watched him and saw how desperate he was. He wanted to breathe, he wanted to survive, and I remembered how he forcefully took my life. I was debating whether or not I wanted to watch him die.

Then I thought of Colton. He wanted to kill them.

Fuck what Colton wanted.

I did the opposite of what Colton would do. Not because I had a good heart, but because I wanted to hurt Colton the most. I saw Colton as my enemy and the enemy of my enemy was my ally.

So, I helped Hunter and saved his life and he thanked me and I smiled at him. He started to cry. I could see how horrified and pained and tortured he was. He told me everything Colton and dad were doing. He told me that Colton was killing parents and families and innocent people. I couldn't believe him. Innocent people...?

Colton was many things, but he wasn't an unjust person. I knew Colton was a dark person, I have always known that, but I also knew he had limits and would never, ever jeopardize the lives of the innocents. It struck me when I listened to all the horrible things he had been doing.

Hunter begged me to ask my father to have mercy on the innocents, and he was on his knees. He was imploring me as if I was his Goddess, his savior, as if I was the Messiah. I said yes to ease his pain, but also because I knew it would piss Colton off. Oh, how I wished he was there to see me bonding with the man he hated the most. To my unexpected surprise, it happened.

Colton came out of nowhere and he was as angry as ever. I thought I would enjoy seeing him angry, but I didn't. I could feel a dark, painful aura around him. He wasn't the Colton I saw few days ago at my garden anymore. He wasn't the Colton with lost, confused eyes begging for forgiveness. He wasn't the Colton that I have always known. He was a complete different person.

He was so cold, enraged, angry and so full of inexplicable hate. Goodness, it sent chills to my heart. I didn't know how, but I felt his darkness inside my heart and it was not pleasant. Colton was in a very cold, dark place. Even his voice held rancor when he spoke. I could feel the deadly, hateful venom coming out of him. He had so much hatred inside of him. That wasn't the Colton Ice I knew.

I was brought back home with Hinata and I went straight to the TV room. I knew Colton would come to me. He said he would deal with me later.

I wasn't wrong. He came to me and boy, was he angry. He was yelling, accusing me, and blaming me for everything that he was doing. He told me many innocent people were dying for me. He told me that he had been through hell for me. He told me Nadia killed herself for me.

Bullshit. It wasn't for me. I refused to believe that. It was for him. Then he started to yell again and again, and I did my best to ignore him. So, he forced me to get up, he was so violent, so angry. He stripped me down in front of a mirror and made me look at my bruised exposed body. He was forcing me to look at myself, to look at my damaged body...the one he would never ever touch... or praise... or love. Then he did something even crueler.

He made me watch a tape of myself getting raped by those monsters.

How could he?

How cruel!

He yelled and yelled and was forcing me to watch. I didn't want to. I closed my eyes and covered my ears, but he was still forcing me to watch and he was yelling and yelling and blaming Hunter so I snapped and told him he was the one I was blaming for all this. I saw sadness and pain in his eyes after saying it, but I did not feel sorry for him at all.

As he let me go, I took advantage of his calmness to shut the horrible painful video and covered my body. Then, he told me that he was doing all this for me and that was the last straw. I grew very angry. As I mentioned earlier, the minute I opened my mouth to talk to him would be the minute I would tell him how I really felt.

So, I started giving him a piece of my mind. I told him how I felt about him and how he didn't give a damn about me and he seemed hurt that I was saying this. Then I started cursing and rage was taking over me. He was stupefied and hurt and wanted me to stop talking, but I didn't. Fuck him! This guy didn't have an idea of what the hell I've been through because of him! He didn't have an idea of what happened to me! He only cared about himself and his pride and other women who were prettier than me! He didn't give a damn about me! That's why he left me all alone to deal with this pain... That's why he didn't visit me... He didn't give a damn about me! He hated me! He wanted me dead.

I was so furious and angry and letting all of my dark emotions out for him to feel it, for him to know it, for him to receive it. I was shouting at him and suddenly he shouted back and then told me something that struck me.

"I am in love with you." He told me.

Love...?

Then he kissed me and our soul clashed together. I was frozen in place...I was trying to find the definition of what love was because I had completely forgotten about it.

Love? What was love?

While Colton was kissing me and showing me his heart, and his feelings for me...I was having a battle with my inner self. It was hate, the disease versus love, the antidote inside me. The disease was fighting and wrestling against the antidote...but the antidote was something I wanted all along. Deep down inside of me, that was what I've always wanted and needed and craved.

Colton's love.

So I found myself kissing him back...I let the antidote in...but then I found myself pushing him again. I was overwhelmed and confused with myself.

He felt hurt, rejected, broken and sad...and I felt horrible. I asked him to leave because all the emotions inside me were swirling and blending and overbearing. I was having an inner battle.

Love...

When he left, and I was alone, I had a complete different view of myself.

Colton was in love with me. Even after my whole entire body was broken, even after my soul was shattered...he was still in love with me. He wanted me. He needed me.

I realized I had a reason to live and enjoy this life again. I realized there was hope. I began to be at peace with myself, to love myself...to love.

Thanks to Colton's confession...I was liberated from all of those vile emotions. I was freed from the darkness. I became kinder to Hinata and my mother and Zero and everyone around me. I realized how much mom and Hinata loved me as well. They would do anything for me. I wasn't sad for myself anymore.

If anything, one could say that I was happy. All because Colton was in love with me.

Love.

Love was all I needed.

I could do this. I could survive. I could fight hate. With the power of love, the power of true love, I knew hate could be destroyed.

I healed myself. I healed my soul, I healed my mind because I knew Colton loved me.

You have no idea how strong love is until you let it take over your mind and soul. Every time I thought about Colton telling me that he was in love with me, I felt cleansed, and free. I was able to forgive everything and everyone around me. I held no hate for this world or for anyone anymore. I was so freed that I honestly forgave my rapists, Dr. Piper and Colton for all the pain that they caused.

I realized that I was enslaved to hate and now that I broke free, now that I accepted who I was and what happened to me...I felt nothing negative for them.

I felt so free, I felt like a bird. I felt one with nature, because he loved me.

Unfortunately, I was the only who was feeling this way. I was the only one who broke free from the darkness. Around me, people were still hating and getting much worse.

One of my rapists attacked my home a week later. He was angrier and even more hateful than he was when he raped me. His disease was getting worse. He told me that it was all my fault. Innocent people were dying because of me. Hunter's innocent brother was brutally killed and so were many more people and I had the luxury to be alive. He wanted to make me suffer again, because he was full of hatred.

Hate...I once knew hate.

Everyone around me had the disease and were contaminating each other. Because of hate, innocent people died that day. Hinata died protecting me and my mother. Mom was hurt too.

Thank Goodness Colton came.

It was when I saw how brutal Colton was toward the angry rapist that I've realized this thing has got to stop. I had to do something about this. Colton freed me from hatred but he wasn't free. He became a monster. His hate was unbelievable and was growing at an alarming rate. I was looking at someone else. He was merciless. He was brutal, he was cold and he was unforgiving. Despite the fact that Hidon was not moving at all anymore, Colton didn't stop. He kept on beating him...and it wasn't until I begged him to stop that he did.

I realized my poor Colton needed me. I realized I've been selfish all along. I wasn't the only one who was suffering...Colton too, was suffering. He was in pain. He was alone. All he had ever known was pain. Forest died, his parents died, Nadia died, I, the woman he loved was hurt. It was a very heavy sorrowful weight he was carrying on his shoulder...and no one was supporting him. Hate was the only thing that made sense to him. My poor Colton...

My father too confirmed my discovery. He grew angrier after seeing mom hurt. He stormed past me and past Colton and shot Hidon's dead body multiple times and was so enraged. I have never seen my father act so violent in front of me. I knew he was a very violent man and killed a lot of people, but he would never ever do anything so violent in front of his family.

There was so much hatred.

Before I knew it, hate transformed everyone I knew into evil monsters. I was the only one who was able to break free from this disease. And everyone needed me. I needed to stop this madness.

———

That's why now, today, four days after the attack in our home, I am speaking with Zero and demanding him to tell me everything that has been going on ever since I was raped. At first, he doesn't want to, but I threaten to have an epic meltdown. I don't really mean it, of course. I just wanted to make him talk. So he panics and tells me everything from the killing of the two security guards who were on duty of the night I was raped to killing Jago, Lazar and his family and his children and the gang members who sold weapons to Hunter's friends, to killing the innocent child and his whole entire family just because he was angry at Colton for hurting his two friends, to the killing of Noah and how they beat him to death and how Hunter has threatened to kill everyone...to Colton being locked in a mental hospital for a week...he was suffering while I was healing...

I am horrified and stupefied and disgusted of how much chaos and destruction is going on between the rapists and my family.

It has got to stop.

I demand Zero to take me to see dad.


I am in dad's office and he is so nervous to see me. Dad has not visited me since I was raped. It's because he would break down and cry if he saw me. Which is what he is doing at the moment.

Dad and I are alone and no one is around and he finally breaks down.

I see how anguished and pained he is. I see how he's suffering. He feels so sorry for me. He doesn't understand why horrible things have been happening to me. He feels so helpless. He cries and cries in my arms and then he stops.

"Are you better now, dad?" I ask him with concern.

He smiles at me. "It's so odd to hear you talk."

I smile back and then become serious again. "Dad, I need to talk to you."

He uses a tissue to clean his face. He is composed now. We're seating on the sofa and he's staring at me, listening to me. "What is it, honey?" he asks me.

"Dad, I have a request to make," I tell him carefully.

He nods at me and smiles. "Anything for you, sweetheart. I will do anything for you."

I smile at him. That's good to know. "Dad, I need you to forgive the rapists for what they've done and I need you to help heal Hunter and those who have lost their loved ones in this hateful war."

His face drops and looks at me in disbelief. When he realizes I am not joking around, he scolds me. "You know damn well that I cannot do that."

I knew he was going to refuse.

Stubborn dad.

"Dad, can't you see what this whole thing is turning you into? Can't you see what Colton is turning into? Aren't you scared and worried for him? Dad, look at what all this madness is leading to?"

"Honey-" he is about to say when I raise my hand up to silence him.

"Please, don't interrupt me," I tell him and continue. "Dad listen to those names: Aaron, Nick, Fiona, Erika, Sonny, Kenna, Sukia, Hugo, Angela, Zeus, Stan,

Ken, Doug, Jon, Yuki, Edgar, Allen, Steve, Sebastian, Belfast, Greg, Andrea, Noel, Tanya, Elisa, Troy, Tyler, Nadia, Noah, Joan, Kenya, Anna, Christopher, Stephan, Milagros, Hinata. Those are the name of the innocent people who died in this mess — the ones who had nothing to do with what happened to me. They're a total of thirty six people and guess how many people are involved in my attack? Ten. Let it sink in, Dad. Thirty six people who have absolutely nothing to do with what happened have been brutally killed and tortured painfully just because they're either related to the rapists in some way or because they were in the wrong place at the wrong time. Dad, how can you sleep at night knowing that you've been killing innocent people? How...?"

"Don't try to make me feel guilty, honey," he argues. "No one hurts my daughter and gets away with it."

"Dad, you're not making any sense. None of those innocents hurt me. You have to stop this madness, this revenge thing...it's only getting worse. You know what you're doing is pointless,"

"No it's not, sweetheart. You're right. It will get worse, because revenge is not about the greater good. It's just an itch that needs to be scratched. I am Lord Fire, a very strong, powerful man in this Island and my daughter has been wronged and hurt by those low lives. I will not let them rest or get away with this. A strong man like me will not let this go," he continues.

"Strong?" I scoff at him. "Dad, you are far from being strong. You are weak," I tell him.

He looks taken aback.

"I am the strong one in this story. You're all weak, you, mom, Colton, the rapists...everyone here is weak. You're letting yourselves taken over by hatred. Look at all this mess, you start with revenge, you want to hurt the ones who hurt me and then you end up hurting their families and some innocent people and when friends of families defend the wronged, you slaughter them all...and then you torment the rapists again, and you all decide to go gang up on Hunter's innocent sick brother and beat him to death? You shoot down Hugo, the ten years old child who was angry because Sony and Kenna the children of Lazar were killed by Colton? How much of a coward are you, father? How could you stoop so low? It's not right dad! What you're doing is not revenge, it's genocide and hatred and it's turning you, Colton and my rapists and their families into cold hearted robots who want nothing but hurt one another! Look at what happened to mom and Hinata and the dozen of guards that were in my house because of all this mess!? Once you give pain and sorrow to someone, once your break him, the person knows nothing else but hatred and the desire to hurt! That is what is happening to the rapists, now Dad. Hidon was filled with so much hatred! He wanted to hurt people and he did! He hurt innocent people! He hurt my mother! Your wife—the love of your life would've been dead if Colton hadn't come! And Hunter! Oh My Goodness, Hunter! Zero told me that he threatened to kill him to avenge his brother's death! Guess what dad, if that ever happens and if Zero ever dies, then you know Zero's brother Light and his sister Lava will be upset and they will want revenge as well, especially Light! He will be filled with hatred and before you know it, everyone will be dead in Terra!" I am raising my voice, completely frustrated and irritated by all of this madness. I can't believe I am the only one seeing the aftermath in all this nonsense!

"Dad, this madness has to stop now," my voice softens and I am talking to him gently. "Please, put an end to it. Forgive and love. I know you're hurt dad, I know this because I was hurt and I suffered too. I understand and it's completely normal for you to feel this way, but don't let it take over you. Don't let it transform you into something you're not. Find a way to love, to forgive. That's the only thing that can set you free, dad. What you're doing is pointless, because even if you kill all of them, I don't know what you'll gain out of this. I will still be the girl who was raped and shot. Nothing will change about it, ever. It will be something I will have to live with for the rest of my life. Their deaths are not going to erase it, dad. I am at peace with myself. I feel free. I feel stronger and more beautiful and more complete than I have ever felt," I take a deep breath and notice that he is looking at me with sadness and contemplation.

"Dad," I continue, "I am alright. I don't have nightmares anymore. I don't hate anymore because I know I have people here who love me deeply and that's all I need to move on. Love is all I need. Love and Forgiveness and is all you need," my voice is pleading.

"Dad, I feel stronger than ever. I was on the verge of becoming like you and hating and wanting to see others suffer...I was really going to, but I didn't, because it's in my nature to forgive and forget. The part of me that I thought was lost, came back to me thanks to Colton. Dad, I am alright. I am at peace. I forgive all of them. So please, do the same for me. For yourself, for mom and for those thirty six innocent people that died unjustly. Please, dad." I beg him.

He listens to me and doesn't say anything at all. I am not expecting him to give me an answer right away. I am not expecting him to tell me he's forgiven them at this moment. I know it will take time and healing and a lot thinking to be able to forgive and be at peace with this and I'm going to give him time. Plus, there's someone else I really want to see and can't wait to talk to.

"Dad, I'll let you think about this for a while," I stand up and kiss him on the cheek. "I love you no matter what and you'll always be my superhero."

"I love you too, my super princess," he smiles at me. "You have matured a lot, Aelita. I am so proud of you."

I smile at him and he continues "The King of Terra is inviting us over for dinner in a week to celebrate Prosperity Day. Will you be able to come this year? "

"Sure dad," I smile. I have never been at any of the royal events, but I would like to go this time and become closer to my father so I can help him overcome this in any way I can. I used to avoid my father a lot because I did not agree with how he ran things, but now I want to help him change. I want to do something about it. I need to help everyone.

"That will mean a lot to me, Aelita," dad smiles with appreciation. He gives me one last hug and walks me out of his headquarter.

"Take me to him," I tell Zero once I am in the car. Zero volunteered to be my chauffeur and my guard for the day so he gets to take me anywhere I want to go. Right now, I want to see and talk to Colton. He needs me the most. He needs healing. We need to talk. I need to confess him what I wanted to confess the night of my rape.

Zero rolls his eyes at me and smiles. He understands and accepts that my heart belongs with Colton and I am so glad that he's handling it responsibly. Can it be the fact that he's been close to Colton and noticed what a great man he is? I hope so.

I am in the hotel and Zero is waiting outside. I feel nervous...gosh, I don't know what to tell Colton. I don't know how to act around him. We never really had a real normal or mature conversation. He either bullied me or ignored me...I really don't know how to start a conversation with him and I am so nervous.

I tentatively knock at the door of his hotel room. No one answers at first, then I knock again this time a bit harder and someone opens the door.

It's a woman and she is almost naked. She's only wearing a huge shirt and I am guessing it's Colton's.

She's very beautiful. She has shoulder length dark wavy hair, captivating grey eyes, a flawless pale skin and a beautiful body. Somehow, she looks very similar but I don't remember ever meeting her. I look inside the room and see Colton lying on the bed. The two of them are staring at me with a very shocked expression written on their faces.

# 21

**COLTON ICE'S POINT OF VIEW**

There is no hope left for me. I'm growing so far, so distant from everything and everyone. Nothing makes sense to me anymore, nothing matters...I can't do this anymore... I don't want to fight. I don't want to...do anything. I just want to die and get it over with. I've seen too much. I've done too much.

I've become the thing, I hate. I've become a vile, foul monster. I've become the slave of calamity. I've turned dark inside. And with that awareness, I can't look into a mirror anymore. I detest myself so deeply to the point where I know I will attack my own reflection and slit my throat with the broken pieces. I do not wish that feeling to anyone. Hating someone else is a very horrible and tormenting feeling, but hating oneself more than anything is unbearable. I am not going to be okay.

How did I come to that tragic truth? Dr. Vancouver showed me that.

———

Four days ago, after I killed Hidon and after Aelita realized what a crazy lunatic I've become, I came to the decision that I wanted to become better for the sake of Aelita and maybe enjoy my last days on earth with a bit of a smile on my face.

So, I went to see Dr. Vancouver for counseling. That night, I was so desperate to talk to him, to make me better. I didn't care what it took, and he realized how desperate I was.

He told me to calm down, and come back the next day since he had other clients. He told me to get a very good night sleep and come back first thing in the morning.

I did so. I slept and woke up the next day, mailed Zero, Warr and Spyros and asked them to take two days off.

I then visited Dr. Vancouver to his institute and we spent the whole day talking about nothing. He told me he just wanted me to relax and forget about all the things I've done. He told me to clear my mind. He helped me do that and we talked about anything but what I was going through. He wanted me to relax for once, and learn to trust him before I opened my entire mind to him. We talked about politics, food, advance in technology and adventures and he told me about the places he travelled, the wonderful things he's seen.

I've grown to like him just in one day. He was such a charismatic, bright person. I thought he was creepy and horrible when I first met him but that was because I was losing my mind. In the end, I liked him. I guess it was mainly because he did not remind me of all the angst and horror I've been through. You know, since the rape, I have not met one normal human being with such a happy, free mind. I've forgotten that this world was actually filled with good people. I really liked Joshua Vancouver.

The next day, things were not so bright anymore. Vancouver wanted me to talk about my past, my childhood. "What was your family like?" he asked me as he poured me a cup of flavored tea. We were in his office. It had a very nice atmosphere and accent to it.

"...My family?" I asked a bit uncomfortable.

"Yes, your mother and father and... your brothers," he said very carefully.

"B-brothers...?" I frown. "I only had one brother."

"No, Colton. You had two brothers. Sebastian and Caleb," he corrected. I cleared my throat and began to feel uneasy. What was he talking about?

"I don't remember having two brothers...anyways my family is a very touchy subject. I don't like talking about them. Can we talk about something else...?"

"Colton," Dr. Vancouver sighed. "Eventually we will have to talk about your family. You are the only person who can help yourself. I am only helping you find the source of your problems and guiding you to the right path. You have to open up and trust me and trust yourself. We will get nowhere if you don't share this information. Remember, you're doing this not just for yourself, but for Aelita."

I took a deep breath and complied. "Alright...what do you want to know about my family?"

"Let's start with the basics. What were they like? Describe each of them."

"Well," I cleared my throat. "My family was very old fashioned. My mother... her name was Rosa. She had soft dark hair like mine and brown eyes...she was calm, quiet and conserved. She was a housewife and my father controlled her a lot. She wanted to be sweet and gentle toward us but because of my father, she ended up being strict. My father, John Ice, was serious all the time. He believed in perfection and was extremely strict toward us. He was an engineer. I admired him a lot because he was very smart and bright and hardworking...and extremely good at his job. People looked up to him and respected him a lot except my older brother Caleb," I sighed.

"Why is that?" Dr. Vancouver asked

"Caleb was incredibly smart, smarter than me and our father. He had lots of unique and rare potentials. He was a prodigy child, my father's pride...but they never got along. During his teen years, Caleb wanted to think for himself and do things his own way. He did not want to follow our father's path. He wanted to do what made him happy, not what my father thought was the best for him. Caleb did not want to go to college. He just wanted to live a simple life and travel the world and my father was not going to let him. They fought a lot, especially when I was in high school. My family was...not very united."

"Hmm," Dr. Vancouver nodded. "It must've been very hard on you."

"I suppose," I shrugged.

"What was your relationship with each of them?"

"Well..." I clear my throat. "Rosa and I never really bonded. I never called her mom. I don't why. She was good to me, she nurtured me and cared for me when I was sick but...I never really had any close relationship with her. I was somewhat closer to my father. He was my role model and I wanted to be like him...I always tried to impress him by studying hard and getting good grades and doing extracurricular activities but he was never impressed because Caleb did way better when he was my age. I was a bit jealous of Caleb when I was a child, but I was closer to him than anyone in our family. He cared about me...he was a good brother but eventually things became worse with him and my father...my father did not believe in fun...so Caleb withdrew himself from me...and I withdrew myself from all of them when I met Forest."

"How did you meet Forest?"

"Kindergarten...I've known him since I was five. He was a little rascal," I chuckled thinking back. "He was loud, hyper, attention seeking and always wanted to play. At first, I did not want to affiliate myself with him because I thought having fun was wrong and I wanted to impress my father...but, at the age of six, when I realized Caleb was withdrawing from me and my family was growing darker, I decided I wanted to know what it's like to not be serious all the time. I wanted to be like Forest. At first, I was too proud to go to that blonde kid and become his friend, so I would just stalk him and follow him around after school to the playground or by the lake. And I observed him and his friends play. One day, I almost drowned at the lake where he usually played with his friends."

Dr. Vancouver frowned and I continued. "They were playing soccer and I was watching from a tree and the ball rolled to the lake. They were too scared to get it because none of them knew how to swim properly and I thought I was an excellent swimmer. I never swam or took lessons in swimming but Caleb was an excellent swimmer and so was my father and I was only six and thought it was just a natural talent. I knew that getting the ball for Forest would be the best way to make Forest thank me and see me as his hero and beg me to be his friend, so I didn't think twice before jumping off the tree and throwing myself in the lake. The current was so strong and I could barely stay on the surface. The moment I jumped was the moment I started drowning. The kids ran away because they thought they were in trouble, but Forest didn't run away. He jumped in the river, he had no idea how to swim either, but was smart enough to hold on a strong branch and drag me out. He saved my life and was worried about me. I was very embarrassed that he had to save me, so I wanted to leave but he wouldn't let me. I couldn't really walk because my ankle was sprained so I was pretty much at his mercy. It was getting dark out and Forest carried me on his back and walked to his house."

"Wow," Dr. Vancouver raised his eyebrows. He seemed impressed. "Forest sounds like an angel!"

I nodded. "He was. He always had my back."

"So what happened afterwards?"

"When we arrived to his house, it was a completely different atmosphere. It was very strange, Forest's mother was a pediatrician and she was the one who healed my ankle, she was fun, energetic, outgoing, she held conversations with Forest's father. They were happy and joyful and kind, and they even did the dishes together and helped one another with the house shores. Mr. Guardian was easy going, very tolerant, and optimistic. He was far from strict and he let Forest do whatever he wanted. Mr. Guardian was a talented painter. My first day with them was strange because I thought it was completely weird for a family to be this fun and open. But with time, I grew used to it because Forest took a like in me. I was the smartest in our class, I was very good at playing soccer and running, I could keep up with him, we competed a lot, but in a fun away. He liked me and thought I was his brother. He told me he had always wanted a brother like me, and his parents considered me as their second child."

"What about your parents? What did your father think of that?"

I inhaled and cleared my throat. "Well, I felt like I did not exist around them. I felt as if I was not worthy of my father's time. He never really said anything about Forest. He was very obsessed with Caleb. Caleb was a genius and his pride and I was not a genius. Don't get me wrong, my father and mother loved me and Caleb very much, but they had a difficult way showing it. Anyways, I was not very scolded or disciplined by father for hanging out with Forest and having fun all the time. My grades were always excellent and I wanted to be an engineer like him… so I think he was okay with me...his main focus was Caleb."

"Did you envy Forest's family or did you feel like they should be more like yours?"

"I envied Forest a lot," I promptly replied shamelessly. "I loved his family and how his parents loved him no matter what. Of course they were not perfect. They fought sometimes and Forest sometimes gets in trouble with his mother and gets grounded but they were happy overall. He had a healthy family...I considered Forest like my brother. I detached myself from Caleb, I spent less time with him and more time with Forest. He was always around me. Even though he was popular and had many friends, we hung out more with each other. He was my only friend and I did not want to share him...and Aelita Fire came two years later,"

Dr. Vancouver smiles, "What was your relationship with the Fires?"

"I was very intimidated by Mr. Fire. He always had a poker face around everyone but he loved Aelita. He spoiled her a lot. I would say that I was tolerated by Mr. And Mrs Fire only because Aelita loved me. I was very mean and cruel to Aelita, and Mrs. Fire saw that and I think if it wasn't for the fact that both Forest and Aelita adored me, I would never be allowed in the Fire Residence. However, I admired them a lot. Compared to my family, they were in love and happier and they loved Aelita to death. They were willing to do anything for her to just see her smile. They were not strict at all. She was never grounded or lectured. Forest got lectured and grounded a lot but Aelita's parents had no discipline or rules for her," I frowned.

"Did you have a problem with that?" Dr. Vancouver asked as he noticed my mood changing.

I nodded, "I did. I thought they were not helping Aelita at all. I mean, of course she deserved to be spoiled and loved and pampered by her parents but I don't think it helped her situation. You see, Aelita was not only mute, but very introvert and shy and very fragile. They treated her like an egg and never let her come out of her little shell. I felt like they were telling her that it was okay to feel sorry for herself just because she had a disability...and in result of that, Aelita never tried to explore the world. If it wasn't for Forest, I don't think she would ever have friends or leave her castle."

"Is that why you disliked her in beginning?"

I raised an eyebrow. "Well...I'm not sure. I disliked Aelita for many reasons, I-"

"Actually, let's not talk about her yet," he interrupted me. "Let's focus on Forest for the moment. Tell me, did he have a dog?"

I shook my head.

"Did you have one in your family?"

"No," I answered.

"Did you or Forest wanted a dog?"

"No, I never really cared for a pet, and Forest wanted a dragon as pet," I rolled my eyes. "Aelita had lots of pets but I was not really attached to any of them."

"Are you sure you did not have a dog when you were a kid?"

"Yes, I am sure." I breathed getting a bit annoyed.

"Maybe you forgot," Dr. Vancouver insisted. "Like you forgot about your fraternal twin brother."

I glared at him. "I'm telling you, I didn't have any brother other than Caleb. I don't know what you're talking about."

"Colton, you-"

"And even if I did, how come my parents or Caleb never talked about him?"

"Colton, you were born with a twin brother. It's in your family records," he took out a folder and handed it to me. I reluctantly took it.

"In this, you'll see the copies of all your birth certificates and medicals records of your family and also, you will see your twin brother's death certificate."

"Wh...?" I was speechless, not understanding how this was possible. "This must be a mistake. I did not have a twin brother. I would know if I did," I was bewildered and confused while I continued to look through the documents.

"Do you remember anything before the age of five?" Vancouver questioned, his expression was calm and his voice was gentle.

"No," I replied with a sarcastic tone. "I don't think most kids do. The brain is still developing."

"You're right, but something traumatizing happened to you at the age of four. You watched Sebastian fall off a cliff and die," he announced bluntly.

A moment a silence stretched between us, and I could not find my tongue to speak. What the hell was he talking about? I had another brother and he died in front of me? That's not possible. I am sure I would remember something like that. "You are making it all up," I accused him in a defensive way. I started to feel very hostile toward him.

He simply flipped his hair and gave me a comprehensive smile. "I have a wild imagination, but I'm not that fucked up in the head to make something like this up. It's in the documents I handed you. Trust me, this happened."

I am left speechless. "...How come I don't remember this...?" I asked a while after.

"Maybe because it was very traumatizing...you were there when Sebastian fell off the cliff. You were the last person he saw before dying."

"...I don't remember any of this," I grunted feeling frustrated and uneasy.

"Try to," Dr. Vancouver was still calm which annoyed me even more. "It's normal to forget traumatizing moments of our childhoods...you were young and your body must have been in shock, and to protect yourself, you forgot everything that happened because it was so traumatizing, but now I think you should try to remember it. It may be the reason why you're this way."

"I don't know how to remember this...I–I don't know!" I was trying to grasp the idea that I had a twin brother and for some reason, I believed what Dr. Vancouver was saying. Maybe I did...maybe something really bad happened to both of us and I forgot. I was so scared and felt an eerie chill down my spine.

"We could try hypnosis," he proposed, observing me. When I don't answer, he continued. "It's a very simple process. You don't have to worry about anything. All I will be doing is helping you relax and focus hard enough to go back to that time."

"...I still can't believe I have a twin brother..." I shook my head still distraught and in shock. "But sure...yes, why not?"

"So you're agreeing to let me hypnotize you?"

"Yes, I am."

He smiled approvingly and we started the hypnotizing process.

I was able to relax and drift away eighteen years in the past. I was a four years, and Rosa, my mother, was holding my hand. We were...apple picking in the woods and I was happy. I was joyful and singing along with my her to a friendly tune. It's strange, I don't remember ever being this happy around Rosa, but I was. I wasn't alone, it was me and another boy. He resembled me and was the quieter and calmer than I was. However, we were close. We were happy. I remembered feeling happy at that moment. I was with my two most favorite people in the world. As we continued apple picking, my brother and I started playing hide and seek while Rosa was picking more apples and suddenly, out of nowhere, a bear appeared and growled at us. We both grew scared and started to run. I remembered being so afraid. We were both screaming and the bear was chasing us. Sebastian tripped and was going to fall off the edge of the cliff and he screamed for help and I wanted to help him, but the bear was coming after me and I was so scared. I remembered my mother screaming for us and I was crying, and afraid and the big bear was coming after me.

When I woke up, I saw the bear and it was standing in front of me, growling at me. Instead of running away like last time, I had a sudden urge to fight and kill the bear. So, I jumped up from the sofa and grabbed the lamp on the desk and started beating the bear with it. It was struggling, but I did not want to let it overpower me. I continued to beat it until it drew blood. I felt angry and vengeful...and by the time I gained consciousness and awareness, it was too late. I found myself seating on the floor with Dr. Vancouver's dead body by my side. I came to the realization that I had just killed him.

"No..." I started to shake him, desperately hoping that he would survive. "Doc, please wake up! Please! Doc! Joshua!" I continued to shake him and he did not budge at all. He had no pulse, and was dead.

I had just killed another innocent human being. I felt like a monster. I was so shaken and so traumatized that I did not know what to do anymore. My problems were becoming worse when I was trying to get better. There was no hope for me.

After hours of panic, I decided to let someone know that Dr. Vancouver was dead. I couldn't just let his body stay there and have his someone find him the next day.

I did not know who to call at first. I did not want any of my crew members knowing what I had just done. I did not want them to think of me as an unstable psychopath, so when I picked up the phone, I dialed Lava's number.

"Who's this?" she answered, her voice was suspicious. I was slightly shaking, and could barely talk. I did not know how to tell her what I've done. Heck, I did not even know her. "Hello?" she said again, getting annoyed. "Whatever, I'm hanging up," she warned and I managed to say something.

"It's...Colton Ice."

"Mr. Ice?" she sounded surprised. "Um...how may I help you?"

"I...didn't know who to call...that's why I called you...I have a situation..."

She was silent for a moment.

"Please..." I insisted. "I don't know what to do...please..."

"Where are you?" she asked with a little bit of concern in her voice. I told her my location and she promised she would be there as soon as she could. It took her less than half an hour to come.

She was standing by the office door and looking down the floor, staring at me and Dr. Vancouver's dead body. She seemed a bit shock and surprised, but her face remained calm and she was not freaking out. Why should she be freaked out? She had probably kills people on a daily basis.

"What happened here?" she asked me, walking in the office and looking around the place.

"I..." I felt sick, but did not have the energy to vomit. "I murdered him."

"Murder?" She raised an eyebrow and continued. "Okay, so? How is this a situation?"

"I thought he was a bear...and I killed him..."

She looked at me and blinked once. "You're confusing the shit out of me...are you okay?" she walked closer and bent down and touched my forehead. "Your body is so cold, and you're so pale. Are you dying or something?"

"I don't...know what to do. I didn't mean to kill him," I continued to stare at Dr. Vancouver's dead body horrified and disgusted of myself. "I don't know what's wrong with me...I'm a monster..." I wipe the tears from my face and pull my hair.

"Okay, calm down Mr. Ice," she sighed and dug in her pocket and tossed me a bottle of medication. "Don't worry, I'll take care of the body. You just try to go home and take this. It will calm your nerves and help you sleep."

She turned her attention back on the body and I took two of the pills she gave me. It took less than a minute for the pill to start working on me. I felt drowsy and sleepy and everything around me started to fade away slowly. Before I knew it, I was unconscious.

———

I wake up the next morning. I am in my hotel bed and the sunlight is blurring my vision. I squint my eyes and frown a bit, feeling discomfort. I start to remember who I am and what kind of hell I live in.

"You're finally awake," Lava says, her voice is a bit grumpy. I turn around to stare at her. She's not in her navy blue uniform anymore. She's wearing one of my shirts and nothing else.

"Gee Mr. Ice, you gave me a scare yesterday!" she glares at me, scolding me. "You only needed to take half a pill and instead you took two! I thought you were going to die. You're lucky you're Lord Fire's son-in-law or else I would've abandoned you and left you for dead."

"You should've," I shrug not really feeling grateful for her little act of kindness. "Why are you in my shirt?"

She continues to glare at me. "Well I got Dr. Vancouver's blood on my uniform and I'm not wearing it."

Dr. Vancouver...

"What did you do with his body?" I whispered, my heart filling itself with angst and guilt.

"Don't worry about it, I took care of it." She grumbles, walking toward the window and opening the blinds letting more sunlight on my face. "You know my brother's gonna be pissed that you killed his psychologist," she whispers but I don't really understand what she says.

I feel numb and empty with no desire to do anything. I really want to die. I am a monster. How could I continue to live with myself knowing that I have been taking innocent lives? Dr. Vancouver only wanted to help me, he meant no harm and I brutally beat him to death. What's wrong with me?

"You look so miserable," Lava says as she looks at me with hunger in her eyes. "You're so handsome, Mr. Ice. I have a weakness for handsome men like you," she's slowly crawling toward me on the bed. Her grey eyes are filled with lust. "I would love to put you out of your misery," she's seating on top of me as my dead, lost eyes blankly stare at her. "It'll be fun for you at first, I would fuck you to the point where you wouldn't know who you are anymore, and when all your senses condense into a strong, overwhelming one, while you're pouring yourself inside of me, I will dig my sharp nail into your chest and pierce your heart, then slowly rip it out." she smirks and licks her lips and continues to purr while brushing away the strands of hair from my face. "I love collecting men's hearts...they're the most precious things on earth. Don't worry, I'll be gentle with you," she's running her hands against my chest, her eyes darkening but she brusquely stops and gets up. "I must control myself. Lord Fire will have my head if I lay a finger on you." she breathes, while staring at me with a desire to kill. She suddenly reminds me of her brother Zero, and I have a feeling that she's worse than him. She's craving to take my life, not because she dislikes me, but for self-pleasure. I find it very disturbing.

"Anyways, you must be hungry. Should I order something for you?" she asks, changing the subject.

I don't answer her. Like I mentioned before, I have no desire to do anything. I don't want to talk, I don't want to eat, I don't want to get up, I don't want anything. I just want to be dead.

"Oh you're not going to talk? Fine, be that way. I'm ordering something for myself," she dismisses and walks toward the phone. She's in the process of dialing when suddenly, there's a knock at the door.

"Are you expecting someone?" Lava asks me, but I ignore her and continue to blankly stare into space. There's another knock at the door and I feel Lava rolling her eyes at me and storming toward the door while muttering something.

She opens the door and I see someone I never expected in a million years to see.

Aelita...

"Aelita?" I rise up from the bed and look at her shocked. I feel suddenly awake, and all my senses are coming back to me. She looks at me with those beautiful honey brown eyes of hers and then blinks and then looks at Lava...then her face falls.

"I...I'm sorry. I should've called before..." Aelita says a bit embarrassed then starts to walk away.

It takes me a moment to realize what she is thinking. I have a woman in my hotel room and she's wearing nothing but my shirt.

I jump out of the bed and chase after her in the hallway. "Aelita, Wait! Wait!" I say, catching up to her and securing my hand around her wrist. "It's not what you think. It's not what it looks like, I swear," I try to explain her. I am not sure if it's a good idea to go into details.

She doesn't say anything. She is avoiding eye contact with me and her facial expression tells me that she does not believe me. I don't blame her. I mean, all I've ever done since we've been married is sleep with countless girls. I don't blame her for thinking that I'm doing something with Lava.

"Aelita, I haven't touched her," I promise her. "That woman is Zero's sister. I would never affiliate myself with anyone related to that psychopath, I swear." She finally looks at me and then turns back to stare at Lava.

"She does resemble Zero," she whispers, giving a kind and acknowledging smile to Lava.

"A whole lot," I agree.

I feel her relax a bit more.

"What is she doing here with you...?" she asks, determined to understand the situation.

"Let's go inside and I'll explain you everything," I propose.

"A-alright." she reluctantly agrees. I am still holding her hand while we're walking inside.

Once we're inside my room, Lava grins at Aelita.

"You must be Aelita Fire."

Aelita smiles back at her kindly and a bit nervously. "I am, and you're Zero's sister."

"It's very nice to finally meet you in person. Zero talks a lot about you," Lava's eyes soften in appreciation. "I think he was understating it when he said you have the beauty of a Goddess,"

I clear my throat and glare at Lava who completely ignores me.

"Thank you," Aelita replies timidly and turns to me. An awkward silence stretches between the three of us and Lava decides that it is best for her to leave.

"I think I'll leave you two alone," she clears her throat and starts to pick up her uniform from the top drawer. It's drenched in blood and Aelita notices it too.

"Thank you, Lava for...your help," I open the door for her and she bites her lip. I know she wants to say something mean but she refrains from doing so because Aelita is here. She just forces a fake smile and says goodbye. I am now left alone with Aelita, and for some reason, I find it hard to maintain eye contact with her.

"What happened here...Colton?" she softly asks me, standing in front of me. Her eyes are searching for mine as if she is trying to look inside my soul. I feel hypnotized. I feel the urge to let everything out and reveal myself to her and I do so.

I tell her everything and I explain what happened between Dr. Vancouver and I and how I brutally killed him, and how Lava came to clean the mess. When I finish, I don't dare look at her in the eyes. I know I scare her. I know she will be thinking of me as a despicable monster. She must be thinking that I am worse than Zero. She is probably right.

"Colton...I'm sorry you're going through so much pain all by yourself," she gently tells me. I glance at her and she is slowly tearing up. She does not look afraid, she does not look disgusted. She just understands me.

"I don't understand why you're not running away from me right now. I killed an innocent man again. I am a horrible person. He was my psychologist, and he wanted to help me and in return, I killed him."

"I did something similar too when I was in the darkness..." Aelita explains. "I rejoiced my psychologist's death. I felt happy when he died...it was wrong. But that was because I was filled with hate for the world and no one was around to take it away from me. But I'm here for you Colton, I'm here for you no matter what. I will not let you carry all this heavy weight all by yourself."

I frown, not understanding why she would be happy that her psychologist died.

"Why were you rejoicing his death?" I ask her.

She slightly widens her eyes and looks away, as if she regrets telling me that. I stiffen and narrow my eyes at her confused and when she doesn't reply, I begin to panic.

"What did he do to you, Aelita?" I ask her, standing in front of her.

"L-let's not worry about me," she tries to change the subject. "It's about you now, Colton."

"No," I take a strong hold of her face in my hand and make her look at me. "Tell me, Aelita. What did he do to you?" I receive no answer from her.

I suddenly start to feel shivers run down my spine and start to think of the worse. "Did he hurt you?" I ask her again painfully. My throat is aching as I utter those words. Her reaction makes me feel even worse about myself. And here I thought nothing could hurt me even more...

She looks away with pain in her eyes and still doesn't answer me. Her silence is confirming my assumption.

My heart clenches and my mind is starting to twirl, trying to grasp and digest what I am finding out but it's so hard. This is too overwhelming. My brother's death, Dr. Vancouver's death and now this...no, I can't anymore.

I let go of her jaw and turn away from her so she doesn't look at me. I walk toward the window and pretend that I am starting out, but I'm not. My eyes are far, far away and distant and my body is starting to shake visibly.

# 22

## AELITA FIRE ICE'S POINT OF VIEW

Colton turns away from me and he's walking toward the window. His back is facing me and he begins to shake.

"Why didn't you tell anyone?" he whispers, his back still facing me. His voice is so quiet and I can feel it tremble.

"I tried to, but no one believed me. He made mom believe that I was unstable and delusional," I explain.

His body is trembling even more and I know he's upset. I start taking few steps toward him. "But it's alright now, none of this matter anymore. He won't hurt me ever again. He is gone."

He's not saying anything.

"Colton..." I whisper and tentatively touch his shoulder. I make him turn around to face me and I see something that breaks my heart into million pieces.

He's crying.

"Oh, Colton!" I say and hug him. "It's alright. It's all over now."

I hear him gasp slowly and breathe deeply. His face is buried in my hair.

"It's okay..." I continue to tell him.

Then, he breaks down completely and holds me tightly as he starts to bawl. He's soundly crying harder and harder by the minute. I can feel his pain, his sorrow and his despair and I feel so horrible. I want to take it away from him. I want to make him better.

My poor Colton... What can I do to help him? What can I do? I feel so helpless. His pain is too much for his body to handle, so he crumbles down on the floor and I follow him. I'm trying so hard to comfort him, but it's not working.

He is crying even harder. His head is resting on my lap as I am patting him and slowly running my hand through his hair. "Aelita..." he continues to bawl. "It hurt so much...the pain...it won't stop...it won't leave me alone...I...I...I can't...it anymore...I...I...it hurts...it hurts...so much...Aelita..." he's gasping holding me tighter. "I'm so drained...my insides hurt...my body hurts...it's like I'm turning black inside...it hurts...I can't...take it...just can't...I can't...I..."

He continues to cry for a while. He is in so much pain. He has been suffering more than I have been and no one was around to comfort him, to be there for him...

My poor Colton...

I just want to take away the pain. "Colton," I start. "It's going to be okay. I'm here for you. I love you, I...I've always had since I first saw you on my seventh birthday party. You captivate me. You're a great person to me. You've always been my other half, my raison d'être. I love you so much, and I want to be there for you. I want to help. I want take away this pain from you. Please, just tell me what I can do. Please...just tell me," I beg him.

He slowly stops crying and raises his head up. He sniffs and wipes his tears, but his eyes are still red. They're filled with so much pain. "There's nothing you or anyone can do anymore," he tells me.

I shake my head refusing to believe him. "No. Colton you're so wrong. I am capable of helping you. I have become stronger than you could ever imagine thanks to you." I take his hands in mine and continue with a smile on my face. "You saved me when you told me you're in love with me. You saved me. Colton, I can't explain the epiphany I had when you told me you love me...it was like revelation. You became my strength when I felt weak, you lifted up when I couldn't reach hope, all because you love me. Your love saved me from the hatred and resentment I once held... I used to be so angry, but all this is now light years away...I feel strong and free. I was a bird encaged and you freed me. I hold no hatred or anger toward anyone, toward Hunter or Dr. Piper, I forgive them and I feel so free…it's such an amazing feeling, Colton...and I have you to thank for. I am everything I am right now because you love me. Colton and I want you to feel the same way. I want you to let me help you. I want you to trust me. I want you to let me love you. Please,"

He shakes his head. "There isn't much to do anymore, Aelita. I'm hopeless. You can't...do anything."

I refuse to let him think that. "No! Listen to me," I say, putting both hands on either side of his face and holding him in place so he can look at me. I stare at him with so much determination in my eyes. "I love you! I am your wife and you are my husband. I'm your lady and you are my man. We belong to each other and it's my duty to help you. So whenever you're in need, it is my duty to do be there and do all I can for you. I won't let you suffer alone. I won't let you feel hurt anymore. Trust me, Colton," I plead him, "Let me in, let me help you. Believe in me. Please, I want to help you. I want to always be by your side from now on. I want to always be the one you run to when nothing makes sense. I want to be your comfort, I want...you. I love you. I love you so much that I can't explain. I love you, I love you, I love you and I will always love you, and I won't give up on you, so please, please don't give up on me."

But my words are not reaching him. He is still holding this sad, lost look in his eyes. He is still pained. "Let's run away!" I suddenly say. "Let's just leave this crazy island and everyone in it. Let's go somewhere else. Let's forget about all this and start over. We can change our names and who we used to be. We can start fresh. I want to start over with you. Let's start over, Colton. Let's break free from this place, from this hate, from this cursed town, let's forget about everyone here. Let's just go, no one needs to know where we'll be going. We'll just go and settle somewhere and I swear every day will be fun. You won't ever have to cry ever again. As long as we're together...as long as you let me help you, as long as you're with me, I won't be scared anymore and you won't suffer ever again. We'll be happy as long as we're together, I promise."

He listens to me carefully and smiles painfully. He leans toward me and kisses me so sweetly. His mouth is cold, yet, I feel my body burn up. I feel warm fireflies illuminate me. I feel my body stimulate by his touch. I love him so much. I can never get enough of his kiss.

He then slowly breaks the kiss and gently removes my hands from his face. He kisses my hands and finally speaks. "Oh Aelita, you're so naive."

# 23

## COLTON ICE'S POINT OF VIEW

Aelita, oh Aelita…she still has the mind of a child. She still is so innocent. Even after all she's been through, she still sees the good in this hopeless world. Sweet, innocent little girl. I pity her.

"Oh Aelita, you're so naive," I tell her as I remove her hands away from me. She frowns, as if she isn't expecting me to say something like this. Well, it's the truth. "All of what you're saying is wishful thinking. Nothing can ever get better," I tell her, standing up. "I have lost all hope and desire to survive. I don't see any reason why I should look forward to a better day...nothing is going to be okay."

I turn back to her. "You're strong Aelita...you really are. I was wrong about you. I am so sorry for ever calling you weak. I'm the weak one. I'm weaker than you and I can't ever be strong."

"Yes you can," she insists, standing up. "Time can heal everything."

"No," I shake my head. "There's too much, way too much that time cannot erase Aelita. I'm broken, I'm gone...and it's not just because of you. It's because of everything I've done and seen in this world. I've been suffering since I was a child. All I ever see, all I know is pain and suffering. My twin brother died because I was too much of a coward to help him...Forest died heartbroken because I betrayed him. My entire family died because I wasn't wise enough to reach out to my brother and accept him for who he was. You...were raped because of the pain and anger I've brought in so many people's heart. You suffered the consequences of my actions," I look at my hands. "I have so much blood on my hands, so many people I've killed both good and bad and every night when I sleep, all I can see are their faces, and their horror...they're hunting me. They're taking over my soul and there's not the day that I don't think about the people I've ruthlessly destroyed," I look back to her. "I'm not free Aelita, I can't be freed like you. You're breathing and you're embracing everything around now, but the air you're breathing, that same air feels like a cage to me...I can't be saved. I don't want to be saved. I don't want to go on in this world...I won't want to be with you even though I probably love you more than you love me...I can't...be around you. You remind me of all the pain I've caused...of all the deaths and suffering...I can't be with you. We can't be together...this relationship is doomed...it can't be helped." Her eyes sadden as she slowly shakes her head. I continue, "I'm weak, Aelita. I am so weak and so hopeless and I am facing reality. I don't want to move on. It's impossible for me. It's too late. I'm far, far gone. So please, don't fight for me anymore...that's the only way you can help me."

I feel weak as if my legs can't support me anymore, so I seat at the end of the bed. "If you love me like you said...let me go. Leave me alone. If you want to run away, go ahead...Go be someone else, go start over...it's good idea for you...you need this. I...I can't come with you and to tell you the truth, I'll be so relieve if you disappeared from all this. I won't be able to see you or hurt you or remind myself of what I've done to you. I'll be free if you go away...you bring me pain, Aelita. You do...and there will never be a happy ending in this... my heart is too dark, to tainted to see the light. There will never be any light. So go, leave me alone, leave me to my fate...let me be."

She starts to cry. "No, stop talking like that! I won't leave you. I can't do this, Colton. I won't be happy without you. I swear, I'll find a way… I'll find a way to save you… to help..."

She's not giving up and it's irritating me. I look up to her with cold eyes. "How? How are you going to help me? How are you going to wash away and the blood I have in my hands? How are you going to ease my heart and soul knowing that I've killed innocent children, innocent people with no remorse and regret? I've come to hate myself so much. I hate myself more than I hate those who hurt you. I've become a monster, something I thought I would never turn into. I hate myself so deeply that if I look into a mirror, I promise you I'll attack it and break it, grab the broken pieces and slit my throat with it. I hate myself so much that I would enjoy see my soul burn in hell for eternity...how can you ever help me overcome that feeling, Aelita? How, Aelita?"

She doesn't answer.

"HOW!?" I fume at her and she jolts.

"I don't...know..." she says slowly.

I rise up and glare at her, and start to storm toward her as she slowly starts to back up. "That's right you don't know. You don't know shit. You don't know what I'm feeling. You don't know what I'm going through. You haven't walked in my shoes, yet. You haven't endured and seen what I have. You don't know shit."

I'm suddenly growing angrier at her for wanting to help me, for being so naive, for being so innocent, for not seeing the world as it is.

I suddenly grab her by the throat, my large hands are circling her very small neck and I can feel my fingers ruthlessly press hard on her flesh. I push her back and slam her porcelain, fragile body against the wall. She slightly gasps, but does not show me any hint of fear or pain. Her soft little neck is trapped in my angry, tainted hand and I'm squeezing her so tightly as I hiss at her face.

"You don't know what I'm going through, so save your breath, I won't hear you. I won't listen to you. You think love is enough to help me? You're so naive, so fucking naive. Too fucking good for your own good..."

She's gasping for air and I can see a bit of panic in her teary eyes. I realize that I am squeezing her neck too tightly so I loosen my grip around her, just a little bit.

My eyes soften a bit and I tilt my head to one side. With my other hand, the casted one, I start to caress her face and wipe the tears from her eye. "You're so beautiful," I whisper at her. "Such a saint...so angelic...so...pure...I don't deserve you, I don't deserve to have you...I only wish I didn't love you…"

My grip around her neck tightens again, this time harder than before as I snarl at her like the demon I have become. "…so I could hurt you even more and kill you like the rest. I wish you weren't so pure, so I could take you down to hell with me and make you endure what I've been enduring all this time."

She is trembling under my grip and is crying more. She's shaking her head, trying to talk. I know she wants to insist on helping me but I don't want to let her. So I tighten my grip around her neck even harder, so hard that I can feel every small veins on her neck throbbing. "I'm done with you, Aelita. I am letting you go. I have no hope or no desire left in me to save us. Don't you hate me...? Don't you fear me...?"

She shakes her head stubbornly and I grow even angrier, so I start to threaten her. "If you don't leave me alone, the love I have for you will transform into hate and I will kill you. I will kill you next time you come to me. I will finish what Hunter started,"

I let go of her neck and she begins to gasp out for air and cough. Her face is completely flustered and eyes teary. I don't feel sorry for her. I don't want to feel sorry for her. She needs to understand, she needs to get in that thick skull of hers that there's no hope left. There will never be. "Let me go," I say, looking down at her shaking body. "Forget about me. I don't see what you see in me, and I don't even want to know. I don't want ever to know the good thing you see in me."

"I need you..." she gasps out.

"No you don't," I growl at her, taking a menacing step toward her. "You never needed me. You never once needed me. You overcame this suffering I landed upon you all by yourself. I didn't do anything. You're strong on your own. You don't need me and even if you do, I won't help you. I am filled nothing but hate and darkness and sorrow. I don't have the desire to help anymore. I won't come to you if you need me. I won't help you anymore. I won't be there for you." I tell her cruelly.

She is looking at me with so much sadness and heartbreak.

It's better that way.

"My days are numbered now and if you want to help me die in peace, let me go. Leave me alone. Do you understand?"

She doesn't answer, so I walk toward her and force her up, then I shake her. "DO YOU UNDERSTAND? LET ME GO! LEAVE ME ALONE! LET ME GO! LET ME GO! LET ME GO!" I am fuming at her.

I start to drag her toward the exit of the room. "GO AWAY AND NEVER COME BACK. LEAVE ME ALONE!"

"No!" she is refusing.

"If you still care about me, if you still love me let me go!" I push her out and slam the door at her. She's crying and banging on the door.

"No! Colton! No! Don't shut me out! No! Please! Don't! Don't leave me!"

I slide down against the door and start to breakdown as she is desperately banging on the door. "Go away..." I sob, I'm crying again and I feel her slide down on the door too, still banging and now sobbing like me.

"Colton..." I hear her whisper. "Please..."

I can't stop crying...it hurts even more...and I can't wait...I really can't wait for my execution day to come...I don't want to endure this anymore...I don't...I don't want to think about her...I don't want...It hurts so much....Please...make it stop...Please...Please God...

# 24

## AELITA FIRE ICE'S POINT OF VIEW

"It's a beautiful view, isn't it?" Zero asks me, as we're both on top of the highest mountain of Terra. My mind is somewhere else, remembering the awful confrontation I had with Colton few hours ago. He needs me, and he is completely lost and alone. I cannot disappear from his life. He needs me now more than ever. It just hurts a lot that he wishes me to disappear...it hurts knowing that he is willing to reject my help just because he hates himself.

Poor Colton.

"Aelita, stop crying," Zero tells me softly, bringing me back to reality. I stare at him and realize that my eyes are clouded with tears. He walks toward me and takes a tissue from his pocket and wipes away my tears.

I smile at him and start to cry even harder. Zero gently pulls me toward him and hugs me. "It's okay," he consoles me as I continue to cry.

"Colton needs me," I explain him minutes after. "He needs me, he needs help, and he won't take it because he hates himself so much. He is not letting me in..."

Zero looks at me with sympathy and clears his throat. He clears his throat a lot when he's about to say something serious. "Aelita..." he starts, and looks down the grass not making eye contact with me.

"What?" I ask him with a concerned tone. His grey eyes are eyeing everything but me. He mumbles something, but I don't hear him.

"Speak clearly Zero," I demand him feeling a bit annoyed. I have the feeling that he's trying to tell me something I don't want to hear.

"You should give up on Colton," he finally turns to me moments after. He is staring at me with his grey, ghostly eyes. I inhale and stare at him in disbelief, not believing that *he* of all people would say something like this.

"How could you say something so taboo?" I glare at him, scolding him. "Zero, how could you? You do know how much I love him. You of all people know how much I love him. How could you look me in the eyes and tell me to give up on him?"

He doesn't answer me, instead he turns around and stares at the view before us. I grow angrier at him. "Zero!" I snap at him, making him turn to me. "How could you say something like this after spending time with him?!"

"Spending enough time with him is exactly why I think you should give up on him," he answers.

I frown and look away.

"Look, Aelita...I tried," Zero says. "I hate him so much, but for you, I tried to tolerate him. I tried to see the good in him, I tried to have hope and faith in him, but Aelita, Colton is a lost cause."

I frown again, offended that he is talking about Colton this way.

"Your love for him is forlorn, Aelita...I'm sorry," he whispers, observing me with an apologetic look.

"No it's not," I hiss at Zero, growing impatient. How could he say something like this about Colton? I understand that he still has feelings for me, but I've made myself clear that night, that Friday night when he confessed to me. I told him exactly how I felt about him and how deep my love for Colton was. Zero knows that, and still he calls my feelings for my soulmate forlorn. How dare he?

"Yes it is," Zero insists. "Colton is in a very, very dark place. He is hopeless. It's not about you not being able to save him, it's just that he doesn't want to be saved. You cannot help someone who does not want to be helped. He is too far gone, Aelita...and I don't think anyone can reach him. I think he has always been this way..." Zero snorts, shaking his head. "He is such a pessimist, Aelita. He is the complete opposite of you."

"You're talking nonsense," I argue. "Colton has always been...dark and gloomy ever since I've known him, that's for sure...but he is not unreachable. I can reach him! I can save him...I can stop all this madness."

"Aelita," Zero takes a step closer to me and takes my hand. "Give up on Colton."

I want to argue, but he hushes me and smiles at me kindly, as if he's talking to a child. "Listen to what I have to say first before saying anything else, okay?"

I slowly nod at him and he continues, "I know you have deep regards for him, and I can see that even today, even after he hurt you, despite all the pain and suffering you've been through because of him, you still love him. I don't know why you love him this much, and I wish I understood the reason...I mean, he hasn't given you any reason to love him and you still do...and you love him so purely, so unconditionally and...it hurts me," he swallows and looks at me painfully. "Aelita, it kills me that you, the kindest and most loving human being I have ever met, are willing to give your heart and soul to a man who does not even appreciate it. Aelita, you don't deserve him and he sure as hell doesn't deserve you. He's miserable and he doesn't want to get better. He's so into himself, into his own pain and suffering that he doesn't want to see a way out. The proof is you. You told him how you felt and you told him that you're willing to forgive and forget all this, and start over and he still doesn't want you and he still doesn't want to give himself a second chance. He...he's a goner, Aelita. There's nothing you can do for him..."

My face starts to crumble and I feel my heart sinking like a boat.

"Forgive me, Aelita for telling you something that you don't want to hear..." Zero apologizes sincerely. "But, it's the truth and you have to hear that," he sighs and runs his hand through his long, dark hair. He turns to me and looks at me with contemplation. "I love you Aelita," Zero breathes. "I love you so much that I don't know what to do with myself anymore...I have never had such strong, powerful feelings toward anyone. I guarantee you that I will treat you right, I will appreciate you every single day, I will love you more than I love myself, I will do everything that is for your best interest. I love you, Aelita Fire."

I look away shyly and guiltily, not knowing how to reject him once again. I know how much he loves me, and I respect him for trying again a second time. I know he will never mistreat me...I know that for sure, but...Colton is the one I love. I glance back at him wanting to reject him when I notice his nose bleeding.

"Zero, you have a nosebleed." I frown a bit worried.

He immediately digs into his pocket and grabs another tissue that is already stained with blood. Then, he starts to wipe his nose with it.

"Zero, are you-"

"I'm okay. Just got in bad fight, it's fine," he cuts me off quickly and puts the tissue back into his pocket. I continue to stare at him with concern.

"Let's run away," Zero changing the subject and successfully taking my attention away from what just happened. I widen my eyes at the sound of this, and he continues. "Let's leave Terra and start over. I will stop killing, I will stop following Lord Fire's orders, I will never take a life ever again if you follow me. We can go anywhere you'd like. We can both be vets and build our own little hospital and shelter and save tons and tons of animals. We can have a big garden in our house. We can live in your utopia. We can make it happen, just come with me. I know it will take time to forget about Colton and I am willing to be patient for as long as you need, but just come with me Aelita. You deserve to be happy."

"I will only be happy with Colton Ice," I reply calmly, staring at him. The wind blows and some leaf gets in my hair. Zero takes it away.

"I do not understand why you're so stubbornly in love with him," he shakes his head.

"I don't need a reason to love Colton. I love him unconditionally. I can't explain why I love him either, I have tried to give myself a reason, but I can't find one...the only thing I know is that when I look at him, I am looking right at the other half of me...I need him like a heart needs a beat. I will never be complete with anyone else in my life. It's him. I love him and that's just it..."

Zero sighs and looks down disappointed.

"I love you Zero, I have feelings for you too but they're simply familial. I see you like my brother, I see you as someone I would love to call big brother, and you hold a very special place in my heart. I assure you that but I will never be happy with you as my lover. I only will be happy with Colton."

"He will drag you down, Aelita. He will drag you down with him," Zero insists, shaking his head at me.

"I will try my hardest to bring him up, to lift his spirit and I will give in my all so he doesn't suffer anymore. I know it's going to be hard, and I am prepared to walk straight through hell to get him out of there. I will give in my all," I feel so confident and so powerful as I utter those words. I know I can bring Colton back to me. I know he is not unreachable, I just know it. I feel so connected to him. I know I can get him back.

"What if you're not able to?" Zero stares at me, slightly glaring at me. "I know you're the type to fantasize about happy endings, Aelita, but this is real life, and what's happening to your husband is seriously dangerous. I respect the fact that you're so confident and are not giving up on him, but what if you give in your all and still don't save him? You can't force someone to be happy, Aelita. What if Colton still chooses to suffer and go down? What will you do then?"

Without thinking twice, I answer. "That's simple, I'll go down with him as well."

Zero's eyes widen in shock and disbelief.

"Colton is the other half of me and I will never be complete without him by my side. I will defy the laws of nature, I will go against The Gods and The Goddesses to bring him back to me, but if I fail to, I will happily follow him down to hell. That's how much I love Colton."

Zero softens his eyes and gazes at me. "Is that what you really want, Aelita?"

I nod. "That's what I really want,"

He nods and smiles with defeat in his eyes. "You're My Goddess, Aelita," he whispers, "And if that's what you wish, if you see Colton Ice as the other half of you, then I will respect him and honor him as well. I respect your decision...and I want you to know that I will never, ever stop loving you."

I can't help but hug him tightly. "Thank you," I whisper as I burry my face on his chest. "Thank you so much for understanding, Zero. Thank you."

"You're welcome," he whispers back, his voice is so gentle. I hug him even tighter, feeling very terrible for rejecting him. I know he loves me so much and I know that I am breaking his heart once again, but I can't help it. I only belong with Colton.

"Say, are you coming to the royal party in a week? Do you feel okay and healthy enough to come?" Zero asks me after we're done hugging.

"Um," I walk toward the hanging wooden swing tied under the giant tree. "Dad wants me to come since mom won't be able to...I might come, why?"

"Well I..." he helps me seat on the swing and he gently starts to push. "I'm going this year too as well."

"That's awesome," I grin.

"Lord Fire selected me, and three other guards to escort him and you during that party," he mutters, pushing me again a bit harder so I can go higher.

"You don't sound pleased," I say carefully, when he doesn't reply, I decide to go further. "Is it because your brother is going to be there as well?"

"He's not my brother, Aelita," Zero says, slowly pushing me.

"Zero, he is your triplet brother," I insist.

"As far as I'm concerned, he is nothing to me," Zero stubbornly retorts. I find him to be acting quite childish.

"Why are you so angry with him anyways? You never told me what happened between you two."

"And I never will," he counterattacks, and then adds. "Can we not talk about him?"

"Fine," I sigh and think about Lava. "I finally saw your sister in person today."

"Yeah, she ran into me in the hotel's lobby,"

"She is the female version of you," I smile. "And she's very beautiful. I wonder how Light will look–sorry, I won't speak of him again, sorry..." then I continue, finding myself curious to know more about Zero's sister.

"What's Lava's specialty? What does she do as a Spark soldier?"

"...Uh..." Zero seems to be searching for a careful way to describe his sister's job. "Uh...she likes to torture people, especially men. That's it."

"Is she good at it?" I ask.

"Very," he clears his throat. "Can we not talk about her either, please?"

"Alright..." I nod and keep silent as he continues to push me. Zero, Lava and Light are triplets. He never mentioned that to me. I once mistook his brother Light Noire, The Head of Kingdom Security for Zero. I've never met Light in person either, I only saw him in the newspaper and he resembles Zero a whole lot. The only difference is that Light wears glasses and has shorter hair.

At first, I thought that Light was Zero, but Zero corrected me and informed me that he is his triplet brother. I want to know more about Zero's family and his siblings, but he is always reluctant when I bring the topic. I wonder what happened between the three of them and why is Zero so hostile toward them.

"Did you know that Colton had a twin brother too?" I start a conversation.

"Did he now?" I can sense the sarcasm in his voice, but I choose to ignore it.

"Yes, his name was Sebastian Ice," I say smiling, trying to picture Colton and his twin brother. It's so unfortunate what happened to him.

"What happened to him?" Zero asks me.

"He passed away at a very young age," I whisper sadly, recalling how distraught Colton was when he was telling me the story.

"Was he sick?" Zero questions, sounding a little bit curious.

"No. He fell off a cliff," I answer him.

"I'm sorry to hear that," Zero whispers, pushing me forward but I feel him trying hard to stifle a laugh.

I become frustrated with his childish behavior. "Stop the swing," I order him and he does so. He helps me down and I glare up at him, he's clearly biting his lip and trying hard to not bust out laughing.

"I don't find that funny, Zero. I really don't," I continue to glare.

"I'm sorry," he clears his throat, but can't help smiling. "I'm really sorry. It's not funny for you and I should not be laughing."

"Just take me home. I don't feel well," I roll my eyes and start to walk away.

"Aelita, are you mad?" he follows me and I don't reply. "Aelita, I'm sorry. It wasn't funny and it was rude of me to laugh at your husband's misery."

"It was rude," I agree with him, still storming away. He continues to try to apologize and get me to laugh. In the end, I end up forgiving him, but still cannot find myself to laugh or be happy. Colton needs me, how can I be happy, how can I be smiling when I know the other half of me is suffering?

I will get him back. I know this for sure, I will get him back to me and everything will be alright in the end.

Everything always turns out okay in the end, I just have to think positive and do something.

I won't give up on you, Colton...so please, don't give up on me.

# 25

## COLTON ICE'S POINT OF VIEW

Aelita has been stalking and harassing me ever since I rejected her. To think she'd back away and let me be and respect my wishes...

She's unbelievable.

My phone has been ringing and she has been giving me countless miscalls and voicemails.

Then, the next day she was knocking at my hotel's door, demanding to talk to me. I never opened the door or said anything. I wanted her to think that I wasn't there. She knocked and knocked and insisted on talking to me. She eventually left five hours later when it became dark and she said she would try again the next day. I wasn't going to let that happen therefore, I changed another hotel that night.

I went to a motel a bit far from where I booked my previous hotel. I went to talk to Zero, Spyros and Warr the next day to plan our next target which was Cain Smith. We gathered information about him and it turns out that Peter Stone, the brother of White Stone was his assistant working at my company. Cain had some balls and he was daring. I'll give him that. If I wasn't numb from all the hatred and sadness and sorrow I had, I would've been so mad, but I didn't care anymore. I was going to kill him soon anyways.

Our plan was to kill Cain and Peter the same day at the same time. It was happening tomorrow.

After the meeting, I went back to my motel. I made sure no one was stalking. I even took the long way back.

When I entered the motel, the first thing I noticed was the strands of golden curly hair laying out just inches away under the bed. She was there, hiding under the bed. I sighed and rolled my eyes. Aelita was persistent and stubborn.

But I still don't want anything to do with her anymore.

So I leaned down and peaked under the bed. She was asleep. That's why she didn't react when I came in. She looked really good and really beautiful asleep. She looked so peaceful, so angelic...I'm very psyched and shocked of how alive she became after this awful thing that happened to her...she's acting as if nothing bad ever happened to her. It's as if every time she gets hit and falls, she forces herself up and becomes stronger than she's ever been. She's so amazing.

That's what makes her special. To tell you the truth, my love for her, has grown stronger ever since the fight we had. She is so unselfish...so caring, so strong and she doesn't want to give up on me. I really love her so much.

No, I can't. I can't think about her like this anymore...it's too late for her and I. It's too late for me. I am not at peace with myself so I can't be at peace with her...the only way for me to find peace is to leave this world.

So I let her sleep under my bed and instead, I left the motel.


It's the next day now and here I am booking another hotel.

"There's going to be a black girl with golden curly hair and honey brown eyes," I tell the receptionist. "She's going to demand to see me. She's the daughter of Henry Fire," the receptionist turns pale. "Don't let her in."

"B-but sir...like you said, she's the daughter of Lord Fire ...I'll be in trouble if I disobey her..." he argues.

I glare at him. "She won't hurt you like I will if you let her in," I threaten with a smile. "I will kill you in the most painful way you can ever imagine and burn this hotel down to the ground if you let her in. You have no idea what I'm capable of."

"Y-yes sir." he stutters, turning pale.

I then make my way inside the hotel and do a complete tour of the room to make sure she isn't hiding somewhere. At this point, I won't be surprised of what she does anymore.

As I am sure she's not hiding somewhere in the room, I unpack my belongings and get ready leave the hotel because today is the day Cain Smith dies.

As I am about to leave, I get a phone call from the hotel receptionist.

"S-sir, I have Mrs. Ice...here and she is insisting to let me give her your room number..."

I should've known. "No," I refuse.

"S-sir...she threatened to kill herself if we don't let her in..."

She *would* say something like this.

"She won't do that," Actually...I'm not sure. She tried to kill herself once...but that was because she was in pain. This time, she's better. She won't do that. The last thing she'll do is take her own life when she thinks I need her. "She won't do that. She's just trying to get you to let her in and if you do, remember what I said will happen to you. I was not joking."

I hang up and take a deep breath.

I can't go anywhere now knowing that my wife is downstairs trying to see me. I don't get her, why does she still want to have something to do with me? Since I've ever known her, I've been the biggest prick to her.

---

For example, when I first met her on her seventh's birthday party, when I found her under the bed, and I told her I was here to save her, she was too shy and too scared to take my hand. I grew impatient and annoyed and pulled her hair instead so she could be forced to come out. I've never been nice to her from the beginning. To think that seven year old girl would get scared of me for pulling her hair, she didn't. Instead, she kept on staring at me with wonder and amazement.

On her first day in elementary school, Forest was so glad to have her in our class and she even sat next to Forest. She stole my seat and I hated her for it. Forest was my friend. I didn't want to share him with that weird mute girl, however Forest completely ignored me and paid more attention to Aelita and shared his crayons with her. During recess, while we were playing duck duck goose, Forest chose her instead of me. I was angry and jealous and officially hated Aelita. I even tripped her during recess on purpose so she would fall behind and maybe go to the nurse office and disappear. She was a crybaby back then, so when I tripped her, she cried and was overdramatic. My plan worked, she was sent to the nurse office only that Forest followed her. I even threatened to stop talking to Forest if he continued to be friends with her. I told him that I disliked Aelita and he was my best friend so he better hate her just as much as I did or else our friendship would be over. He did not take me for serious because he knew I would never do that.

With time, I gave up on trying to separate Aelita from Forest because each time I tried to scheme something and tear those two apart, it would only get them closer. Aelita became Forest's favorite and I reluctantly accepted her as Forest's 'second' best friend. It became her and I and Forest all the time. We were the trios. We always played and spent time together. When Forest was around, I would try to acknowledge her and treat her as a human being. When I happened to be with her alone or when Forest wasn't looking, I would just either ignore her or bully her. For example, when we were twelve, one time we were taking swimming lessons at her house. Our coach gave us a break because he had an important phone call, so he left for a while. Forest took advantage of that to go inside the house and use the bathroom. It was her and I left in the pool and somehow, we glanced at each other and she smiled at me. Her smile used to annoy me the most, no matter what I did to her, she would smile. It annoyed me and I didn't want to see her face, so I shoved her head down the pool and attempted to drown her. I let her go seconds later when I saw the coach coming back. She never told on me and never stopped freaking smiling at me. It seemed like the crueler I was to her, the kinder she became. I was her first bully.

I remember in eighth grade, that was when she started getting bullied by others. During lunch time, she was pushed and slapped by a new kid who was annoyed with her because she wasn't talking to him. He didn't know she was mute but it still didn't give him the right to raise his hand on her. When I saw someone else other than hurt her, I felt uncomfortable. I had a very unpleasant feeling inside. Maybe it was because she was a girl getting hit by a boy and I didn't think it was fair... I wanted to beat the crap out of that guy. Forest was ahead of me. Before I even stood up and rushed toward the guy, Forest was already attacking him and beating the crap out of him. I just stood there and watched because I was confused with myself. I thought I hated Aelita, but when I saw someone else hurt her, I felt so angry. I didn't want to admit that I cared about her or acknowledged her as a friend, so I ignored her and every time she would get bullied, Forest would always be the one to save her first. She would cry and Forest would comfort her and tell her nice things and I grew angry with her. She was such a crybaby and everyone always spoiled her. I didn't like that. I was the only one who never gave into her pouts or cries. I was bossy, demanding, and mean. I never spoiled or pitied her.

During freshmen year, Forest told me Aelita had a crush on me and I was a bit surprised. Why would she? I have been nothing but a jerk to her. Why the heck would she have feelings for me? If anything, Forest should be the one she should fall for because he was always sweet and caring to her. It didn't make sense and I was angrier because I knew deep down, I was trying to sort out how I felt about her. I was unsure. I hated her, but cared for her because she was my friend...but when Forest told me she had a crush on me...all those feelings were becoming even more confusing. I didn't want to think too deep about it, and thankfully, Nadia came and she was a distraction. She was beautiful and could talk, she was different compared Aelita. She had a very strong willpower and would never let anyone bully her or get in an argument with her. She could defend herself...and I wanted her because I thought she was better than Aelita. I completely started to ignore Aelita and spent more time with Nadia instead.

Then we went cliff jumping during the spring break and I was a complete jerk to Aelita again and became more and more obsessed with Nadia.

A day before Forest's death, he threw a party. Aelita wasn't really the party girl because she was shy and an introvert person, but she always came to Forest's parties and stuck along with us. But that night, she wasn't there and it bugged me. Aelita was always around me no matter what. She was my shadow. I thought I'd be relieved not to have that crybaby girl around, but to my surprise, it bugged me.

"Where's Aelita?" I asked Forest a while later.

"She has a really bad cold, her mother won't let her come," Forest answered.

I lost all desire to enjoy the party knowing that Aelita was not feeling well. I was worried. Forest, on the other hand wasn't because he said Mrs. Fire was taking good care of her and Aelita was resting and besides, at the moment, he was in love with Nadia and nothing else mattered to him but Nadia. I was worried about Aelita. I wanted to see her and confirm for myself that she was alright. I told myself that I was only worried because I finally acknowledged her as a friend and that I only cared about her as a friend that I had stronger, deeper feelings for Nadia. So I left the party, and went knocking at Aelita's house.

Mrs. Fire was the one to open the door. "Ah, Colton, what are you doing here? I thought you were at the party with Forest..." She said a bit surprised to see me. It was unusual for me to visit Aelita all by myself without Forest. I didn't blame her. I was just as surprised as she was.

"...Is Aelita alright?" I found myself asking carefully and avoiding eye contact.

"Aw, it's so nice of you to think about her," Mrs. Fire smiled at me. "She's still feverish and very exhausted and has a loss of appetite," she sighed worried. "I've been trying to make her eat soup, but she doesn't want to. Maybe you could feed her?"

I looked at Mrs. Fire surprised. "W..wh...?"

She leaned down and whispered in my ear. "I don't know if you know this, but Aelita has a big crush on you. You hold a very special place in her heart...I'm sure she will be delighted and actually eat something if you ask her to."

I was flustered and angry that even her parents thought I should be by her side and lead her on. I had feelings for Nadia, not Aelita. "I'm not her babysitter!" I snapped at Mrs. Fire and left immediately.

No, I didn't want to have anything romantic or affectionate to do with Aelita. So, I went straight back to the party, and Forest was playing pool with some classmates and Nadia was talking to other girls. I rushed to Nadia and asked her if I could have a private moment with her.

She followed me to a private room. We were alone I got close to her and stole a kiss from her. She didn't reject me.

"Finally," she told me and closed the door. "I thought you would never make a move,"

I realized she also wanted me, and she kissed me and I kissed her back too with all the strength I had. I forgot about Forest and that we were at the party. I was telling myself I had feelings for Nadia. I wanted her.

We were in the middle of having sex when Forest barged in.

"Hey Colt, can you..." he started but then he saw Nadia topless, on top of me, riding me and he dropped whatever thing was in his hand.

"No..." he shook his head not believing what he was seeing.

*Shit*. I told myself.

He looked at me and at Nadia and looked back at me again. "How could you...?" he asked me and then before we even had the chance to talk to him or try to soothe him, he left the party.

The next day, his parents told me he got in a car accident and was in critical conditions. By the time I came to the hospital, he had already passed away.

That's when I started to hate myself.

Aelita tried to comfort me in her way, to make me feel as if it wasn't my fault and I didn't want her pity, comfort or support.

Nadia and I stopped talking ever since his death because we both felt guilty and knew it was our fault. He was driving recklessly and wasn't thinking...because of us. We betrayed him.

I wanted to be left alone, but Aelita wouldn't let go of me...and that time, I didn't really have a choice but be around her because she was getting bullied more and more and I knew that if Forest was alive, he would defend her...so I sometimes, defended her for the sake of Forest . I eventually grew tired of it.

In eleventh grade, I cut all bond and ties with Aelita because I found out I had feelings for her even though she wasn't my type. I decided to get my focus back on Nadia because she was different from Aelita.

Nadia, however, didn't want to continue the relationship with me because she had finally moved on from Forest and had eyes for William. She rejected me.

Aelita tried to befriend me again, but I didn't want her at all. I was alone.

Months later, my whole family died within a week. I was even lonelier. Lord Fire then took pity, and took care of me and even asked me to start living in his mansion with Aelita. I had no idea back then that Aelita was the one who begged her father to not abandon me.

Even though I was living under the same roof as Aelita, I was rarely around her. I never really bonded or talked to her. I became a workaholic and started working hard and took interest in business and engineering. I wanted to follow my father's footstep. As soon as I graduated high school, with the financial help of Lord Fire and my master mind, I was able to create my first company. I was distracted from everything because of Cain Smith. He was my rival. Our companies were born around the same time and we were competing and I didn't like losing. I wanted to dominate the business world. So, I asked for Lord Fire to let me take over his electrical company since it was the most successful and popular. At that same time, I was about to convince Nadia to be my partner, my girlfriend or my wife or anything she wanted. I told her I was going to give her the world if she was by my side. She refused of course, because her and William were really serious, and Lord Fire agreed to let me take over his company, in exchange I had to marry the woman I've been trying so hard to forget about.

Aelita just wouldn't let go of me. I was angry at her for that. I accepted of course, because I didn't want to lose to Cain, but I was cruel and mean to Aelita. I blamed her and ignored her and barely acknowledged her as my wife ever since we got married. I would cheat on her and come home with another woman's perfume on me and she could smell it. She knew I was cheating on her, but never once confronted me about it. She never once broke down or cried or hated me. I've been an asshole to her since the beginning and she never ever, ever got angry with me.

---

Even now that she has been raped and tainted and suffered because of me...she still doesn't want to let me go. If anything, I feel like she's fallen even more in love with me. I don't get her. I don't understand her.

Why would she want to waste her time with someone like me? I don't understand her at all...and the fact that she is not giving up on me is hurting me even more. I feel like she's killing me with kindness. As if it's her way of torturing me. I hate myself even more because she still loves me even after all this. I really hate myself.

I am pacing around the hotel room, it's been half an hour since the receptionist called me and I am pretty sure Aelita is probably there, still trying to convince him to let her see me. I can't believe the situation I'm in right now.

My phone suddenly rings. It's Zero. "Mr. Ice," he starts and I cut him off annoyed.

"I know I'm half an hour late. I'll be there as soon as I can. I just have a situation."

"Actually sir," he continues, sounding annoyed as well "I was in the process of informing you that we will have to cancel our mission today."

I fall silent and frown. "Why is that?"

"We're being summoned to an emergency meeting with Lord Fire in ten minutes."

"Alright," I grunt and continue to pace around my room and at the same time, I hear a noise outside my window. I glance out and see Aelita at the balcony tapping my window glass. My jaw drops, my heart skips a beat and I drop the phone.

*What the...?*

I rush toward the window and open it. "What the heck are you doing here?!" I glare at her as she gives me a tentative smile. "How did you even get up here?" I step in the balcony and start to look around. My room is on the fifth floor, I don't know how the heck she got up here.

"Aelita," I turn to glare at her annoyed.

"Colton, how are you?" she hushes me softly. My heart starts to beat fast as we stare at each other. She's so beautiful. The sunlight is setting down on her, brightening her face up and making her glow. She's absolutely stunning.

"You look pale," she continues as she takes few steps toward me, bringing her hand to my face. I love the way she touches me, I love how her small, warm palm feels on my cold, dried skin.

"Have you been eating, Colton?" she tilts her head to the sides and looks at me with concern.

Oh Aelita, how much I love her. I find a part of me wanting to take her in my arms and kiss her and hug her and spend the rest of my life with her...but the other part, the realistic one doesn't want to give myself that luxury.

"Don't concern yourself with me anymore," I remove her hand from my face and glare at her. "I told you this already."

I make my way back into my room and she follows me. "Colton, you don't really expect me to abandon you, do you?" she starts, her voice is firm.

"Yes, as the matter of fact I do." I bluntly say as I turn to her.

"But you love me, and I love you," she insists.

"That's exactly why we can't be together," I snap and she raises her eyebrow. I roll my eyes and open the exit door for her. "I'm not in the mood to argue with you. Just go, Aelita."

"Please come to the Royal party with me this Friday," she begs me.

The what?

"It's Prosperity Day," she answers my unspoken question. Prosperity Day, huh? Another way for Mr. Fire to feel like a God.

"I'm not going," I refuse.

"Please," she insists. "It'll be fun for both of us."

"I don't want to come, Aelita," I tell her firmly, sounding annoyed.

"Colton–"

"Aelita, please leave. I'm asking you nicely. I'm very exhausted and would like to rest," I tell her calmly and softly.

Her face drops and she nods. "Have a good afternoon, Colton," she whispers and walks out of my hotel room. I sigh and roll my eyes.

"Aelita, wait," I call after her. She stops immediately and turns to me with hope and excitement in her eyes.

"You'll go with me?" she almost squeals, grinning at me like an idiot. I can picture her wagging her tail in excitement if she was a dog. I keep myself from snickering at her.

"No," I tell her, and her face drops once again. I take off my jacket and wrap it around her. "It's a bit chilly outside. I don't want you to catch a cold."

She smiles at me with appreciation. "Thank you,"

I want to smile back at her, but I keep myself from doing so. However, I can't help but soften my eyes. "Take care, Aelita." I open the elevator door for her and watch her as she enters. She stares back at me and smiles gracefully.

"I love you, and I will never stop loving you," she tells me before the elevator door closes. I stand there for a moment, staring at the door as I find myself whispering. "I love you more, Aelita."

# 26

"Well, well, well. Look who decided to show up?" Mrs. Fire tells me with a smirk on her face. Since Zero, Warr and Spyros have been busy and caught up with a lot of work this week, I have decided to stop staring at the ceiling for the whole day and visit Mrs. Fire at the hospital. I have not seen her since the attack in my mansion, and I thought it would be polite and thoughtful of me to drop by and see how she's doing. After all, she's the mother of my wife and she protected Aelita with her life. I ought to visit her.

"How are you feeling?" I ask her as I drop the white roses I bought her in a vase.

"I've never felt better," she says sarcastically and pushes the vase away from her. "Those are the ugliest roses I've ever seen. My, look at this. They're just as good as dead...like you."

I keep myself from rolling my eyes or saying something smart to her.

"Anyways," she continues. "Have you seen Aelita, lately?" she smiles at me. "She's happier and brighter, I told you my daughter would be able to overcome all this." she continues to boast proudly. "Aelita may seem weak, but she's the strongest of all. She has been through so much since her first day in this world...she really suffered and any normal person would have completely crack down but here she is still up and carrying on and caring about others. She's so amazing,"

I can't help but smile. "I agree. She's very strong. She never ceases to amaze me."

"And yet, you take her for granted."

"I..." I want to argue, but there is nothing to argue there. I do take Aelita for granted.

"It's a shame that she still thinks of you as someone worthy of her time," Mrs. Fire continues, not holding back from insulting and demoting me. She really is not fond of me at all.

"Well, she has always loved me ever since she set eyes on me and I love her too," I counterattack.

"Please, don't make me laugh. This is not even funny," Mrs. Fire scoffs. "You love my daughter?"

"Yes I do," I nod, admitting it.

"And yet you made her life miserable and continue to? Is that what your definition of love is, Colton?"

"I don't want to make her miserable anymore," I explain. "That's why I'm cutting all ties with her. I am letting her go because I love her."

She wants to say something, but her phone beeps and she ignores me. "Aww," she smiles at her phone and then shows me the picture. "Henry just sent me a picture of Aelita and Zero together at the royal party, aren't they cute together?"

I stare at the picture and see Zero dressed up in a suit wrapping his hand around my wife's waist proudly and they're both smiling at the camera.

I feel something starting to boil inside of me. I start to clench my jaws.

"If you ask me, Aelita and Zero would be the perfect couple. They look so happy together, don't you agree?" Mrs. Fire asks me, smirking arrogantly and enjoying my very displeased reaction.

I glare at her and leave the room, ignoring her calls. Zero and Aelita are at together at the ball. My wife is with another man, let alone Zero.

No way.

# 27

## AELITA FIRE ICE'S POINT OF VIEW

"You look absolutely stunning, Mademoiselle," His Excellence, King Leon, bows to me and kisses my hand with grace. "It's a pleasure to have you with us,"

"The honor is all mine, Your Highness," I respectfully bow to him and smile. I am pretending to be having fun, but deep down...I don't want to be here. I want to be with Colton, I want to make sure he's okay, that he's eating, I want to see his face, I want touch him. I crave Colton's presence as if he is my drug.

"Your mother loves your dress, sweetheart. She is happy you're having fun," dad tells me after taking a picture of Zero and I.

"That dress sure fits you perfectly, Mrs. Ice." Spyros, the short redhead guard compliments me.

"Thank you," I thank them all. "You're all very well dressed as well."

Dad and I are accompanied by four Sparks. Zero, Spyros, Warr and Lava. The male Sparks are wearing navy blue suits with gold tie on. Zero's hair is well combed and groomed and put in a ponytail. He looks quite majestic. Spyros too looks quite handsome, and he has a very strong perfume on. It's a pleasant one, it's just very strong. Warr as well looks honorable. The golden tie brings out the rare color of his eyes. His grey hair is nicely combed as well, only thing odd about him is that he is still wearing his mask. I thought he covered his nose and mouth for work hazard purposes but it seems more like he is hiding his face. I feel suddenly curious to see what's behind the mask. Warr's hands are also covered with black gloves.

Lava, Zero's sister is wearing a long sleeved short navy blue dress and black stockings. Her dark hair is let down and her grey eyes are popping out due to the dark mascara and the red lipstick. She looks absolutely gorgeous...compared to me.

I bet Colton would've slept with her if she wasn't Zero's sister.

"Aelita, cheer up," Zero nudges me, giving me a kind smile. I see that he has been observing me for a while. I smile back at him halfhearted.

We continue to walk around the ballroom of the Palace and greet many important individuals. Minutes later, the King gives a welcoming speech to everyone and thanks my father for helping make this Island a safe, blossoming kingdom full of prosperity, joy and happiness.

My dad receives countless of standing ovations and awards and recognitions. He is very happy and proud of himself. I am not sure I feel the same way.

I respect my father for being a great help to this Island, that's for sure. He has never refused to come in aid when needed. He shares his goods and abundant natural resources with the citizens of Terra and thanks to him, there is almost no starvation or hunger in this Kingdom. Thanks to my father's resources, doctors are able to use medical herbs and plants to fight diseases and save lives. Thanks to my father's army, Terra has been a safe and peaceful island. He does play a very important and positive role in this Kingdom in the eyes of many, however, I can't admire him like everyone does.

There's a dark side of him that very few people know. He is a cruel tyrant. He kills those who stand in his way. He destroys lives... he hurts people and likes to control things and decide other's fate...he is a coward and I don't think I can ever look at him as a noble person. Because of him, my Colton is turning dark. I don't think he deserves all the praises and recognitions that are being awarded to him when I know what he has been doing.

After the speeches, we start to dine. I am seating with my father, on the royal dining table along with the King of Terra and a foreign royal guest. He is the new successor of Appland.

Appland is a nearby island that has been under the dictatorship of a very cruel leader. The previous leader has tried many times to take over Terra creating tension between the two islands. Now that he has passed away, the new successor wants to have a peaceful relationship with Terra and try to ease the tension and become allies.

They discuss about a lot of things, they seem to be so relaxed and carefree and I look around the dining hall and notice everyone around me is happy.

My heart starts to clench as I think about Colton. He is not happy. I wish he could be with me tonight, and just forget about everything even for a minute and just let go. I wish this world could share its happiness and virtue with him.

What will it take for things to go back the way it was, when we were children, when Forest was around?

Forest...I bet he would be able to make Colton change and see the light. Forest had a natural way of convincing and bringing people together. Forest was so important to Colton...I am so sure that if he was still alive, everything would be okay. I miss Forest so much.

"Aelita, are you okay?" Zero's velvet and concerned voice brings me back to reality and I notice that I am crying. Everyone at the table is staring at me with concern.

"Oh," I wipe my tears away. "I'm sorry, I have something in my eye. Excuse me," I say and stand up.

I rush to the washroom and hydrate my face with cold water. I stare at my reflection in the mirror and for a moment, I see the love of my life in the reflection. He looks so lost, so empty, so scared and I have the urge to go to him and pull him out of the mirror and embrace him. The only thing I am able to do is place my hand on the mirror and stare back at Colton. He's staring back at me as well and I slowly whisper to him. "I love you more than anything you could imagine."

"Wow," I hear someone clear his throat. I gasp and turn around and see Zero standing by the door of the washroom and raising his eyebrow and trying to stifle a smirk. "Aelita, I had no idea you were that deep into yourself," he's fighting back a laugh.

I retract from the mirror and walk toward the exit, glaring at him annoyed. "I was talking to Colton," I mutter walking past him.

"Okay..." He says following me. "That's even more disturbing,"

"What were you doing in the ladies room anyways?" I grunt at him, stomping on the carpet a little harder.

"Making sure that you were okay," he answers smoothly now walking by my side. "I am responsible of you. Lord Fire will have my head if something ever happens to you."

I don't reply to him, I am not in the mood to have a conversation with Zero or anyone. I don't want to be here, so I walk in another room.

"Where do you think you're going?" Zero asks me curiously.

"I want to be alone," I snap at him.

"Aelita come on," he starts, still following into the room. "It's time to dance and feast, and you need to participate."

I ignore him and look around the room. It's a beautiful vast reading room with an open door leading to the balcony. I walk out to the balcony. The sunset is nostalgically beautiful and the wind is gently blowing on my face, drying away my tears. I remember when I used to see beauty and happiness in the simplest things...

"Aelita, it's a beautiful day," Zero is right behind me, his voice is soft and yet firm. "Don't be a party pooper."

I roll my eyes knowing that he is trying to make me smile or laugh but that's impossible. "I can't enjoy this day when I know that Colton is not happy. If he's not happy, I am miserable."

Zero inhales for a moment and walks in front of me, making me face him. He has a serious look on his face. "Aelita," he starts softly. "You told me you wanted to save him, right?"

I nod.

"How can you do that if you're choosing to be just as miserable as he is?"

I don't know what to answer him.

"Aelita, you told me yourself that you needed to be his light and that you will do everything in your power to make him see the good things in life...to me, right now, you're not being his light. You're being dragged down in the darkness...you're not trying at all."

"I..." I want to say something, but he hushes me by gently wiping away the tears from my eyes. "Aelita, if you want to save Colton, you have to cheer up. You have be different from him. You have to light up and take care of yourself and be happy. Not for you, but for him. If you fall, he will fall completely and will never be able to get back up, and neither will I."

The wind continues gently blow on us as he continues to talk. "I'm hurting, Aelita. I'm hurting bad and I am heartbroken because I can't have you, but I still love you and I want to see you happy. That's why I am trying to be happy too. You need all the support and love and attention you can get and I am willing to bury away all the sadness I feel inside and make sure you're happy. Do the same for Colton if you really want to save him. I believe you're his only way out."

I gratefully smile at Zero thankfully. He's right, I can't cloud my mind and heart with sadness right now. I can't afford to be sad if Colton needs me. He needs me to be strong for him. He needs me so much, and it's time for me to stop being selfish and think about what's best for him.

"Thank you, Zero," I whisper.

He winks at me and walks back inside the reading room. "You know what? I know what will change your mood," he digs into his pocket and takes out his iPhone then looks around the room and finds a speaker.

I curiously observe him as he plugs in his phone into the speaker and a familiar music starts to play.

"Music always makes everyone feel better," Zero announces as he takes off his suit and loosen his tie. He starts to move around the furniture to make more space. "Music and dance," he corrects and starts to move to the beat in a very silly way.

"What are you doing?" I find myself giggling.

"Just having fun," he grins at me and continues to move as I find myself giggling and laughing at his silly moves.

"What are you laughing at?" he asks me.

"You're a terrible dancer"

"Yeah?" he raises his eyebrow and then completely changes his dance moves. I gape at him with dropped jaws as he breakdances in front of me like a professional. I had no idea he knew how to dance like that, I would have never guessed.

"Surprised?" he moves toward me, still dancing.

"How is this even possible?" I continue to giggle and applaud.

"What? Just because I'm your dad's soldier doesn't mean I can't dance," he teases.

"What? I never said that." I say in a defensive way still laughing.

"Well, why don't you come show me your moves, huh?" he dares me, and I shake my head and join him.

We continue to dance and laugh, and fall and make silly moves and for a moment, I let go and find myself allowing the music to take over me. I untie my hair and start to move to the beat as well, forgetting about everything around me. I dance with Zero and when the music stops, he grins at me. We're both sweaty and breathing hard, and I feel awake.

"Well you look better now," Zero approves, nodding his head at me. I slightly laugh and turn around to put my shoes back on when I see Colton standing tall and handsomely with his hands in his pockets by the door.

My heart skips a beat as if it's the first time I am seeing him. He's wearing a light blue sweater on a grey pant and he looks deliciously handsome. Or so I thought until I see his face. He's glaring at me with fury.

# 28

## COLTON ICE'S POINT OF VIEW

As soon as I leave Mrs. Fire, I drive to the Palace feeling angry and jealous. Aelita and Zero together? I can't allow that. He doesn't deserve her. She can do so much better than that psychopath.

I arrive at the Palace two hours later because of the traffic. Since it's a holiday, the streets are packed with citizens and kids and marching bands. When I arrive to the palace, I have a hard time with the security guards but they let me in after looking me up in their data. Once I'm in, I start to look around the ball room for any sign of Aelita and Zero.

I see familiar faces like Spyros dancing with Lava.

I walk to them and interrupt their dances.

"Mr. Ice," Spyros is surprised to see me. "I'm glad you could make it."

Lava rolls her eyes and smirks at me. There is nothing pleasant about her smirk.

"Well,well," she purrs. "What do we have here? Do we have another situation?"

I glare at her. "Where's Aelita and your brother?"

"Oh," Spyros answers. "Zero went to check up on her fifteen minutes ago, she was not feeling well."

I clench my fists as I start to think about Aelita and Zero alone. That little prick is probably going to be trying to take advantage of her.

"What direction did they disappear to?" I glare down at Spyros who smiles at me nervously.

"This one, Mr. Douchebag," Lava flips me off and points her middle finger to the hallway. Without wasting an instant, I walk in the direction I am given and start to look for them.

Minutes later, I start to hear music blasting from a room, and so I walk toward the door and open it and I see Zero dancing with my Aelita. He has his arms wrapped around her, helping her move as she is flipping her hair back and forth and moving with him as well. They're very close and moving freely. From my perspective, they look like they're into each other.

Once the music finally stops, they stop dancing and stare at each other. I find myself growing angrier and angrier at Aelita. She's such a hypocrite. She claims that she loves me, yet she's letting herself go in the arms of another man. A man she knows has deep feelings for her. How could she?

When they finally notice my presence, Aelita stares at me and I see her honey brown eyes dilate with excitement. She's stunning.

She's wearing a gold and white short dress with a bowtie belt. The dress fits her perfectly and she outstands any woman in the palace. Her curly hair is let down and her dark skin is glistering and glowing. She's breathtaking. I want to walk to her and take her, but then I remember Zero in the background and I remember how she let him touch her body while dancing, so I stand still and glare at her with fury.

"Colton!" she squeals and rushes toward me, with bright welcoming smile on her face. "I'm so glad you're here."

I continue to glare at her and when she sees that I am not responding to her, her smile slightly drops and she frowns.

"What's wrong, Colton?" she asks me innocently, making me even angrier. I glare up at Zero and he understand why I'm mad, I can see almost see a mocking smirk on his face.

I clench my jaws and look down at Aelita, glaring at her. "You from me to zero, huh?" I glance at Zero and he understands I'm using his name as an insult. I glare back at Aelita. "You're a whore," I tell her coldly. She widens her eyes in disbelief and steps back. I can see the amount of pain in her eyes almost making me feel bad for throwing such a vile word at her.

"Hey-" I feel Zero taking few steps toward us, I ignore him and continue to talk down on Aelita.

"You tell me that you love me and that I'm the only person for you, yet I catch you dancing and grinding on the guy who wants to fuck you," I snarl at her and she slightly glares at me.

"First of all," she starts. "I am not a whore. I don't ever want to hear you call me like that. You do not get to disrespect me anymore," her voice is firm and she is standing up for herself. I am almost proud and surprised that she is not breaking down and crying. She has really grown. "Secondly, Zero is my friend and he is cheering me up because I have been down and miserable. He treats me with respect and appreciation and we were simply dancing and having a fun time forgetting about all the misery and sadness around us. Lastly," her serious face disappears and I see her crack a smile. "You're jealous."

I swallow and continue to look at her now confused that she finds it amusing. "So it makes you happy that I'm jealous?" I scold and she nods at me.

"You've never been jealous before," she continues to grin and I don't find it funny at all. "It means that you really care and love me."

I open my mouth to say something mean to her, but then close it. I smirk to myself then open my mouth again to talk. "Aelita," I start. "I do love you and I care about you, and you're playing with my feelings," I whisper the last words slowly and look down hurt.

"What?" her face becomes serious. "I'm not, I swear..." she shakes her head.

"Yes you are." I insist. "You're spending time with Zero, one of my mortal enemies and you know he has strong feelings for you and you still spend time with him,"

I feel Zero intently glaring at me, but I ignore him and continue to reprimand Aelita. She's easy to manipulate and I know I can easily get her to do whatever I want her to. I'm the only one she listens to.

"If you love me and don't want me to suffer more than I already am, you will stop spending time with Zero."

She looks at me with sadness in her eyes and two women come in the room.

"There you are, Mrs. Ice," the ladies smile genuinely at her. I take few steps back from her and my eyes lay on Zero who has been glaring at me with unashamedly hate. I glare back at him with a triumphant smirk.

"Excuse us, gentlemen," they bow to Zero and I then, to Aelita. "It's time for the inauguration and picture-taking, we need you to come with us, please," one lady tells Aelita.

Aelita clears her throat and nods. "Of course," she gives me one last apologetic glance and follows the two ladies out.

"I'll be right behind, Aelita," Zero tells her, watching her leave. She turns around and stares at him and shakes her head. "Please don't follow me," and she disappears out to the door.

Zero looks down the floor and clenches his jaws, then looks back up to glare me. We're both alone.

"You're a fucking cruel douchebag," he snarls at me. His voice is trembling with anger.

"I know," I tell him not feeling offended at all. "Stay away from my wife from now on, Zero. I mean it," I warn him. I know for sure that I will kill him next time he tries to make any move on her.

"What do you want?" he starts to look at me as if I am a code that he can't crack. "She confessed to you, and poured her heart out to you. She has been thinking about you nonstop every single day! This past week has been miserable for her because she cares so much about you," he's seething. "Even today, she was not feeling well because you were not there and you are not okay. I have absolutely no idea how far she will go for you, Mr. Ice but I know she loves so much, so deeply, so unconditionally and yet you still reject her and push her away, hurting her even more. You say you don't want her, but have the audacity to tell her that she can't be happy with anyone else. What the fuck, Mr. Ice? How fucking selfish and inconsiderate are you?" he's really angry with me. "I love Aelita and I respect her. I want her to be happy more than anything else. Her happiness and well-being is all I want and you are the key to that. I don't know why, but you're the one for her and I respect that. If you love Aelita, then make her happy. Let her in your life and stop being a little bitch. She's willing to start over with you and you have no idea how lucky you are. I respect her wish and decision, but if you don't start treating her like the Goddess she is, then I will and I will do everything in my power to change her heart and help her fall in love with me because I know I can make her happier than you ever will."

I cruelly smirk at him and insensitively start to speak. "Hey listen kid, you can never outdo me. The love Aelita has for me is absolutely unique and she will never feel the same way she feels about me with anyone else. You can try to be a man to her, but even if you do, you will never come close to being even half the man she sees me as."

He clenches his jaws and glares, knowing that I am right.

"Stay away from my wife, Zero," I give him one last warning, and start walking away.

"By the way," Zero calls after me, touching my shoulder and making me turn. "This is for calling Aelita a whore," he gives me one hell of a hard punch, almost breaking my face. I stumble back, trying to retain my balance. I feel blood dripping out of my mouth and I wipe it away, glaring at him.

"And this is for playing with her feelings," he wants to throw another powerful punch at me, but all of the sudden he loses his balance and I frown. He isn't acting like himself at all but I take advantage of the opportunity and grab his wrist and twist it, he's in shock that I am fighting back this time.

I take advantage of his surprise and sprain his wrist. Zero grunts out in pain and falls to his knees. Then, I punch him as hard as I can in the stomach. He starts to cough, bringing his other good hand to his stomach.

"You're so unoriginal, Mr. Ice," Zero starts breathing hard. "That is my move."

"Yeah," I smirk down at him, kick him hard in the stomach and turn to his back. "You've been my role model for the past month, Zero," I grab his tie and start to strangle him.

"I've decided to kill you," I tell him truthfully. I have had enough of him. I cannot stand him, and the world would be better off without a psychopath like him anyways. If anything, I'm doing Aelita and this world a favor.

"You've fallen so low," Zero continues to grunt, trying to loosen the tie around his neck, but I don't let him. I pull harder. "Lord Fire will crucify you if you kill me, and Aelita will hate you," he continues.

"Didn't you just say that her love for me is unconditional?" I smirk cruelly down at him. "Besides, I want her to hate me...and concerning your Lord, I don't give a shit about what he'll do to me. I don't give a shit about what will happen to me anymore," I continue to tighten his tie around his neck, meaning to kill him and taking pleasure at doing so. But before I know it, I feel myself being thrown against the wall with an immense, inexplicable power. I feel my back bone slightly crack and I grunt in pain.

Before I even get the chance to register what just happened, I feel a very cold, heavy metal against my chest, making it hard for my lungs to expand and breathe.

I look at Zero who is staring right back at me with calmer eyes, but I see another Zero seating down on the floor and coughing hard, trying to pick up his breathing. That is when I realize that the man in front of me, who is on the brink of breaking my lungs is not Zero.

However, he is the exact replica of Zero. He has the same pitch black hair, the same ghostly grey eyes, the same pale skin, the same emotionless expression, same height, and same body posture. The only difference is that his hair is shorter than Zero's, he's wearing glasses and his right arm is a metal weapon.

"What the fu..." I try to cough out and push him off of me, but his arm is as heavy as a boulder. I feel as if I am trapped under a giant rock.

"Who the fuck...are you?" I manage to grunt.

"You have just made the most fatal mistake of your life, sir." he finally speaks. His voice is calm and yet deadly. "You tried to kill my brother," he furrows his eyebrows and presses his metal arm a little harder on me and glares hard. "I'm going to annihilate you,"

He continues to press his arm against my chest and I slowly start to give out. I feel compressed and can even feel the wall behind me me crackin. I have nowhere to go, I can't push him off and cannot defend myself. All I can do is stay there and let him crush me. For a moment, I think I am done for, but Zero's brother suddenly stops crushing me.

"I wouldn't do that if I were you, Light," I hear Warr's voice. He is right behind Zero's brother and has a knife to his neck. Spyros is pointing a gun to his head and Lava has her hand blocking his. The three of them are protecting me against Zero's brother.

However, the maniac still has his metal hand pressed against my chest and he is still glaring at me. "Warr, it's been a long time," Light says, his voice is still calm and a bit friendly.

"Indeed it has," Warr answers cautiously gaining my attention. My eyes drift away from Light and stare at Warr and I notice that he looks agitated. It's not like him to lose his cool at all.

Spyros too, does not look composed. His hand is shaking while pointing the gun at Light and I can even see his body tremble slightly. It's so unusual to see Spyros scared. He is usually the one to attack first, but this time, he looks like he wants to run. Why are the two so afraid of this guy? Who is he? I glance at Lava and notice that she is the only one who is remaining somewhat calm...of course she is. It's her brother.

God...Zero has triplets?! Fucking triplets?! What the fuck?!

I turn back to Light and glare at him. He is still suffocating me with his arm and still staring at me with his ghostly eyes.

"Let him go Light," Warr says again in a warning tone.

"Why should I?" Light's voice is neutral and holds no emotion. "This douchebag tried to kill my brother."

"I'm sure Zero could have handled himself and this is Colton Ice, the son-in-law of Lord Fire and it is our duty to guard him and protect him at any cost. If you hurt him, then you're going against Lord Fire. Now, I'm going to ask you one last time," Warr presses the knife harder on Light's neck and I can see his eyes glaring seriously. He is more composed, but still agitated. "Let Mr. Ice go or we will terminate you."

Light continues to stare at me dead in the eyes and I see his lips slowly forming a smirk. "Colton Ice huh?" He utters, still pressing his arm on me. "Interesting..." he then lets go of me and I take a deep breath, able to breathe normally. Light turns his back at me and is now facing Warr. Warr still has the knife in his hand and is guarded cautious as if he is ready to attack Light at any moment. Spyros too is still pointing his gun at Light, and still trembling. Lava lets go of Light's hand and is more relaxed. She gives me a slight glare then walks toward Zero who is still seating on the floor, his back faced to us. He does not seem a bit interested in what's happening here.

"My, my..." Light starts to talk with a very relaxed, kind voice. I notice that his metal hand is now changing form and turning back into a humanlike hand. He put both his hands in the air. "You guys did not have to go to this extreme for me,"

"We can never be too careful with you, Light." Warr responds.

"Hmph," Light continues his voice still calm and composed. "Warr, you said that if I hurt Colton Ice, I go against Henry Fire. I shall also remind you that if anyone related to Henry Fire hurts my brother, that individual is going against me as well. You and Henry Fire know to what level I will go to protect Zero," his voice becomes dark. "I shall also let you know that I chose not to kill Colton Ice not because of you, but out of respect for Aelita Ice, a dear friend of my precious brother. Next time Colton Ice tries to harm Zero, I will certainly kill him," his back is still turned to me, but I know he is talking directly to me.

There is a very cold silence between us again. It is as if Warr and Spyros are expecting and ready for Light to strike, they're on their guards and extremely serious. I have never seen them so perturbed. Spyros is starting to tremble even more and I am afraid that his legs will give out at any moment. Light suddenly shoots him a cold look, startling Spyros, then Light carelessly smacks the gun off of Spyros's hands and walks past them. He is walking toward Lava who is helping Zero up.

"Are you alright, brother?" Light's voice is sympathetic and gentle as he attempts to put his hand on Zero's shoulder.

Zero shrugs his hands off and coldly replies to him. "Don't touch me, and you're not my brother."

Lava sighs and rolls her eyes. "Light, Zero's fine...it's just a sprained wrist. Don't worry, I will take good care of him," her voice is gentle and sweet. "Thank you for protecting him."

"Very well then, thank you Lava," Light says nodding at her sister and Zero. "I shall go back to the party. It was good seeing you, Zero," he starts to walk toward and talks a bit louder, he is addressing to Warr and Spyros and possibly me. "Please try and pretend to behave like civilized humans in the King's palace. It's prosperity day and it will be rude of you if we end this night with casualties. Behave yourselves," before closing the door behind him, he adds. "By the way Spyros,"

Spyros stiffens. "Y-yes...s-sir?"

"You dropped your balls...again."

Spyros slightly blushes and forces a smile. "T-thank you for notic-" he starts to say but Light does not wait for him to finish. He leaves the room.

Once he is gone, Warr and Spyros finally sigh out of relief. They relax their shoulders and put away their weapons.

"...Who the heck was that and why did you get so worked up over him?" I finally ask Warr.

"That was Light Noire. He's the triplet brother of Zero and Lava and also the Head of Our Kingdom Security.

"Zero's brother is Light Noire?" I raise my eyebrow. I have heard of him of course, but never really took interest in knowing what he looked like. "He doesn't work for Lord Fire?"

"No," Warr clears his throat. "He answers to the King and only works with Lord Fire when in absolute need of soldiers to defend Terra from invasion."

"...I've never seen you so agitated and worried...he is only one guy. Why were you guys so sc-" I retain myself from saying 'scared' because I don't want to hurt their feelings.

"Scared?" Spyros finishes my question. We hear Lava scoffs in a mocking way.

"I'm not ashamed to admit that I'm still terrified of your brother," Spyros looks at her. "I can handle Zero, but Light? Fuck that. I'm never going to put myself in a situation where I'll have to confront that...demon again...no, fuck that."

"I couldn't agree more with you, Spyros," Warr admits as well.

"...How dangerous is he?" I am finding myself feeling curious.

"He is dangerous, Mr. Ice. More than I am. I am one of the strongest and agile soldiers that Lord Fire possesses and I can honestly tell you that I am no match to Light Noire."

I feel goosebumps starting to form on my skin. "...Who trained him? The King?"

"No," Warr answers. "He was trained under Lord Fire. Light Noire is possibly the most deadly killer in this Kingdom. You are extremely lucky that you're still alive, Mr. Ice. You owe your life to Zero."

I frown raising an eyebrow and glancing at Zero who is walking toward us while rotating his wrist.

"Zero?" I have a hard time believing that.

"If he hadn't paged us, signaling that you were in danger, you would have been done for."

"Maybe he paged you because I was trying to kill him," I corrected, glaring at Zero.

"No," Spyros refuses. "We're only allowed to request back up when we're unable to protect someone alone. The alarm is never for us. Zero saved your life, Mr. Ice."

"Now," Warr's voice is now serious and slightly severe. He is glaring at Zero and I. "What the heck is going on between you two? What were you two doing in this Palace?"

"We were just talking," Zero says, fixing his tie. I can see the red marks around his neck. I really tried to kill him. "I just have learned that Mr. Ice can speak my language," Zero looks at Warr and turns to me. "I'm impressed, you have come so far in such a short term."

He stretches his hand to shake mine. I take it, half-hearted. "I told you you've been my role model."

"Whatever beef you two have seriously needs to stop," Warr's tone is still severe and I can tell that he is very upset at us. It's rare to see him lose his cool. "Listen Mr. Ice, it is our job to look after you until Lord Fire decides your fate. Please, do not make it more complicated and I sincerely am stressing that you stop antagonizing Zero because his brother-"

"He's not my brother," Zero corrects Warr, but Warr shoots him a glare.

"Shut up," he growls at him. I am a bit taken aback. Warr is *really* angry. Zero quiets down and doesn't say anything else. Warr continues to talk to me. "We do not want Light Noire to get involved in any of this matter. I kid you not when I tell you that he has a knack at creating calamity and will cause mayhem if Zero gets hurt by anyone, especially if that someone has any connection with Lord Fire. It will end badly for all of us. I've watched hundreds of my comrades die in his hands and I never want to witness this ever again. Now, Mr. Ice, I get that you are suicidal and don't care much about what's going to happen to you, but if you've forgotten, I shall remind you that you still have the strong desire to kill those who have hurt you and have hurt Mrs. Ice. You still have to get Cain Smith, Hunter and Veronica Cross and we are here to assist you in any way possible. But for that to happen, you need to try to stay alive and out of trouble. Once we're done with the killings, you can choose to do whatever you want, but for the moment, please settle down. If not for yourself or for Zero, or for your wife or Lord Fire, please do it for me. I am asking you a favor."

He then turns to Zero "And you," he starts, his voice is meaner and it is as if he is lecturing a child. "Your job is to be a guard and respect and obey Mr. Ice at all cost. You promised Lord Fire not to let your emotions take the best of you, yet you've been breaking that promise since day one. You've been acting as if your actions will not have consequences, but I shall let you know that I can convince Lord Fire to remove you from this mission and replace you with someone else. You know damn well that he will listen to me. I am one step away from getting you replaced, Zero. This is not bullshit."

Zero turns paler and Spyros is staring at both of them, a bit worried as well. I have never seen Warr this angry, and this mean. All because of Light Noire.

"Now both of you, let it be the last time you have act recklessly and immature. We have a job to do and you're not children. I do not want to come back on this subject, have I made myself clear?"

"Crystal," Zero and I say in unison. We both slightly glare at each other but decide that it's best if we don't start arguing.

"If the four of you are here," I start once Warr seems relaxed and calmer. "Who's keeping an eye on my wife?"

"Do not underestimate Lord Fire," Spyros tells me with a proud smirk. "He can protect her better than anyone in this room."

"Besides, I had Christopher come just in case so he's probably watching over her too," Zero adds.

"Well boys," I hear Lava yawn and I glance at her. She is seating on the sofa and looks very comfortable. "Even though this was quite an interesting talk, I would like to go back to the party, and," she grabs her phone and looks at it. "It seems like Lord Fire is summoning the four you in a meeting room."

Warr checks his phone as well. "You are right," he turns to us. "We should get going."

"Are you going to be okay, Zee?" Lava asks Zero once we start walking out of the reading room.

"Yeah," Zero replies a bit coldly and walks away from her. I notice that he is not in good terms with any of his siblings. I wonder what happened between them...

We make our way to another room in the ground floor of the palace and we see Mr. Fire smoking his cigar and contemplating the art works.

"Sir," Spyros, Zero and Warr salute him as I just stand there and watch him with an emotionless expression.

"Colton, you're here." Mr. Fire exclaims as sees me. His expression holds displeasure and resentment, but he is calm.

"How can I help you?" I neutrally ask him.

"Cain Smith," he starts, his voice is cold and sharp as his eyes darken. "Why is he still breathing? And most importantly, why did he feel safe enough to show his balls here at this party?"

I frown and stiffen, my heart and mind goes immediately out to Aelita.

"Aelita-" I want to rush out the door but Mr. Fire stops me.

"You think I'll leave my daughter in the presence of Cain Smith? How dare you?" he growls at me. "My men have discreetly captured him before he escaped. The

King is willing to lend us his royal forest to take care of him tonight. I want him dead, today."

"Yes sir," Zero answers.

Lord Fire turns to Zero and shoots him a glare. "And by the way, Zero."

Zero stiffens.

"I am aware that you told everything that has been going on to my daughter. I trusted you to keep everything we've been doing strictly confidential and you let me down. Now my daughter sees me as a monster and is calling me a coward."

Zero looks down in a guilty way while Spyros and Warr give him a silent, accusing glare.

"It won't happen again, Lord," Zero apologizes.

"You *will* be sanctioned for your unprofessional behavior," Mr. Fire nods, "I am going to give you two choices. You can either choose to be removed from this assignment permanently and go back to the headquarters or cut all types of communication with my daughter until I say otherwise," Mr. Fire turns off his cigar and looks at Zero. "Which one are you willing to give up son, the mission or my daughter?"

*Why not both?* I think to myself.

Zero clenches his jaws. Although his facial expression is emotionless, I can see the hurt in his eyes when he answers "Your daughter, sir."

I can't help but smile a little bit.

"Alright then it's settled," Mr. Fire continues, addressing to all of us but he is looking at me. "Now it's time for you to go end Cain Smith...tonight. He is patiently waiting for you in the freezing room. Do it outside, in the woods. The guards will give you privacy."

"Yes, sir!" Spyros, Zero and Warr say in unison. We turn around and in the process of making our way out when we all freeze.

Aelita is standing at the door and staring at us with horror. Lava is running after her, and has joined her seconds after. My heart starts to beat fast as I see the pain in her eyes.

"You..." she is staring at her father with trembling lips. "You're still killing people, dad...?"

Mr. Fire too, is frozen in place and doesn't know what to say.

"Dad, answer me!" she yells at him, but no one dares to utter a sound except me.

"Yes, Aelita. We're still killing people,"

She then turns to me, she's aggravated and angry. "You promised me there will be no more killings!"

"I promised you I won't hurt any more innocent lives–and I broke that promise. Cain Smith is not innocent and he has to pay for what he's done to you. So does Peter and Hunter and Veronica. I am going to pulverize them all," I growl feeling angrier now that I am thinking about Hunter.

"I already told you, I forgive them! I forgive them!" Aelita is shaking her head. "You should do the same too!" She looks at her father. "All of you!" she turns back to me. "It will set you free, I promise!"

When she sees that I am not convinced, she continues. "Maybe all of this hatred toward them is the reason why you're feeling so lost and hopeless, Colton! Please! We don't need any more blood to be shed! Colton! Please!" she's getting angrier. Her honey brown eyes are blazing and her lips are pursed.

I exhale a bit frustrated with her and then I take her by the arm and direct her in the corner of the room for a little bit of privacy.

"Aelita–" I want to start, but she interrupts me.

"I love you so much, Colton." she says desperately. "I don't know how many times I have to say this for you to understand that you're not alone and that you can still turnaround from all of this. I...I love you so much and it hurts me to see you act like this, my love." her voice softens. "We can start over...we can just leave and–"

"Your father is going to kill me in less than eight days," I announce bluntly, staring at those beautiful honey brown eyes of hers. I was trying to hide it from her, but I don't want to anymore. She really needs to let go. She needs to start planning her life without me in it.

Aelita stiffens and frowns. "W-what?"

"That's a deal he and I made. He'll take my life after I finish killing all those guys responsible for hurting you. I am not going to survive and live happily ever after with you."

She shakes her head in disbelief. "No," she glances at her dad and back to me. "Dad will never hurt you...like that. It's not true..."

"It is," I tell her nonchalantly.

"Then I'll talk to him!" she suddenly says, glaring and him and trying to walk toward him but I block her from doing so and I glare.

"Aelita, you will do no such thing," I hiss at her. I have never been this serious in my entire life. "I want to die. I don't want to be part of this world anymore. I don't want to go on. This is what I want."

"Colton..." she says sadly, tears starting to fill her eyes. "What about me?" I look away, feeling even more guilty and horrible.

"You'll get over it with time."

She shakes her head furiously at me. "No. I won't be able to come back from this one...Colton I can't let that happen...I...I can't let you leave me..." her voice is breaking.

"You have to..." I tell her. "If you stop your father from killing me, I will take my own life. That's the only way I can cleanse myself and heal myself. Death is the only way out for me."

She starts to cry and I realize that this is very painful for her. I'm really being selfish...and cruel to her. My eyes soften while I continue to stare at her.

"Hey..." I tell her softly. "Don't cry."

"It's not fair..." she's sobbing looking down the floor.

"Aelita, please look at me," I ask nicely. She does so and I pull her to my arm and hug her. I feel her warmth against my body. It feels so good..."Aelita," I break the hug and wipe the tears from her face. "This is what I want. This is the only way I can be saved, the only way I can be at peace. I'm not sad about it and if you really want to make me happy, if you really want to help me ease this pain...you'll let me die. This is my only wish." I caress her face as she frowns. "I know this is hard for you to accept and understand, but you have to...and you'll need to. You'll be fine without me, Aelita. You've always have been...you're strong and young and beautiful and have the heart of a saint, and you have this whole entire life ahead of you. I've done nothing but brought pain in your life, if I disappear, you will be completely free. You will be happier and I am sure someone else will treat you million times better than I've ever treat you. You'll be–"

"No," she interrupts me, raising her tone and breaking away from me. She's storming toward her father. "I will not be okay! If Colton dies, I will not be okay!" she shouts at her father. "And you're going to have to stop this madness now. You're going to have to stop killing people! I have had enough of all your childish behaviors!"

"Sweetheart..." Mr. Fire wants to calm her down but she gives him a death glare.

"No! Don't you sweetheart me! How dare you, dad? How dare you look at me in the eye, how dare you stand in front of thousands of people tonight and say that all you care about is the safety and the happiness of the Terrans! You're a liar! You're a murderer!" she screams. "You disgust me!"

Mr. Fire is looking away pained and ashamed, not knowing what to say to his daughter. I start to feel a bit irritated with Aelita's little tantrum. She has no idea what's going on. She doesn't understand that all of this is for her own sake.

"If we don't kill them Aelita, they will kill you," I tell her and she turns her attention back to me.

She looks up at me with very cute, sad teary eyes and she says. "Then stay alive and protect me. Please! Don't hurt anyone, don't take your life. Just...come with me! Please, Colton. It's wrong what you're doing. It's very wrong!"

I don't answer her, she then turns to Zero. "Zero, tell him! I know you feel the same way I do! Please help me stop this madness!"

Zero looks away with guilt and regret in his eyes, not saying anything.

"Zero!" Aelita continues to call after him. "What about what you told me earlier? Is that how you're helping me...? By killing more people and letting Colton go down as well?"

"Aelita stop," I tell her and move forward, signaling the crew that it's time to leave but she is blocking my way again.

"No! I won't let you go. I won't let you hurt anyone else! You can't do that! I refuse! I refuse! I refuse!" She's glaring at me with determination in her eyes.

I smirk at her. "You know Aelita, you've actually completely changed your personality since the rape," I start.

She frowns.

"You used to be so shy, so reserved and calm, so weak...now you're hot headed, stubborn, like to take risks and have the gut to defy me and on top of that, talk a lot. Maybe the rape was actually a good thing for you," I feel Zero and Mr. Fire glaring at me, but I continue. "Maybe you should've gotten raped sooner."

Then, I feel the palm of her hand slam against my cheek, with a burning sensation. She has just slapped me. Hard. Very hard actually. So hard that my head was turned to the other side.

It hurts...a lot. My left cheek is burning. My hand slowly rises up and I touch my cheek...to feel the burning sensation.

I finally turn to look at her. She is glaring at me furiously and tears are rolling down her face.

"Don't say hurtful, cruel things to me! Don't say things like this, Colton! Don't! It hurts..."

I glare at her. "Maybe that's what you need to hear from me so you can understand that you will get hurt when you're around me!"

She shakes her head. "No! You won't push me away like this. I...I won't leave you and I'll do anything to stop you from killing yourself and hurting others! I'll save you!"

"Get out of my way, Aelita," I whisper. This argument is pointless.

"No," she tells me firmly.

"Get out of my way or I will push you," I threaten.

"No!" She says again strongly. "I'm not letting you hurt anyone."

I stare and take a menacing step toward her. She is trembling, but holding her ground, determined to not let me pass. I don't want to get physical with her. I'm afraid I will hurt her bad if I touch her with the level of anger I'm trying hard to conceal.

Zero comes to my rescue and slowly walks behind her, takes out a cloth and grabs her. She gasps.

"No!" she is trying to fight and struggle, but Zero is stronger.

"I'm sorry, Aelita," he tells her softly and then places the tissue on her nose. It's probably drenched with chloroform. She struggles for a second more but then her body becomes limb, her arms drop and her eyes slowly close. She's unconscious. Zero looks down at her sadly.

I sigh and take her away from Zero's arms. I stare at Aelita's sleeping face and my eyes sadden. She's still crying even while unconscious. She's in pain because of me.

*See Aelita?* I think to myself while wiping away her tears. *It's going to be like this every time for the rest of your life if you stay around me.* I continue to stare at her, blocking away everyone around us.

"I'll take care of her," Lava comes toward us and takes Aelita away from me.

"Please do," Mr. Fire finally speaks.

"Yes sir," Lava nods, carrying Aelita on her back.

"Make sure Christopher is with her at all times," Zero calls after Lava.

"Roger that," Lava replies and leaves the room with my unconscious wife.

I take a deep breath and turn to Zero, Spyros and Warr. "Let's go," I walk out of the room, with a cold burning feeling inside. I have a rival to kill.

# 29

## HUNTER CROSS'S POINT OF VIEW

I care about nothing else but killing Zero Noire, Spyros Cardenas and Warr Van Der Vart. Ever since Noah died in their hands, all of my self-pity and desire to persevere have diminished. I hold nothing else inside of me but anger, and the dark urge to retaliate. I don't care about anything else anymore. I don't care about protecting Veronica or other people. I don't care about trying to save my own life. I don't care if I die tomorrow. All I care about is to make those three monsters pay for the crime they've committed.

It's not just about revenge, it's about justice. As much as I want to make them feel what I felt when they were bashing my innocent brother's skull, as much as I want to hunt their family members and make them suffer just as bad as Noah did, I chose not to because I don't want to be like them. Too many innocent lives have been paying for our mistakes and I still have a little bit of conscience and moral left inside of me. I will get justice and revenge for my brother and I will do it before I die.

I have been tracking Cain Smith for the past two weeks now. I know that he is going to be the next target because Colton wants to kill me last. I know that if I have Cain Smith with me, then Zero, Spyros and Warr will show up and I will be able to deal with them.

I have searched for Cain Smith, but have not been able to find him. He has been able to hide and cover up his back.

Fucking rich people.

Thankfully, I've guessed that there will be a high chance to have Cain Smith at the Royal Palace today. Rich pricks like to fit in with their own.

I am right.

I am not able to enter the palace. There are too many guards, so I decide contour the palace, merge myself with the outside entertainers and hide in the bushes. I wait and wait for hours to pass by.

Once the night starts to fall, I notice the security guards starting to leave while a group of men are walking toward the woods. Two of the men are dragging another man. My eyes narrow at the men and I start to recognize them all.

Zero and Spyros are dragging Cain Smith while Colton Ice and Warr are walking behind.

My body starts to boil with fury. The three men I want to kill the most are there, and I fight the urge to run after them and kill them. I watch them as they continue to drag Cain Smith deeper in the woods.

I slowly follow them from distance. They stop fifteen minutes later in the middle of the woods by a stream and throw Cain on the ground. I hide myself four trees away under a small cave. It's dark and they can't see me, but I can hear them.

"Colton Ice," Cain says nonchalantly, standing up and fixing his suit. "It's good to see you well."

"The pleasure's all yours," Colton answers acidly. I can almost feel the venom in his voice. Colton Ice has been growing darker and darker as days go by. He is not the same guy who begged me to not hurt Aelita, nor is he the guy who authorized the death of my brother. He is...something else. Something I can't describe. I sense in his aura that he's neither happy, nor miserable. As if his existence does not matter anymore.

"How's Aelita doing?" Cain dares to ask, and I jolt as I see Zero throw a punch at Cain and start to beat him senseless. I clench my fist as I remember when Zero beat Noah with a baseball bat with the same cruelty. Even though I am angry, and hateful, I am also scared and worried. Zero has the strength of a monster and I know I am no match to him. My idea is to confront the three of them at the same time, but I need to rethink that idea.

If I want to be realistic and bring all of them down, I need to think logically. It will be very hard to bring them down even one by one. I have to be smart, and think clearly. I have to set my feelings aside and find their weaknesses.

My first idea was to find Cain Smith before they did and trade him for the lives of those three guards. But they are one step ahead of me. Cain Smith is going to be dead within minutes and I will be next. I have to think of something else and I have to stay alive until the three of them pay for their mistakes.

After Zero finishes beating Cain half dead, he starts to tie his hands and legs together behind his back. Warr and Spyros are building something that is starting to look like a spit roast. Once they're done, Zero attaches Cain on the steel pipe who now looks like a pig in process of being roasted...alive.

"W-what are you doing?!" Cain starts to grunt and struggle but he can't move a muscle. "Colton–you can't possibly do this to me!"

Colton doesn't answer at all. He is just standing there looking down at him.

"Y-you killed Nadia...we're even! We're even! You can't kill me! And, and I have been taking care of your company!"

Cain tries as hard as he can to change Colton's mind, but he only receive silence as a response.

Spyros pours gasoline under the spit along with black coals. Warr then gives a lighter to Colton.

"Please, Colton! Don't do this!" Cain begs, continuing to struggle. Colton says nothing at all, it is as if he doesn't want to bother with Cain anymore. I am expecting him to maybe curse him out, wish that he goes to hell or ask him why he did what he did, but Colton has not uttered one word to Cain. He just wants to torture and watch him burn.

"Colton!" Cain continues to cry out, but Colton throws the lighter in the coal and it starts to catch fire.

"Ah!" Cain grunts in pain, but he is not enflamed yet. He is just inches away from the flame. The rest of them just stand there and watch him, circling him and not looking a bit tensed or horrified. I, who despise Cain as well, feel so sick and so bad for him. What's happening to him is inhumane and cruel. I highly doubt that I will have the stomach to do something like this to any of them. I hate them and want to destroy them...but I am not a monster.

Cain continues to scream of pain as I see his face and chest start to redden, burn and bleed. He is also starting to cough. The smoke is suffocating him and probably burning his lungs.

"Just shoot me already!" Cain screams minutes after but none of them react as his skin continues to roast while he is still breathing. About ten minutes later, Colton stares at his watch and finally speaks.

"Just kill it, I don't want to stand here all night. It's not worth the time." As he says that, Zero grabs the bottle of gaoline and pours it on Cain's body. Cain is now enflamed and screaming even more. He's being burned alive.

Colton starts to walk away from the screaming Cain and the three guards follow him. I make myself as small as possible under the cave as they pass by me. They seem so careless and not bothered by what they've just done.

Monsters...

As soon as I am sure they've completely vanished and left the woods, I step out of my cave and rush toward the burning Cain. I want to save his life.

I can still use him against them. I can still get my revenge.

I start to push the spit roast as hard as I can away from the burning coal while Cain is still screaming his lungs out. My hands are burning as they make contact with the hot steel pipe.

"Ugh," I grunt and continue to push. Once I succeed in doing so, I take off my shirt and attempt to stop the fire. It fails.

I then start to roll him on the ground full of pebbles, but the fire still continues to burn him. So, with force and the willpower to endure the pain, I find myself dragging the very hot pipe toward the lake. I grunt and scream in pain as the palm of my hands are gluing to the hot metal bar and melting my flesh away.

I manage to endure the overwhelming pain and throw Cain in the lake. The fire starts to dissipate from his body, but Cain is grunting and moaning in pain.

I use my teeth to untie his hands and legs and drag him out of the water. His entire body is a mess. He is completely burned, his face is bloody and disfigured and I can't tell if he still has his right eye or not.

Cain continues to grunt in pain. He is weak a helpless and I can do whatever I want with him and he won't be able to do shit. I smirk at the thought.

"Can you hear me, Mr. Smith?" I ask him. He is breathing hard and painfully but manages to slowly nod.

"Do you recognize my voice?" I receive another nod from him.

"Very well," I smirk. "I am going to throw you back in the coal and let you finish burning," I feel his body slightly stiffen and he starts to moan again.

"You don't want that? Very well then. The only way you get to have me save your life and not leave you for dead is if you agree on one thing. The tables have turned. You will become my little bitch and you will help me destroy Warr, Zero and Spyros. They're the three guards who set you on fire today. I want to kill them and I cannot do it alone. I need your help to make this happen. After you're done helping me accomplish that, you can do whatever the fuck you want. Do we have a deal?" he slightly nods and continues to cough.

"Good," I smirk at him as start to slowly and gently wiping the blood off his face. I stare at the flames from the burning coals and feel my eyes glisten with anticipation and the desire to kill. Fire and Ice won the battle, but I will win the war.

# 30

## COLTON ICE'S POINT OF VIEW

"May I say something, sir?" Zero asks me as we're parting. It's late at night, I feel exhausted, and my sweater smells like smoke and human flesh. I feel dirty and want to take a shower.

"By all means," I mutter walking to my car. He reluctantly follows me.

He hesitates as if he is searching for the right words and then he starts "I think...I think you'll hurt

Aelita more if you die. You should live, and try to make her happy."

I turn to him and raise an eyebrow. "If I'm not mistaken, this is what you told me about three weeks ago word for word 'sir, with all due respect, the only reason why she's still your wife is because everyone is too busy trying to fix the mess you've created to think about divorce. We all know that marriage is already over.'" I quote and stare at him. "And didn't you mention just few hours ago that I don't deserve her at all and that she's way too good for me?"

He exhales sharply and shakes his head. "I'm sorry sir, I didn't mean that. I was very resentful of you in the beginning,"

"Really? What changed your feelings toward me?" I ask him sarcastically. Not that I care or anything.

"Even though I still dislike you, I have learned to know and understand you," he continues, "and I can admit that you care about Aelita a lot."

"Fascinating, Zero" I tell him sarcastically. "Is your father captain obvious?"

"Sir," he is getting irritated, "Aelita is making great improvements. She's smiling, she's alive and she's better because of you. She told me that herself. She said you're the reason she wakes up every single day and sleep peacefully. She told me you confessed to her that day when you found her with Hunter and she had an epiphany and everything bad, everything dark and painful that was hunting her body, soul and mind completely vanished. She told me it is almost like you washed away all the dirt and darkness from her just by confessing her....she's been happy ever since and you're the reason. If you were to die...I don't think Aelita would handle it."

I'm silent for a moment, trying to remember Forest's death and how Aelita handled it. "You know Forest, the human? Me and Aelita's best friend?" I start.

Zero nods.

"He was her first friend. He was the one who always got her back day and night. He was the one who made her come out of her little shell and explore the world. He put a smile on her face every day. He was her little guardian angel and she loved him. When he died...I never saw Aelita shed one tear in front of me for him. I don't know how she did it, but she quickly got over him and never mentioned him to me."

"The only reason why she never cried in front of you was because she wanted to be strong for you," Zero explains me. I look at him with disbelief. Mr. Fire told me something similar...I didn't believe him at first. "You were the reason why she was strong enough to let go of Forest. There's not the day that she doesn't think about him, but it hurts less because she has you. The only one she will ever really love. I kid you not when I tell you that you give her strength just by being around her, sir." His voice is firm. "If you leave this world, she'll be crushed."

"If I stay, I'll watch her get crushed eventually," I answer sharply. My voice softens. "Everyone...I know gets hurt in the end. Anyone that gets too close to me gets hurt. I don't want to get close to her, get my hopes high and then watch this fucked up world crush it right in front of me. That's what it's been doing ever since. I can't...I'm doomed. I am not happy with myself and I can't make her happy and eventually, I'll hurt her...everyone I get too close to eventually dies. I'm cursed."

He pauses for a moment and for the first time, I see his ghostly cold, emotionless grey eyes warm up a bit as he looks at me with...compassion? "I'm not dead,"

I chuckle darkly. "You will soon if you get close enough."

He smiles at me for the first time, a very kind warm friendly smile. "I've been fatally sick as a child, beaten to death, stabbed in the neck, and drank poison and I'm still alive. It takes a lot to kill me so I don't think your curse can have an effect me. I'd like us to be friends, Mr. Ice. I'd like to help you see the good in this world."

"I don't think you can help me do that. I don't think anyone can. Plus, I don't deserve it. My life is pointless."

"There you go again," he rolls his eyes. "I swear, Mr. Ice it's like you're a narcissist and a masochist. You're so into your self-hate that you ignore everyone else around you...it's like you love to hate yourself." He looks at me and continues. "Sir, you're not pointless. You've saved and completed Aelita's life. You saved her from killing herself, you've saved her and her mother from Hidon and you've cheered her up and made her feel better about herself. Your life is not pointless,"

I sigh and roll my eyes. If only he knew that I didn't save Aelita...the dog did. I would've never saved her from killing herself if the dog hadn't show up...and cheering her up? No...she has been cheering herself up. She's strong. She has been handling herself without my help. I have not done anything. All I bring her is pain. It's because of me she's in this situation in the first place...

"Why do you even care, Zero?" I stare at him a bit confused. We've been trying to kill each other hours earlier and now he's trying to praise me? What's his deal?

"...Because I can see that you're fighting your inner demons and losing the battle, sir." he tells me.

I feel goosebumps start to build on my skin. *That's creepy.*

"When I look at your eyes, I see they're dying and I see how hopeless and lost and conflicted you are with yourself. You've changed a lot, Mr. Ice. You used to be a bit more emotional, a bit more alive in the beginning, but now it's almost as if you're becoming an empty shell. I used to be like you, sir. I used to not know what to do with myself, I used to think I was horrible because I was not wanted, and...I was weak. I used to not care about what happened to me. I hated everything around me. The only thing I've ever loved were animals, but even them did not want me around them at first. I felt like a disease. I thought this world would be better off without me...but when Lord Fire laid his eyes on me, he accepted me for who I was. He told me I was worth it. He told me he saw talent in me. He told me that I could be useful. He saved me...he and Aelita and Dr. Vancouver. Thanks to them, I've found a purpose in life. My life is not pointless and neither is yours. As bad, and as horrible as you think you might be...Aelita still admires you and is still in love with you. She accepts you completely for who you are and I am sure that if you open your heart to her, this world won't seem so bad anymore."

"That was pretty deep, Zero." I tell him sarcastically then I scoff. "Why are you trying to get me to be with her? Aren't you in love with her?"

"I am very in love with her," he admits without shame. "That's why I want her to be with you. She loves you and is happy around you and her happiness is all I want. It hurts, I won't deny it and I am heartbroken and I know you don't deserve Aelita at all, but like I have mentioned before she is only going to be happy and complete with you and I am willing to accept and respect that."

I don't say anything anymore.

Zero is...very mature. He's a better man than I'll ever be. He's willing to let the love of his life be with someone else for her sake. I won't ever be able to do something like this, I am so selfish. I will do the exact opposite... I mean look at what I've done to my best friend? I screwed his girlfriend.

I don't deserve Aelita and I can't make her happy. I know that for sure.

"That was all I wanted to say. Have a good night, sir." Zero says a while after since I don't have anything else to say.

"We're meeting first thing tomorrow morning at 10 AM to discuss our next target," I tell him.

"Yes sir," he nods.

"...Call me Colton," I say and enter my car.


It's the next day and I am downstairs, in the conference room with the three guards discussing our targets. Zero informed me earlier that Aelita had woken up and is alright. She's under Christopher's protection. I'm surprised that she hasn't been calling me or been knocking at my door. Maybe she's finally realized what a monster I am and is taking her distance away from me.

Good.

"So we've eliminated so far Jago, Lazar, White, Hidon, Cain," Spyros starts, showing the faces of our enemies through the projector. "Jon and Otto have taken their own lives and Peter Stone was run over by a car three days ago. Unfortunately, he died of a quick and painless death," he sighs shaking his head. "So now we're left with Veronica and Hunter...who's our next target between those two? Would you like them to die at the same time? We can torture and kill Veronica in front of Hunter before killing him since he is madly in love with her," Spyros proposes.

"No, I don't think he cares much about Veronica anymore." I remember the look Hunter had on his face when he watched his brother die. I know his brother's death hurt him more than anything else. Killing Veronica in front of him won't really matter anymore.

"We've already killed his brother in front of him. Noah was the most important person in his life. Veronica's death won't have any effect," I continue. "We kill Veronica next." I see Zero's face finally light up

"Finally," he sighs.

Warr turns to him. "You've been hating on Veronica Cross more than any other targets, why is that?"

Spyros and I turn to him too, expecting an explanation. I'm curious because Zero doesn't really show much of emotion toward the people we've killed...but he's excited that Veronica's about to die? Why is that?

Oh no...Don't tell me he fucked her too.

"Well," he clears his throat. "She reminds me of someone I have resented in the past. Her death will satisfy me the most."

Spyros smiles and shakes his head while Warr's eyes soften at him, as if knows who Zero is talking about. Warr then turns to me. "Well, what do we do with Veronica, sir?"

I stare at Zero and then back at Warr and shrug. "Let Zero decide." Honestly, I don't really care what happens to Veronica. I was planning to disfigure her face first before brutally killing her, but I'm sure Zero will think of something worse.

Zero looks at me stupefied and then blinks. "Sir— Colton," he corrects, "are you saying that I am in charge of what happens to Veronica?"

I nod.

"Really?" his eyes widen.

"Yes," I say.

It's the first time I see him grin. He looks like a child on Christmas. There's so much excitement showing on his face.

Warr and Spyros can't help but laugh at his reaction. It is very amusing.

"But we're doing it today," I tell him now very serious. I want to get over all this killings as soon as possible. It's becoming boring to me.

"Y-yes, sir. I have an idea," Zero says, getting up.

"Already?" Spyros raises his eyebrow.

"What is it?" Warr asks.

"I have to show you," he tells us and then asks us to follow him.

We do so, and we're driving to his house. It's a small cabin in the woods. He's isolated from the whole entire world.

"Why are we at your house, Zero?" Spyros asks him as we exit our cars.

"Follow me and you'll see," Zero replies.

We follow him around the house and to our surprise, we see a gigantic dome arena made of solid glass. It's vast and is about 400 feet wide. Inside, I see three wolves who are growling at us angrily. They're twice the size of an average wolf and they're very, very aggressive. I can tell that all they want to do is kill and eat us.

"So, um...why the fuck do you have three wolves who look like they're about to kill all of us in a dome in your backyard? And why do you have a freaking dome in your backyard?" Spyros asks Zero. He's pale.

Zero has a mischievous and yet gentle smile as he is looking inside the dome at the wolves. "I'm a vet and I like helping animals—not only domestic animals, wild animals as well. I built this dome for the wounded wild animals that I can't bring in my home. They're used to the wild and to the outside world and I'd like to make them as comfortable as possible. That's why I built this dome. I don't want it to be like a cage, I want to give them as much space and freedom as possible while they're healing," he clears his throat and continues. "Those three wolves have been wounded about three days ago by a hunter. He captured them, held them in cages, and then let them out in the wild so he could hunt them for fun. I managed save the three wolves and healed them. Their wounds are not bad so they healed fast. They're ready to be left back into the wild in about a day or two."

"What happened to the hunter?" Warr questions Zero immediately, narrowing his eyes at him. "We are not to kill freely. We are only to take lives under Lord Fire's permission."

"Of course," Zero slightly glares at Warr. "I know that. I left the hunter off with a warning and a broken arm."

"You managed to get close to them and heal them? They don't look like animals that can be tamed," Spyros says suspiciously, staring at the wolves.

"They aren't," Zero repeats. "They were very defensive and aggressive when I was getting close. They felt threatened because they were weak. I had to give them each two doses of tranquilizers while healing their wounds. But they've been getting more and more aggressive lately and I have not been able to feed them yesterday or enter the dome because they're very hungry. All I've been feeding them is artificial meat and it's not enough, plus they want to join their packs and hunt...I would say that they're famished..." his face saddens. "I want to let them out, but I fear that they'll eat me the minute I open the gate...the only way they can be tamed and less aggressive is if they hunt and eat real flesh and I think Veronica can help them," he says with a mischievous smile.

I look at him with disbelief...wow...

"You want to feed Veronica to the wolves," Spyros repeats.

Zero nods.

"Zero..." Warr too is amazed by how sick and psychotic Zero really is.

"That's a good plan," I finally say. "It's better than what I had planned for her, plus it'll be entertaining to watch. She values her life more than anyone else. She will try to put up a good fight before getting eaten...

I nod at Zero who's smiling at me as if I am suddenly his God.

"Let's do it then, Warr, Spyros, go get Veronica." Zero tells them.

They both sigh and decide to walk back to their car, before they disappear, I call after them.

"Veronica is very smart and very paranoid at the moment. She will be watching out for anyone who tries to get in her house. She might try and escape the minute she sees you two this black car. I advise you guys to not be obvious."

"Yes sir," Spyros says and then he and Warr take off. I'm left alone with Zero and he is the happiest, and the most excited today. I have been wrong when I thought he wasn't much of a talker. He only acts professional and quiet when he's on the job. But the real him is just as talkative as Forest. Less annoying, but just as talkative.

He tells me about all the animals he's encountered and how he healed them and how amazing he thinks Aelita is. He continues to babble for as long as possible. But most of all, I've noticed his passion and love for animals which makes him seem less of a monster.

We're waiting around and he's still telling me tales of all the animals he's saved and encountered and finally his phone rings.

"Oh, it's Warr," he announces and then talks on the phone for quite a while then hangs up and looks at me very excited.

"They got her, Colton" he tells me. "They're going to be here in about twenty minutes or so. It wasn't easy. She fought. Spyros is very pissed because Veronica bit one of his ears off while she was struggling to run."

I'm not surprised. She really wants to live. She had no regret when Hunter's brother took her place to die. "Ah...well how are you planning to get her in the dome without the wolves attacking everyone else when the gate is open?" I ask Zero.

He gives me a reassuring look. "We're going to drug them and put them to sleep for few minutes."

How the hell is he going to do that?

"I'll be right back," he says and goes inside his house then comes back minutes after with big chumps of pink looking flesh."

"It's artificial angus meat,." he tells me. "I've drugged it."

Okay...still, how is he going to feed them this without opening the gate?

I watch him as he slowly walks toward the dome with the wolves who are angrily growling at him. They want to kill him.

He doesn't open the gate. Instead, next to the gate, is a very small hole...small enough to pass the food through.

Wow.

He throws the meat through the small hole. The wolves hungrily rush and each start devouring the meats.

Zero walks back toward me and sighs, "It pains me to see them like this. I can't wait for them to be fed and then let out of this dome. They really need to start living in the wild."

The wolves slowly start to calm down and slowly lie down and are now sleeping.

"How long do we have until they wake up?" I ask.

"The most is half an hour," he stares at his watch. "They should be here in about ten minutes," he is talking about Warr and Spyros and Veronica.

Ten minutes later, we see a van park next to the dome. I am sitting on the porch of Zero's house, about fifty feet away from the dome. Zero immediately rushes toward them, but I don't feel like doing the same. I don't want to see Veronica's face or her annoying begs and cries.

Spyros and Warr exit the van and open the back of the van. They drag her out. There's a black bag covering her complete body. Her body is not moving.

"Why do you have a bag over her?" I faintly hear Zero ask them.

"Because she wouldn't stop trying to bite me with her satanic mouth! I had to wrap her before throwing her in the car!" Spyros is shouting.

"That's okay," Zero continues. "The bag over her is perfect. I want to see her reaction when she takes it off once she's in the dome with the wolves."

Spyros is cursing and muttering something as he takes out a knife and cuts the duct tape wrapped around the bag. He then goes even further and stabs her leg through the giant black plastic bag with the knife. "Here take that you bitch, the wolves will want you more if they smell your blood," Spyros growls.

Her body is still not moving, actually it's starting to...but faintly. She's knocked out.

"Ready?" Zero asks them as he starts to use a key to open the gate of the dome.

"Yes," Warr and Spyros force Veronica's limb body up and they throw her inside the dome. Her body falls on the ground. Zero closes the gates with the key. Spyros grabs the key from him and throws it far away. "There! She can't ever, ever get out of this!"

Gee. Spyros is really angry with Veronica.

"Hey," Zero scolds him. "How am I going to open the gate and let the wolves out after they finish her off?"

"...Don't you have a spare key?" Spyros retorts.

Zero shakes his head still glaring.

"We'll find a way, first let's enjoy the show." Spyros says and they're all standing in front of the dome looking through the glass.

I decide to join them. I won't get a good view from where I'm seating and I definitely want to see Veronica devoured alive by those animals. I really hate her. She's a spiteful woman. I don't even know why I ever fucked her...She had a nasty attitude from the beginning.

"Why is she knocked out? Did you hit her?" Warr asks Spyros.

"No I didn't...I don't know she probably knocked herself out while in the back of the van. She was trashing and making noises," Spyros explains.

"Oh well she's waking up," Zero says excited.

I am in front of the dome, staring inside and I see her body slowly moving and rising up. She's just sitting there with the bag over her head. The wolves too are starting to wake up from their nap. They're disoriented. The next events happen so fast.

523

I suddenly hear a dog bark, it's Forest. He comes out of nowhere and is barking at me and at the dome. I am confused and scared and worried all at once, why...what is he trying to tell me? Does he not want us to kill Veronica? Then, out of nowhere, the van that was parked suddenly takes off and drives away. Me, Zero, Spyros and Warr are looking at it even more confused...who is driving the van?

"What the..." Then Zero turns back and look inside the dome. His eyes widen in horror.

I do too and I see her slowly removing the black bag from her head.

The woman who is in the dome isn't Veronica.

It's Aelita.

## END OF BOOK ONE

> ## HOW DID AELITA END UP THERE? WHAT WILL HAPPEN NEXT?

...**Find out in the second book** *"For Colton"* **coming soon...**

---

Meanwhile, visit the author's website www.feudragon.com for more information and share your thoughts…

# Thank you for reading!